NIGHTSTALKER

NIGHT STALKER

BY

TIMOTHY RIZZI

DONALD I. FINE, INC.
NEW YORK

All rights reserved, including the right of reproduction in whole or in part in any form. Published in the United States of America by Donald I. Fine, Inc. and in Canada by General Publishing Company Limited.

Library of Congress Cataloging-in-Publication Data

Rizzi, Timothy.
Nightstalker / by Timothy Rizzi.
p.   cm.
ISBN 1-55611-290-4
I. Title.
PS3568.I835N5   1992
813'.54—dc20   91-58662
CIP
r91

Manufactured in the United States of America

10 9 8 7 6 5 4 3 2 1

Designed by Irving Perkins Associates
Maps by Richard Granald/LMD

ACKNOWLEDGMENTS

I would like to thank the following people for helping me along the way:

Paul Fling, for your insight, constructive criticism and the many meetings we had discussing this project. Yes, you did warn me about this.

My sister, Chris R. Tobin, for her hours of helping prepare the manuscript.

To a true warrior and lover of freedom, Capt. Miles Crowell, USAF. You saved me from making some embarrassing mistakes.

Roberta Pryor and Donald I. Fine, this wouldn't be possible without the both of you.

To my children Kirk, Jason, Lindsey and Dixie for your patience and understanding. I know it wasn't easy.

Most of all to my wife Diana. Words alone cannot significantly say what I feel for all you have done to help complete this important project in my life. I can only say . . . Thank You.

To Diana, my wife and partner

GLOSSARY

AAA—Anti-Aircraft Artillery

AA-8 (NATO "Aphid")—Soviet-made highly maneuverable close range infrared homing air-to-air missile. Range 3 miles.

AA-9 (NATO "Amos")—Soviet-made radar-homing long-range air-to-air missile. Reported to be in the same class as the USN AIM-54 Phoenix. Range 45 to 93 miles.

AA-10 (NATO "Alamo")—Soviet-made radar-homing long-range air-to-air missile. Performance is along the same lines as the AA-9. Range 18.5 miles.

AA-11 (NATO "Archer")—Soviet-made radar-homing and infrared-guided air-to-air missile. Medium-range equipped with a 20 lb. fragmentation warhead. Range 7 miles.

AFSATCOM—Air Force Satellite Communications.

AGM—131C SRAM—Short-Range Attack Missile carried by the B-2 *Nightstalker*. Powered by a Hercules solid-propellent rocket motor. 14 feet 0 inches, diameter 1 foot 3.5 inches. Warhead: Super-cooled Metastable Helium.

AGM—136S TACIT RAINBOW—Supersonic radar homing "fire and forget" cruise missile.

ALCM—Air Launched Cruise Missile.

9

AWACS—Airborne Warning And Control System. Built on a modified Boeing 707 airframe.

"Back Trap"—Developed as a successor to the P-14 "Tall King" early warning radar. Operates on A-band around 172 MHz. It is used to give early warning to SA-5 SAM sites.

"Big Bird"—Deployed with SA-10 "Grumble," this long-range early warning radar operates on F-band at 3.3 GHz.

BUFF—Nickname for a B-52 Strategic Bomber, "Big Ugly Fat Fella."

CINCPAC—Commander in Chief Pacific

CINCPACFLT—Commander in Chief, Pacific Fleet

COCOM—Coordinating Committee for Multilateral Export Controls. Essentially this is a handshake between western countries to disallow high-tech equipment which can be used for military purposes to be exported to unfriendly countries.

COMIREX—Committee on Imaging Requirements and Exploitation. This committee approves the movement of satellites in orbit, and those areas of the world they should cover.

CRTs—Cathode Ray Tube

DIA—Defense Intelligence Agency

DoD—Department of Defense

ECM—Electronic Countermeasures

ECCM—Electronic Counter-Countermeasures

ELINT—Electric Intelligence

EO—Electronic-Optical

EWC—Early Warning Center

"Flip Lid"—I/J-band system operating at a frequency of 10 GHz. This system is used to control SA-10s.

HUD—Heads-Up Display

ICBM—Intercontinental Ballistic Missile

IFF—Identify Friend or Foe. A radar transponder is used so the aircraft can be identified by ground control radar.

IR—Infrared

IRST—Infrared Search and Track

KGB—Komitet Gosudarstvennoy Bezopasnosti. Soviet secret security and intelligence service.

KH-11—Known as a "Keyhole" the KH-11 is an advanced reconnaissance satellite incorporating real-time capability using high-resolution cameras and IR detection.

KH-12—A more advanced version of the KH-11.

NSA—National Security Agency

NSC—National Security Council

NRO—National Reconnaissance Office

P-12 (NATO "Spoon Rest")—A-band early-warning radar. Operating frequency of 147–161 MHz.

P-14 (NATO "Tall King")—A-band early-warning radar with an effective range of over 300 kilometers. The "Tall King" operates at 150–180 MHz.

P-14CX—A-band frequency radar operating on 157 HMz beam.

P-15 (NATO "Flat Face")—This is an early-warning radar used to direct SA-3 "Goa," SA-4 "Ganef," SA-6 "Guideline" and SA-8 "Gecko." The "Flat Face" operates on C-band.

PVO—Voyska Protivovozdushnoy Oborony (Troops of Anti-Air Defense) or Troops of Air Defense. Responsible for the air defense of the Soviet Union.

RADAR BANDS:

Band	Wavelength (cm)	Frequency (MHz)
A/B	300 – 100	30 – 300
B/C	100 – 30	300 – 1,000
C/D	30 – 15	1,000 – 2,000
E/F	15 – 7.5	2,000 – 4,000
G/H	7.5 – 3.75	4,000 – 8,000
I/J	3.75 – 2.5	8,000 – 12,000
J	2.5 – 1.67	12,000 – 18,000
J/K	1.67 – 1.11	18,000 – 27,000
K	1.11 – 0.75	27,000 – 40,000

RCS—Radar Cross-Section

RPV—Remote Piloted Vehicle

SAC—Strategic Air Command

SAM—Surface-to-Air Missile

SAR—Semi-Active Radar

SA-2 (NATO "Guideline")—Soviet-made surface-to-air missile. This missile has been operational since 1959, is land-transportable and was used extensively in combat over North Vietnam and the Middle East. Power Plant: Solid-propellant booster, liquid-propellant sustained burning nitric acid and hydrocarbons. Guidance: Automatic radio command along with radar tracking of target. Warhead: 288 lb. high-explosive. Performance: Maximum speed Mach 3.5; range 33 miles with a ceiling of 83,500 feet. SA-5 (NATO "Gammon")—Soviet-made long-range high-altitude surface-to-air missile. Over 9,000 SA-5s are deployed throughout the Soviet Union. Power Plant: Two stage consisting of four wraparound solid-propellant jettisonable boosters. Guidance: Semi-active radar homing. Performance: Maximum speed Mach 3.59; range 190 miles with a ceiling of 95,000 feet.

SA-6 (NATO "Gainful")—Soviet-made mobile tactical surface-to-air missile system. This system took a heavy toll on Israeli aircraft during the 1973 war. Power Plant: A single solid-propellant booster. After booster burnout the empty casing becomes a ramjet combustion chamber mixing the exhaust from a solid-propellant gas generator. Guidance: Semi-active radar terminal homing backed up with radio commands. Warhead: 176 lb. high-explosive. Performance: Maximum speed Mach 2.85; range 18.5 miles with a ceiling of 59,500 feet.

SA-8 (NATO "Gecko")—Soviet-made short range, all weather tactical surface-to-air missile. The fire control equipment and missile launcher are mounted on a rotating turret. Surveillance radar has a range of 18 miles and folds down behind the launcher. The tracking radar is a pulsed-type with a range of 12 to 16 miles. Power Plant: Solid-propellant dual thrust motor. Guidance: Semiactive radar and infrared for terminal homing along with command radar for proportional navigation. Warhead: 110 lb. High-explosive. Performance: Maximum speed Mach 2, range 6 to 8 miles with a ceiling of 50 to 20,000 feet.

SA-10 (NATO "Grumble")—One of the most advanced surface-to-air missile systems deployed by the Soviet Union. This system uses multitarget tracking and engagement and has the capability to defeat low altitude targets with extremely small radar signatures. Its all-altitude capability allows this system to engage targets such as ballistic missiles and low flying cruise missiles. Power Plant: Solid propellant, single stage. Guidance: Semi-active radar command. Warhead: 210 lb. high explosive. Performance: Maximum speed Mach 6 plus; range of 72 miles with a ceiling of 125,000 feet.

SA-11 (NATO "Gadfly")—Soviet-made surface-to-air missile designed to destroy low- to medium-flying high-performance jet aircraft. This system is mounted on tracked vehicle which carries the engagement radar and missiles. Power Plant: Solid propellant. Guidance: Monopulse semiactive radar command. Warhead: 315 lb. high explosive. Performance: Maximum speed Mach 3; range of 1.9 to 18.5 miles with a ceiling of 100 to 46,000 feet.

SA-12A (NATO "Gladiator")—Soviet-made land-mobile tactical missile system. This surface-to-air system can intercept aircraft at all altitudes and is capable of engaging cruise or ballistic missiles. Power Plant: Solid propellant. Guidance: Semiactive radar command. Warhead: 330 lb. high explosive. Performance: Maximum speed Mach 3; range 3.5 to 45 miles with a ceiling of 250 to 98,000 feet.

SA-13 (NATO "Gopher")—Soviet-made mobile surface-to-air missile system. The system is deployed on a tracked vehicle. Power Plant: Solid-propellant. Guidance: Infrared homing. Warhead: 13 lb. high explosive. Performance: Maximum speed Mach 2; range 0.2 to 7.5 miles, effective ceiling 145 to 17,000 feet.

"Square Pair"—H-band engagement radar operating on 6.62–6.94 GHz. Used to control SA-5s

"Straight Flush"—G/H-band engagement radar operating on 4.9–5, 6.45–6.75 GHz. Used to control SA-6s.

TALD—Tactical Air Launch Decoy. Used to distract MiGs and surface-to-air launched missiles away from the B-2 *Nightstalker* by broadcasting a false radar signature.

TDT—Tactical Decoy Transmitter

TFR—Terrain Following Radar

TID—Tactical Information Display

TWP—Threat Warning Panel. Informs crew of which radar band is painting or sweeping over their aircraft, and prioritizes its threat.

USEUCOM—European U.S. Command

VDT—Video Display Terminal

ZSU—23-4—Highly mobile 23 mm. radar-directed air defense cannon.

ZSU—57-2—Mobile 57 mm air defense cannon. Considered less of a threat than the ZSU-23-4.

CONTENTS

NIGHTSTALKER

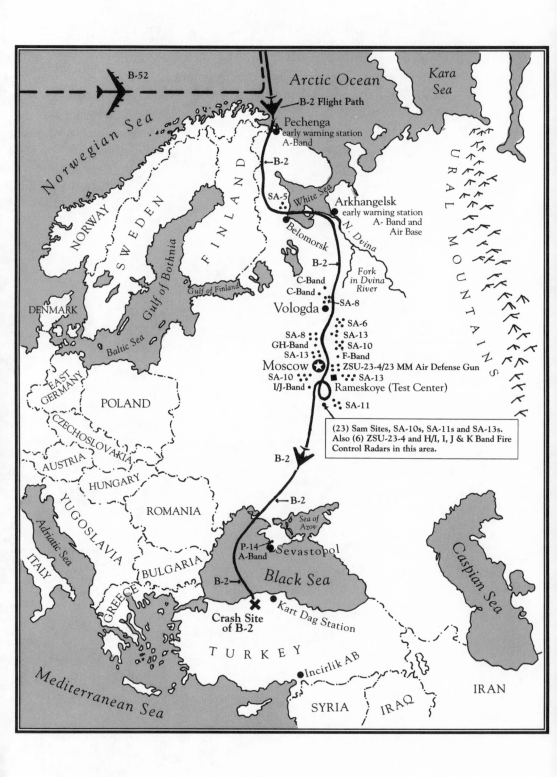

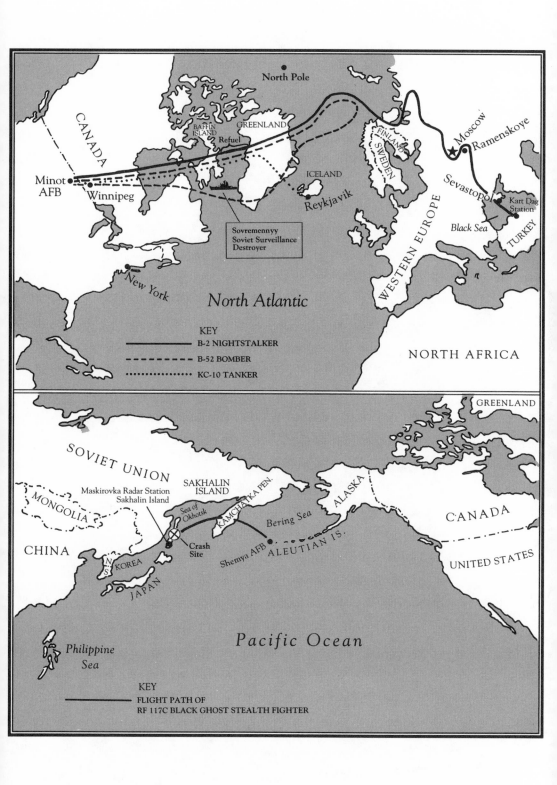

North Pole

CANADA

GREENLAND

BAFFIN
ISLAND

Refuel

FINLAND
SWEDEN

Moscow

Ramenskoye

ICELAND

Minot
AFB

Winnipeg

Reykjavik

Sevastopol

Kart Dag
Station

WESTERN EUROPE

Black Sea

TURKEY

Sovremennyy
Soviet Surveillance
Destroyer

New York

North Atlantic

NORTH AFRICA

KEY

———————— B-2 NIGHTSTALKER

– – – – – – B-52 BOMBER

· · · · · · · · · KC-10 TANKER

GREENLAND

SOVIET UNION

SAKHALIN
ISLAND

CANADA

Maskirovka Radar Station
Sakhalin Island

MONGOLIA

Sea of
Okhotsk

KAMCHATKA PEN.

ALASKA

Bering Sea

C·ANADA

CHINA

N
S
KOREA

Crash
Site

Shemya AFB

ALEUTIAN IS.

UNITED STATES

JAPAN

Philippine
Sea

Pacific Ocean

KEY

———————— FLIGHT PATH OF
RF 117C BLACK GHOST STEALTH FIGHTER

1

BLACK GHOST DOWN

SHEMYA AIR BASE, ALASKA 7 OCTOBER 1984

Two guards wearing olive green Air Force winter parkas and carrying M-16 automatic rifles stood silently in the snow. They watched as the ugly black insect-shaped RF-117C Black Ghost stealth fighter rose slowly from its underground hangar. The heavy lift elevator struggled to push the fully loaded 52,000-pound aircraft up into the ice-cold Alaskan night as it leveled with the ground. The hangar had been built over twenty years earlier for the older SR-71 Blackbird.

The pilot, Major Danny Sheldon, waited until his aircraft was being towed into position for boarding before he started to approach. He watched his icy breath float off into the night air.

The Black Ghost had been stationed at the Alaskan base for the last six months. The odd-shaped fighter was bigger than it looked. Equivalent in size to an F-4 Phantom or an F-15C Eagle. The RF-117C was a more advanced unarmed reconnaissance version of the F-117A, of which only six had been deployed. The stealth fighter had been developed out of the Senior Trend program in the early eighties. The Air Force had been able to pull off an intelligence coup by keeping the existence of the F-117A's development, flight testing and ongoing deployment under total secrecy.

The F-117A was designed to perform low-level air strikes on

23

high-priority, heavily defended targets such as command posts, antiaircraft artillery or radar guided surface-to-air-missiles. The C-model, Reconnaissance Fighter, was equipped with afterburning turbofans which allowed it to accelerate out of an area very quickly. This particular Black Ghost was also crammed full of radar and electronic equipment. The Air Force was killing two birds with one stone by test flying it down the Soviet Union's Pacific coastline. The aircraft could also monitor the radar frequencies the Soviets were using in their long-range search and short-range tactical radars. So far all the missions had gone off without a hitch. The Soviets had not detected any of the test flights.

The boxy delta-winged aircraft wasn't a fighter in the true sense of the word. If the Black Ghost ever did get into a dogfight chances were it would lose. The airframe of the reconnaissance version wasn't designed to take the stresses of aerial combat. Its prismatic cut-diamond shape was composed of many flat surfaces and a short stubby V tail. The stealth characteristics of the plane would reflect the radar beam in angles away from the emitter. No matter what direction, a radar illuminated the fighter. Only a very small part of it was reflected back. This allowed it to fly in close enough to take out SAM sites and leave the sky open for the F-15s and F-16s to do their stuff. The radar emissions that weren't reflected were absorbed and turned into heat. The Black Ghost was made mostly of graphite and kevlar and covered with radar-absorbent material, RAM. Hand-built by Lockheed at the Skunk Works, it was easy to understand why the fighter was one of the most guarded secrets of the U.S. Air Force's inventory.

"I am not sure if I like the cold or wet better," Major Sheldon said under his breath as he approached the Ghost. The former F-111 pilot had been stationed with the 48th Tactical Fighter Wing at Lakenheath, U.K., before transferring to the F-117A. After growing up in central Wyoming and attending the Air Force Academy in Colorado Springs, going to the United Kingdom was quite a change. He never thought he would miss the cool damp air but now he would welcome it. After two months of temperatures right at zero, wet sounded good.

His training for the Black Ghost took place in the Nevada

desert north of Nellis Air Force Base. The major was part of a specialized group of pilots that made their home at Tonopah. They called themselves the Team One—Furtim Vigilans, which meant covert vigilantes or stealthy vigilantes. Danny liked flying the Black Ghost because it was tough and demanding. His instructors always told him, "If they can't find you they can't hurt you." He liked that thought.

The smell of the JP-4 burned his nose as he slid his helmet over his head and buckled in. The mission tonight would take him east across the Kamchatka peninsula along the northern coast of the Okhotsk Sea. Then he would turn south and run straight at one of the Soviets' newest radar stations on Sakhalin Island. The satellite photos Sheldon had reviewed showed a large number of new SAM sites surrounding the station. The CIA and Air Force were sending the Black Ghost in to find out what was going on. As with all operations of this sort, Danny knew he would be alone during his flight into Soviet airspace. He was under orders to maintain radio silence, and if he did run into any trouble the only way he could call for help was to radio an RC-135V Rivet, which would be flying off the eastern coast of Sakhalin Island. This converted Boeing 707 spy plane, code-named "Rivet Joint," routinely patrolled the area around Sakhalin. So presumably it would not be suspicious when the big four-engine jet showed up on the radar operators' screens at Maskirovka station. After completing his mission Sheldon would land at Misawa Air Base in Japan, and a C-5A heavy transport would be used to take the fighter back to Shemya AFB.

He swept the instruments before advancing the throttles a half inch and taking his fighter to the edge of the dark runway.

"Specter eight two seven, you are clear for takeoff. Take a heading of 203," the tower squawked.

Sheldon looked over his checklist for the second time. The air in the cockpit was still a cool forty-three degrees. He would let it warm up to only forty-eight degrees. At that temperature the inside of the canopy wouldn't freeze and his IR signature would still be too low to detect from the front.

Major Sheldon swung his fighter around and lined it up on

the center of the runway. He increased power and felt the aircraft leap into the air as it hit 139 knots.

RC-135V, RIVET JOINT FLIGHT

"Set the autopilot for eighteen thousand. I'm going to see how
the rest of the crew is doing," the captain said.

"Yes, sir. I've got it," responded the right-seater.

The sleek four-engine jet was on a routine mission. It was
headed north just outside of Japanese airspace. The standard
RC-135 could cruise at over 550 miles an hour, though most
missions were flown at the lowest possible operational speed to
keep the plane in the area of the target for as long as practical.

The crew had left their base on Okinawa five hours before
and had refueled off the southern coast of Japan. They were
now making their way along the Kuril Islands. Soon they would
be diving down to a few hundred feet above sea level. Then the
big jet would turn and fly toward Sakhalin Island to see what
trouble they could stir up. This particular RC-135 was no
stranger to Soviet airspace. The crew was very proud of the
half-dozen red SU-24 Fencer silhouettes painted on its side.
One for each time it had penetrated the Soviet Union and snuck
out undetected.

The captain, thirty-two-year-old Douglas "Buddy" Brooks,
walked back through the gunmetal gray partition separating the
flight deck from the rest of the aircraft. He had been sitting for
over five hours and wanted to get up and move around before
beginning the toughest part of the mission, flying just outside
Soviet airspace. Brooks had never imagined he would be putting his neck on the line when he entered the Air Force after
college ten years earlier. He had figured it would be a safe way
to learn how to fly multiengine jet transports, serve his country
for a few years, get experience and then take a job as the first
officer of a 737 or MD-80 for a major airline. Next would be a
move to a big city, marriage, family, a BMW and six figures a
year. Those old yuppie plans weren't working out, and to his
surprise Captain Brooks found he wasn't sorry, he loved what
he was doing. Sneaking in and out of enemy territory gave him
a rush he knew he could never get from flying from Boston to

Miami every day, an airborne bus driver. The airline job was on hold, and as for getting married, he was too busy even to look.

Brooks now entered the aft section of the RC-135 to the sight of four rows of technicians sitting behind their multipurpose consoles. The technicians were responsible for monitoring everything from the RC-135's weather radar to the most advance on-board avionics and electronic recording devices. As Brooks walked through the shadowy cabin he could easily make out the data dancing on the various four-color screens. When he was satisfied everything appeared to be running smoothly he returned to the flight deck to get ready for the run along the Soviet coast.

"Everything looks good, lieutenant," Brooks said as he glanced out the cockpit windows into the clear night sky. "I can't believe how clear it is." He reached for his shoulder strap and started buckling his five-foot-ten-inch frame back into his seat.

1st Lieutenant J.D. Hill did not take his eyes off the instruments. He wasn't sure if he should be scared or flattered that the captain had left him alone to fly the 135. After all, this was only his second mission as a copilot. Maybe that was Brooks's way of helping him build confidence. Or maybe, he thought, I'm such a good actor he doesn't know my gut's in an uproar. Either way Lieutenant Hill was glad his C.O. was back in the left seat ready to take over again.

"Anything happening out there, Hill?" Brooks asked as he put on his headgear.

"I show a Comair fifteen miles to the east. That's the only traffic in the area, probably a 747 or DC-10 on its way to Japan or Hong Kong with some rich civilians."

"Okay, take a heading of two four five and start to ease her down, slowly." They were now heading for the southeast corner of Sakhalin Island. It would be a few more minutes before the long-range early-warning radar at Maskirovka Station would begin to pick them up. For the time being Brooks could relax—

Suddenly a red warning light flashed on in the center of the instrument panel.

"Oh shit, what's this?" A hostile radar was sweeping from the north. "They've never been able to detect us this far out before." Brooks looked at Hill. "Get this baby on the deck and let's take a closer look. I want to find out if those emissions are coming from Maskirovka, or if the Sovs have themselves a new radar site . . ."

RF-117C BLACK GHOST, SOUTHBOUND

Major Danny Sheldon finished his long slow turn and started his run to the south. It would be at least fifteen minutes before the Soviets could even start to detect him. Even then he would just show up as a slight smudge on the long-range radarscope. He could imagine the scope operator trying to adjust the sensitivity of his radar. After a few unsuccessful tries at clarifying the target the operator would just write it off as a large flock of birds or some kind of atmospheric condition.

He looked over his instruments quickly. On the upper center panel of his cockpit were warning lights for all the different radar frequencies and their representative wavelengths. A/B and B/C on the long-range long-frequency side, C/D, E/F, and G/H in the midrange and I/J, J, J/K and K on the shortwave. A different light would come on indicating what particular band of radar was sweeping his fighter.

Danny dropped the nose of the airplane and throttled back to adjust the airspeed. His extra wide HUD and the night-vision device built into his helmet gave him an excellent view of his surroundings. He could make out the coastline of Sakhalin Island rapidly coming into view straight ahead.

"So far so good." Danny turned on his ground-tracking laser letting it cycle before he turned it to active tracking. The laser sent out short pulses of light every second. The reflection was then recorded and fed into the Black Ghost's three navigational computers. Danny just had to monitor the plane. The computer would keep him at the right altitude and correct heading. The laser was silent, so it couldn't be tracked, unlike a noisy conventional ground-hugging radar.

Three minutes later the major passed over the coast. He checked his altitude and punched the proper coordinates into the NAV computer. He switched on the ELINT, Electronic Intelligence computer. The ELINT, with its very high speed integrated circuits, would catalog the operating frequencies of the PVO's different radars. This mission was intended to catalog the radar transmissions used in the Maskirovka long-range search radar. The information gathered would then be shared with Japan to help coordinate their northern defenses.

Danny felt a chill go up his spine. The cold was going right through his Gore-Tex Thinsulate flight suit. When I get done with this I'm going to spend a week in Hawaii baking in the sun with a hot woman, he fantasized.

Just then the A-Band light on his Threat Warning Panel came on. The Soviet's long-range radar at Maskirovka was sweeping his fighter.

MASKIROVKA RADAR STATION, SAKHALIN ISLAND

The Soviet operator leaned forward for a closer look. The fuzzy shape on his scope faded in and out with every pass of the beam. The second lieutenant tried to make sure he really was looking at something before he said anything to the general. He pointed now to the shape on the screen.

"What is it?" the general asked.

"I am not sure, it could be a snow shower but it's moving very fast. Look, now it is gone."

Both men stared at the screen to see if the image would reappear. In a minute it did.

"What do you make of it?"

"I'm not sure." The operator's eyes came off the scope. "I have seen this before."

"An aircraft?"

"I can't get a lock on it, sir. But it is moving like an enemy target trying to hide itself."

"Lieutenant, get me General Yefimov on a secure line."

RAMENSKOYE TEST CENTER,
THIRTY MILES SOUTH OF MOSCOW

Deep inside a concrete bunker fifty meters underground, in a room half the size of a football field, sat the supercomputer. They called it Zashchita, meaning "as a shield."

A single glass-walled control room overlooked the main computer center below. The operators on the floor could see the ominous looking computer in the next room through several large windows. It looked like a huge black ten-legged octopus. Its main terminal was in the center and ten smaller units surrounded it with large cables connecting them together. By Western standards the computer was enormous, but the Soviets, with their limited technology, had been able to construct a supercomputer that could challenge and surpass anything the West had in operation.

A single PVO general, of the Troops of the Air Defense, was trusted to man the command center, and his technicians worked the computer terminals below him.

General Yefimov picked up the phone after it rang twice. "Standard command," came his coded answer.

"General . . . this is Maskirovka station. We are tracking a possible target. It fits the test profile you have set out."

Yefimov smiled. "So soon?" he asked softly. "Have you boosted your power levels?"

"Yes, general . . . we cannot clarify. Each time we pick it up it has moved farther inland, out of the north. I believe it is an American aircraft."

"I understand. The system is ready. You may deploy it at will. I have received clearance from Moscow." The line went dead without a reply.

"Prepare yourselves, we will be operational within five minutes," Yefimov told his people. The control room grew quiet as each man took his place.

RF-117C BLACK GHOST

Major Danny Sheldon froze as he watched each of the radar-warning lights flash on and off. The Soviets were sweeping him with every radar band they had.

What the hell . . . ? This had never happened before. He looked to see if any of the radars had locked onto his fighter. None had. He pushed the stick to the right to see if the radar would change at a different angle.

Okay, let's see what you've got. I got ten-to-one back at the base I can fly this thing right down your throat.

The major had been in Soviet airspace over the Sakhalin Island for twenty minutes. The radar complex at Maskirovka was still over 300 miles away. Sheldon recalled what intelligence officers had told him about the long-range early-warning radar the Soviets were operating at Maskirovka Station—a mono-pulsed long-frequency A-Band, which meant it had the potential of detecting his Black Ghost at maximum range. However, Danny Sheldon knew as he flew closer to the radar's antennae and the electronic signals became stronger, the stealth characteristics of his aircraft would become more effective . . . the angular shape of the Black Ghost would deflect the radar waves as they rolled across his aircraft. So the closer the major got to the radar station, the less likely it was that he would be acquired and tracked by their system.

He reprogrammed his computer for 150 feet above ground, and the Black Ghost, as though protesting, slowly responded.

MASKIROVKA RADAR STATION, SAKHALIN ISLAND

The young Soviet radar operator could feel the tension in the air. He knew by the sound of the general's voice this was the target they'd been waiting for. It was a chance for his leaders to test The Project.

His eyes moved across the screen as he looked for the target. An instant later a computer tone told him his radar had just locked up on an unidentified aircraft off the eastern coast of

Sakhalin Island. Its strong radar return told him it was an American RC-135 reconnaissance aircraft—a spy plane.

"Lock-on, general . . . new target bearing zero eight eight. It's an RC-135."

"Break off. I don't want them to record this. Have you found the new target to the north yet? That's the one we are most interested in." He paced the floor behind the large amber-colored scope.

The operator focused back onto the upper part of the radar-scope. "I have it, general. Heading one seven eight, altitude four four meters, speed three hundred seventy knots. It is heading straight for us—now I've lost it, no, now it's back."

He watched the screen as his target faded in and out. It would be gone for ten seconds, then back for three.

The general was looking over his shoulder. "You lose it but it comes back long enough for us to follow it. Do not go for a lock-on until I give the order. Lieutenant, double-check to make sure none of our aircraft is in the area." He turned to the communications officer. "Put me back in contact with General Yefimov, I want him to follow this. Where is the target now?" The general's eyes went back to the scope.

"It is heading one eight two, altitude fifty meters, speed three hundred sixty-five knots. The target is three hundred twenty-two kilometers to the north and on a constant course for this station."

RF-117C BLACK GHOST, CONTINUING SOUTH

Danny Sheldon pulled out a plastic water bottle from the upper part of his flight suit and shot a burst of cold water into his dry mouth. He watched the computer generate multicolored holographic images on the HUD. The outline of the horizon was an orange red while the direction, speed and altitude of his fighter showed up in green. If another aircraft came into the area the on-board computers would classify it as either friendly or hostile. A friendly would be projected as a blue triangle, an enemy would be yellow. The 3-D effect of the HUD helped him make quick and accurate decisions. One wrong decision could be his life.

The lights of a small Soviet village passed on his left side. He rolled the fighter to the left behind a large hill. The ground-following laser kicked back in as the nose of the jet pitched up to go over the hill. There he spotted a long canyon to his right. He banked a few degrees toward it and pushed the nose down. Danny saw what looked like a microwave relay station. Its white dish showed up clearly with his night-vision device.

He checked the ETA readout. Twelve minutes and he should be right on top of the radar station. No sweat.

Suddenly a loud birdlike chirping sounded through his headset. A Fan Song. The thought made his insides jump.

He watched the C-Band and E-Band warning lights flash on, telling him the radar had just locked on. His HUD showed two long yellow cones pointed upside down toward his aircraft. The cones simulated the SAMs' radars that were directed at him. If the Soviets had had their radar turned on sooner he could have flown between the two search radars and avoided them. If . . .

Ten miles to the south a single Soviet SA-2 radar operator sat in the command van and manipulated the controls of his CRT display. The two fan-shaped radar beams illuminated from the twin radar dishes that swept across the sky in an even pattern. The vertical beam quickly flip-flopped from side to side while the horizontal beam worked in unison up and down. The tracking data was displayed on the operator's scope where he could handle range, altitude and azimuth. The Fan Song could track while it scanned and simultaneously engaged up to six targets.

The SAM operator prepared for launch. The order had already been given to fire at the target. He watched it, on his yellowish scope, slowly approach his position from the north.

The chirping sound continued in his helmet. There was no question in Danny Sheldon's mind why the pilots two decades before him had code-named the radar Fan Song. The electronic noise produced by the radar beam was like music—seductive, scary music.

The Soviets had achieved a lock-on to his fighter with not one but two radar bands. This was new. Danny scanned the priority threat panel directly below his HUD. It told him the missiles had not yet launched. He jinked his fighter left and right. "I should have been more mentally prepared. *Damn* it."

The Black Ghost's lowest radar cross section occurred when the fighter was pointed right at the antennae. The fighter was designed to deflect 99.8 percent of the radar emissions that hit it from this angle and the rest would be absorbed. Danny pushed the stick hard to the right and the fighter banked fifty degrees. He added power and started to climb. He watched his altitude increase at 1500 feet per minute. He passed through 700 feet, pushed the nose down and came out of the climbing turn with wings level.

The operator didn't need any more time. The radar was clearly locked up on the unknown aircraft. He let the target get well within the maximum range of the SAM system.

"Now," the operator said under his breath as he hit the launch button three quick times.

Two thousand meters out in front of him the solid fuel motor of the first SA-2 ignited in a plume of fire. Its rearward pointing C-Band uplink transponder immediately started to receive targeting information from the Fan Song's fire control computers. It was headed straight for the target.

The yellow radar warning cones on the HUD were now pointed directly at Danny Sheldon. A white flash appeared in the distance followed by a second and a third. The Soviets had just launched on him. He watched as the burning white pillars of fire grew closer. The first was going to miss by half a mile as indicated on the Threat Warning Panel. The other two were tracking on target. If he maintained course the missiles would hit him.

Only seconds had passed since he had first spotted the SAMs. He waited until the warning light on his HUD went to red, then pushed the nose down and dove straight down. The two SAMs streaked overhead and exploded 200 feet away. He could hear pieces of shrapnel hitting the back of his fuselage.

Major Sheldon took a deep breath as his eyes swept the instruments before going back to the horizon. He guided the fighter into a canyon just ahead, keeping Black Ghost at eighty feet above ground level. None of his radar-warning indicators were on. He nosed the fighter up and out of the steep granite walls and into the open air above, then cursed as he looked over at his electronic countermeasures. Turned off. If he turned them on, the Soviets could possibly track him by their emission. Track me hell, they're *already* tracking me. He turned ten degrees south and continued his climb.

As he watched the altimeter needle move through 2500 feet he was completely defenseless. He could not fight back. He glanced back over his instruments. His right engine was running a little hot. He adjusted his infrared-suppression system that mixed cool air with the hot-engine exhaust to mask his heat signature.

Another radar warning tone sounded. He looked up, they were sweeping to the southwest—his HUD showed an SA-6 this time. He banked away from the SAMs' search-radar and stayed on course to the radar station. Nothing else to do.

MASKIROVKA RADAR STATION, SAKHALIN ISLAND

"General, I have just received confirmation there are no other Soviet aircraft in this area," the lieutenant said. "Air Defense Command does advise, though, to get a visual before attacking. If it's a commercial airliner you are instructed to force it down."

"Visual . . . ! That is not an airliner. The Americans are trying to play me for a fool. You tell them our situation and that I believe we have some sort of American stealth aircraft in our airspace. And tell those idiots to shut down those acquisition radars. I want him to draw him in closer. In five minutes the target will be over our heaviest SAM belt. I want him brought *down*."

The lieutenant gave the order to shut down the SAMs' radars.

"And contact command at Ramenskoye. Tell them Mas-kirovka station reports we have been able to track and engage the target," the general ordered.

A few moments later the lieutenant in charge of communications sent a coded electronic signal via satellite to the newest and top-secret radar complex located at Ramenskoye test center south of Moscow. Unknown to the lieutenant, they were operating one of the world's most advanced supercomputers and radar-acquisition systems linked to the A-Band radar at Maskirovka station; this had enabled them to track the target. The message stated they had tracked and locked onto what was believed to be an American stealth aircraft. It was something the commander of the underground complex at Ramenskoye already knew.

RF-117C BLACK GHOST

"Nothing . . . it doesn't make sense," Danny Sheldon muttered to himself. An odd feeling had come over him, as if he had just imagined the whole thing. The radar-warning lights on his instrument panel were dark. The standard information was being displayed and the HUD was clean except for the long-range A-Band search radar based at Maskirovka station that continued to sweep back and forth to the south of him.

There was no question in his mind the Soviets were shooting at him. He was the only aircraft in the area and there was no other way to explain what had just happened. In a way it didn't surprise the major. The Black Ghost was a new aircraft and this was all part of its ongoing tests and evaluations. He also knew it was his choice whether to proceed or break off for a friendly base in Japan.

Sheldon considered. They had not come close to shooting him down, so they couldn't have had a precise lock-on. And the Black Ghost was working as advertised, or he'd be dead. Plus the information he was collecting might well help save the lives of others in a similar situation. He dropped the nose of his fighter and turned back on the terrain-following laser, then set the computer to maintain an altitude of 200 feet. But if they shoot at me again I'm out of here, he thought. Until then, I've got a mission to complete.

The little fighter accelerated toward the ground.

RC-135V, RIVET JOINT FLIGHT

Captain Brooks felt the adrenalin pump into his veins. Something was happening over Sakhalin Island and he didn't have a good feeling about it. He adjusted his grip on the steel yoke as he refocused, looking from the red lights of the instrument panel to the black sky in front of him. Stars winked overhead and the weather radar revealed only a small cluster of clouds to the north. He didn't hear the sound of the computer-fax printer as it signaled an incoming message.

"Captain Brooks, this just in off the faxcoder."

The sound of Lieutenant Hill's voice brought him back to the cockpit.

"It's marked High Priority, sir."

Brooks waited until his copilot had one hand on the yoke and control of the aircraft before he took the message and opened it. "Holy hell, intelligence says the Soviets may be shooting at one of our recon planes flying over Sakhalin."

"What kind of aircraft, sir?"

"Doesn't say." Brooks's mind raced. "His being there must be one of the reasons we're out here tonight . . . Command says if he gets into real trouble the pilot will contact us, we've orders to stay on course and keep recording."

Captain Brooks keyed the internal intercom. "Attention, crew, we have a situation developing over Sakhalin Island. Make sure every recording device is turned to maximum power and be damn sure to keep me informed of anything out of the ordinary."

"This whole thing sounds kind of out of the ordinary, captain," Lieutenant Hill put in.

"Well, lieutenant, you sure got that right." The rookie was coming along.

RF-117C BLACK GHOST

Sheldon double-checked to be sure the ELINT computer was on and running. The computer recorded the pulse repetition frequency, antenna beam width and rotation rate of the Soviet search radar. The Air Force wanted to know the number of pulses that hit his aircraft with each pass of the antenna. The buildup of the echo or "on" time, the amount of time the radar beam was in actual contact with the aircraft, could then be compared with the width of the beam and total time it took the radar to make one pass. From that the radar cross section could be computed and an equal amount of pulse-frequency energy could be fed into the ECM equipment and radioed back to the antenna—thereby jamming it.

Danny Sheldon added power to the RF-117C and started to climb to position himself head-on for maximum reflection of the radar. *Man, in one hour I'll be in Japan drinking a beer—*

The HUD had turned yellow. A SAM search-and-track radar was sweeping him.

Quickly he jinked his fighter into hard-crossing turns. His HUD showed a gap in the radar coverage about three miles away. He nosed over five degrees to gain some airspeed and headed for the hole. Without thinking, he flipped the switch for his electronic countermeasures, watched his airspeed increase to 400 knots, then pulled the side-stick control back a little and came up level at 1200 feet. The Threat Warning Panel showed nothing.

But his HUD showed four shortwave SAM search radars scanning, two behind him, two still ahead, one on each side of his flight path. Suddenly all the radar-warning lights flashed on. He was being scanned on all bands again.

What is this shit, Danny wondered. The two search radars in front of him were now pointed toward him, both locked on E- and C-Band again. But this time it wasn't a Fan Song, it was something new. He heard the rattle in his helmet. The Threat Warning Panel showed three SAM missiles lifting off the ground, at eleven o'clock and easily spotted against the dark ground. He rolled right, squeezed the chaff button and yanked the stick up hard and added power. Careful, he warned himself, don't go into afterburner.

He needed more altitude to outmaneuver the SAMs. The first two missiles headed for the chaff cloud, they would miss him by a couple of thousand yards. The third, the last to launch, stayed on track. He pulled into a hard left turn. The missile was now at his one o'clock and still climbing. He pushed the chaff button again, continued left and did a split S. He was down to below 300 feet, felt the Gs fall off, then pulled his nose up and added power. Again the missile overshot and exploded, the bright flash making him lose his night vision for a few seconds.

Danny climbed and turned to the northwest, his body shaken from the sudden rush. His radar warning lights continued to flash on and off but his threat panel showed nothing. Below and to his left he could see the flash of antiaircraft artillery. Obviously they were shooting behind him.

His mission now, he told himself, was to get the hell out of there, save the aircraft—

Suddenly the fighter rocked violently back and forth. It felt like being hit by a freight train. A 55mm. armor-piercing round had smashed through the left side of the RF-117C, shattering its graphite skin. Danny watched his airspeed fall, fought to come level at 3500 feet and added power.

"Engine left, engine left," the female voice announced from a small speaker left of his VDT, his Video Display Terminal. Danny looked to see the RPMs still falling. He hit the switch to turn off the annoying sound of the engine warning. The fighter yawed to the left as the engine died. He added right rudder and attempted to trim up the wounded fighter.

He continued to hold his fighter at 3500 feet, but now the Threat Warning Panel lit back up—I/J, C- and E-Band radars were now locked onto his plane. He pushed the throttles forward and went into afterburner with his only engine. The fighter shuddered as he pulled the stick back and again began to climb. At 5000 feet came another launch-warning. Two SAMs left, at ten o'clock. He watched as they made their way upward, curving toward him, waited till the last possible second before reacting . . . He hauled the stick back and nosed up forty-five

degrees, hitting the flare button and a magnesium flare fell from
the undercarriage of his fighter. He banked to the left and inverted his aircraft, pointing the nose straight down. His airspeed
increased to 550 knots.

"Now," he grunted. The major yanked back on the stick hard
as he could. He pushed the chaff button and watched the
G-meter increase . . . three . . . four . . . five. At six Gs, he
knew, the fighter would break apart. Five-and-a-half . . . he
pushed the stick forward, felt the Gs bleed off and came wings-
level at 240 feet. His airspeed was 300 knots and steady. Both
SAMs raced past the flare and exploded a hundred yards apart.

Danny nosed his aircraft down. "Now let's see if you can
follow me," he yelled into an empty cockpit.

He checked the instrument panel. He had lost his automatic
leading-edge control on the left side of the fighter, which would
make his fighter even harder to control and maneuver.

He glanced at the computer-driven HUD display to check his
airspeed at 300 knots and an altitude at eighty feet. He eased
the fighter down another thirty feet and added power. He felt a
drop of sweat run down the side of his face.

RC-135V, RIVET JOINT FLIGHT—INBOUND

"Turn right, take a new heading of two three three and take her
up to eighteen thousand," Brooks said. "I'm going to see if I can
contact that reconnaissance aircraft." He keyed his mike. "Specter eight, two, seven, this is Home Base, do you copy?"

No response.

"Damn it, Specter, come in," Brooks said and repeated the
call.

Lieutenant Hill broke in. "Captain, the navigational radar
shows us eighty miles off the Soviet coast and closing."

"All right, when we hit fifty miles out turn due north and
let's head up the coast. Take her up to twenty-two thousand."

Hill eased back on the yoke and brought the nose of the big
jet up three degrees, then nudged the throttles forward.

Brooks keyed his internal mike, tying him directly to Staff
Sergeant Walter E. Nelson. The sergeant, nearly fifteen years
older than Brooks, also had fifteen more years of experience. It

was Nelson's job to monitor Soviet radio and radar transmissions coming out of Sakhalin Island. If anyone could give Brooks a clue about what was really happening the white-haired Nelson could.

"Sergeant Nelson . . . what's happening out there? Any more SAMs?"

Nelson didn't look up from his console as he keyed his mike to respond. "Yes, cap'n, I now count eight. Five in the last twenty minutes. As far as I can tell they haven't hit anything yet. There's nothing on my radar but sure as hell they're trying to bring down our recon bird . . . wherever it is."

"What about their radio transmissions, are we picking anything up?"

"It's all coded, sir. We're copying them but I'll have to wait until we get back to the base and use the mainframe to decode it." Nelson paused. "There's one other thing I think you should know, cap'n . . . I've been flying this route for two-and-a-half years. The Sovs have never operated this type of radar before. Right now we're being swept on all known radar bands . . . and all *at the same time*."

Captain Brooks didn't respond right away as Nelson's words sank in. "Roger, I understand. Keep me informed, out." But did he really understand?

MASKIROVKA RADAR STATION, SAKHALIN ISLAND

"The target is now heading northwest. Altitude is below thirty meters and speed is constant at 350 knots. It will be entering zone seven in thirty seconds, general."

"Good, it can't hold out much longer. What about that American surveillance aircraft off our eastern coast?"

The operator behind the eastern-looking scope answered, "It is still out there. Now approaching 140 kilometers. Moving up our coast to the north."

"Good, they're close enough to be jammed. I want full power."

"Yes, sir, and the Soviet lieutenant gave the command to transmit the high-power microwave beam at the RC-135.

RF-117C BLACK GHOST

A flicker of light caught Danny's eye. Two SAMs had just lifted
to the west. He watched as they climbed out of sight. A warble
sounded in his helmet and the Threat Warning Panel flashed
back on. Two more search radars locked onto him. Danny took
a deep breath and tried to concentrate. He banked right to increase his crossing-angle to the search radar and watched as his
HUD showed where the radars were located on the ground. The
launch light came on and the warning panel showed the missiles lifting off. Danny counted one, two, three and a fourth
missile as they rocketed into the night sky at his eleven o'clock.
He strained as he watched them make a high arching semicircle
above him and start to nose over, then fall toward the ground.
The solid-fuel rocket motors of the SAMs burned a bright white
and had an almost eerie beauty to them.

The signal-detection indicator on his HUD showed C- and
E-Band radars again. Damn it, SA-6s, Sheldon thought. The
SA-6 was radar-guided but also had a semiactive terminal-
seeker head that could track his IR signature. After its solid-
propellant booster burned out, the missile's empty casing
became a ramjet that could follow an aircraft through its entire
flight envelope.

Danny jinked his fighter right to left. The first missile was
turning and coming right at him. He broke hard right and
pulled the nose up hard, popped a flare and pumped the chaff
button. He came across the beam of the remaining missiles and
let go with three more flares, then watched his G-meter climb.
The first SAM tracked on the flare and failed to explode, slamming into the black ground and disappearing in a fireball. The
second and third missiles corrected themselves and raced for the
cluster of flares that were slowly falling to the ground, and exploded into a fireball.

Danny watched his altimeter needle pass through the thou-
sand-foot mark. He pushed the nose of the fighter down and
felt his lap belt hold him in his seat. He looked over his shoulder
and watched the fourth SAM accelerate toward his fighter. He
slammed the stick down and to the right.

The RF-117C twisted and shuddered toward the ground. Again Sheldon hit the chaff button and popped the flare canister. It was too late—the missile exploded only 100 feet from his fighter. The 176 pounds of warhead rocked the RF-117C. The specially treated laminated plexiglass panels of the canopy shattered. Danny Sheldon felt pieces of burning hot metal slice into his neck and left arm.

It was the shock of the cold air pouring into the cockpit through the broken canopy that brought him back to life. He pulled the fighter out of its dive and tried to level out at 250 feet. But the plane was sluggish and slow to respond. He looked over his instruments. The HUD and Threat Warning Panel were out. The fighter was pitching up and down. The in-flight computers were chasing the flight controls. Danny tried to look out the left side of the aircraft but could barely move his neck because of the pain. Large pieces of the fighter's graphite skin were missing.

Try to make it out to sea, he ordered himself. If you crash on the island the Soviets can learn too much about this plane and . . . He made a slow turn to the right and moved the throttle to full power.

RC-135V, RIVET JOINT FLIGHT

The Soviet jamming had shut down the electronic eavesdropping systems on the aircraft. The operators sat behind their CRTs looking at their scopes that were now nothing more than a combination of broken and wavy lines.

"Captain, this is Nelson, it's no use. We can't break it. Their jamming is too strong. They must be using maximum power. The only other time I've seen this was when they were testing their ICBMs and didn't want us to intercept their signals—"

"*Keep trying*, damn it. I've got to find out what's going on out there."

RF-117C BLACK GHOST

Danny Sheldon could feel the energy leaving his body. He was losing blood, fast. His left arm was numb, he couldn't feel the

handle of the throttles. Two more SAMs launched to the south.
He couldn't tell if their radars were locked onto him or not. He
flipped the On and Off switch to his countermeasures hoping
the fluctuating signals would confuse the SAMs. One of the
missiles raced by his windscreen in front and above him. His
reflexes somehow pushed the stick forward and the Black Ghost
snapped into a roll and nosed down toward the ground. He
pulled the stick back and tried to come wings-level . . . no response. He popped open the air brake, trying to slow his fighter.
His airspeed slowed, he pumped the stick back and forth, trying
not to overstress the airplane. He had lost track of the second
missile.

"Where are you?" he shouted to no one.

Just ahead was the coastline he could barely make out. He
put the fighter in the steepest climb he thought it could handle.
Still no sign of the other missile. At 3500 feet he leveled out. In
one minute he should be over the water. At least if he went
down in the sea the Russians would have a tough time finding
his broken aircraft.

He closed his eyes and put his head against the back of the
headrest. He had trained for a moment like this in the simulator . . .

Think, man, think. What the hell am I supposed to do? He
opened his eyes and looked at a small red light next to the
control stick. Just behind it was the ELINT computer. He waited
for the computer disk to stop cycling. The red light went out.
Danny quickly hit the bright orange switch next to it and
dumped all the radar information he had gathered and stored
on the disk to an orbiting relay satellite . . .

Danny couldn't see the SAM approaching from his rear. By
its very nature, his aircraft had poor all-around visibility. The
infrared-suppression system that cloaked the fighter's IR signature from behind wasn't designed to be used with the engine in
afterburner. He had pushed the throttles all the way forward to
get as much power as he could out of his one remaining engine.
He had also inadvertently put his fighter in afterburner.

The SAM hit the port side of the airplane and turned the little
black fighter into a yellowish orange ball of flames. The main

fuselage emerged from the opposite side of the fireball, flipped over and glided down to the earth below.

Danny Sheldon died before his ghost made it to the sea.

Like too much in the military, payback came after the fact. In this case the death of Major Danny Sheldon. But it was coming, for his memory, for his family, for the Air Force . . . and from the most unlikely of places, deep in the confines of the Soviets' most secret and lethal installation.

2

FREEDOM

KART DAG STATION, TURKEY

The sun was just breaking through the clouds of the cool October morning when 1st Lieutenant Bart Bowlings reached the Early Warning Center located on a remote ridge just twenty miles south of the Black Sea in northern Turkey. Young Bowlings had hoped for a more scenic first assignment after graduating number two from the Electronic Systems Division School at Hansom AFB in Massachusetts. Maybe Alaska, where he had heard one could see the northern lights splash across the sky when the nights were twenty hours long and fish for silver salmon or rainbow trout in the summer. What he really wanted was an E-3 Sentry on AWACS Airborne Warning and Control System, but he knew those assignments were hard enough to get even if he had graduated number one. For now the lieutenant had to be satisfied with the challenges of his new command and make sure everything was running smoothly.

In one way or another the Air Force had always been a part of his life. He was born on his father's first overseas tour at Kunsan Air Base, Korea, in 1963. The next year his father died when his F-100 Super Sabre flipped over, crashed and burned when attempting to land in heavy fog. His mother moved back to the States and married a college professor four years later when Bart was five. By the time he was eight Bart Bowlings knew what he wanted to do the rest of his life. At twenty-two, after graduating from Central Washington University with a Bachelor's degree in electronics, he joined the Air Force. A year later he found himself in charge of one of the Air Force's most advanced and strategically located Early Warning Centers in NATO.

The Kart Dag Station was responsible for monitoring all air traffic in an 800 mile radius. Most days were filled with tracking commercial aircraft that crisscrossed the skies to the south. To the north, however, was the Black Sea, and 200 miles north of the Turkish border was the Soviet Strategic Naval and Bomber Base of Sevastopol, where the Soviets had both the TU-26 and the new TU-160, the Soviet equivalent of the B-1B, stationed for training—and use—on NATO's southeastern flank in the event of hostilities.

Lieutenant Bart Bowlings was just starting to make out the luminous green glow of the radar room as he walked down the hall, then stopped and paused for a moment before entering the main control room. To his right were the two large radar-scopes that kept a watch on everything that flew into their sector. The scope on the right was for the dish looking south. If anything out of the ordinary came up on it a computer tone would immediately alert a technician to start tracking the aircraft. The scope on the left, which was always manned, looked north for any activity in Soviet airspace. To the left of the two scopes sat the Soviet communication and code-breaking equipment, which looked more like a dozen pieces of the latest high-tech stereo devices all stacked on one another. It ran by computers until a radio signal was picked up and then it was also manned. To the right of the scopes were the station's communication radios. From his desk, which sat four feet higher than the equipment in the front of the room, the lieutenant overlooked the operation.

Now he walked over to the coffeepot in the rear of the room, reached up and grabbed his cup. Glancing down, he noticed that all the Sweet and Low was gone, put his cup under the spout and pushed down on the lever. A thick black liquid filled his cup.

"Sergeant Roundtree must have made the coffee this morning," he muttered to himself.

"Good morning, sir, I didn't hear you come in," Kevin Roundtree said without taking his eyes off the northern scope.

"Morning, sarge. Anything happening with our friends to the north?"

"No, sir, all's quiet on the eastern front. You did get a Faxcode from headquarters. I put it on your desk."

Lieutenant Bowlings tore the perforated edge off the envelope, pulled out the message and read:

KZT819G1219DO71090
TO: KART DAG STATION
FR: 2717th ABG USAFE

1. INTELLIGENCE HAS NOW CONFIRMED THAT A FULL SQUADRON OF MiG-29 FULCRUMS HAS BEEN DEPLOYED TO SEVASTOPOL.

2. REPORT IMMEDIATELY ANY ACTIVITY IN YOUR SECTOR.

From the station's records Bowlings remembered the Soviets had rotated in several squadrons of MiG-23s six months ago. They had been used to train the bombers in evasion tactics and at the same time allowed the fighters to practice their interception techniques. The fighters were there for eight weeks and then were rotated out. Was this maybe the case this time? He walked over to his Faxcoder and typed in a message that sixteen seconds later appeared at headquarters, then sat back and began his routine.

Sergeant Roundtree sat watching the northern scope with his usual dead-on intensity. People like Roundtree made the younger Bowlings glad he had chosen the military. Roundtree, himself, was a lifer, he and his wife had built their whole life around the military. He was intelligent and damn good at what he did, took pride in his work and his heritage—a direct descendant of Chief Fighting Bull of the Winnebago Indians in upper Minnesota and Wisconsin. His father Mitchell Roundtree had won the Congressional Medal of Honor for valor in the Korean War. Kevin Roundtree had followed in his father's footsteps and enlisted in the Air Force the day after he was married, not exactly the honeymoon his bride had hoped for.

Bowlings had just started to refill his coffee cup when he heard the Faxcoder, looked at his watch, noted it had only been five minutes since he'd sent the message.

"Must be more important than I thought." He opened the reply:

1. CONFIRMATION: AT LEAST 14 MIG-29 FULCRUMS ARE NOW STATIONED AT SEVASTOPOL.

2. COMMAND BELIEVES THEY FLEW IN UNDER YOUR RADAR COVERAGE WITHIN THE LAST FORTY EIGHT HOURS.

3. IT IS BELIEVED THEY ARE ON A TRAINING MISSION.

4. ALL OTHER QUESTIONS WILL BE ANSWERED ON A NEED TO KNOW BASIS.

Bowlings smiled to himself. In other words, shut up, do your job and let us know if those MiGs do anything. "Sergeant, headquarters reports fourteen MiG-29s are now stationed at Sevastopol. Let me know if anything comes up on that scope."

Roundtree felt prickles at the back of his neck. This was the first time the Soviet air force had deployed Fulcrums this far south. He had some familiarity with the new MiG. He had seen satellite photos of the squadron based at Kubinka near Moscow, and he had recently received new computer software to enable him to identify them on radar. Nevertheless, the prospects tracking a Fulcrum for the first time had put him on edge.

Bowlings now looked over at Sergeant Roberts, who was just seating himself at the communications and code-breaking console.

"Roberts, let me know pronto if you pick up anything on those Soviet communications channels."

SEVASTOPOL AIR BASE

Captain Grigori Koiser wiped his lips with the faded red napkin that had been sitting on the left side of his plate. Breakfast tasted unusually good this morning. Maybe the base commander was trying to impress his new arrivals. Koiser was hungry, he had been up since 3:30 A.M. preparing for his first training mission since arriving at the base.

Captain Koiser was the oldest son of a family that the party system had developed into one of their finest. A product of the party, Koiser nonetheless considered it a failed party and government. The party had lied to him and his family too many times to ignore. His parents had killed themselves working in the coal mines of southwestern Russia believing that hard work would give Grigori a better life. When his father finally decided that the system wasn't going to work and his family's life would not get any better as a civilian, he steered Grigori toward the military, and Grigory followed his lead. As a pilot he received the best of everything; food, lodging, transportation and hard-to-get consumer goods. But after Koiser joined the Soviet air force he began to see Soviet society in a new way. He learned about the concentration camps used to "reeducate" people who had the courage—and temerity—to challenge the party and speak their minds. He learned that the more corrupt and dishonest a man was, the further he got. More goods were available underground through the black market than on the open market. Life, he was convinced, would not change because the system would not change. The system didn't work, no matter what they'd taught him. No matter what was shown to the world. Many young officers talked about democracy but Koiser knew it was just that, talk. If his country was ever to change the people would need to do more than talk. *He* would need to do more . . .

Koiser was not the PVO's standard MiG-29 pilot. He was several years ahead of other pilots his age in experience, training and education. He had spent the last five years at the Soviet test center of Ramenskoye, thirty miles southeast of Moscow. He had been part of the elite team of pilots, engineers and designers that worked on the Central Committee's most secret projects. He was allowed to see his wife and little girl only once every six weeks and then only for a short time. His daughter had been six months old when he received his orders to report to Ramenskoye, originally for a maximum stint of two years. But two years turned into three and then four and finally five. He had missed his daughter's first steps and first words. As his daughter grew his young wife changed, and soon they were all but strangers with little in common except their child . . .

Koiser stopped such thoughts and forced himself to concentrate on the immediate. His aircraft, the MiG-29C, was the best fighter in the Soviet air force. He had flown it at Ramenskoye almost exclusively. The new radar and avionics were state-of-the-art by Soviet standards and the Ministry of Defense was counting on the new MiG to help close the gap in the West's edge in fighter technology. Koiser's chief assignment at the secret base had been how to intercept strategic bombers and advise engineers on the best ways to build and use radars. The Soviet high command was very worried about the U.S. B-1B and terrified of the new B-2 stealth bomber. Koiser's team had been involved in developing and testing new radar-detection technologies that would allow the PVO to track the West's latest aircraft. Nine times out of ten when Koiser was vectored to intercept a simulated American bomber attack he did just that. The bomber came under simulated attack and was brought down.

This morning Captain Koiser had other things on his mind. The day he was told he had been assigned to Sevastopol he knew his fortunes had changed. His dreams, more like fantasies, of a new start in the heady atmosphere of freedom were about to come true . . .

"Final briefing in five minutes, full flight gear," Colonel Igor Belikov's voice boomed throughout the mess hall, sending a special chill into the air.

Koiser watched the base commander move across the front of the room. His navy blue flight suit was neat and pressed, fitting his narrow-waisted muscular body. Young pilots in the room looked on the fifty-one-year-old colonel with respect, someone to model their careers on. Not so with Grigori Koiser, for whom Belikov represented what he'd come to hate. A man purposefully blind to the truth about what the party had created, what it was doing to the people, including Koiser's parents. Grigori had long ago decided he was willing to risk death to avoid turning into a Colonel Belikov.

Belikov himself stood five feet ten inches, with thick curly red hair. He had flown with the North Vietnamese in 1971 and 1972, and as a young lieutenant was credited with shooting down one American F-105 and participating in several dogfights with F-4 Phantoms. Belikov had worked his way up through the ranks by eliminating his enemies one at a time, with the blessings of his senior commanders, who were not unaware that it was widely speculated that Belikov did a lot of the general's dirty work when it came to taking care of dissident officers.

There was not much conversation as Koiser entered the mission ready room and opened his locker. His fellow pilots kept their thoughts to themselves as they dressed. Each knew he would be evaluated on everything that happened in the air, which in turn would reflect on their careers.

Koiser took his time. He had been working on his plan from the first day he learned he would be stationed at the Black Sea base. A dream for years, now maybe it would have a chance to come true. Koiser had more hours and more experience in the MiG than anyone except Colonel Belikov, and the colonel's experience and intelligence were the biggest threats for Koiser.

He closed his locker door gently after taking one last look at his only picture of his wife and daughter. Actually Koiser had nearly forgotten what it felt like to be in love, to hold a woman. He hadn't touched or been with his wife for two years, not since the night he had surprised her in the arms of another man on an unannounced visit home. It was the end of the end for the marriage. As for Alexandria, his daughter. . . . the captain would miss his girl, very much. At least the *idea* of her had helped keep him going through the pain. But the fact was he had seen so little of her over the last several years she was less real than imagined.

Koiser sat in his assigned seat now, waiting for the final briefing. He saw the colonel enter the room, watched him push through the pilots still milling around the front of the room and head straight for the huge map hanging over the blackboard, pick up the pointer and start to pace the floor. Within moments everyone had taken their seats. Koiser studied the colonel as he readied himself for the briefing, reminding himself to be very careful not to give away his plan. One thing was sure—if he failed Belikov would see to it he could never try again. He would get one chance . . .

"As I speak, eight of our newest and finest bombers, the TU-160s, are taking off," Belikov was intoning. "The bombers will head east, turn south and head back toward this base and attempt to bomb it. Our mission is to intercept them." The colonel indicated the point where the TU-160 Blackjacks would make their turn back to Sevastopol.

"To score a kill, missile-lock must be maintained for a minimum of twenty seconds. To familiarize each of you with the latest weapons your MiGs will be carrying live missiles." The colonel paused and stared right at Captain Koiser, or so Koiser felt. "I will be watching, the Defense Ministry will be watching. I want *all* those bombers shot down." Colonel Belikov turned around and faced the wall. "Take off in twenty minutes. Dismissed."

The sleek twin-tailed MiG-29C sat at the edge of the runway as Koiser approached. The two-tone blue gray camouflage would make the aircraft difficult to see under most conditions. The blended wing and fuselage design of the MiG and the jet black radar dome made this aircraft one of the most fearsome looking fighters in the Soviet inventory. Koiser's MiG carried a standard mix of radar and infrared homing missiles plus a cannon, none of which made the captain feel more secure as he walked around the fighter, performing his preflight checks.

Three minutes later Koiser climbed up the ladder and started going over his internal checklist. Sergeant Petrov followed the captain up the ladder to the cockpit and helped Koiser strap himself into the ejection seat. The rest of the ground crew finished fueling the plane and gave the signal that the MiG was ready.

"Looks like a good day to fly, captain," the sergeant said.

Koiser didn't respond.

Petrov could take a hint. He checked the last buckle on the seat and helped the captain fasten his helmet, climbed down the ladder, turned and gave the signal to start engines. The auxiliary-power unit kicked to life and Koiser could feel the hum as the RPMs started to build. The twin Tumansky R-33D Turbofans fired up with a loud roar. Everything checked out.

The captain snapped Petrov a quick salute, the canopy low-ered and the ground crew pulled away the tire blocks. Koiser released the brakes and started to taxi to the runway, then stopped just short, waiting to get his takeoff clearance.

He thought about Belikov's last remark, how he seemed to be looking at him when he said it. Was it possible Belikov knew something? Did he make a mistake? But if he knew, or sus-pected, why would Belikov allow him to fly? Stop it, he ordered himself, the time for such thoughts was over.

Koiser pulled his MiG onto the runway, lining up its nose with the center stripe. He waited for his fellow pilots to get into position. He pushed the throttles forward and felt his aircraft come to life.

KART DAG STATION, TURKEY

"They're maintaining 087, altitude is 11,000 feet and still climb-ing, speed . . . 600 knots and accelerating. I don't know where they're going but they sure are in a hurry to get there," Round-tree said while tapping on the computer keyboard, trying to get the most out of the software.

"How far are they from their base?" Bowlings asked.

"200 miles, sir."

"Can you give me a positive I.D.?"

"Not yet, I need to watch them a little longer. The informa-tion we have in the memory of the RCS computer isn't com-plete on the Blackjack, if that's what they are."

"All right, but if those bombers turn south let me know. I need to alert command right away." Bowlings backed off a lit-tle, inched forward on his desk chair to get a better view of Roundtree's screen some twenty feet away.

"Lieutenant, I'm starting to pick up some new targets leaving Sevastopol. They look like fighters in a tight formation." A short pause. "Heading 203, altitude 2500 and climbing, speed 350 knots. They're coming right at us." Roundtree glanced at the lieutenant.

"I want an I.D. on those new targets. They could be the MiGs," Bowlings said.

"I got them, sir. The RCS computer says they're MiG-29 Fulcrums, eighty percent confident."

"What are the other targets?"

"Still haven't got enough radar data." Roundtree continued to work on the computer.

"Roberts, link me into Colonel Clasp at headquarters," Bowlings said, his voice tense.

SEVASTOPOL AIR BASE

Captain Koiser pushed the stick forward and eased the throttles back. He wanted to be a little below and behind the rest of the fighters as they headed out over the coast. The exercise was to take them southwest for 300 kilometers and then due east. By that time the eight Blackjacks would just be making their turn south and back west toward the base. The MiGs and Blackjacks would meet 600 kilometers east of Sevastopol and engage.

Koiser's MiG was equipped with the new Pulse-Doppler lookdown/shoot-down radar, which gave it day-and-night all-weather operating capability against low-flying targets as well as freedom from ground controllers. It was that freedom Koiser was counting on. The controllers had always restricted Soviet air-defense fighters, and the new MiG was supposed to correct that.

The captain's plan was to stay with the MiG squadron until they broke to the east and started their search for the TU-160" Blackjack bombers. At that point he intended to put his aircraft into a sharp dive, push the throttles forward to afterburner, try to level out at thirty meters above the water and hope the ground-control radar wouldn't be able to find him. He knew the Americans had a base at Incirlik, Turkey . . . If he could make it there without being shot down by his fellow pilots or the Americans, escape and freedom were a possibility . . .

Koiser blinked hard. Despite intensely personal forces driving him to this act, what he was about to do nevertheless went against everything he had been taught to believe in his whole life. He was beginning to feel the pull, the inevitable conflict in his gut. It wasn't easy, what he planned to do, no matter what his good reasons. He had to invoke memories . . . The Soviet system that had made his father die an early death, made him watch his mother waste away into nothing. The party talking a glowing story it never delivered on. Rumors of so-called reforms were just that . . . rumors. Now he had a chance to be free, a dream his parents only secretly, hesitantly talked about. Koiser told himself he knew in his heart that his mother and father would have approved of what he was about to do . . .

He keyed his mike. "Red one, this is Red six, I have a problem."

"State your problem, Red six," Colonel Belikov snapped back.

"The RPMs on the left engine are surging and falling off." A not uncommon occurrence on account of the uneven quality of Soviet jet fuel.

"Red six, state your fuel number."

"Nine . . . comrade colonel."

"Maybe it is *your* fuel and it will just have to run through. Keep me informed and stay with us."

Koiser clicked his mike twice to signal "understood." So far, so good. At least it sounded like the colonel was buying his phony fuel story.

KART DAG STATION, TURKEY

Bowlings picked up the yellow phone located on the right corner of his desk that gave him a secure line to the intelligence center at Incirlik Air Base.

"Colonel Clasp," came the answer.

"This is Lieutenant Bowlings, sir. We have radar contact on nine MiG-29 Fulcrums and eight possible Blackjack bombers. The MiGs are heading 203, altitude is 6000 feet and climbing, speed is 650 knots and accelerating."

"How long have you been tracking them?" the colonel asked.

"The bombers, about twenty-five minutes, the Fulcrums only five."

"What's their position in relationship to their takeoff point?" Clasp was jotting down the information as Bowlings relayed it.

"The bombers are 235 miles east of Sevastopol, the Fulcrums

are twenty-three miles southwest of the base. They just crossed the coast, sir."

"All right, if those fighters break 100 miles south let me know pronto."

Bowlings heard the line go dead, put down the phone receiver and looked at the northern radarscope. "Roundtree, let me know fast if those MiGs break 100 miles south . . ."

INCIRLIK AIR BASE, TURKEY

Colonel Clasp picked up his priority phone. "Give me the base commander," he ordered, wondering what the hell Ivan was up to.

"Colonel, this is Clasp at Intelligence. I need two F-16s standing by for a possible intercept. I'll give you more information as it comes in." Clasp turned to his aide. "Give me General Sweeny on the scramble phone, at once."

OVER THE BLACK SEA

Captain Koiser stopped his drift below the rest of the MiGs, then increased his speed in hopes of giving Belikov the sense that his mock engine troubles were under control. In twenty minutes they would be 300 kilometers south and the fighters would make their turn east.

He reminded himself to drop his auxiliary fuel tank. Although it would still be half-full he wouldn't need it. Losing the extra weight and drag would give him an edge over the other fighters. At least until they figured out what was going on. He tightened his lap and shoulder belts, adjusted his G-suit and started his checklist. Very soon life was going to get very complicated.

KART DAG STATION, TURKEY

Sergeant Roundtree tapped away at the computer keyboard. The radar was being bombarded with new electronic information as the unknown aircraft gained altitude.

"Bingo . . . got you . . . Sir, those must be Blackjacks. The RCS computer is showing seventy-five percent confidence and they're really cooking. I have them at 900 knots, 273 miles east of Sevastopol, heading is constant at 087, altitude steady at 15,000 feet. The Russkies are really in a hurry, they're going supersonic." He caught Bowlings's eye. "What do you think, lieutenant?"

"As far as we're concerned this is a training mission until we get different orders from headquarters. Anything on the communications channels, Sergeant Roberts?"

"No sir, thought I had something earlier but it faded out. I think the bombers are being quiet. Whatever it was came from those Fulcrums."

"Okay, hope you're up to speed on your Russian, you just might need it today."

Bowlings went back to his desk, feeling more anxious than he hoped he showed. "Talk to me, Roundtree. Those MiGs still want to play chicken?"

"The Fulcrums are heading 182, ninety-five miles south of departure, 325 knots and steady at 18,000 feet. Those Blackjacks . . . I can't figure them. Three hundred thirty miles east of departure, now heading 123, speed 950 knots and still level at 15,000 feet."

Bowlings reached for the phone again and reported to Colonel Clasp that the MiGs had just broken 100 miles south.

INCIRLIK AIR BASE, TURKEY

The pair of F-16s sat at the end of the runway, their canopies closed. Both pilots had some experience intercepting Soviet TU-143 Bear Bombers that flew across the northern coast of Turkey to check the reaction time of NATO air defenses. The large four-turboprop Bear could carry long-range air-launched cruise missiles with conventional or nuclear warheads. The F-16s would escort the Bears until they reached Soviet airspace, give them a goodbye wave and send them on their way. However, MiG-29s were a different story, and the American pilots knew it.

"Rover flight, you are cleared for takeoff," the controller's voice crackled over the pilots' headsets. "We have radar contact on nine MiG-29 Fulcrums heading 182 out of Sevastopol, speed 325 knots, altitude 18,000 feet."

"Ah, Roger tower . . . Rover flight on the roll."

The two American fighters accelerated down the runway, one on each side of the center line. Within twelve seconds they were airborne.

"Rover flight, turn left heading zero six eight. You should have radar contact in twelve minutes." The F-16s banked slowly to the northeast, light gray smoke pouring out of their engines as they followed the controller's instructions.

KART DAG STATION, TURKEY

Sergeant Roberts concentrated on finding the base frequency the Soviets were hopping from. If he did he could tie it into the computer and maybe lock onto it. Even if the Soviets hopped back and forth he could follow. He turned the control back to the lowest setting and started his search again.

"Lieutenant, I have something." He held up his left hand before returning it to the keyboard, then typed the information into the computer and hoped the signal stayed strong long enough for it to be locked onto. "I got them, the base frequency. One of the fighters is having some sort of engine trouble. The leader has ordered him to get back into formation . . ."

OVER THE BLACK SEA

"Red one . . . I am still having engine trouble." Koiser reported.

"Are you requesting to return to base, Red six?" from Belikov.

Koiser did not want this. Did not want Belikov to give him an escort. "Negative, colonel. I will try to maintain."

Koiser eased his fighter back into formation. He was still a little outside of the group when he heard the order to break left and increase speed.

"This is Red one, follow my lead. Remember I want all those

bombers." Belikov pushed his stick hard left and moved his throttles forward.

Koiser waited until the last moment. On the outside edge, he would be the last of the group to turn. He watched as the two MiGs on his left broke. He didn't follow. He reached down and pulled the emergency release for his auxiliary fuel tank, pushed the throttles forward and put the MiG into a steep dive—and felt the afterburners kick in, ramming him back in his seat. The altitude indicator on the MiG's Heads Up Display showed him that he was diving at 6000 meters a minute. In forty-five seconds he would be at sea level.

"Colonel, this is Red four, we have lost Red six—"

"What do you mean *lost*?"

"I don't know, I made the turn and when I completed it he wasn't where he was supposed to be," Red four radioed back.

Belikov looked over his shoulder. "Red six, report your position."

No response.

"Red six, *report your position*." The colonel was yelling into his mike.

No response.

"Damn it, Koiser, are you in an emergency situation?"

"Colonel, this is Red four, I have a visual. Red six is in a steep dive." The pilot could see the glowing red tailpipes of the MiG's twin afterburner.

That statement made the blood rush to the colonel's head. It was hard to believe, Koiser was just about his best man, but his instinct told him Koiser was heading for Turkey, a NATO ally, with one of the newest Soviet fighters. Belikov had no way of knowing his country was in danger of losing much more than a MiG-29. The information Captain Koiser had obtained, after spending five years training and working at Ramenskoye, would threaten and damage the Soviet Union far more than the loss of a single fighter if he defected. Without knowing it, Belikov was about to pursue a man that could singlehandedly supply the Americans with knowledge that could bring down the government of the USSR. For Belikov, from his myopic viewpoint, the big reason he needed to stop Koiser and the MiG from reaching Turkey would be to save his own neck . . .

"All fighters return to base at once. Red four, you stay with me." The colonel pulled back on his stick and climbed to 6250 meters. The other MiGs turned hard left and headed back toward Sevastopol. Red four pulled up with the colonel and assumed his wingman position on the colonel's left side.

"All right, Red four, break hard left and see if you can get on his tail. I'll break right and try to cut him off. Break now." And the two MiGs rocketed away in opposite directions.

KART DAG STATION, TURKEY

"Lieutenant Bowlings, look at this. Those MiGs are breaking formation. I count six now heading 337, one heading 176 in a sharp dive and these two"—Roundtree pointed to the location of the other two turning MiGs on the screen—"are splitting off in opposite directions."

Bowlings turned to Roberts. "Are you still locked onto their communications channel?"

"Yes, sir. Those MiG's were ordered back to base by the flight leader. I'm not sure what's happening but I *think* they're going after the MiG that's furthest south."

"Are you telling me that the Russians may be going after one of their own MiGs? What exactly are they saying?"

Roberts repeated what he had heard—and suddenly the unlikely thought hit him. "They just might have a rogue MiG-29 on their hands—"

"Roberts," Bowlings said "that's a wild-hair idea, but if you get any indication at all that that MiG is trying to defect . . . I want to know immediately. The flight commander is obviously worried about something, and I need to be sure what the hell it is before I alert headquarters." Bowlings knew his career could be made or lost on the decision he was about to make.

The F-16s slid through the cobalt blue sky as if there were no resistance. The northern coast of Turkey flashed by in a blur. Both fighters inched their throttles forward until they were supersonic.

"I have contact, bearing 052. Turn right heading 055. Let's

see what this is all about." Rover one readjusted his grip on the throttle and continued his turn.

OVER THE BLACK SEA

Koiser watched his altimeter click off his altitude. As he hit 600 meters he pulled back on the throttles and began moving the stick back. He watched his G-meter climb and felt the stress of the Gs force him back into his seat. Three, four, five, five and a half, he kept up a steady five and a half G-pull until the nose was pointed up and away from the water. His altimeter showed 155 meters. He turned his head left and right to see if anyone was on his tail. He had, of course, heard Belikov's orders over the radio.

His "six" was clear and he saw nothing on his radar. He reached over and turned off his radio. No use listening anymore. He planned to turn it back on when he was over Turkey or came in contact with the American interceptors.

A radar suddenly started to sweep his fighter, the tone fading in and out as the radar came in contact with his fighter. Koiser accelerated and pulled up the nose, he needed more altitude to trade for maneuvering if he had to fight. A high-pitch warning sounded again in his headset and the radar-warning indicator light blinked on the left side of the instrument-warning panel. This time the tone didn't stop. The radar had achieved a lock-on. Koiser strained as he looked over each shoulder. Damn it, where is that plane? he silently shouted to himself.

Belikov's radar had locked onto Koiser's MiG. The colonel could not actually see his target, but glancing down at his CRT located in the upper center of his instrument panel he determined a lock-on with an AA-10 air-to-air missile with eighteen kilometers to the target. He radioed one final warning to Koiser. Again, no response. Belikov launched the missile, pushing a button located on the throttle, and watched the sparkling white missile accelerate toward the target in a cloud of silverish smoke and fire.

*   *   *

Koiser nosed up over 625 meters. The warning tone in his helmet was still sounding along with the flashing radar-warning light. He checked the throttles to see how close he was to afterburner—in afterburner his large infrared signature could easily be tracked by a missile. Koiser squinted hard, looked up, turned his head to the left and saw nothing. To the right, the snaky white trail of smoke needed no explanation.

His timing had to be perfect. If he broke too soon the missile would correct itself and score a hit, too late and it would be over. Within seconds the missile was only 1500 meters away. Koiser didn't need to think, he was operating on experience and instinct. He pushed the stick hard right, stepped on the rudder and put the MiG into a right turn, seventy-five degrees of bank. He turned into the missile at 400 knots, the G-forces slamming him into his seat. It took every ounce of his strength to keep his eyes on the missile as it raced by his MiG, overshooting by no more than seventy-five meters.

Koiser felt the Gs bleed off as he came out of the turn and rolled to wings-level. He scanned the sky in front of him. The warning tone was gone, the radar-warning light was out. He pushed the nose over twenty degrees and went to afterburner. His airspeed quickly increased to over 500 knots. He was down to 100 meters when he leveled out. Let's see if they can find me now, he thought as he headed straight back toward the other two MiGs.

Belikov watched as his missile descended toward the water following the reflecting signals of his locked-on radar. He knew that as soon as the missile came within four kilometers of Koiser's MiG the IR seeker head would pick up its target. After that he no longer had to keep his radar locked onto Koiser's MiG.

Seconds later, though, the smoke trailed off into nothing—he had missed. Koiser must have out maneuvered it, was still below him somewhere.

But *where* . . . ?

* * *

Koiser saw a flash of light six kilometers out and to the far left
of where the missile had been fired. No doubt the second MiG.
He turned off his radar, the other two MiGs would know he was
close by if he scanned them. Surprise would be his biggest advantage.

Koiser strained, trying to spot the MiG as he looked up
through the light haze. The flash must have been the sunlight
reflecting off the canopy of the MiG as it turned toward him. He
told himself it would be easier for him to see the dark image of
the hostile fighter than for him to be spotted . . . the blue gray
background of the water helping camouflage his aircraft. He just
had to find the speck of the other aircraft's silhouette against
the light background of the sky.

Koiser could feel the rush of adrenaline as a hollow, pulsating
tone sounded in his headset. His attention turned from the sky
to his HUD. A bright orange circle, the IR optical sight for his
AA-8 heat-seeking missiles, had appeared in the upper left corner. His MiG's infrared search-and-tracking system was looking
at the hostile MiG. The low tone would change to a high constant pitch when the system had achieved a lock-on. Then he
would have to maneuver into position for a kill . . .

He nosed up fifteen degrees and banked twenty degrees left.
The orange sight on his HUD was now in the upper center. To
get a lock-on he had to get his fighter directly behind the target.
The seeker heads on the missiles would only lock onto the hot
IR signature of the engines to the rear of the aircraft. He looked
again to the sky. The target—he had eliminated its personality,
its being one of what had been his comrade—the target was just
coming into view . . .

KART DAG STATION, TURKEY

No question now in Bowlings's mind what was happening over
the Black Sea. Yes . . . the Soviets had a MiG trying to defect!
He picked up his phone and dialed Colonel Clasp at command,
trying to keep his voice under control.

"Sir, this is Watch Dog, one of the MiGs we've been tracking is trying to defect—"

"What? Are you sure?"

"Yes sir, I mean, Jesus, they're trying to shoot him down . . ."

"Where are our interceptors?"

"Thirty miles south." Bowlings was watching the blips that represented the Sixteens on the radarscope.

"Vector them away unless those MiGs enter Turkish airspace. I want this by the book. Do you *understand*?"

"Yes, sir." Bowlings hung up and ordered Sergeant Roberts to put him through to the interceptors. He plugged in his headset. "Rover flight, this is Watch Dog, do you copy?"

A short pause, then: "Ah . . . Roger, Watch Dog, this is Rover one."

"Rover one, we have a sensitive situation. It seems one of the Fulcrums is trying to defect. Stay out of the area until we have a clearer picture of what's happening." Bowlings swallowed hard. "Turn left heading 035, maintain 15,000 feet, hold at NOVEMBER, X-RAY, TANGO." All of which told the F-16 pilots to take a position thirty miles to the west of the MiGs and maintain a holding pattern until they received further orders.

"Wilco, Watch Dog, we copy you. Rover one out."

OVER THE BLACK SEA

Koiser watched the hostile—yes "hostile," it was the enemy now, trying to destroy him—MiG streak toward him and pass high and to the left. His infrared search-and-track was no longer locked onto the second MiG. His MiG had to be flying at its target before it would start to track again. He kept his eyes on the second MiG and put his fighter into a maximum left-hand turn pulling 8.5 Gs. As he came out of the turn Koiser came wings-level at 100 meters above the water. The MiG was straight ahead and above him. He pulled up the nose twenty degrees and added power, looked left and right—and saw the MiG as it seemed to float in the air in front of him. Since he was directly below and behind the MiG, the other pilot could not see him. He watched his target above his HUD, and gently brushed the launch button with his finger. An AA-8 Aphid air-to-air missile could destroy the other MiG within a heartbeat. Suddenly he felt sick. He could not wash out of his head that he was about to shoot down one of his comrades, a man he didn't know, a man he didn't want to know . . . was freedom worth *this* . . . ? He hadn't considered such a prospect. No surprise. Well, he could still return to base, claim engine and radio trouble, his word against the colonel's. Koiser found himself hesitating.

And then reality came rushing back at him. All Soviet pilots, he well knew, had standing orders to pursue and help in shooting down *any* pilot that varied from the flight plan and appeared to be heading toward enemy airspace. The pilot flying the MiG in front of him would not hesitate to blow him out of the sky. That was why Belikov had ordered Red four to engage.

Koiser watched the missile leave the rail-launcher under the tip of his right wing, pulled the stick back and hard to the right. The fighter nosed up eighteen degrees, banked right. He came wings-level just as his missile impacted the starboard engine. With a bright flash the rudder and tailplane on the right side of the fighter disappeared. Black smoke poured out of the plane where the engine had been.

When the missile hit the aircraft the warhead's explosion tore through the internal parts of the turbofan, causing the compressor blades to rip through the fuel tanks. With the fuel tanks ruptured, the stricken MiG would explode at any moment . . .

"*Eject*, you fool, *eject*," Koiser heard himself screaming into his oxygen mask. The crippled fighter shuddered and rolled slowly to the left, then in a fiery explosion, broke apart. Hot metal and fuselage pieces cartwheeled through the air, falling toward the water below. Koiser waited, searching, searching for a parachute.

He turned left, heading 175, dropped down to sixty-five meters above the water and applied power. In minutes he should be in Turkish airspace.

KART DAG STATION, TURKEY

Lieutenant Bowlings and Sergeant Roundtree watched as one of the MiGs they were tracking disappeared off the scope.

"Roberts, get search and rescue, tell them to send a chopper out there." Bowlings turned to Roundtree. "Can you tell who the hell shot who?"

"I don't know for sure, sir, but I think our defector is heading this way. Roundtree pointed to the light green blip on his screen. "It's accelerating toward our coast and has dropped down to 200 feet. This MiG, over to the right, is staying up higher. It looks like he's in a search mode."

Bowlings watched both MiGs work their way toward Turkey.

"Stay with them, Roberts. How long before we can get S and R out there?"

"They're on the way, sir, fifteen, twenty minutes." Roberts paused, then: "I'm picking up Soviet radio signals. Sounds like the whole Black Sea Fleet is either headed this way or is on full alert."

"That's all we need. Give me a vector for those Sixteens to intercept that lead MiG." Bowlings put his headset back on.

"Rover one, this is Watch Dog, how do you copy?"

"Rover one, loud and clear, Watch Dog."

"Rover one . . . need you to intercept and give us a visual I.D. on the lead MiG. Head southeast to one five niner, descend to an altitude of 5500 feet."

"Roger, Watch Dog, where are the other MiGs?"

"We have MiG two at 5000, speed 450 knots, heading one two niner. Will advise of any change."

"What about MiG three?"

"MiG three is a splash, Rover, I repeat, three is a splash."

"Roger, Watch Dog, we're turning to engage." The two ghost gray F-16s turned into the glowing orange sun.

OVER THE BLACK SEA

Colonel Belikov loosened his grip on the Fulcrum's stick. The cramp in his palm told him he was uptight, needed to relax to think through his next move. Obviously, Koiser had known his radar had locked onto his aircraft. It was the only way he could have expected an attack. This time would be different. He planned to keep Koiser on his radar just long enough to plan an interception course. Then he would turn his radar off and, he hoped, be in position to pick him up on his infrared systems. Then Koiser would have no way of knowing he was being tracked or even fired on.

Belikov banked his MiG to the left and turned his radar to full power. A red warning light flashed on in the upper right side of his control panel. A hostile radar was sweeping him.

"Damn it, probably American interceptors," he said out loud.

He rolled his MiG over to its back and nosed down to the water, building airspeed. He watched his altimeter unwind until he had descended to 600 meters. He snapped his aircraft up-right, completing his roll, punched the chaff button and pulled the nose straight up. The Gs forced him back into his seat. He watched the gray water turn to blue sky. Instinctively he looked over his instruments, saw that the radar warning light was no longer flashing. He banked his fighter around to a new heading of 093.

The sudden blip on his radar screen had appeared sooner than expected. The colonel made a mental note of Koiser's direction, speed and altitude, then reached over and turned off his radar. Within moments he should be able to track Koiser on his IR system. He edged his throttles forward and slid through Mach one.

Koiser scanned the horizon in front of him, straining to pick up the American interceptors that should be coming his way. Many long hard hours in tactics he'd trained to defeat the Americans. Now, he wanted them to find him and lead him to a safe base. His eyes were stinging from the sweat dropping from his forehead. He reached up, closed his eyes, and pushed hard on the bridge of his nose. He felt exhausted, and drained. In two minutes he would be in Turkish airspace. Belikov would not risk following him. Freedom was two minutes away. But it was not altogether sweet.

*   *   *

Belikov watched the steering symbol on his HUD move to the right, his IR tracking system had locked onto Koiser's MiG in front of and below him. The colonel could fire at any time. He waited for the distance to close between them. He wanted to be at least two kilometers from Koiser's MiG to visually identify his kill. He watched the vapor condensation streak off Koiser's wing tips, throttled back and pushed the nose of his aircraft down fifteen degrees. Koiser was now 300 meters below him and only 1500 meters ahead, straight and level. He was heading right for him.

The colonel heard a swoosh as the AA-8 Aphid left his fighter. He watched it track toward Koiser . . .

Koiser readjusted the trim to 500 knots. The mid-morning sun shone bright in his eyes, blue water sparkled less than 150 meters below. The missile accelerated quickly, the supercooled seeker head was locked onto the hot cross section of his MiG. In less than four seconds the missile had traveled over 600 meters and was descending down to the water. The hundred mirrorlike reflections of the sea below suddenly confused and overloaded the sensor head of the missile. The seeker had lost its lock on the target, was pitching up and down trying to find the hottest signature in its target area. Koiser caught the smoke trail of the AA-8 in his right-hand rear-view mirror. He pulled back on the stick and headed straight for the sun, looked over his shoulder and watched the missile fade away, then smashed the stick right and tried to make out where in the hell the missile came from.

Belikov watched the missile twist slowly, harmlessly toward the water. He would have to use his cannon. The colonel banked to the right as Koiser came across his beam. Belikov rolled upright, leveled his wings and watched Koiser's MiG continue its right turn. Belikov adjusted, making a small turn to the right, lining up Koiser's MiG in his gunsight. He led him about twenty-five

meters, pulled the trigger on the stick. The 30mm. cannon, on
his left side, thundered to life.

Koiser first saw the flashes of the orange tracer rounds pass in
front of his fighter. The sudden impact of the explosive armor-
piercing projectiles smashing and tearing into his MiG shocked
him. He watched his instrument panel flash red. His right engine was on fire and his altimeter showed him losing altitude.
He pushed on the left rudder and tried to straighten his fighter.
No good.

An unexpected burning pain in Koiser's right leg took the
breath out of him. He looked down and saw his navy blue flight
suit turning purple with his blood. He fought to control his
fighter, which slowly rolled to the left and pitched up, then
came to a shuddering stall and started to fall tail-first toward the
sea. Koiser pulled himself into a tight ball, straightened his back,
made sure his arms were inside his seat, reached down between
his legs and squeezed the orange handles of his ejection seat,
arming it. He counted to three and pulled the ejection handle
straight up with all his strength.

In a blast of fire and smoke Captain Koiser was rocketed away
from his MiG.

Captain Belikov banked left and watched as Koiser's parachute
opened up below him. He throttled back and dropped his nose
to line up Koiser in his gunsight. The colonel wanted to make
sure Koiser was made an example for the rest of the air force.
Slowly he began depressing the cannon trigger—suddenly an
American F-16 appeared to the right.

"This is Major Miles Wheatley, U.S. Air Force. You are in
Turkish airspace. Please identify yourself and your intentions."
It was delivered to Belikov in perfect Russian.

Belikov pulled up and away from Koiser. I'll get you, Koiser,
I'll get you, Belikov silently swore and he turned his MiG north
and applied power with the F-16 still on his wing.

* * *

Koiser watched as the water came closer. The jerky movement of the harness bit into his groin as he descended. He reached down and pulled the red lever on his flight suit. A life raft dropped and inflated below him. He could feel the energy drain out of him as he hit the water. It was much colder than he'd thought. He unbuckled his parachute and swam toward the raft floating only ten meters away. The pain in his right leg surged as he pulled himself onto the raft. He heard the roar of jet engines above. He lay there looking up at the sky. After a while he closed his eyes and didn't move.

3

REUNION

OAKTON, VIRGINIA

It's no use, I can't sleep, Mark D. Collins said to himself as he rolled over and looked at his clock radio glowing in the darkness, 2:14 A.M. The stark reality of his dream had forced him awake. He rolled back over and stared at the ceiling. The window next to his bed was rattling back and forth as the autumn wind hit it, the first cold front of the season on its way to northeastern Virginia.

Mark wasn't sure if he was ready for fall. It seemed like summer had gone by so fast he'd missed it. Besides, it wasn't the same without his wife Amy. He let out a long breath. The doctors told him the dreams would stop in a few months. It had been eight since her awful death in a car accident and he still couldn't sleep through a whole night.

Well, might as well go to work, it doesn't really matter, the CIA never slept. He pulled himself out of bed and was on his way by 3:00 A.M.

Collins headed north on Highway 123, clouds hanging low in the night sky and reflecting the bright burning lights of Washington back to the ground. He reached over and hit the switch to turn on his car heater, the first time since spring that he'd had to use it. He took the exit for I-495 and continued north, a few flakes of snow reflecting off his headlights. If it kept up, rush hour would be a mess.

Collins pulled up now to the guard post of the CIA's north entrance, stopped his Honda and rolled down the window.

"Good morning, sir, kind of early aren't you?" the security officer said.

"Yeah, couldn't sleep."

"Your I.D., please?"

Collins offered his badge to the guard, who checked it against his computer printout that was updated each day at 12:00 A.M.

"Okay, major."

Collins drove up the hill toward the CIA building. He cut straight through the nearly empty parking lot and pulled into space 216. Since being assigned to work at the CIA two and a half years ago his parking place still wasn't any closer. Maybe when he made Deputy Director they'd move him up. When . . .

The musty clean smell inside CIA headquarters reminded him of his hometown library. Pine-Sol and old books. His father and mother had built their lives around a country-style grocery in Antigo, Wisconsin. Mark had been expected to take over the family business but instead went off to college, where he met Amy. It was then he decided he wanted something different, and after graduating from college enlisted in the army. His grades had been excellent, he had a high IQ and was quickly promoted and given a choice of assignments. He chose the CIA.

Actually Collins knew little about the organization when first he arrived, but he was a quick study and was put in the office of the director, intelligence group, specifically economic research. At the moment he was working with the Strategic Research Department, tracking sensitive, high-tech equipment that could be used to the advantage of the U.S.'s enemies.

Collins made his way now to the fifth floor of the north wing, went through his final security checkpoint and entered the top-secret part of the floor. The clock on the wall showed 3:25 A.M. He walked through the outer office and into his own—"Mark D.," no last name, on the door.

He proceeded to unlock the large cabinet-style safe in the rear of the room, removed the files he'd been working on, put them on his desk and sat down to work.

The unremarkable start of another day at the CIA.

Which would soon change, thanks to a remarkable man in a raft somewhere in the Black Sea.

PALMER PARK, MARYLAND

It took Charles Tyransky a few moments to realize it was the phone ringing next to his bed, that the noise wasn't a part of his dream. He looked over at the digital display on his alarm clock —4:03.

Oh God, now who died? he thought. He turned the light on, reached over and lifted the receiver.

"Hello."

"Mr. Tyransky, this is Lieutenant Bob Davis. I'm with A-2, Air Force Intelligence—"

"I know what A-2 is."

"Yes, sir. Tom Staffer asked if you would meet him at Washington National Airport in an hour, sir."

"What the hell for?"

"I'm not at liberty to say, sir."

"You tell Mr. Staffer I'm *retired*."

"I understand that, Mr. Tyransky . . . but Mr. Staffer did instruct me to let you know we have another Falcon."

Charles sat up in bed, tried to clear his head. Staffer had another defector, probably a pilot, and he must be important if Staffer was trying to bring him back into the picture after all these years . . . He had worked with Tom Staffer at the CIA for longer than he wanted to remember. In fact, Staffer was just a field officer when they were assigned to work their first case together in the late sixties. Even then it was well known that Tom Staffer was on the fast track within the Company. Over the next twenty years he had watched Staffer maneuver his way up the ranks. Now Staffer was a Deputy Director and chances were one day he would head the agency as Director. None of this changed his opinion of his former colleague. As far as he was concerned he always had to watch his back when around Tom Staffer . . .

"Okay, I'll be there. Where do I meet him?"

"Gate seven, Concourse A, Washington National."

Tyransky hung up.

"Trouble, honey?" asked his wife Martha.

"I have to go to the airport, help me pack, okay?"

Oh God, he thought, I'm getting too damned old for this.

WASHINGTON NATIONAL AIRPORT

Charles Tyransky did not like being pulled out of bed in the middle of the night, especially by a man like Staffer that he did not respect or trust anymore. Still, maybe, just maybe, this was his second chance. For sure he had mixed emotions. His years in the CIA had been some of the best and worst in his life. He had promised himself never to return, and now he was going back on that promise.

He grabbed his garment bag and walked briskly to the terminal door, looked at his watch, 5:15 A.M. Not bad, considering the weather. He passed the empty ticket counters and walked toward Concourse A.

"Mr. Tyransky, I'm Russell Hamilton, I work with Tom Staffer. He asked me to meet you here."

"What's going on?"

"I'll leave that to Tom. Would you like some coffee?"

"No, I'll wait." He took in Russell Hamilton, mid-to-late thirties, dark blue suit, white shirt, yellow tie. By the regs.

"I didn't know commercial flights left this early," Charles said, fishing.

"They don't, this one's just for you."

"Don't shit me, young man. I was playing this game when you were in knickers." Come on, he told himself, don't take out your anger on him.

"There she is," Hamilton said, and went to the door of the jetway.

The red and white 727 with navigational lights blinking slowly swung around and moved nose-first to the boarding ramp.

"Charles, I'm glad to see you made it. How have you been?"

Tom Staffer had walked up behind him.

Tyransky turned around. Staffer looked the same as the last time they'd worked together seven years ago. His hair was still salt-and-pepper but with a bit more gray. His mustache was black and neatly trimmed. He carried himself in his usual confident manner. Real cocky, Tyransky thought, taking in Staffer's sharp blue eyes.

"We better get going," Staffer said. "I'll brief you on the way, but first I want to hear how you've been." The two men walked toward the waiting airliner.

No, this sure as hell wasn't any commercial flight, Charles thought. The smell of jet exhaust and the aroma of freshly brewing coffee mixing together swept over him, and as he entered the aircraft memories of the past filled his mind. "Maybe Martha was right, maybe I actually do miss all this." Both sides of the plane were furnished with a couch, a coffee table and two reclining chairs. To the rear were two desks with PCs and FAX machines on each of them. The floor was covered with a thick brown carpet.

"Nice little flying office you have here, Staffer."

"Thanks. We've made a few changes since you were with us."

"What's behind the doors?" Charles motioned to the back of the plane.

"Oh, the galley, a couple of cots and the rest of our communications equipment. I can tie into any country's phone system I choose. Plus I have access to the military command and control transmitting channels of all the NATO powers."

"Nice cover, you sure the airline doesn't mind?"

Staffer smiled. "Not hardly, their veep of operations used to work for me."

Once the plane was in the air Staffer began chitchat about how was Martha, fine, how were the kids, fine, heard you had a new granddaughter in July, congratulations, thanks . . . What the hell else does he know? Tyransky thought.

"You enjoying your retirement?" Staffer asked, getting closer to the point in his elliptical fashion.

Tyransky didn't answer, Staffer got the message.

"Well, Charles, I suppose you're wondering what's going on . . . yes, well, a few hours ago we got a call from our people in

Turkey." Pause. "It seems a Soviet pilot was trying to defect during a routine exercise over the Black Sea. From what we can tell he was shot down by one of his people."

"Do you have him?" Tyransky couldn't flatten the tone of excitement.

"Not yet. A rescue mission is underway—"

"If you don't have him yet, what the hell do you want with me?"

"I assure you we will get him," Staffer said quietly.

"Where is he now?"

"Several miles off the coast. We know he ejected from his MiG. An F-16 got a visual."

"What's the Kremlin saying?"

"Nothing. Look, Charles, I know things didn't go the way you expected when Falcon defected. I can't change that. But things will be different this time—"

"Why?"

"We've learned since then. We are capable of that, you know. Get some sleep, Charles, you'll need it. We'll be hip-deep when we get to Ramstein Air Base. I want this one to go off without a hitch."

Tyransky turned away from Staffer and looked at the picture of the President hanging on the wall. "We'll see," he said, not really believing. They'd screwed up badly with Falcon, the last defector, and made a liar out of him in the process.

CIA HEADQUARTERS

Mark Collins finished categorizing the latest information he had received from COCOM, the Coordinating Committee for Multilateral Export Controls. The Soviets were notorious for taking manufactured equipment that NATO and COCOM thought had little or no military value and using it for designing and producing military equipment.

Collins had recently written a report on the trend in Soviet interest in two key areas. The first was a broad-based missile defense. They had the only operational ABM system in place circling Moscow, but they needed Western technology that could detect the launch of enemy missiles and distinguish real warheads from decoys. And this required a radar and computer system that could process information for the launching of an effective antimissile defense. Obviously they wanted to build a security shield much like the United States' planned so-called Star Wars system. Collins saw an even more persistent trend in their interest in Western computer technology. Every one of their military plans was based on this. It seemed they still lagged behind in computer systems, software and the making of silicon and gallium arsenide chips. Such was the state of the art of the CIA's analysis—something less than as up to date as Collins thought.

He swung his chair around now to the computer console behind and to the right of his desk, switched it on and watched the color monitor come to life, and began to feed information into the ADABAS computer system—a system so secret that a second computer located in the basement had to be used to decrypt it.

Around the Company the ADABAS was called "The Source." But like all technological wizardry, it was no better than the information it got . . .

4

BACKLASH

SEVASTOPOL AIR BASE

"Approach control, this is Red one, I need priority landing clearance."

"Red one, negative on the clearance. We have a full pattern—"

"Approach control, this is Colonel Belikov. Tell one of these bombers to come around again. I want landing clearance *now*."

A short pause. "Red one, maintain present heading, wind is three four zero at thirteen knots. You are clear to land on runway three five right."

Belikov dropped the nose of his fighter and lined up his MiG for final approach, brought the speed brake to the maximum upright position and popped the drag chute. Once on the taxiway and in his parking place, he opened the canopy of the MiG and felt the cool fresh air hit him in the face—a nice sensation but hardly enough to cool his anger as he proceeded to the base commander's office.

"Colonel Igor Belikov reporting, comrade general."

Major General Boris Smirov sat behind his large polished desk with his back to Belikov. Long fingers of light cut through the stale cigar smoke that filled the air.

The general, bald, overweight and in his late fifties, turned his chair slowly around.

"I understand we have a problem." He waved his hand. "Would you care to tell me what happened out there today?"

"Captain Koiser attempted to defect and I shot him down—"

"Is he dead?"

"I don't know, sir . . . I did see a parachute after I destroyed his MiG . . ."

The general nodded curtly. "We have a rescue operation going on. Sit, colonel." Abruptly he seemed to sag in his chair. "Colonel Belikov, you have served me and our country well for many years. I need your help in finding a way out of this mess. I have ordered everyone involved in today's operation to assemble in the debriefing room. I want you to debrief them. Most have already heard what happened. Tell them that as far as we know the traitor is dead and not a word of this is to be repeated."

"What about the other MiG and its pilot? The one Koiser shot down?"

"Tell them there was a mid-air collision or engine trouble and he had to ditch. Colonel, this isn't the first time this has happened," he said wearily. "Eight years ago two pilots stole an AN-22 transport. They tried to fly across the Black Sea to Turkey, just like Koiser. Except we were able to shoot them down and kill both of them. I wish we knew if Koiser was dead . . ."

"At least he didn't get away with the MiG, general."

The general shook his head. "Captain Koiser is far more valuable than the MiG. What Koiser knows is far more damaging . . ."

"What do you mean?"

The general poured himself a shot of vodka, opened his top desk drawer and pulled out a thick file.

"Before being transferred here Captain Koiser was stationed at Ramenskoye Test Center. For the past five years he was involved in a super-secret operation only known as 'The Project.' " The general handed the file to Belikov.

The first two pages were the standard PVO officer profile. On the third page the words CONFIDENTIAL—SPECIAL TROOPS were written across the top. Captain Grigori Koiser, it revealed, was not only one of the best MiG-29 pilots in the PVO, he was an engineer with a degree in microwave electronics from the

Military Science Academy, specializing in ultrawideband radar technology. Which meant he was one of the Kremlin's top radar and fighter-interception authorities with knowledge of the latest Soviet air defenses. He had also been schooled in English and French.

Belikov handed the file back to the general. "This secret project you speak of, does Koiser know of it?"

"Know of it, he—" The general's aide entered and handed him a note.

"We have received word," he said, "that an American Air Force helicopter has rescued Koiser. It appears they're taking him to one of their air bases in Turkey." The general stared at the note. "We must assume he is alive."

The general poured himself another vodka.

INCIRLIK AIR BASE, TURKEY

Koiser lay on his back and watched the fluorescent lights flash by as they wheeled him down the hall to the emergency room. Everyone seemed to be talking at once and very fast. He had listened to other Soviets speak English and couldn't remember if it sounded like this or not. He wished he had practiced it more in school. He closed his eyes, badly wanting something for his headache.

The doors to the emergency room swung open and he was taken to two waiting doctors.

"Captain Koiser, I am Colonel Bradford Clasp, U.S. Air Force Intelligence. Welcome to Turkey." Koiser was surprised at how well the American spoke Russian. "How are you feeling?"

"My head hurts some, I have a cut on my leg."

"Yes, the doctors would like to check you over."

Koiser tried to nod. "May I have some aspirin for my head?"

"Sorry, we can't give you anything yet. Give the doctors a few minutes and then I'll see what I can do."

Koiser lay quietly as the doctors took his blood pressure, typed his blood, looked into his eyes. He guessed they were checking to see if he had a concussion.

"Captain, we need to stitch up your leg, it's a fairly deep cut. Okay?"

Koiser nodded.

"You're very lucky. When you ejected you must have hit your head on the canopy. Your helmet is cracked."

Koiser watched as one of the doctors injected his leg with Novocain in preparation for stitches, then studied the room as his calf started to numb. Along with the two doctors and Colonel Clasp there were two security men standing against the far wall and another outside his room.

When the doctors finished, one of them spoke with Colonel Clasp, then both doctors left the room. A nurse came in with new underwear, socks and an olive green American flight suit.

"The doctors tell me you're going to be all right. They want you to stay here a few hours for observation. I hope you're hungry, I ordered up lunch," Clasp said as he pulled up a chair next to Koiser's bed.

"So, captain, what happened? Did you lose your way?"

Koiser sat up in bed, using his elbows to prop himself up. "I did *not* get lost. I chose to defect."

"I didn't mean to upset you, captain, but this is a very delicate situation . . . what type of aircraft were you flying?" Clasp asked.

An odd question, Koiser thought, coming from an intelligence officer. He didn't realize Clasp was asking questions, like a good lawyer, that he already knew the answers to.

"A MiG-29 . . . a Fulcrum."

"What base were you flying out of?"

"Sevastopol."

"Captain, are you certain you want to defect, or did you just lose your way and—"

"I did *not* get lost. I *chose* to do this. I flew here because I meant to."

"Would you write that down in your own words, what you have just told me, and sign it?"

"Yes."

While Koiser was writing, his lunch arrived, along with two aspirins that he greedily swallowed. He couldn't stomach food.

"Where are you going to take me?"

"Captain," Clasp said, "we'll be moving you to Ramstein Air Base, in Germany. We won't give you back against your will.

Please don't worry about that. We have facilities in Germany, to make you more comfortable, and the security is much better. You'll fly out after dark in a military plane."

In his muddled state, things were happening too fast for Koiser.

"Try to get some sleep, try to relax. You're safe and you'll be leaving in a few hours." Colonel Clasp shook Koiser's hand and left the room.

Koiser closed his eyes. The Novocain was wearing off and he could feel the pain return to his leg. His head, though, was starting to feel better. And with that he started to think a little about what had happened this incredible day . . . Did the pilot he shot down live? He hated to think otherwise. And Colonel Belikov, what was he saying? Most of all . . . Had he made the right choice? No use worrying about it now. No going back now. And then sleep ended the pain of second-guessing . . .

General Sweeny approached the nurses' station. The tall Texan's trademark throughout the Air Force was for wearing nothing but the best in exotic cowboy boots. From python to ostrich, the general had a pair of them all. His tall thin frame hid his age well and he still had that deep-down-country-boy-twinkle in his eye, as some magazine had described it. After graduating from Notre Dame in the late fifties he entered the Air Force and worked his way up the ranks. He was well known around the base for being a strict disciplinarian but most considered him fair.

"May I help you, sir?" the nurse on watch asked.

"Where can I find Colonel Clasp?"

"He's in the cafeteria, two doors down and to your left."

Sweeny found Colonel Clasp sitting at the rear of the room.

"How's it going, colonel? How's our Soviet pilot doing?"

"He'll be all right. A few bumps and bruises and he does have a pretty good cut on his leg. He's sleeping now."

"I got word from USEUCOM. They want us to have him on board one of their jets in less than an hour."

"We'll have him ready."

"Okay, colonel, make him comfortable. CIA is getting everything ready. I don't want *anything* to go wrong. A smooth transition. You read me?"

Clasp did.

SEVASTOPOL AIR BASE

1st Lieutenant Aleksandr Maksimov sat alone in his section of the pilots' barracks, looking up at Colonel Belikov.

"What I told you in the briefing this afternoon was a lie. Captain Koiser did not die in a mid-air collision. He has defected."

The words hit Maksimov, Koiser's roommate, like a bomb. He fumbled for something to say.

Belikov's forced smile grew wider. "Where is your Tokarev?"

"With the rest of my flight equipment, locked away in the squadron's safety area." Maksimov was puzzled. It would be against regulations for him to have his pistol with him. He could be sent to prison.

Belikov pulled a shiny black automatic 9 mm. from under his coat. "Is this yours?"

Maksimov examined the pistol, it was unloaded. His initials were scratched on the soft plastic handle. "Yes, sir, it is mine." He handed it back.

"Good. Now do you have something to tell me?"

"I don't understand."

"You are Koiser's roommate. What did he take with him today? What did he take to the Americans?" Belikov's smile had changed to a stone-cold stare.

"I don't know. I . . . ." Then it hit him. Colonel Belikov was setting him up. "You cannot do this, I did not even know the man—"

"Liar." Belikov pulled a loaded magazine out of his pocket and slid it into the gun, then tossed a small note pad and a pen on the lieutenant's lap.

Maksimov began to panic. "You must believe me, I know nothing . . ."

Belikov jacked the slide back, cocking the pistol. "Write what I say . . . I have shamed my country, I am a criminal." The

Colonel watched Maksimov's hand scribble the words. "I no longer deserve to live . . ."

"NO . . ."

Belikov put the pistol to his head.

Maksimov could scarcely hold the pen as he finished the last words. Maybe this was all a bluff, Belikov just wants to make sure I really didn't help Koiser—

"Now sign it."

The lieutenant handed the notepad back to the colonel, looked him in the face for an instant before turning away.

Belikov pressed the end of the barrel to the side of Maksimov's head. He looked down. The man had his eyes closed and a dark wet spot was growing between his legs.

"Better you than me," Belikov muttered, and pulled the trigger.

General Boris Smirov glanced over the report that Colonel Belikov had just handed him.

"How did the debriefing go?"

"I did my best to make the 'accident" plausible. Also, I have been informed Lieutenant Maksimov committed suicide. Apparently right after I interrogated him."

General Smirov was aware of the colonel's interrogation techniques, dating back to Vietnam and downed American pilots.

"Did you learn anything?"

"No, I guess he chose to take his own life rather than admit helping Koiser . . . General . . . Boris . . . I have been your friend for many years. I flew against the Americans under your command twenty-five years ago in Vietnam. You have never kept anything from me."

"Speak your mind."

"Today I lost two MiGs. One pilot is dead and the other has defected to the United States. Another just killed himself. I know I made the right decision when I shot Koiser down. But why exactly is Captain Koiser so important, beyond his special training?"

The general was quiet for a moment, then leaned forward and placed his arms on his desk and looked directly at Belikov.

"Yes, we have been friends for a long time. You must understand . . . only a small group of officers know about The Project. I am sorry you had to hear about it in such a way . . . What I can tell you is this. The exercise you were to be flying this morning was only partially for the benefit of your pilots. The Voyska PVO has been developing and testing a new computer-driven radar defense network, the best in the world. It can lock onto and continue to track an aircraft, including the American B-1B, flying into this country at any altitude. If we can find them, we can shoot them down."

"Is it operational?" Belikov's voice was full of excitement.

"I believe we are very close. Captain Koiser worked on this project. He flew the MiGs to intercept the bombers after the new radar system found them. He also developed some of the tactics of engagement. He was stationed at Ramenskoye for five years for security reasons, then transferred here because the tests were over."

"What exactly does he know?"

"The KGB is trying to find that out and evaluate the damage," Smirov answered warily.

"General, you were a pilot. You still think like a pilot. What do you fear most from the Americans?"

"What do you mean?"

Belikov could tell by the look on the general's face he knew exactly what he meant. "If it were you out there as one of the fighter-interceptor pilots, and your job was to defend, what would you fear the most coming at you over the horizon?"

"Colonel, I think you already know the answer to your question. I would fear the unknown, the same as you."

"Yes, the unknown. And what is the biggest unknown we face in a battle with the Americans?" Belikov paused for a moment, then answered his own question. "Their technology. Our biggest fear is to be sent out to destroy an enemy aircraft already in our airspace and not be able to find it. The truth, general. Can we or can we not find the new American bomber with this new radar network?"

"The TU-160 is much like the American B-1B. We can track

it. As far as the Americans' new advanced technology bomber, we're not sure. We have no way of testing it. Our own advanced bomber is still on the drawing board."

"Why haven't I seen any new construction around our current SAM sites?" Belikov pressed.

"There's no need for any. The Americans don't know what we have . . ." Up to now, at least, he silently added. "I am not a physicist, all I know is we are very close to full operation on The Project."

Neither man had to speak what he was thinking—that Koiser's defection could blow the secret cover of the most secret of defense systems.

INCIRLIK AIR BASE, TURKEY

"Hello, Grigori, how are you feeling?" Colonel Clasp entered his room carrying a heavy wool overcoat and a black felt hat.

"I feel much better."

"Good, please put these on and we will be on our way." Clasp handed him the coat and hat. Koiser noticed that the colonel was still carrying a brown leather jacket over his left arm.

"Captain, one other thing. We would like to give you this flight jacket on behalf of the 39th Tactical Group here at Incirlik." The jacket had a white wool fleece collar and the squadron's insignia and patches on the breast pockets. An American flag was on the left shoulder. Koiser took it from the colonel, felt the oiled leather with his thumb. "I am sorry, I cannot take this." He handed it back to Clasp.

"It's a gift—"

"I cannot. I don't want a reward for what I've done. My people will call me a traitor—"

"Well, I call you a brave man. Everyone at this base respects you."

"Right now, sir, I don't respect myself."

Clasp thought he understood, but had no more time for making Koiser feel better. "Come, the plane will be here soon," and started for the door.

KGB HEADQUARTERS, MOSCOW

Nikolai Tomskiy had not had anything to eat since breakfast. As Minister of Defense his day had started like most others. He'd had his standard briefing on significant military changes in the world during the night. A review of production schedules for various weapons systems started at 7:30 to last until noon. After that he had planned to have lunch with several top generals and admirals from the air force, navy and army. However, at 10:19 A.M. the first word filtered in that a young air force captain had apparently tried to defect into northern Turkey with a MiG-29C. The rest of his day had been spent trying to piece together who this pilot was and how he could do such a thing and what the consequences might be.

Now it was just past 7:00 P.M. and the rumble in his stomach reminded him how hungry he was. Tomskiy readjusted his position in the chair. He wished he was back in his own office, in his own chair. His right leg was slowly falling asleep. He had been waiting for half an hour for Dimitri Volstad, Chief of the KGB, to show up for the quickly called meeting. He pushed himself away from the table and stood to stretch just as the door opened and Volstad entered.

"Sorry to keep you waiting. Your pilot's background check took longer than I anticipated."

Tomskiy watched the tall leader of the KGB walk around the rear of the table and take a seat next to him facing the door. Volstad's private conference room was neat and practical. The wall at the head of the table held two large cork noteboards, one filled with color maps of Moscow and Washington. Several areas on each map were circled in red. The other was empty, with only a corner full of thumb tacks. The opposite wall was painted white and was used for films and to project color slides. The two side walls of the windowless room were paneled with a dark rosewood.

Volstad put on his reading glasses, his face looked tense and tired. "This is much bigger than I'd thought," he said quietly. "My sources have just confirmed . . . the pilot is alive."

"Do we know who he is?" Tomskiy asked.

"Yes, Captain Grigori Koiser. He had only been stationed at Sevastopol for a short time . . . no more than a couple of days. He was transferred there from Ramenskoye test center—"

"Ramenskoye! What was his assignment there?"

Volstad pushed the file toward Tomskiy. "Read for yourself."

Tomskiy skimmed through Koiser's top-secret service record. There was nothing to indicate he was capable of betraying his country. Each commanding officer that Koiser had served under had given the captain nothing but high marks and top recommendations. As Tomskiy read on through the last pages of the profile he felt his face burn. First from surprise, then from anger. "He spent five years working on The Project." He knows about it, this could put our whole strategy in serious jeopardy . . ."

"Agreed," Volstad said. "At least we can use this to force the General Secretary to make a final decision on full deployment of the radar network. We don't need another test." Volstad reached over and took the secret KGB file from Tomskiy.

"You want to force the General Secretary?" Tomskiy didn't like Volstad's choice of words. "The General Secretary's strategy has already been set. The radar network will remain secret until the Arms Reduction Treaty is signed with the Americans. Only then will he allow us to deploy it." Tomskiy was suspicious of the KGB Chairman, who had been present during the Council of Defense meetings. He always had to wonder what the man was up to.

"I feel it's a mistake for us to sign a treaty cutting our nuclear forces before the new radar network is operating fully," Volstad said smoothly. "Even you admitted after the American fighter was shot down that it worked better than expected. We should proceed, you're too cautious. Further testing is a waste of time."

Tomskiy felt even more that the KGB head was driving at some unstated agenda. "Do you actually believe the Americans will sign that treaty if they know we have such a defense? We have poured billions of rubles into the project, turned the energies and talents of hundreds of our top engineers and scientists away from other projects just so this network could be finished on time. If we deploy it the Americans will know about it—"

"What about the pilot?" Volstad said as he stared at Tomskiy over the top of his half-moon glasses.

"I agree that is a real concern, but it's one we can't control. Why make it worse by confirming what this Koiser may tell them? Will they believe him? Won't they be concerned, at first at least, that he's a plant? And if we openly deploy, the Americans won't sign the treaty—"

"I disagree," Volstad said, thinking that Tomskiy should have been in the KGB. "The American President has been building this treaty into his big step toward world peace. I don't believe he will change his mind because of some allegedly defecting Soviet pilot." Volstad was now pacing from wall to wall as he spoke. "I want that system deployed and so do your generals."

"I think I know what my generals want . . ."

"Let me say this . . . there is some . . . concern about your higher ranks staying loyal to the new General Secretary. As you know, not all are in complete agreement with him, and the other side talks of reforms. I have already had to put the KGB in command of the 103rd Air Assault Division. And there could be more if we do not show your general staff that the party has no intention of allowing the West to dominate us. Politically, economically *or* militarily."

"I can control my men," Tomskiy protested.

"I am sure you can, but your concern is only to protect our country from external threats. Mine is to protect our leaders from internal threats as well." Volstad, a skilled negotiator, had planted the seed. "Consider this, Nikolai," he went on. "The Americans are in no position to upset their already fragile alliances by backing away from the treaty. Western Europe is calling for total disarmament. West Germany no longer wants U.S. forces in their country. My agents tell me this treaty is needed to keep the NATO countries together, especially West Germany in NATO. Europe no longer looks at us as the bear ready to gobble them up."

Tomskiy had to give some respect to Volstad's opinions about America. Volstad had worked there as a diplomat when he was younger, in the early sixties. He had graduated from the Moscow State Institute of International Relations, the MGIMO.

From there he had worked his way up to head the powerful KGB.

"Why don't you take this to the General Secretary and present your case?" Tomskiy said.

"I have, but he has many other problems . . . Lithuania, the food shortages and the strikes. And I am KGB, not military. He has a great deal of respect for you, Nikolai, you can convince him full deployment is needed."

"I think both of you are right," Tomskiy said. "Yes, we should deploy the system but the General Secretary is correct in his belief that surprise is the best weapon of all. If the Americans don't know we have the network how can they defend against it? Except, of course, there is the defector Koiser, how much he knows, how much he tells them, how much they believe what he does tell them . . ."

"But surely it is a powerful additional argument to go operational and deploy the system," Volstad added.

Tomskiy nodded. "I am not as sure as you he will listen to me but I will try. I too am very tired of having to reconsider our every move because the Americans are always in the way. Each time I move our ships or one of our allies participates in maneuvers with us an American carrier task force shows up to observe. I look forward to the day when I can sit in front of my generals and tell them we no longer need to fear the Americans flying into our airspace and slipping into our waters undetected. Now we can intercept them and if need be shoot them down."

Volstad nodded his approval, suppressing a smile.

5

REVELATION

ABOARD CIA 727

Charles Tyransky was glad to be in the air and heading for West Germany again. The two-hour layover in England Staffer requested seemed a waste of time.

"All right, good work, we'll be in Germany in a few hours to get everything set. If you have any questions you know where to reach me," Staffer said on the phone.

"We have the Soviet pilot," he told Tyransky. "He's a little beat up but he'll be okay. When the Soviet government finds out he's alive they're going to demand to see him. I've told them we don't want any leaks this time. We'll let them make the first move on this."

Staffer sat in the seat across from Tyransky. "Charles, we worked together a lot of years. I can tell you haven't changed your mind about me. Which makes me wonder why you're here."

Tyransky stared out the window. "Tom, never mind what I think of you, I still care . . . I want to make damn sure what happened with Falcon *doesn't* happen this time."

"Charles, I can assure you—"

"You can assure me nothing. I told you and the Director, if you didn't stop parading Falcon around they'd track him down. For Christ sake, *lectures* at air force bases and universities. Security wasn't nearly tight enough. He rejected his family, his friends, everything to be a free man. Not to mention that he brought a top secret aircraft with him."

"I know he was a friend of yours—" Staffer began.

"You still don't get it. We came from the same country, the same background. He wanted to help us work for the day when the Soviet Union would change and the world, including the U.S., would be a better place for it. I was *with* him through it all. The defection, the months of debriefing, the readjustment . . . He was more than a friend. He was like my . . . my brother."

"I know, and Falcon couldn't have done it without you. The information he provided us with was invaluable—"

"Then why didn't you place him in deep cover? As I asked. They would never have found him. He deserved better than to be gunned down like some criminal in Nowheresville, U.S.A., by the KGB." Both men stared at each other.

"I am sorry, Chuck, it was a screw up. This time will be different, I promise you." Stafford put his hand out. Tyransky eyed him, slowly reached out and shook his hand.

"I give you my word, I mean that."

"You better," Tyransky said. "You owe that much to Falcon."

CIA HEADQUARTERS

Darkness had given way to daylight as Mark Collins checked his watch, 7:48 A.M. The rest of the building was starting to fill up.

"Good morning, Mr. C., I didn't expect you in already." Mark looked up and saw his assistant Maddie O'Connel in the doorway. She had worked in Strategic Research for more than ten years and Mark was smart enough to rely on her a great deal. She was old enough to be his mother and at times she fussed over him as if she were.

"I came in early, couldn't sleep." The wrong thing to say to Maddie.

"You need to take better care of yourself," she instantly warned.

The computer had finished typing up a report, which Collins tore off the printer and began reading.

"Maddie, please get Clayton Boyle on the phone. And see if I've gotten that info I requested from Euratech."

"Clayton, what's up?" Collins began when he got through to Boyle.

"What can I do for you, Mark?"

"Well, you know more about computers than anyone else in this department. Could you come over to my office? I've a few questions . . ."

Thirty minutes later Collins glanced up to see Maddie offering Clayton Boyle a cup of coffee as he entered the office. Clayton always reminded Collins of the typical mad scientist. Bald, short and stocky with a pot belly.

"So, what's on your mind, Mark?"

"Well, I'll tell you what I can. Tom Staffer, I'm not sure if you know him, told me if I ever needed any expert advice I should call you. I've been trying to track and stop the transfer of high-tech equipment to the Soviet Union. What I've found is that because of our expanding trade with them it's almost impossible to stop much of it. So I try to block the most damaging computers and related systems. We've identified areas where the Soviets are applying special effort. The first is their ABM systems to shield military networks of command and civil authority. They rely on a layered defense. We know, though, that they lack and need advanced Western technology. With it they could detect the launch of our missiles and be able to distinguish between the real warheads and the decoys. We're way ahead of them in that technology. They need the means to immediately process radar information if they ever want to come up with a security shield like we are trying to develop through SDI. They've made big gains in integrated circuitry and microelectronics by stealing some of our best computers. Now Russian engineers and scientists have duplicated our radars, acoustic sensors, lasers, signaling and guidance systems."

Boyle nodded. "Yeah, I've seen our technology turn up in almost every piece of military equipment we've been able to acquire from them."

"Right, and that's why they're closing the gap so quickly. We spent the money and time to design, develop and deploy new systems and then they steal them. We know for sure that they've improved the accuracy of their weapons-and-guidance systems. Their communications systems are more reliable, which cuts the time it takes to make a battlefield decision. All thanks to our technology. What the whole thing comes down to, Clayton, is our computer technology and equipment. Every advance the Soviets achieve or hope to achieve is based on Western computer systems. From the software systems all the way to chip-making. If I sound pissed, I am."

"Mark, that's not exactly true. I've learned never to underestimate them."

"What about the MiG-31? Once we got one we found it wasn't in the same league as our front-line aircraft."

"Right. But we were wrong on our *assumption*. As a fighter the MiG-31 can't hold its own in air-to-air combat, but it wasn't *designed* to. It was designed to be an interceptor, Mark. Take off, climb fast, make one pass and fire its weapons. Period. They built it for one mission only and in that role it does very well. I was on the team that took the plane apart. Look, Mark, my point is this, the Russians will go to any lengths to meet their military requirements, and in spite of their deficiencies in technology they usually meet their goals."

"By stealing what they need from the West."

"Not all the time. During the Yom Kippur War, you were probably still in high school, I learned my first lesson in what the Soviets can do. Egypt attacked Israel and the Israelis got their butts kicked the first few days. They lost over forty aircraft. The Soviets surprised us with their SA-6 missile. Their new SAM launched and accelerated a lot faster than we expected and its guidance system used radar bands that the EMC equipment we supplied the Israelis didn't cover. What surprised us the most was that after we got our hands on one of the SAMs we didn't have the technology to build the tools we needed to reconstruct one."

Boyle looked at his watch. "Anyhow, you said you had some questions about computers."

"That's right, what can you tell me about an Intell 8224 chip?"

"Oh, it's been around awhile, over ten years. It's mostly used in calculators and video games."

"Come on, what do they use it for?"

"What *don't* they use it for? That chip is in almost every weapons system they have. Starting from the navigation to their newest and deadliest SA-10 ground-to-air missile."

"And in 1982 they smuggled in two Digital Corporation VAX 11/782 computers by way of South Africa, which enabled them to mass produce the chip."

"You've been doing your homework," Clayton said.

"How long before those computers would wear out?"

"Probably fifty years. They're damn good machines."

"What else could they help the Soviets achieve?"

"Mark, you onto something?"

"I really don't know. It could be something or nothing."

"Well, I'll say this, if the Soviets wanted to use those computers for something else they could. Remember what I said, Mark. Don't underestimate them."

Collins watched Boyle leave his office, then opened the dark brown envelope marked with red letters: CONFIDENTIAL EYES ONLY. He removed the papers inside and read:

X0942762DO610-SSQ
CONFIDENTIAL *EYES ONLY*
FM: CIA OPERATION - BONN, WEST GERMANY
TO: MAJOR DELATTRE, OFFICE OF STRATEGIC RESEARCH
INFO: EURATECH CORPORATION

1. MANUFACTURE: PRIMARILY CALCULATORS AND RADAR DETECTORS FOR PRIVATE AUTOMOBILES. RATIO: 55% CALCULATORS; 40% RADAR DETECTORS; 5% OTHER.

2. YEARS IN BUSINESS: 3

3. SALES: EXPORT PRIMARILY, NEW ZEALAND, OTHERS: BRAZIL AND ARGENTINA

4. GROSS REVENUES: FOR CURRENT YEAR, $875,572.83.

5. LOCATION: STESTBURG, WEST GERMANY.

6. PRIVATE COMPANY, NO OUTSIDE FINANCING.

Collins read it twice. Red flags were going up. Euratech had imported more than 200,000 Intell 8224 chips in the last five months. Their revenues for the first eight months didn't reflect a great deal of sales in relation to their chip purchases. Who was selling to them, and more, what were the chips being *used* for?

He was, indeed, onto something. More than he could imagine. Captain Koiser, late of the Soviet Air Force, had the answers.

RAMSTEIN AIR BASE, WEST GERMANY

Colonel Clasp and three Air Force MPs escorted Koiser up the stairs to the second floor of the officers' quarters, where Staffer and Tyransky were waiting. Staffer introduced himself and Tyransky, using near-flawless Russian.

Colonel Clasp moved in quickly and reviewed the events of the last eight hours. Koiser stood quietly, his leg smarting, listening, and surprised at the Americans' fluency in Russian.

"Grigori, I'll be leaving you now," Clasp said. "These are good people and they'll take care of you." Clasp took Koiser's hand and shook it firmly. Koiser barely nodded.

"Captain Koiser," Staffer began, "it's been a long day for all of us and we have a lot of work ahead of us. In the next few days Soviet representatives will be demanding to meet with you—"

"Do I have to meet with them? They will try to take me back."

"Captain, if you feel uncomfortable meeting them, you don't have to," Tyransky said. "If you do choose to see them I will be there with you. I know their tricks. I was once one of them. I also defected, I am here to help you."

"May I sleep?" Koiser asked.

He badly needed rest, but he also needed to think. Meeting another defector was not what he expected. What did he expect? Thoughts and feelings swirled until sleep mercifully intervened.

NO.10 KOSYGIN STREET, MOSCOW

Defense Minister Nikolai Tomskiy entered and stood in the
doorway of the General Secretary's private study. He was wearing his long black coat to protect him from the frigid air outside.

Tomskiy watched the middle-aged man rise from his chair in
the corner of the room. Many questions were still unanswered
about his country's new General Secretary. The one question
Tomskiy didn't have to ask himself was how the General Secretary had won the election by such a wide margin. The KGB had
made sure of that.

"If I didn't feel this was important I wouldn't be bothering
you, sir, but because of today's events I strongly feel we need to
proceed with deployment of The Project as soon as possible."

"Come and sit. Please explain."

Tomskiy entered the dimly lit room. The walls were book-
shelves filled with books on all sides. In one corner sat the Secretary's desk with a Macintosh computer resting on it. The
Secretary had been sitting next to his desk reading a novel.
Tomskiy couldn't make out the title. He didn't bother to remove
his coat. This meeting would be short.

"General Secretary, earlier today one of our pilots defected
into Turkey—"

"I am aware of that. I have been briefed. The pilot was shot
down and the Americans now have him. Is there more?" Actually, he knew there was.

"What I am concerned with, sir, is what the pilot knows.
Grigori Koiser has knowledge of The Project. I would like your
approval to bring the system into operation as soon as possible."

"How close is it to being operational? And why are you so
particularly worried about this defection?"

"I am worried about the pilot because he has worked on the
new computer-driven radar system at Ramenskoye, sir. I am
still trying to find out just what he knows. To answer your first
question, I'm told we can have our Far Eastern theater network
tied into the computer and ready to operate immediately, and
the entire country set up in less than a month—"

"Nikolai, I put you in charge of this project because I respected your judgment. Do what you have to do. Maybe we have waited long enough. The Americans are not in a position to change world opinion. I have pledged to cut our conventional forces in Europe and have agreed to cut our strategic forces. In three months I am going to the United Nations and will be signing the Arms Reduction Treaty. In return the United States will cut its land- and submarine-based ICBMs. We have agreed to cut ours. The United States will be allowed to deploy their new B-2 bombers. I made that concession *only* because of your wonderful new radar network." Was this a hint of sarcasm here? "We are going through the motions but staying strong. Their backs are against the wall. And this pilot, if we don't make him into someone too important, then I suspect the Americans will not either."

"I hope you are right, sir. It would be tragic to have this destroyed by a traitor."

6

FACE TO FACE

THE PENTAGON

Secretary of Defense John Turner tossed the report into his briefcase and closed it, then checked his watch, 9:50 A.M. He had been in his office since 5:30 preparing for a hastily called meeting of the National Security Council that was set for 10:30. He slipped on his suit jacket and made his way to the car waiting to take him to the White House.

At only thirty-nine years of age John Turner was the youngest member of the President's cabinet. He looked even younger with thick black hair and a slender, athletic build. His father was a university professor of economics and business who had steered him to Wall Street after college and pushed him to stay active in New York politics. It was there young Turner made his first contacts in Washington and proceeded to make a name and build a reputation for himself within the defense industry. His education and experiences in business and management gave him the background for the top Pentagon job.

Turner's black limousine made its way now up the ramp to the rear entrance of the White House. He quickly exited and entered the waiting room, where the President's Chief of Staff Alan Manning was waiting.

Turner didn't shake the former New York congressman's hand. As far as he was concerned the forty-two-year-old Man-

100

ning was in a class by himself, even by Washington standards. Turner considered him the most *political* person he had ever met. To Manning, what mattered most was where the political polls were pointing each week. Manning was also hard-working and talented, no question, but when it came to such matters as national defense Turner considered him at worst unreliable and at best inconsistent in his support of Defense's projects. Indeed, many felt it was that inconsistency that had lost him his seat in the congress. Five months later he landed a job on the President's campaign committee and from there he had worked his way up to his current position. Like it or not, Turner had to work with him.

"Am I the first one here?" Turner asked.

"Yes, sir."

"Well, I might as well get down there," he said, picked up his brief case and headed for the Situation Room.

In ten seconds he was several stories below the ground floor of the White House, then walked down the short hallway and into the thirty-by-fifty-foot room. On the far wall was a huge map of the world with three television monitors set to one side and a big screen in the corner. Below the map was a row of eight telephones used to contact the nation's military command and control centers. Two aides were placing a tray of sweet rolls and donuts along with a pitcher of orange juice and two pots of coffee on the table.

"Good morning John, I thought I would beat you this time," the President said as he entered the room. The Chief of Staff followed close behind.

"Good morning, Mr. President," Turner said, and rose from his seat.

Ten minutes later the council had assembled. To the President's right was Larry Robinson, the Secretary of State and Anthony "Tony" Brady, the Director of Central Intelligence. On his left sat Major General Jack Dawson USAF, the Chairman of the Joint Chiefs of Staff, Leo Lewis, National Security Adviser, and John Turner. The Vice-President was not present. A single chair separated each man at the table.

Secretary of State Robinson took a drink from his glass of orange juice and began. "Approximately thirty hours ago a Soviet MiG-29 pilot defected into Turkey. He is asking for political asylum in the U.S.—"

"How are the Soviets reacting, Tony, anything yet?" the President quickly asked the CIA Director.

"They're still quiet, Mr. President. The pilot was shot down and we got him out of the sea. One of our tracking stations was able to determine that he was trying to make it to Turkish airspace. We now have him at Ramstein Air Force Base."

"Well, if we knew he was trying to defect, who the hell gave the order to shoot him down?" the President looked around the room. He still had not been fully briefed.

"No one, sir. The Soviets shot him down. I guess we should be more exact," Turner said, trying to save the President from embarrassment.

The President smiled. "Excuse me for jumping the gun. Okay, we have a Soviet pilot." The President looked around the room again. "You didn't bring me down here just to talk about a Soviet pilot."

The room was silent.

"No, sir." John Turner looked up at the President and took a deep breath. "Mr. President, last night we also lost a reconnaissance aircraft. An RF-117C fighter. We believe it went down about five miles inland on the Soviet island of Sakhalin."

The President rubbed his right temple. "Is the pilot alive?"

"We don't believe so, sir."

"Larry," he asked the Secretary of State, "what kind of diplomatic fallout will this cause?"

"It's too early to tell. It depends on how the Soviets decide to handle it. After they downed Powers in 1960 we promised not to overfly their country. We've broken that promise. It can't help us. Whatever progress I've made in the last few months with their new General Secretary could go up in smoke." He paused staring at John Turner. "Possibly, Mr. President, you could use this to your advantage. It may be wise for you to contact the General Secretary and resolve this in person. It couldn't have happened at a worse time."

The Secretary of Defense knew that last was pointed at him. "Goddamn, John, how could you allow this to happen?" The President stared right at him. "I was on national television last week telling the American people this administration would be signing the arms reduction treaty after the first of the year. We've worked hard on that treaty and this will give the Russians every right to walk away from the table and make us out to be the bad guys. I authorized those flights with your assurances that nothing would happen."

"Mr. President, let me explain what exactly concerns me. Do you know what a RF-117C is?"

"Yes," the President said, annoyed. "It's a stealth fighter. I believe each one costs about fifty-five-million."

"That's right. A stealth fighter, sir. The same stealth fighter that we've been running in and out of Soviet airspace for the last six months. Only the C-model is more advanced, faster, better avionics and better stealth characteristics. Up to this point the Soviets have never been able to detect one."

"Explain."

John Turner stood, walked to the map and pointed to the tip of the Aleutian Islands. "This is where the fighter was stationed, at Shemya Air Force Base. This was the planned flight path of the aircraft . . . Jack, if I skip something just jump on in," he said to Jack Dawson, Chairman of the Joint Chiefs . . . "it flew across the Kamchatka Peninsula and then turned to the south." John showed the flight path with his finger.

"It was supposed to run the length of the island and land in Japan. Right here, on top of this mountain ridge, is the Soviet long-range radar station of Maskirovka. The Soviets shut it down three months ago. Well, it became operational again last week. Our photo-reconnaissance satellites show that the Sovs had deployed approximately twenty-eight new SAM batteries around the radar site, SA-2s, SA-6s, their standard air defenses."

"What makes this radar base so important?" asked the President.

"That is exactly what we would like to know," Jack Dawson cut in. "The only thing that makes it different from the other Soviet stations is its location. We can get fairly close to this one and still be in international waters."

"But our aircraft wasn't in international waters. Was it?" snapped the President.

"No, sir, it wasn't, but that's not the point." said Dawson.

"I am still waiting to hear the *point*, gentlemen."

John Turner walked back to the table and sat down.

"Mr. President, we have key Soviet bases that we routinely monitor and the Soviets have key bases of ours that they monitor. We fly into their airspace to check the reaction time of their air defenses. They do the same thing to us. For instance, in Alaska we are constantly intercepting their Bear Bombers. As far as the RF-117C, they know we were using Maskirovka as one of our test stations. I think we were set up," John Turner said.

"The Soviets use the same basic search-and-warning radars all over their country"—Dawson spoke with a mouth full of sweet roll—"the base at Maskirovka is no different. If those bastards were able to track and shoot down that fighter then they're a lot of years ahead of where they should be—"

"There's no evidence of that. My men in the field would have heard something," interrupted CIA Director Brady.

"What the hell do you call a downed stealth fighter? A mirage?" Joint Chiefs Chairman Dawson took another bite of his roll.

"All right, what do we know, John?" the President asked.

"We also had an RC-135 in the area. They recorded at least eight SAM launches at the same time the fighter should have been approaching the base. After that the Soviets jammed our detection devices."

The President turned to National Security Adviser Leo Lewis. "You've been quiet, Leo."

Lewis looked at Robinson before speaking. "I agree with Larry. This can hurt us, particularly with Western Europe. We need to wait and see what their reaction will be before we can try to repair any damage."

"Okay . . . we wait. John, get me hard evidence and a clearer scenario of what happened out there. Tony, see what you can dig up on your end. Go to work."

The President left the room followed by the Secretary of State, the CIA Director, the Chief of Staff and Leo Lewis.

"Jack, I'd like to talk with you," Turner said to the Chairman of the Joint Chiefs. The two stood for a moment waiting until the rest were out of earshot. "I should be getting the computer data back from the National Reconnaissance Office by mid-morning. It will give us some answers." Turner buttoned his coat. "Jack, I am going to ask the President to meet with me privately. If the Soviets have come up with something to defeat our RF-117C then the Advanced Technology Bomber could be in trouble."

"I agree, but you know the President. You'll have a hell of an argument. Robinson is peacock-proud of that treaty. I don't have to tell you Congress and Europe are looking to see how the President will work with the new Soviet leadership. I don't think the President is going to do anything to jeopardize our relations with the Kremlin."

Turner knew he was right. Neither of them had so much as mentioned the downed Soviet pilot that apparently had defected. Their eye was not on the sparrow. Not yet.

RAMSTEIN AIR BASE, WEST GERMANY

Staffer, Tyransky and Captain Koiser sat quietly in the east conference room of the officers' quarters. It was mid-morning and Koiser was wearing a green flightsuit they'd given him in Turkey. Tyransky was conducting the debriefing and taking notes at the same time. Staffer was quiet, sitting with his arms folded across his brown suit jacket.

"You need to understand, Grigori, if the Soviets have a chance to get you back it will be in the next twenty-four hours. You are the most vulnerable right now."

"I will be careful, I know how they think . . ."

Good God, I hope so, Tyransky thought.

There were two knocks on the door and an Air Force intelligence officer entered the room. "A Soviet delegation is at the front gate demanding to meet with the captain."

"Damn it . . . I said no leaks," Staffer muttered.

"Not everything is a leak, Staffer," Tyransky said. "Obviously they tracked what happened to him with their own resources."

"Tell them we don't know what they're talking about—"

"I tried, sir. They demand to see him and they gave me this.

It's for the captain." The officer set a video cassette on the table.
"I checked it, it's for real."

"Get back out there and tell them again we don't know what
they're talking about. Admit nothing. If they refuse to leave
have them escorted off the base."

"Yes, sir." The officer left, silently calling Staffer an asshole.

"It's started," Tyransky said as he picked up the cassette. "It's
for you, Grigori, from a Colonel Lizichez."

"My wing commander at Ramenskoye . . ."

"You know we don't have to look at this," Tyransky said,
seeing the tension and pain in Koiser's face.

"I know . . . go ahead." Koiser nodded in the direction of
the VCR and the television set in the corner.

Staffer turned the machine on. The television tube turned
from black to gray as he fine-tuned the controls. The sound
started before the picture:

"I have good news for you, Grigori. Your wife and daughter
are waiting for your return in Moscow. They have been very
worried about you." Now there was a picture of a Soviet colonel. "Captain Koiser, you are a Soviet military officer. We have
studied the radar and radio telemetry of your last flight and we
know your radio and navigation equipment failed. This is why
you lost your way. Your fellow countrymen understand and I
assure you that you will not be punished. You will be welcomed
home as a hero . . ."

"A lie," Koiser said quietly.

In a flash of light the screen showed a picture of Koiser's
grandmother. "My grandson, you have always been a patriot. I
know you are strong-willed, I know some terrible misfortune
happened to you. I am deeply pained, Grigori, that the Americans will take advantage of you . . . prevent you from returning home . . ."

Koiser watched the screen without saying a word. Tyransky
sat next to him, shifting his eyes from the television screen to
Koiser's face. The screen went blank for a few seconds, then a
young woman appeared. Tyransky guessed she was in her mid-
twenties:

"Grigori, please listen to me. I know things haven't been the
best between us lately but they will get better. I promise you.

Remember how you pledged your life to me, told me you would love me forever . . . What about Alexandria, how will I take care of her without you?" She dropped her head in her hands.

The screen then switched to a small girl holding a doll and sitting in a large arm chair. "Daddy . . . please come home, I miss you . . . I love you . . ."

Koiser suddenly stood up, grabbed the television with both hands and threw it to the floor.

"They use everything, even my little girl. She is only *five* years old. And what lies . . . my wife doesn't love me, she lives and sleeps with another man. A party official . . ."

"Grigori, we understand your pain." He put a hand on Koiser's shoulder. "You are a very brave man." In more ways than you know, he added silently.

Koiser looked down at his black flight boots as his stomach churned. Anger at the Soviet officials, pain at the separation from his child and his country that he had spent a lifetime believing in. "I don't like myself," he muttered, "I left my little girl behind, I'll never see her again . . . I hate them for using her, I hate myself—"

"Captain," it was Tyransky again, "what you are feeling is to be expected. You would be monstrous if you did not have such feelings. All I can say is that time does heal. Believe me . . ."

Koiser abruptly turned and walked into the bathroom, shutting the door tightly behind him. He closed his eyes and forced his body to come under control. After a few minutes, more under control, he reentered the room. Staffer and Tyransky looked expectantly at him.

"I have things I must tell you," Koiser said.

"Grigori . . . this can wait," Tyransky said quietly.

"No, it cannot." He sat at the table next to the two Americans. "I am more than a MiG-29 pilot that was based at Sevastopol and at Ramenskoye test center."

They waited.

"I was stationed at Ramenskoye for over five years on a very special assignment."

"What were your responsibilities?" Staffer asked.

"I mainly flew MiG-29s and helped refine fire-and-control

systems. But I also helped develop tactics to counter your manned bomber force. The military leaders of my country consider the American strategic bomber the greatest threat to their security. For the last two-and-a-half years I worked with a new radar-tracking system considered top priority by our commanders. It is considered *most* secret. The best engineers, mathematicians and research scientists in the country are involved in it.''

"Go on," Tyransky gently prodded. "I'm no military man. What exactly is this top-secret radar designed to do?''

"If it works as planned the new system will make your new B-2 bomber obsolete before it ever flies.''

That statement hit Staffer like a brick.

"The stealth . . . are you sure—''

"Yes, I am sure. I've been to the complex. It is much like your NORAD and I know where it is located—''

"How the hell could that be? How could they have built something like that without our knowing . . . ?''

Tyransky bit his tongue, figuring this wasn't the time to say what he thought of some of Staffer's CIA assets. The human element had been played down for too long in favor of gadgets, he firmly believed.

Staffer looked hard at Koiser. "Captain, would you be willing to tell what you know to the CIA and the members of the United States National Security Council?''

"Yes, sir. I would. Especially now after . . .'' He didn't need to finish. It was obvious he was still shaken by the concocted video. Revenge was very much on his mind, in his bones, and understandably.

Koiser turned to Staffer. "When do we leave for the United States?''

"Immediately. I'll call Washington and set up a meeting for first thing tomorrow morning.''

THE WHITE HOUSE, OVAL OFFICE

"Not a word, Mr. President. I spoke with the Soviet ambassador for twenty minutes today," Larry Robinson, Secretary of State, was saying.

"It smells fishy, Larry." The President's desk speaker sounded a short buzz. It was his Chief of Staff saying Secretary of Defense Turner was there for his four-thirty meeting.

John Turner entered the Oval Office, obviously not happy to see Robinson there.

"Hello, John," the President said, "I hope you don't mind, Larry and I were just discussing the topic of the day." Of course, he well knew that Turner minded. He had long ago learned the value of playing one against the other to get closer to the truth.

The three men sat in a circle on the right side of the President's desk. Turner put his briefcase on his lap and took out a small binder, which he opened.

"I just received this from the National Reconnaissance Office. It's the data gathered by the flight computers of the RF-117C Black Ghost before it was shot down. It shows some things that, well, frankly, scare me," Turner said as he handed the report to the President.

"Well, it seems the Soviets are going to let this incident blow over, as we should," Robinson said.

The President thumbed through to the last page to read the conclusions of the report.

"Well, as the saying goes, I am not a rocket scientist but from what I read here the Soviets may or may not have the technology to detect that stealth fighter." He flipped the last page over and handed it back to Turner.

"Mr. President, that's right. The key words are "may" and "may not." That aircraft has flown within four miles of the Soviets' most advanced radar installations before. It has never been detected, let alone scanned on all known Soviet radar bands."

"What are you saying, John? Have the Soviets made some sort of breakthrough that we don't know about?"

"The evidence does tend to point to that, Mr. President," Turner replied.

"John, the report says the fighter could have been tracked by a number of other things. Like a malfunctioning radio transponder. Or possibly the fighter lost several graphite skin panels." The President took the report back and went to the back page. "It says here that if the fighter lost two skin panels on just one of its wings the radar cross section would raise to that of an F-16. John, can the Soviets track an F-16?"

"Yes, but the pilot made no mention of losing any panels. What you read were just possibilities . . ."

"Mr. President, I don't believe the Soviet government wants in any way to break the spirit of détente. If they did, believe me, we would have heard about it by now. It is not any different than when one of their Badger reconnaissance aircraft crash-landed in Alaska two months ago. We returned the bodies of the pilots and nothing was said." Robinson looked at Turner.

"*It is a whole lot different.* A TU-16 Badger is a thirty-year-old bomber, not a state-of-the-art fighter with the latest stealth technologies." Turner's voice resonated with his irritation. "Secretary Robinson, we have based the future of this country's defense on stealth technology and if the Soviets have come up with something to counter that, then we are in deep shit."

"I understand, Mr. Turner. You and your friends in the defense industry would like nothing more than to see the negotiations fail. The Soviets don't have the means to compete with us in high-tech weapons and you know it," Robinson stated, his heat rising.

"Larry, that's enough. I know you have worked very hard on our relations with the Soviets. Particularly with the new General Secretary. But, it's John's responsibility to inform me of his concerns." The President turned back to Turner. "Go ahead, John, you have my attention."

"Mr. President, I still worry we are being inveigled into an agreement harmful to us. We've only had one spy satellite in operation for a long time. Unquestionably as a result we missed a lot of important information. When we launched the new KH-12 last year we spotted things we still can't explain. If the Soviets have come up with some sort of detection device to spot a stealth aircraft then we must not sign a treaty that reduces our capabilities . . . *And*, I recommend we think seriously about destroying any such detective device once we more clearly identify it—"

Robinson laughed. "John, you're beginning to sound like Dr. Strangelove."

"What *proof* do we have, John?" asked the President quickly.

"Very little, sir, I realize that. But I would recommend you delay your meeting with the General Secretary until we know for sure," replied Turner.

"John, without proof?" The President shook his head.

"Sir, in my report I requested we send a carrier force up the Japanese coast in the direction of where we lost our fighter," Turner said.

"Why?"

"I believe the Soviets tested some sort of advance new radar system on the only thing they could. An American RF-117C. That's probably why nothing has been said about our overflying in their air space."

"I need more proof, John. More hard information. God, if what you say is true, the strategic balance of the free world vis-à-vis the Soviets is in danger. All right, you're authorized to deploy the carrier force. Larry, inform the Soviet Ambassador that they are on a training exercise. Maybe that will turn up the heat a little."

"Yes sir, but he won't like it—"

"I don't like it when we lose an airplane, no matter where it is," said the President.

"Mr. President, I would also like to draw up some response plans. If we do dig something up I want to be ready to strike," Turner said.

"You are *way* out of line, Turner . . ." Robinson put in.

The President let out a long breath. "John, I can't authorize that until you can get me more facts. I'm sure you understand. I can't be seen as a shoot-from-the-hip cowboy."

Neither Turner nor Robinson had anything to say to that.

7

CONFRONTATION

CIA HEADQUARTERS

Mark reviewed the notes he had taken when he met with the customs agents the day before. One, Al Snider had been involved with sting operations and had a fundamental understanding of why Collins was concerned about the Intell 8224 chips. His friend Bob Rawlins hadn't been able to find a single company in New Zealand doing business with Euratech. So Collins had decided to become more aggressive in his pursuit of more information.

It was only 5:15 A.M. in California. It would be at least five hours before he heard from the agents sent out to interview the company supplying Euratech for the Intell 8224 chips.

The phone rang. It was Peter Valk in Bonn. Valk worked for the German government but had direct ties to the CIA and the U.S. Embassy. He was a man that never turned down a free meal or a free drink.

"The information I received from World Wide Express freight company says the shipping crates containing those chips you wanted traced is being sent to an airport storage warehouse in Auckland."

"When does it leave?" Collins asked.

"On the last flight tonight. You'll have the hard information shortly."

Collins had barely hung up when Maddie informed him that Al Snider of Customs was on line two and said it was very important.

"I didn't expect him this early." Collins's heart began racing as he picked up the line. "Al?"

"I have some information for you."

"Can you get it to me right away?"

"Five minutes."

It was 8:20 A.M. "I have a messenger on the way now."

CAMP PEARY, VIRGINIA

Captain Koiser lay in his bed and listened to a crow cackling outside his window. The sun had been up for a half hour and Koiser was almost relaxing in the peace and quiet.

He had been transferred to the secure CIA training facility in southeastern Virginia. Camp Peary, "The Farm," was also used to provide CIA agents with basic courses on espionage. Located northeast of Williamsburg, just off Interstate 64 and disguised as a testing and research plant for the Pentagon, it resembled a large military reservation. Koiser had only arrived at the base the night before. He had been told he was approximately 150 miles south of Washington and would stay at the military base for an "adjustment period."

Koiser slid the covers off, walked into the bathroom, showered and dressed. What he had seen so far hardly lived up—or down—to the strictures the party had tried to indoctrinate.

He heard a knock on his door and Charles Tyransky came into his room.

"How you doing, Grigori? I hope you understand your stay here is only for a little while. It's for your safety . . ."

"I understand. I was just thinking." Koiser spoke in English, that was coming back to him more easily than he'd expected.

"About why you defected?"

"No . . . I think I know why."

Tyransky sat down across from Koiser. "You took a great risk doing what you did . . . you could have been wrong . . ." Tyransky was probing, trying to see into the man's head.

"The West should not be so trusting. The leaders talk about

wanting to live in peace. Why do you think they built the radar system? Defense is offense, we all know that . . . Before I made my decision I read accounts about how your pilots in Vietnam, the ones that flew the F-105s, would risk their lives by flying over the SAM sites trying to get them to fire at them. They were called . . ."

" 'Wild Weasels,' " Tyransky filled in. "And today they fly F-4s and F-16s."

Koiser shook his head. "Do you know, my instructors told me some of the pilots were high on marijuana and cocaine, others were just mercenaries. I didn't believe it. How could a pilot fly a jet fighter when his mind wasn't clear. And while they told me about how our equipment and technology was unequalled, I read the secret performance chart on the American F-15 fighter. It scored over sixty kills against our MiG-23s and MiG-25s. It took us ten years to put anything in the air to counter your F-14s. Our system will never change, unless . . . unless there is no alternative . . ."

Tyransky listened closely. Koiser not only seemed sincere, he was smart. "Captain, I'm impressed, but I must warn you this won't be easy. The people that will be debriefing you aren't fools and they *are* skeptical. Until they're convinced otherwise they operate on the theory that you're the enemy . . . a plant . . ."

"How do *you* consider me?"

"I see a reflection of myself many years ago when I defected . . . I consider you a friend, and I believe in you."

"How long has it been?"

Tyransky's eyes went blank as he tried to remember. "Thirty-five years."

"Do you ever regret your choice?"

"I did . . ."

"If you had to, would you turn your back on your people for a second time?"

Koiser's question rekindled Tyransky's long-buried feelings.

"Grigori, I want you to understand that you have *not* turned your back on our people. Neither have I. I have come to believe that keeping America strong and free is working *for* our people." Tyransky stared straight at Captain Koiser. "How do you see me?"

Grigori Koiser looked at the yellow tile floor. "I see a reflection of my father and what he stood for. I also, I hope, see myself. You have put your trust in me. I will not betray you . . . and I know you will not betray me."

Was there a question mark in that last statement, Tyransky asked himself. He reached out for Grigori's hand. The two men stood, said nothing. The handshake said it all.

Tom Staffer entered the small waiting room. His I.D. was checked and he was asked to wait. He sat down and lit a cigarette.

The door to the main room opened and Tony Brady appeared. "Tom, come on in."

"Tony, how the hell did you get here so fast?"

"We hopped on a military helicopter. It only took us thirty-five minutes." The CIA director smiled.

"Who came with you?"

"Dawson and Turner. I wanted you involved for obvious reasons." Brady wasn't blowing smoke, Staffer was good and he knew it.

"What's with all the security? I thought no one knew the Soviet was here."

"No one does. It's Tyransky's idea."

"Of course," Staffer said under his breath. The two men entered the conference room of the main building. Sitting around a large rectangular table Staffer saw the Secretary of Defense and the Chairman of the Joint Chiefs.

"Hello, how's everyone doing?" Tom asked. They all exchanged greetings, sat down and coffee was served.

The focus of the room shifted to Turner, since it was clear he was in charge.

"All right, let's get started." Turner glanced at his watch. Staffer wondered how late he was. "Tom, I've briefed everyone here. You probably know more than most of us about this so I'm going to get right with the program." He walked over, opened the door to the adjoining room and told Koiser and Tyransky everything was ready. Koiser was introduced.

"Grigori, would you tell us what you told Tom Staffer and me yesterday?" Tyransky would interpret the conversation for those in the room.

Koiser slowly, deliberately repeated the details of his knowledge of the radar system and how it had evolved over recent years. Jack Dawson scribbled some questions on a yellow notepad and then flipped through his file and reviewed the data that had been learned from the crash of the RF-117C.

As Koiser talked it became increasingly apparent that John Turner's worst fears were reality. The technical data the CIA and Air Force intelligence had tried to piece together from the computer records of the downed RF-117C had answered some questions, but Koiser was answering many more. Koiser, who did not know a stealth fighter had been shot down, confirmed what everyone had most feared. The Soviets had developed a new technology with multiband sweeping radar. It was tied directly into a new supercomputer which then linked to all their existing radar and SAM sites throughout their air-defense network.

Staffer knew what Koiser was saying before the others did. As Tyransky translated and Koiser talked he watched as Turner's face turned increasingly pale. When Koiser finished everyone in the room looked pale.

Dawson was first with the obvious question. "How the hell do we know he's telling the truth?"

Tyransky was ready for it. "Everything he's told us checks out. Everything we can check, at least. And consider the circumstances of his defection . . . he was shot down by his own squadron. Also, the radar station at Kart Dag recorded where Captain Koiser was forced to shoot down one of his fellow pilots in order to survive. Something he feels rotten about. I truly believe he is telling us the truth—"

"Charles, *why* is he telling us this?" Brady demanded.

"This man has a personal history . . ." And he proceeded to fill them in on Koiser's family, his parents, his anger at and profound disillusionment with the Soviet system and its leaders. "And because of his rank and position in the Soviet air force he had access to secret information that let him do something about how he felt and believed. He is independent and intelligent, forms his own conclusions." Tyransky looked around the room. "Gentlemen, something like this happened before. Grigori Koiser is a man much like Falcon. Except his information is far more valuable."

"Well, we've also had KGB plants before—" Brady was cut short by Tyransky, who was clearly getting angry.

"Are you prepared to sit here and tell us how the Soviets, out of the blue, were able to find, track and shoot down one of your invisible war planes?" He turned to Staffer. "Tom, you've been with him, do you believe he's for real?"

"Yes, and what he just told us is way too damned important for us to shrug off because of screw-ups in the past." Staffer was looking at Brady as he spoke. Tyransky was a little surprised, if pleased, by Staffer's support.

"Charles, ask him if he can tell us where this radar computer complex is located if we show him some satellite photos," General Dawson said.

Tyransky did and Koiser nodded yes.

Secretary of Defense Turner had been silent up to this point. "All right," he now said, "your job, gentlemen, is to get me more information." He turned to General Dawson, "Jack, I'm going to need your help coming up with a plane to neutralize that radar complex."

Staffer spoke up. "I want to keep this compartmentalized as much as possible. The fewer that know about it, the better."

"I agree. Anything else?" Turner asked, and looked around the room.

"What about Captain Koiser?" Tyransky asked.

"Transfer him to the CIA," Turner directed.

Tyransky gave Staffer a look. "Well, I'd like to take it a little slow. How about tomorrow before we move him?"

Turner and the general agreed.

The meeting over, Staffer now followed Tyransky and Koiser back into the Soviet's private room.

"How are you doing, Grigori?" Staffer asked in fluent Russian.

"I am fine, Mr. Staffer, thank you for coming."

Tyransky did not join in the pleasantries. "Damn it, Tom, transferring Grigori to the CIA undermines me. You told me I was in charge. I can see it happening all over again. Next thing I know, you'll have him speaking at the White House Press Club and breaking bread with the Joint Chiefs."

Staffer kept calm. "I told you this time it would be different. What do you want from me?"

"I don't want him at the CIA, it is too dangerous."

"Too dangerous? Give me a break. Besides, we don't have a choice. That was Turner and Brady in there, in case you have forgotten. And if I have to I'll put him in a safe house—"

"No way." Tyransky took a deep breath and tried to calm down. He had pushed Staffer as far as he could. "Let me approve the security."

Staffer nodded. "Like I said before, as far as I'm concerned you're in charge of Captain Koiser and his well-being. I'll spread the word."

Tyransky looked at him. It seemed a decent compromise. And Staffer had backed him during the meeting . . .

THE PENTAGON, GENERAL JACK DAWSON'S OFFICE

"Are you sure about this?" Jack Dawson asked.

"You tell me, you're Air Force," John Turner told him. "I had a team from advanced research and scientific intelligence check out the information and they both came up with the same thing . . . This couldn't have happened unless the Soviets have come up with some sort of monstrous breakthrough that we don't know about. Or at least didn't until Koiser told us about it."

"What do you propose?"

"You were in the meeting when Robinson crawled all over me," Turner said. "He's so damned proud of that treaty the Soviets could be marching down Pennsylvania Avenue and he'd be wanting to negotiate." Turner paused, "I've called a meeting in thirty minutes in my office. Brady, you and I will be there. What do you think, Jack, am I out in left field or not?"

"Have you talked with Lewis about this? I'd think the NSA should be involved."

He'd answered the question with a question, Turner noted.

"No, I haven't talked with him since the NSC meeting. We both know he's got a direct line to the White House, whatever I say to him goes to the President. I want my ducks in a neat row before I do that again. Then I'm betting, hoping, I can get him on my side."

As General Dawson thumbed back through the report again, Turner said, "Jack, I made a mistake . . . I had a meeting with the President with just the preliminary results of the RF-117C's computer report. There were loose ends and he picked them apart."

"You know how he is, John, he isn't afraid to make a decision but you got to give him the information to make that decision."

"I know." Turner shook his head.

The general put the report back in its folder and handed it to Turner.

"You know, I can't believe the Soviets haven't said a word. At least they could throw us to the political wolves if they wanted to . . ."

"Unless," Turner said, "they figure we'll discount the truth if they seem to be indifferent to it . . ."

Turner entered his office, set his briefcase on his desk and opened the drapes, allowing a burst of sunlight to fill the office. General Dawson pulled up two chairs in front of Turner's desk and sat down. Turner's personal aide escorted CIA Director Brady into the office.

"This won't take long, Tony," Turner said. "I've gone over it with Jack and I think he's better qualified to go into this than I am." Turner handed each man a copy of the report.

General Dawson picked it up. "What this says is really disturbing. It confirms what the defector Koiser told us this morning."

Brady opened the file. "Are they sure about this?"

"I know what you're thinking," Dawson said. "We've been trying to develop a multiple-radar-scanning system for twenty years. Our R & D departments understand how to build one in principle but they're still at least five years away from practical hardware. Then it would have to be linked together so the data from each processing station could be computed. We're talking ten, maybe fifteen years before we can even think about a practical system."

"How does it work?" the CIA director asked.

"Well . . . let me give it a try," Dawson said. "As you know, radar is a sensor, it operates by transmitting electromagnetic energy into the air and detecting the energy that's reflected back from the object it hits. The Soviet Union uses about a dozen different bands that designate the radars' frequencies and wavelengths. Most of their long-range search-and-track radars use long A, A/B and B bands. Their mobile SAM and air-defense radars use shorter J, J/K, I and I/J bands for tracking, target-acquisition and fire-control." The general stopped and turned to the fourth page of the ten-page report. "On page four, about halfway down the page, is the part that scares the beejesus out of me. According to your rocket scientist, John, that fighter was being swept on all bands at the same time . . . by the same antenna."

"Isn't it possible to have more than one radar scan on an aircraft at one time?" Brady asked.

"Oh, yeah, that happens all the time, but not from the same *radar site*. Besides, that plane was designed to avoid detection. It shouldn't matter what bands the Soviets were using. They shouldn't have been able to find it, let alone track and shoot it down."

"What was the President's reaction?" Brady said. "I can't believe he doesn't understand the strategic implications if the Soviets have made such a breakthrough."

"He does understand. I asked him to authorize moving a carrier task force off the eastern coast of Sakhalin Island and into the area where the fighter was shot down. I also asked for permission to draw up a contingency plan. He gave the okay on the first, thumbs down on the second."

"What kind of plan did you have in mind, John?" Dawson asked in a surprised tone.

"Well, that's the second reason I called for this meeting. I need information from your side, Tony, the CIA. I need to know what we're up against from the military side. That's your job, Jack."

"I'll put one of my very best on it and see if the boys in the satellite department have anything," Director Tony Brady said.

Turner turned to Dawson. "What about you?"

"I've already contacted experts at SAC. I can't come up with a plan to defeat something I know so little about. Hell . . . why don't we just take out the radar site at Maskirovka and be done with it."

"I wish it was that simple," Turner said. "Just remember, when I go to the President next time I'm going to have an airtight case. All clear?"

CIA HEADQUARTERS

Tom Staffer was glad to be back at his desk. Having to take off without notice gave life an edge but it also piled up the paperwork. He planned on working into the evening. Since his divorce he didn't have a home life. Occasionally he got together with his children and ex-wife for dinner, but that was it. His oldest boy was twenty and had moved out before his marriage had split. The daughter was eighteen and lived at home with her mother. On the right corner sat a picture of his family that he studied for a few moments, his thoughts drifting to better times . . .

His secretary's voice abruptly announced that Director Brady was there to see him. What the hell was up that brought him all the way over to this wing?

"Tom, I don't need to tell you the NSC is concerned," the DCI said. "Here's a copy of the report drawn up by the National Research Office. It deals with the RF-117C stealth fighter that was shot down over Sakhalin Island and what we've learned from this Koiser." Brady handed Tom the report. "As you know, that fighter was mission-capable, *not* one of our protos. They found it, tracked it and downed it."

"What's the President's view?" Staffer asked.

"Right now he's a skeptic. Of course, he's under a lot of political pressure at home and in Europe to finish off that treaty. Tom, I need you to turn over every stone to see if anything crawls out. I'm meeting with operations at three. We have some contacts in the Soviet Union that we haven't had to activate for a while. This is the time."

"Do we know where the fighter went down?" Staffer said.

"It crashed five miles inland and about eighteen miles north of Maskirovka radar station. Our satellite photos showed where the Sovs have constructed a series of new SAM sites and we believe the fighter crashed in an area between the newest sites and the coast."

"How old are our latest recon photos?" Staffer asked.

"Two days. We have the photos, they just haven't been analyzed. And we've had some problems." Brady didn't want to admit that Defense Secretary Turner had pushed the President and had gotten backed into a corner.

"I need to have authorization to get to that recon info if you expect me to find anything."

"You got it."

"I'll start digging." Staffer stood and opened his office door for Brady.

"We don't have much time, Tom," Brady said, and left.

Staffer buzzed his secretary and told her to get Bernard Simmons from the National Photographic Interpretation Center on his secure line.

OAKTON, VIRGINIA

Mark Collins finished off the last of his Diet Coke and looked at the empty plate sitting in front of him on the portable tray. After a while a man could get used to anything, even TV dinners.

The last of the 11:00 local news was on. His small dark living room was only lit by the changing picture of the television set. His thoughts drifted to the evening he'd spent with Clayton Boyle and his wife three nights earlier. Clayton had invited his niece Christine to dinner the same night and pretended it was a mistake, both of them showing up at the same time. Sure. Maybe Clayton was right, after all, the only places Mark knew were the office, home and the highway in between. Amy's death had taken a lot out of him. He liked his job and it kept him going but . . . he closed his eyes and let a picture of Chris-

tine fill his mind—short blonde hair, clean clear complexion
. . . reminded him of Amy—

The phone rang.

"Hi . . . Mark?" A female voice.

"Uh, yes."

"This is Christine, I hope I'm not calling too late—"

"No, not at all."

"Oh . . . well, I just wanted to call and apologize for my
uncle's behavior the other night. He sort of put me and you too,
I imagine, in an awkward situation. I hope you didn't mind too
much."

"I didn't mind. Maybe I could give you a call some time and
we could get together."

"I'd like that."

"Okay. When's a good time to call?"

"In the evenings after six, except on Wednesday. I'm taking a
class . . . Well, like I said, I just wanted to apologize for the
other night."

"Hey, no need to. I'll call you later this week." Or sooner, he
thought.

8

FINDERS KEEPERS

U.S.S. *CONSTELLATION*

Admiral Gorham Alton on the command bridge walked the eight feet to the large four-by-four plexiglass windows. He watched as his ship was resupplied and refueled. The U.S.S. *Camden* was steaming in a parallel course to the *Constellation*. The seas were relatively calm.

"Admiral, I've told the pilots the purpose of this operation," Commander Dick Kelley, the F-14D squadron leader, said.

"Good, any questions?"

"Yes, sir, we just finished similar exercises two weeks ago. My men are asking why they're scheduled again."

"Because the old man said so." Alton looked up from his written orders sitting in front of him on the window ledge. "I think they want us to test the opposition."

"Should we be expecting anything? You know how the Soviets feel about Sakhalin Island."

"Right, but I don't know what mood they're in. I want a Hawkeye in the air at all times and tell your men to be alert and prepared to defend themselves."

NATIONAL PHOTO INTERPRETATION CENTER

The street lights glistened off the shining galvanized double rows of barbed wire that sat on the eight-foot chain-link cyclone fence surrounding the center. The five-story windowless beige cement structure, Federal Building 213 on M and First Street, was eight blocks down from the Capitol. An outsider might consider the building just another guarded government warehouse if it weren't for the huge airconditioning units next to it. The cooling system was eighty feet long and only a few feet shorter than the building. The airconditioners were needed to cool the supercomputers operating inside the NPIC, computers used to process the billions of information bites that were supplied by the U.S.'s most advanced spy satellites. The information was then daily fed into the computers' data base.

Bernard Simmons was sitting behind a computer terminal in a small ten-by-ten cubicle on the third floor of the NPIC. On the left side of his desk was a four-inch stack of files containing five to six photos each of the area Staffer had asked him about. By punching in the computer codes on each photograph Bernard could call up the raw data stored in the computer. He finished putting the last of the code numbers from a series of photographs taken over Sakhalin Island into the system, and by the time he had placed the last of the color pictures back into the file the computer screen produced the menu.

An older KH-11 spy satellite had taken the photo passes in a north-south polar orbit over the western edge of Sakhalin Island. Along with the daylight photographs it transmitted back infrared images of trucks, aircraft, ships from their heat emissions. He typed in a series of command codes and the color monitor flashed from red to green and back to red as the huge computer integrated the information he had entered. Forty-five seconds later the screen jumped to life with a three-dimensional color picture of extraordinary clarity and depth. The software that drove the computer had taken the stored electronic images of the same scene that had been taken from varying angles and reconstructed them into the present picture. The scene Simmons was viewing showed trees, large rocks and steep cliffs a few miles from the coast that rose out of the flat terrain five miles inland. The nearest road to the crash site was almost fifteen miles away. He typed in a second command and waited. No change. He then instructed the computer to zoom in on any changes that had occurred from the first to the second picture. The screen rolled and twisted in a series of quick flashes until the computer monitor zoomed in on a one-square-mile area.

There was a long burned section of grass and weeds located on top of a high rocky plateau. At the end of the burn area was a twisted gray-and-black wreckage. He knew it had to be some sort of plane because he couldn't see any tread or tire tracks into or out of the crash site. Next he analyzed the infrared emissions the area was giving out at the exact time of the photo pass. From those he could tell the aircraft must have crashed the night before. The center of the charred fuselage was still hot and smoldering. He punched in a new command and the computer multispectrally analyzed the smoke rising from the wreck.

"Okay, let's see what else is going on," he said quietly as he called up the next days' photos. The first were useless, cloud cover obscured the crash site by mid-morning. By late afternoon, though, the high thin clouds had drifted away and Bernard could see the satellite photos taken at that time showed something very different. On the ground only fifty yards from the downed airplane was a Soviet Mi-8 helicopter. The large, dark green transport chopper with five long rotary blades looked like a giant bug sitting on the brown landscape. Bernard zoomed closer.

If this is one of our planes, he thought, I sure as hell can understand Staffer's concern.

He scanned the rest of the computer-generated picture by manipulating the cursor buttons on the lower right corner of the keyboard, rolling the images in a counterclockwise direction that enabled him to view the wreckage on all sides. He froze the picture above the wreckage, and counted six Soviets in and around the burned airplane. Soviet air force technicians, he figured.

Bernard Simmons could feel the excitement building inside of him.

THE *LENINGRAD*

The smoke from Captain Volkov's cigarette slowly drifted upward and swirled down in the face of the ship's political officer, Kaspars Kanovich. He ignored it, or tried to.

"Kanovich, my ship has been anchored here for more than twenty hours. No doubt it's been pinpointed by the Americans and Japanese. If the wreckage of the American fighter is not on board my ship in six hours we sail. I will not sit here like a Siberian ground hare waiting to be eaten up by the fox."

"I assure you this ship is not in danger," Kanovich told him. "The American carrier is under constant surveillance from our reconnaissance aircraft and we have air cover from the base on Sakhalin." Volkov was glaring hard at him. "Captain, like it or not, we sit here until that cargo is transferred to the deck of this ship. Is that clear?"

Volkov turned his head and stared ahead. "If anything happens to this ship or the men aboard it, I'll hold you accountable. Is *that* clear?"

SAKHALIN ISLAND, THE CRASH SITE

Kicking up a cloud of dust and flying gravel the Mil Mi-10 heavy transport helicopter hovered fifty feet above ground. Its pilot pushed the stick slightly forward and changed the pitch of the whirling blades, then lowering the control stick with his left hand he put the helicopter, all 60,000 pounds of it empty, into a slow descent to touchdown.

"Let's get to work, we only have a few hours of daylight left," the commander of the six-member Soviet team shouted as he ran toward the helicopter. "Did you bring the cargo nets?"

"Yes, major, and they were reinforced as you requested," the pilot told him as he climbed down from the cockpit. The helicopter was only thirty yards from the wreckage. The pilot didn't take his eyes off the fighter. "What is it?"

"It's American . . . that's all I can tell you. We need every available man, where's your copilot?" the major demanded.

"I wasn't allowed to bring one. Now I know why."

CIA HEADQUARTERS

Director Brady stood to introduce Secretary of Defense Turner to Bernard Simmons. "He's one of our best at the NPIC."

"I know who you are," Turner said. "I've seen some of your work. The threat scenario you put together for the Air Force on Iran was right on the mark."

"Okay, Bernard, it's your show," Brady said a bit impatiently.

"What I have, gentlemen, is a series of KH-11 photos taken over Sakhalin Island, which is the area around Maskirovka radar station." He handed the first photo to Turner. "This one was taken two days ago . . . all normal. A day later in the same area there's a downed aircraft. From the IR signature and a multispectral analysis on the smoke still coming from the wreckage I was able to tell that over half the aircraft was made from a graphite composite material. The same sort of material we would use in our stealth aircraft . . ."

This got a reaction. Especially from Brady, who liked to keep secrets . . . it was, after all, the essence of his job . . . and this involved stealth technology. "Go on," was all he said.

"Well, sir, they obviously figure they have something very important and I'd suspect they want it off that island as soon as possible to check it out. I believe the purpose of this meeting you see is to arrange within the next few hours to have that wreckage picked up and transferred to one of their ships now anchored off their eastern coast."

"You mean they are going to pick the whole thing up?" Turner queried.

"Yes, sir, it sure looks like it."

"Why not just take it apart?"

"As you can see in these next five photos, they've been trying that." Bernard handed the stack to the Secretary.

Turner studied each picture and handed them to Staffer.

"You jump from morning to afternoon. Why?" Turner looked at Bernard, like a challenge.

"Cloud cover, sir. Considering where that plane went down we're lucky to have this information." He turned to Staffer. "Tom, did the pilot make it?"

"We don't believe so."

"Well, with everything burned black around the crash site it's hard to tell how much of the fighter is intact," Turner said. "What makes you think the Sovs are going to pick it up and haul it away?"

"In the third to the last picture you will see a Soviet Mil Mi-10 Harke heavy-lift helicopter next to the crash. It landed about two hours before dark last night, their time. And they've been working all night."

Staffer flipped through the recon photos until he found the one Bernard Simmons was talking about.

"That chopper," Simmons went on, "has the capacity to lift over 25,000 pounds. Its range is 500 miles and it can cruise 155 miles per hour at 15,000 feet. On the next satellite pass ninety minutes later, the second to last photo, the ground crew is unloading two large cargo nets. In the last photo, Mr. Secretary, you can see the Soviet helicopter-cruiser *Leningrad*. Our White Cloud ocean reconnaissance satellites have been tracking her for the last two days. She's been steaming at full power from the Indian Ocean. The Soviets have anchored her fifteen miles off the coast." He paused and glanced at Brady. "I believe they're going to try to airlift that downed plane to the *Leningrad*."

"What's the battle capacity of that cruiser?" Brady asked Turner.

Before he could answer Simmons cut in. "I've already pulled that data . . . We classify her as a heavy cruiser, over 20,000 tons displacement fully loaded, top speed forty-one knots. She's armed with two twin SA-N-3 SAM launchers with forty-eight missiles each and four twin 57 mm. guns. From what I can tell there's at least eight KA-25 Hormone helicopters on board. The *Leningrad* was originally designed for antisub work in the eastern Mediterranean but the ship is so versatile they use it for a lot of other duties. She's big, tough and heavily armed. Her captain is a veteran of the Soviet navy and he's well-respected within our own service."

"I want to know how much of that fighter is still intact," Turner persisted. "Maybe we can at least minimize the damage if we know what they might be able to learn. If they're smart they'll wait until our satellite is out of range and then move. Where is the *Conny*?" Meaning the U.S.S. *Constellation*.

"About a hundred and fifty miles southeast," Simmons said.

Turner nodded. "I'm ordering the *Constellation* to get a reconnaissance aircraft in the air when they start to move that aircraft off the island. It should get us some pictures when they put that fighter's remains on the deck of their ship, give us more of an idea about what's going on . . ."

"What's the range of those SAMs, Bernard?" Staffer asked.

"They're carrying the standard SA-N-3 Goblets. They have a ceiling of a little over 100,000 feet and can attack targets as low as 300 feet. As long as an aircraft is in that window, and is within eight miles, it's fair game."

"Gentlemen, I'll contact CINCPAC, I want air support for that recon bird. We'll have Alton send up a couple of F-14s to keep Ivan busy while we shoot some pictures. The Soviets could be on edge, which is dangerous. This is a hell of a big catch for them."

U.S.S. *CONSTELLATION*

"This just came in, sir." One of the ship's communications officers handed the eight-and-a-half-by-eleven manila envelope to the Officer On Deck. He took the envelope and opened to his new orders.

DEL1104MDO25NS–D1017.
TOP SECRET
FM: CINCPAC
TO: CONSTELLATION
RE: RECONNAISSANCE OVER FLIGHT

1. URGENT—RECONNAISSANCE OVER FLIGHT TO COMMENCE IMMEDIATELY.

2. AIR SUPERIOR ROLE REQUESTED.

3. SOVIET INTENTIONS COULD BE HOSTILE.

4. *LENINGRAD* ANCHORED ON EAST COAST OF SAKHALIN ISLAND. BELIEVED TO BE AWAITING AIR DROP OF DOWNED AMERICAN RECONNAISSANCE AIRCRAFT.

5. LATEST SATELLITE INFO ON SHIP AND SUB LOCATIONS TO
   FOLLOW. END.

The OOD was not surprised, this would explain their rede-
ployment. The support mission would be carried out by the
Conny's F-14Ds. The reconnaissance flight would be carried out
by an RF-14A flying totally defenseless.

The OOD picked up the clipboard sitting next to him and
reviewed it. The glowing red and yellow lights from the control
panels around the bridge gave off enough light for him to read
by, but still allowed him to retain most of his night vision. The
E-2 that was currently on station wasn't scheduled to land for
another hour and a half. He turned to the junior deck officer.

"Get down to flight ops. I want two Fourteens and a fresh
Hawkeye on deck and ready to go in thirty minutes. Put our
first team in those fighters. Get them up and ready for briefing."

"Aye, aye." As the junior DO left the bridge, the OOD moved
to the communication center on his right, from which he had a
direct tie into the admiral's quarters. He hit the intercom and
waited for an answer, knowing that Admiral Alton hated to be
disturbed before 0600 hours.

"Yes . . . what is it?"

"Sir, we just received orders from CINCPAC. They are requesting an RF-14A overflight of the *Leningrad* with air support."

"You woke me up for that?"

"Admiral, the orders stated possible hostilities. I thought you
would want to be present in the event the situation does become hostile."

"Anything else?"

"Yes, sir, we should have complete details from CINCPACFLT
in eight minutes."

"Very well, I'll be on the bridge shortly."

Commander Dick Kelley entered the combat-information
briefing room. The lights were on but no one else was in the
room. He had hurriedly showered and dressed. His hair was still
wet and the feeling of the cool morning air moving through it
reminded him of his days at Annapolis. Kelley was a large man
for a fighter pilot, six-two and weighing in at one-ninety. There

was just enough room for his broad shoulders to squeeze into the Tomcat's cockpit. He had started flying F-14s three years ago after spending six years of his life behind the stick of an F-4 Phantom. Currently he was the most experienced F-14 jock on the *Constellation* with more than 800 hours flying time. Kelley and his back-seater Lieutenant Burt "Skip" Colby were one of the few F-14 teams that had completed a training section at the Navy Fighter Weapons School.

Kelley heard footsteps behind him and turned to see his RIO, his Radar Intercept Officer, making his way down the narrow hallway toward the briefing room. Skip Colby was only the third man in Kelley's career who had flown behind him in the tandem-seat Tomcat. And in Kelley's opinion the young lieutenant was without a doubt the best RIO he had flown with. Colby, of Italian descent, had a dark complexion, green eyes and good looks that tended to get him in trouble. He got the moniker Skip because of his tendency to cut and run out of more than one involved romance. Colby claimed he always made it clear that a lasting relationship was not in his immediate future, but there was some disagreement on that from some of the ladies. When it came to flying, though, Colby was totally committed. His job was to work the F-14's big radar, its radio and complex weapons systems as Kelley piloted the fighter. He also served as Kelley's extra pair of eyes.

The two men now joined up and took their seats in the front row, waiting for the rest of the pilots to arrive and the briefing to begin.

The ship's Combat Situation Commander entered and stood at the podium. He had been up all night. Kelley, Skip Colby, and three other F-14D crews listened as the commander outlined their assignment. It seemed routine enough to Kelley, but the expression on the commander's face indicated otherwise.

"Gentlemen, Pacific Command made it clear that the Soviets view this area as high priority. Do not hesitate to defend yourselves . . . understood? Questions?"

"Commander," Kelley said, "what is it that they're moving?"

The Situation Commander shook his head.

"Sorry. That's a need-to-know, Dick. If you get close enough to that chopper it will be apparent. Anything else? Okay, we have a fresh E-2 in the air now and as soon as it sends word that the chopper is moving, Kelley you and your wingman move. Keep your heads up." The briefing broke up and the crews made their way to the flight deck, Kelley and Colby in the lead.

Colby and Kelley reached the F-14D at the same time, climbed the ladder and started to strap themselves in. The night sky was now a dirty gray in the east and a briskly cold wind was rolling over the flight deck.

"Hurry up, I'm freezing my ass off," Colby shouted over the noise of the running engines. The canopy closed and Colby flipped the cockpit heater switch to high. "You know, commander, it really pisses me off they wouldn't tell us what the Soviets have out there on that sacred island of theirs. If we put our asses on the line I'd at least like to know what for."

"Sometimes it's better not to know." Kelley started his preflight checks. Ahead of him a KA-6 Intruder tanker roared off the number-one catapult, its afterburners glowing orange in the darkness. Kelley watched as the Intruder climbed and did a slow banking turn to the left. At 2000 feet the pilot shut the burners off and Kelley lost sight of it. His F-14D would launch next, followed by his wingman.

THE *LENINGRAD*

The grinding metal of the cruiser's heavy anchor chain being hauled aboard could be felt on the bridge. A single link of the chain weighed over 200 pounds and each one made a distinctive thud as it rolled into the storage compartment in the bow.

"I have waited long enough," Captain Volkov told Kanovich. "Your helicopter with its precious cargo will have to find us. I will no longer just sit here and wait for something that may never show up." The captain could stand it no longer. Being anchored in open sea went against his every instinct.

"How will they find us if we move?"

"They can radio us. I will no longer endanger this ship . . . the sun is up now. That helicopter was to be here at dawn. Dawn is over, we move."

SAKHALIN ISLAND, CRASH SITE

"Everything is ready, major," the military engineer said.

"The major nodded. "I will be going with the pilot, after we deliver the plane to the *Leningrad* we will return for you and the rest of the men." The major looked up and made a swirling motion with his right hand to signal the pilot to start the engines of the huge helicopter. The two turbines came to life with a loud bang and a cloud of dark blue smoke as the blades began to turn, then slowly accelerated until the major could feel pieces of sand hitting his face.

"We will wait until you return," the engineer yelled over the sound of the spinning rotary blades. The major gestured with his left hand, acknowledging him, then shielded his eyes with his forearm and quickly ran to the waiting helicopter.

F-14D TOMCAT, MUSKIE FLIGHT

"Commander, they're moving. Godmother reports they're airborne and heading toward the coast with our fighter. Our recon bird is to launch in thirty seconds." Lieutenant Colby had the radio set so only he could hear the incoming transmissions. By Godmother he meant the E-2C Hawkeye early-warning orbiting above the *Constellation*.

By God, Kelley thought, it was happening . . . Fifty miles to the southeast a single RF-14A reconnaissance aircraft sat on the flight deck of the *Constellation*. Any second it would be catapulted into the air and climb to 20,000 feet. After that its pilot would firewall the throttles and run straight for *Leningrad*, cameras running.

"Tell Godmother we're on the way," Kelley said as he snapped his oxygen mask back into place. Time to move. The Soviets would be over the water in minutes and that meant the RF-14A reconnaissance aircraft would need their help.

"Roger that, commander . . . take heading of zero five eight," Skip Colby told him.

"You with us, Muskie two?" Kelley radioed to his wingman.

"We're with you," the response crackled through his helmet.

"Let's descend to angels twelve, it will give them a chance to look at us." Kelley did a slow banking turn with Muskie two to the northwest. He pushed the nose down five degrees and came wings-level. Robin, his wingman, stayed 500 feet off Kelley's left side and a little back.

THE *LENINGRAD*

"Captain, radar shows two unidentified aircraft 190 kilometers southeast and approaching on an intercept course."

"Contact Krakntov Air Base on the island and tell them I want air cover *now*." Captain Volkov was looking directly at Kanovich when he said it. "Go to combat conditions, weapon systems up and ready."

Everyone on board the *Leningrad* waited in anxious silence for further instructions.

"Captain," the radar operator reported, "radar shows a slow-moving object bearing 257 degrees, altitude 650 meters, speed 137 knots."

"That's our cargo, it's on the way." The political officer Kanovich didn't try to hide his excitement.

Captain Volkov walked over and with his binoculars glassed the area where the helicopter should have been. "I see it, bring her around to one six seven. One quarter speed. Quick and smooth."

F-14D TOMCAT INBOUND, MUSKIE FLIGHT

"You got anything yet, Colby?" Kelley asked, meaning the *Leningrad*.

"No, sir, we're still too far out. I can't see it through the haze." Colby was using the fighter's long-range optical tracking system, the camera under its nose.

"I'm switching to radar," Colby told Kelley as he reached over and switched the AWG-9 radar from standby to active, then switched the navigation mode to ground. The tactical information display radar screen came to life in front of him. He scanned the instruments making a few last checks. TACAN and

radio . . . on. IFF . . . off. AWG-9 liquid-cooling switch . . .
on. Weapons arms switch . . . off.

"Okay, everything is up and running."

Kelley nudged the throttles forward. The airspeed Mach
meter climbed to .8.

"I got 'em. Turn right, heading zero four two. They're seventy
miles out." Colby's screen showed a long narrow object in the
upper center.

"Muskie flight, Muskie flight. Be on Juliet station in six." The
instructions came from the Air Control Officer aboard the E-2C
Hawkeye orbiting above and south of Kelley, telling him to start
his run at the *Leningrad.*

"Roger, Godmother, we copy. Muskie flight inbound and
ready to dance," Kelley radioed back, "let's earn our pay,
Colby."

Each pilot tightened down his torso harnesses and lapbelts.
Their plan was simple: The two fighters would drop down to
several hundred feet above the ocean and head straight for the
Soviet cruiser. They would pop up from time to time to make
sure the radar operators on board the ship knew they were
coming. Coming in above and a little behind them would be the
RF-14A reconnaissance fighter. The Fourteen had been stripped
clean for maximum speed and acceleration. There was little
chance that Soviet naval weapons systems would have time to
engage it, and if the plan worked the *Leningrad* would be preoc-
cupied with the F-14s and wouldn't know the reconnaissance
aircraft was in the area until its mission was over.

"Muskie two, follow my lead." Kelley's wingman responded
by clicking the trigger on his mike twice. Kelley readjusted his
oxygen mask and banked the big jet into a dive.

THE *LENINGRAD*

The dark speck on the horizon grew larger and more defined. In
the distance it looked like two aircraft flying formation, one on
top of the other. After a few minutes crew members on deck
could make out that the two objects were connected with a
large cable. Many had never seen the enormous Mi-10 helicopter, let alone wreckage of one of the West's most secret aircraft.

"Bring her to a full stop," Volkov ordered. Ten seconds later the turning of the mighty ship's props came to a stop.

"What's the position of the American fighters?" Kanovich asked.

"Sixty kilometers out, heading straight for us," the answer came back. Volkov swore.

"Where is our air support?"

E-2C HAWKEYE, GODMOTHER

"You got them?"

"I got 'em," the radar and combat information officers said, referring to new unidentified targets that had just appeared on the radar screen.

"From their airspeed and size they look like fighters out of Sakhalin. Angels 3100 feet and descending. Speed 600 knots and accelerating, heading is one six three degrees." The radar operator paused. "They're on an intercept course for the Tomcats."

The air control officer took over. "Muskie leader, we have two unidentified bogies heading one six three. Closing at 630 knots and accelerating. Altitude, 3000 feet and descending. They should be in your radar range in two minutes."

Kelley confirmed the transmission.

The radar operator kept his eyes on the screen. The second needle of the threat-direction indicator was now pointing at the two targets moving across his screen. He waited for the computer to stop cycling and tapped in a new set of instructions. Now the background noise in his headset was clearer, he heard the static separate into four distinguishable rhythmic tones followed by a click and then repeated again once every two seconds. He was hearing the radar emissions being sent out by the two unidentified aircraft scanning back and forth. The signal was growing stronger with each sweep.

"That's a Pulse-Doppler flashdance radar." He paused for a few seconds. "They're Flankers . . . SU-27s," the operator announced loudly enough so the two other men could hear.

"We now have positive I.D. Muskie flight. You are closing on two Soviet Flankers. Repeat, two Flankers."

THE *LENINGRAD*

"I understand, general. As you say, time is of the essence."
Captain Volkov replaced the radio receiver and looked out over
the flight deck. The helicopter was now hovering directly overhead, resembling a huge bird of prey with its night's catch
hanging beneath it.

F-14D TOMCAT, MUSKIE FLIGHT

Kelley was totally visual. He strained to see the cruiser or the
Flankers in front of them. The heavy morning haze was limiting
his view to only five miles.

"What's happening out there, Skip?" he asked Colby.

"*Leningrad* . . . straight ahead on our current heading, eighteen miles out. Their ECM is up to full power and we're still
being swept by their radar," Colby said. "They could have
locked up on us ten miles ago."

"What about those Flankers?" Kelley asked, looking straight
up through his canopy as he spoke.

"Nothing, I don't see them on radar or hear their radars
searching for us any more. I'm switching to air-to-air search-
and-track."

Kelley tried to picture the scene. The Flankers were coming in
at low level. They had turned their radars off and were coming
in behind the cruiser. Which was why Colby hadn't been able
to find them. In minutes Kelley had a choice to make. He could
break left or right around the ship, going over the top was out
of the question. The Soviets obviously knew the American reconnaissance aircraft would soon be over the ship. Question
was, what did they intend to do about it . . . ?

"Lock-up, commander, the cruiser has us on I/J Band . . .
dog blue." Colby was giving the code designation of the enemy
radar, which he got from the RHAW, the Radar Homing and
Warning system that kept them up to speed on enemy radars
sweeping the area.

"Jam it, I'm taking her up . . . Robin, you with me?" Kelley
radioed his wingman Robin McGuire.

At the same time Kelley saw the gray glimmer of the RF-14A reconnaissance aircraft streak overhead straight for the *Leningrad*.

THE *LENINGRAD*

The enormous sonic boom told the crew that the reconnaissance version of the Tomcat had come and gone. Chances were the Americans had gotten the information they wanted. Still, the sailors on the flight deck worked quickly to secure and cover the wreckage of the RF-117C fighter.

"Radar reports targets still on interception course, now nineteen kilometers out, speed constant at four hundred and fifty knots," the Soviet radar operator relayed in to Captain Volkov.

"Keep our fighters updated," ordered the captain. "Engine room stand by. When I give the order set a course of one seven eight full power."

SU-27 FLANKERS

Major Gichko could just make out the light gray shadow of the *Leningrad* ahead of him. At just forty meters above the ocean the air turbulence from the rapidly warming morning air shook the big fighter. The major and his wingman had been flying at low altitude, silently, the *Leningrad* seeming to mask their presence. At least so far Gichko's passive on-board sensors had not detected any enemy radar scanning the air space in front of them. The Americans were vulnerable, they shouldn't have exposed themselves. He looked forward to taking them on for the first time.

Major Gichko had some experience flying intercept missions against American RC-135s and Japanese F-16Cs that tried to penetrate Soviet airspace. The F-16Cs, some flown by American pilots, would fly at high-Mach speed directly at the naval base in Petropavlovsk, but they had always turned away before Gichko could make visual contact. The RC-135s were different. They were big, slow and relatively easy to see. He had escorted about a dozen of the spy planes out and away from Sakhalin.

Now Gichko could feel his confidence beginning to waver as

he thought of the F-14s. They were something new, he thought uneasily.

F-14D TOMCAT, MUSKIE FLIGHT

Kelley watched the early morning haze all but disappear when his fighter broke through 2000 feet. Ahead was clear blue sky, the sun at his back.

"Anything yet, Skip? I don't want to take her up any higher than necessary."

"Not a thing. All I have is that ship. I don't like this, commander. They're still locked-up on us, our ECM hasn't the power to jam them." Colby continued to scan his instruments, wishing they had an EA-6B Prowler up there with them.

Kelley took over. "Arm your weapons." He keyed his mike. "Muskie two, go defensive. In thirty seconds we'll be at the target area. When I break left you go right, I'll meet you on the other side. Look out for those Flankers. You follow?"

"Roger, lead, I follow."

Kelley readjusted his restraint straps and turned his oxygen air-mix to one hundred percent.

Major Gichko heard the warning from the *Leningrad* that the F-14s were now sending out hostile radio signals, the Tomcats had armed their weapons. He brought all his systems, radar and air-to-air missiles, up and ready. The major's Flanker carried a mix of AA-11 medium range and AA-8 close-range infrared homing missiles. He nosed the fighter up a few degrees and turned his all-aspects Pulse-Doppler radar to full power to sweep the sky above and ahead of him.

"Break now, Muskie two," Kelley ordered.

The navy commander snapped the large fighter into a hard left turn. The bow of the *Leningrad* flashed below only 500 yards away.

"Got 'em, two bogies heading zero two seven on a direct course for Robin," Colby announced.

Muskie two had the sun directly behind him. The two Flankers were some 3000 yards straight ahead and only 100 yards below in a tight formation. Flankers and Tomcat were closing on each other at over 1100 knots.

"You see them, you see them?" Gichko shouted to his wingman.

"Nothing, I see nothing."

Gichko slapped his sun visor down over his eyes as a high-pitch warning tone sounded in his helmet, telling him the F-14 had just locked onto his fighter. With visor down, he could barely make out the black outline of the American fighter for a second or two, then it would disappear again in the burning orange sun.

Expecting a sidewinder to tear through his aircraft any second, Gichko keyed his mike for help from his wingman. "Has he launched, has he launched . . . ?" He hated the panicky sound in his voice. He had badly wanted to be successful in this first engagement with the Americans, but that very eagerness and excitement had diminished his concentration. In the confusion he had failed to fully depress his communications' trigger on the Flanker's stick, so that his wingman only heard a broken message with two "launches."

The fighters were now only 1200 yards apart and closing fast. An AA-8 Aphid heat-seeking air-to-air missile blasted away from under each wing of the Soviet Flanker a split second apart. The American F-14D broke high and to the right trying to evade. The first missile, its seeker-head confused by the sun, failed to track. The second, accelerating to 1500 miles an hour in less than two seconds, arched to the right following the Tomcat. Lock-on. In a flash of white fire the rear half of Robin's fighter disappeared.

Kelley watched in disbelief as the smoking fuselage of his wingman spun violently toward the water. It happened so fast that neither he nor Colby had been able to call out a warning.

"Ambushed us," Colby said through clenched teeth.

"Call for back-up *now*," Kelley shouted. The commander swept his instruments, smashed the throttles forward and watched his airspeed climb to over 500 knots.

"Bogies heading . . . splitting, zero seven two and three six four," Colby said, reading off the new headings.

"I got 'em." Kelley could see the black smoke pouring out of their Tumansky turbofans, snapped the Tomcat into a ninety-degree roll and turned hard right. He felt his G-suit fill with air and the pressure build around his legs and torso. The HUD clicked off the Gs—three, four, five, six. A sudden pop in his back told Kelley he was just about at his limit.

"All right, you bastards," Kelley muttered, and brought the fighter wings level at 2000 feet. The Gs fell off rapidly. He pushed the twin throttles all the way forward until he felt a definite click and the Tomcat burst into afterburner, the forty percent added thrust compressing both men back into their ejection seats.

Kelley chose to attack the Flanker on the right. He could hear the whine of the Tomcat's electronic motors as the variable wings swept back for maximum speed. His HUD showed airspeed just passing 600 knots.

"You watch that other Flanker. He's going to try to get in around behind us," Kelley warned Colby. "This mother is mine."

Kelley pushed the stick back, nosing the fighter up fifteen degrees. The sudden warbling tone in his helmet told him the sidewinders were trying to lock onto the Soviet fighter ahead of him a little more than three miles.

Suddenly two bright objects appeared, falling away from the enemy fighter. Infrared flares designed to confuse heat-seeking missiles. The Soviet fighter then pointed its nose straight up and rocketed away. Kelley followed. His F-14 had a higher thrust-to-weight ratio than the Flanker, which meant he could out-climb and outturn his opponent. If that second Flanker stays off my tail just long enough . . . Kelley thought.

"He's coming around, eight o'clock now," Colby grunted, telling Kelley the position of the second SU-27.

Tomcat and Flanker were now in a parallel vertical climb. Kelley was waiting for the Flanker to start bleeding energy, to

fall in behind and fire. He watched the vertical-velocity indicator show his airspeed climbing. He was overtaking the Flanker.
A few more moments . . .

"Come on, push over, push over," Kelley yelled out. His concentration on eliminating the first fighter, he forced himself to
put thoughts of the other Flanker out of his mind.

Abruptly he saw the air break open just before he could react.
As the Flanker's speed fell off Kelley overshot him by several
hundred yards. The Soviet rolled his fighter left and went into a
dive. Muttering, Kelley pushed the stick forward to drop his
nose. The wing-sweep indicator showed his wings moving to
twenty-five degrees as he pushed over and rolled left. He
chopped the throttles and cut across the beam of the now-
diving Flanker, banked hard right and left again and slid in
behind. Now both planes were in a steep vertical dive for the
ocean 7000 feet below. The piercing tone in Kelley's ear told
him the time was right.

"Fire," he said loud enough for Colby to hear. He squeezed
the trigger once, twice to make sure the sidewinder launched.
The white missile tracked straight for the enemy in front of him.
His first reaction was to pull up and away, but Kelley forced
himself to wait . . . And he saw the white smoke-tail of the
missile end in an array of orange flames and black smoke.

Kelley leaned back on the stick and pulled out of the dive.

Major Gichko watched as his wingman's fighter went up in
flames. He pushed the stick harder to the left, increasing his
turn rate to five Gs, completing his 360-degree turn. The American fighter was now 1000 meters above him and just over four
kilometers in front. Gichko leveled his Flanker and pushed the
throttles forward, keeping his eyes fixed on the Tomcat.

The American fighter was coming out of a steep dive, but
Gichko couldn't tell if the Tomcat was heading away or toward
him. Never mind. The sight on his HUD changed from yellow to
orange, telling him an AA-11 medium-range semiactive radar
air-to-air missile had just locked onto the F-14. Engage, engage,
Gichko thought. *Now*, and he squeezed the button on his stick,
sending the fifteen-foot-long missile racing on its way.

* * *

Commander Kelley pumped the stick back twice, leveling his Tomcat at 550 knots . . . and as he did so the bright flash of light accelerating toward him needed no explanation.

Steady, steady, Kelley told himself, keeping his speed constant and altitude right at 3000 feet.

"We got enemy radar lock-on . . . I got a launch. I'm trying to jam," Colby told Kelley. "Goddamn, not enough time, I can't jam it . . ."

Kelley could no longer wait. He hauled back on the stick with all his strength at the same time pushing the throttles forward in the opposite direction. The G-meter on his HUD jumped from .5 to 7.5 in a fifth of a second. Both pilots were slammed with 1200 pounds of force into their seats. The nose of the Tomcat pulled straight up and away from the approaching missile. The AA-11 raced underneath them, missing by only fifty yards, just outside the radius of its proximity detonator.

Kelley could feel the Gs starting to loosen as he broke through 5500 feet and throttled back, taking his fighter out of afterburner. He rolled the Tomcat over 180 degrees, turning his head right and left to look for the Flanker somewhere below.

"I've lost him, Skip, I've lost him," Kelley said.

There was no response.

"Colby, I need some help here. Where is that Flanker?"

Again, no response.

"Hey . . . what the hell . . . ?" Kelley turned around and looked over his shoulder. Colby's head was bobbing like Jell-O. Apparently he had blacked out.

"Hey . . . wake up, Skipper!" Kelley yelled as he pushed the stick forward and eased the throttles back again. At the top of his 8000 foot climb he leveled off inverted, again looked right and left, trying to catch sight of the Flanker somewhere below. The Soviet would be tough to see against the blue gray background of the water.

Gichko watched the American above him. In a few more seconds he would pass under the Tomcat.

Perfect. He checked his instruments, no red warning lights. He knew in a lesser plane, like the older MiG-23 he used to fly, the American would have the advantage being above him. But not in the new SU-27. He broke hard left, banking seventy degrees and increasing his speed to over 600 knots, keeping his eyes on the Tomcat now arching above and behind him.

His vision slowly coming back, Colby rubbed his eyes with his fingertips, shook his head back and forth.

"Skip, you back yet?" Kelley asked.

". . . Ah, yeah, I think so." And suddenly it hit Colby what had happened. His mind was clearing and he remembered they were in a fight for their lives against a Soviet Flanker.

"Where is he?" Colby shouted.

"Somewhere below us." As he spoke, Kelley saw the black trail of smoke in his right-side rearview mirror. "He's coming in behind us," Kelley called out. Colby swung around just in time to see the Flanker leveling off behind them.

"He's right behind us, get the hell out of here, Kelley," Colby shouted.

Kelley banked his Tomcat hard right, then left, repeated the maneuver three more times. Each time the Flanker stayed with him just inside his turn-radius. With each turn he could actually feel his body receiving a shot of adrenalin.

"Missile at five o'clock. Brake hard left," Colby warned.

Kelley smashed the stick left and turned his head in the same direction, trying to get a visual on the Soviet heat-seeker.

"I don't see it," Kelley shouted, and then caught sight of the Aphid between the two tails of the Tomcat. He kept with his left turn until the missile was in a perpendicular course to his fighter, then rolled level at 7500 feet, speed 520 knots.

"Come *on*, Kelley, come on," Colby was saying.

"Flare *now*," and Kelley yanked the stick back, forcing the F-14 into a sudden climb. The missile raced past, hitting the flare and exploding only forty yards below them. Kelley eased his throttles back and dropped his right wing banking steeply. He watched his airspeed drop off on his HUD—500, 300, 150, 50 knots. Zero Gs were indicated at 10,000 feet. Both pilots seemed to hang suspended in their seats for a moment, their fighter shuddering almost to a stop. Kelley then dropped the nose and rolled the Tomcat ninety degrees to his left.

"Gotch ya," Kelley said under his oxygen mask. Three thousand feet below and to their south the Americans saw the Flanker rushing away.

"He's heading for the deck trying to lose us," Colby said, his voice rising.

"I see him," Kelley said, pushing the throttles all the way to afterburner. The dull gray nose of the Tomcat pointed down forty degrees as it accelerated toward the Flanker straight ahead.

"I got 'em three miles out, heading 235, altitude 3000, speed . . . I can't tell," Colby said as Kelley pulled the Tomcat out of its dive.

"Lock up a sparrow," Kelley ordered.

"I got radar lock."

Kelley's round gun-sight on his HUD turned yellow to flashing red. "Fox one," he said as the radar-guided sparrow left his Tomcat with a giant *swaasshh*.

"Come on, baby . . ." Colby said as both pilots watched the sparrow speeding toward the Flanker at Mach three.

A sudden flash told them that the sparrow had hit its mark.

"Yeah . . . hot damn," Colby shouted, "now let's get the hell out of here."

"I'll second that," Kelley said, banked hard to the southeast and leveled out his fighter at 4000 feet. He unsnapped his oxygen mask and wiped the perspiration from his face, took a deep breath and let it out slowly. He could feel his legs shaking beneath him.

9

ILLUSIONS OF TRUTH

THE WHITE HOUSE, SITUATION ROOM

The President got right to the point.

"What information do you have, general?" he said to the Chairman of the Joint Chiefs. *General*, not Jack, Dawson noted.

"Mr. President, details are still coming in, but here it is so far. At about 3:06 P.M. local time two F-14s from the carrier *Constellation* flying support for RF-14A were confronted by two Soviet SU-27 Flankers. At approximately 3:10 a Flanker fired an air-to-air missile and downed one of the F-14s. A dogfight followed and our flight leader returned fire and shot down both Soviet aircraft."

Secretary Robinson jumped in. "We've never been in a situation like this, and if you don't keep your hotheads in line—"

The President broke in. "Mr. Brady?"

"We've intercepted transmissions from our listening posts in Japan and our Jumpseat Three ferreting satellites. The Soviets seem to have instructed their forces to cool it," the CIA Director said.

"We'll see if they mean it . . . What else?"

"I'll tell you what else," said Secretary of State Robinson. "There shouldn't *be* anything else. This could put everything I've worked for at risk, again. This stealth fighter of Turner's isn't worth a war."

"Mr. Robinson, we all know how serious this is." The President's tone was low and quiet.

General Dawson picked it up rather than answer back to Robinson, who was so worried about his treaty. "The *Constellation* reports that more of the RF-117C was intact than we'd first thought. The Soviets could very easily learn too much about stealth construction." Dawson handed the file of photos to the President.

National Security Adviser Leo Lewis, who had been quiet up to now, moved in. "If they learn from the Black Ghost it could jeopardize our SIOP-15 strategy. Our plan to defeat the Soviet Union in the first hours of a nuclear conflict. It calls for us to use our force of stealth reconnaissance planes to ferret out the locations of their heavy and light mobile ICBMs. If the Soviets can find an RF-117C they can also attack it and down it. That will leave us blind. And that's linked to a bigger threat. The more they learn about our stealth technology, the more our plan to attack their secret computer-radar complex with B-2s . . ."

Turner bit his lip. Lewis was getting ahead of himself. The President didn't have all the facts and their meaning about Koiser and the computer complex.

The President looked hard at Lewis. "What the hell don't I know?"

Lewis looked at Turner who looked at CIA Director Tony Brady. "Tony?"

"Well, sir, the Soviet pilot that defected two days ago has given us some additional information . . . we're still checking on it—"

The President shook his head, annoyed at the buck passing. "How soon will you be finished *checking*?"

"It shouldn't be more than a day. We're going to move him tomorrow from Camp Peary so he's closer to CIA headquarters," Turner said.

"Let me know," the President said, not masking his annoyance. "Meanwhile, to use the vernacular, the word is cool it. No posturing, no apology."

VOYSKA PVO HEADQUARTERS, MOSCOW

Nikolai Tomskiy sat in the back of his black staff car. The streets of Moscow were dead quiet as he and his driver made their way to Red Square and the party headquarters. He closed his eyes and rested his head against the back of the seat, and his thoughts turned to an earlier time when he was a Deputy Defense Minister in charge of the strategic rocket forces. Things seemed so much easier in those days. The United States and Western Europe let their nuclear and conventional forces lag behind, allowing his country to catch up and even surpass them in some areas. He remembered the day when the Americans decided to cancel their B-1 bomber program and rely on cruise missiles launched from old B-52s. The Minister of Defense threw a party that night and everyone celebrated the ignorance of the American government. It fanned the fire in the USSR to become bigger and stronger on all fronts, nuclear and conventional. Whatever new program he had asked for he got. Times had changed. The economy was in trouble. And if The Project didn't work as he had promised, he and the others would be fired or worse.

The cold night wind cut through his heavy wool coat as he hurried to the stairs of the Kremlin's main entrance . . .

THE WHITE HOUSE

"John, you were pretty quiet in the meeting today. You were holding back on me. Let's have it."

"Mr. President," Turner said, "I'm now confident the Soviets have developed a new kind of radar-detection system that could render our entire force of stealth aircraft obsolete."

"Go on. How would it work?"

"In order for them to detect a stealth aircraft they would have had to have a breakthrough in computer-assisted target acquisition and radar imaging. The information provided by the RF-117C before it went down and the new information from the defector, the Soviet MiG pilot, has told us without question that the PVO has been working on a new detection system—"

"*What* exactly has the pilot told us so far?"

"The defector Koiser flew MiG-29s at Ramenskoye test center, where he was based for five years. Ramenskoye is sort of the Soviet equivalent of Edwards Air Force Base in California. He told us while he was there he worked on a secret project. They've built a huge computer complex that's tied directly into their air-defense radar network and is capable of detecting stealth aircraft. They had not yet tested it . . . until they shot down the RF-117C."

"If this pilot knows all this, it makes him very important to the Kremlin. Yet they haven't said a word . . . nothing. Don't you find that strange?"

"Yes, I do. Except it goes with them saying nothing about their shooting down our stealth fighter over their territory."

"Anything else?"

"At this time . . . no, sir . . . we're still working on it. You know, there are skeptics like Robinson—"

"I feel like you're trying to tell me something, John."

"Yes, sir, I am." He took a deep breath. "I've taken the liberty of starting work on plans to . . . to destroy this computer complex—"

"Taken the liberty? I'd *say* so. Last I checked I was still President. No more, damn it, without authorization."

Turner expected even worse, and was relieved. "Absolutely, I'm sorry, sir, there was a time crunch and the plans are only preliminary. But of course you're right . . ."

"Any more surprises, requests . . . ?"

"Yes, sir," knowing he was pushing his luck, "I'd like your authorization to fly into their airspace again—"

"John, I can't risk more life—"

"But now that we know what we're looking for I could order a pilotless recon drone into Soviet-controlled air space. We have one that's stealth proven."

"Where would you fly it?"

"Right at one of their most advanced warning stations in East Germany. We can learn the most about the new system and collect the most data there. As a preliminary to . . ."

The President hesitated, then: "I'll authorize that flight. I also want you to locate exactly where this computer complex is.

And tell the hotshots in research to figure out how the hell the Soviets could have built such a system."

Turner nodded and pushed on. "Mr. President, will you then authorize an attack?"

"I don't know. How long will it take to set up your intrusion flight?"

"A few days."

"John, I want you personally to update me on this at least once a day. Is that real clear?"

"Yes, sir," Turner said, feeling excited and grateful all at once.

THE KREMLIN, MOSCOW, 10 OCTOBER

"I assume you have brought us the current information," the General Secretary said to Tomskiy.

"Yes," Tomskiy said as he sat down next to him and across from KGB Chief Volstad.

"Well, let's have it," Volstad said. Tomskiy explained to the two men what had happened over the Okhotsk Sea, shooting down the American fighter—the F117 stealth reconnaissance, now on board the *Leningrad* on its way to the Soviet Union for analysis—the dogfights . . . "I had not planned on the Americans being so aggressive. I am concerned. They may well know we have a superior radar network, they have the defector who worked there. We have, as you instructed, said nothing to play it down, to make it seem we are not concerned and thereby undermine their confidence in what he says and in their intelligence. Still, they aren't stupid . . ."

Volstad shook his head. "My agents in America tell me the American press loves the idea of living in peace with us. They want to see the new General Secretary succeed. They'll blame the American navy, not us. Now we can pressure the West to sign the treaty, knowing our shield works even on their most advanced spy plane. And, of course, a treaty is just a treaty . . ."

"Is The Project fully operational now?" the General Secretary asked Tomskiy.

"We are progressing. The southern theater was tied into the network just two days ago. There are needed adjustments in the northern sector because of the numbers and differences in our defense radars."

"Nikolai, I sense something still bothers you. What is it?"

"I hope Chief Volstad is correct in his assumptions. But let us at least be prepared. I would like to reinforce our defenses around The Project. I would also like to have a squadron of MiG-29s on alert at all times at Ramenskoye."

"I understand," the General Secretary said. "You may proceed . . ."

UNITED STATES EMBASSY, MOSCOW

The front of the United States Embassy on Tchaikovsky Street looked placidly quiet from the outside. Four large street lamps with gas-burning lightbulbs gave a yellow glow to the warehouse-type office building. Inside, on the ninth floor of the ten-story structure, a half-dozen agents from the NSA, the CIA and the State Department were working to decode the volumes of messages being transmitted to the Embassy via a standard AT&T telecommunications satellite.

Victor Baxter opened the huge vaultlike door to the Communications Program Unit, the CPU. The hour was late, 4:06 A.M., and Baxter could feel his lack of sleep starting to affect him. The Ambassador, Marshall Dixon, was currently at the Kremlin meeting with officials there over recent developments. As Deputy Ambassador it was Baxter's responsibility to keep things running while the Ambassador was gone.

Baxter picked up the latest batch of transmissions from the CIA. The top message was from the Secretary of State on the meeting with the Soviet Ambassador and his thoughts about how Dixon should handle further conversations with the Soviet leadership. Several of the other transmissions said the Soviets' military had pulled in its horns and had no discernible intention of escalating hostilities. Discernible . . .

Baxter signed the logbook and jotted down the time and date next to his name, verifying he was taking the top-secret correspondence out of the CPU, then returned to his office.

Baxter sat down at his cluttered desk and reread the latest assignment that had come directly from CIA Director Tony

Brady. It was no trick to sense the urgency in it. It told him to reestablish contact with a mole deep inside the Kremlin, a man he hadn't seen or talked to for over five years, and he felt uneasy about directly reactivating the agent. In the past "Andre" had always been reliable. However, a lot could happen in five years. The information the Director wanted had not surfaced through the CIA's standard network. That in itself made him very damn nervous . . . Baxter had put together a contact package explaining to Andre what the CIA needed. It said that U.S. Intelligence had learned of a new Soviet air-defense radar technology and a super-computer that operated it, and that there was an underground complex containing the system located south of Moscow. The CIA needed to know if there were any holes in the system, any weaknesses or bugs that could be exploited. Was the system fully operational? Partially? And was it tied directly into the Soviets' radar and SAM sites? The message would be delivered, as before, at the gravesite of one of Andre's old friends.

Baxter pulled out a tattered file containing what information he had on Andre and began rereading its contents. For security reasons, Baxter didn't have any details about this man. His real name was Sergei Ilyich Karpukhin. He was born and raised in Azerbaijan next to the Caspian Sea. The son of an Armenian sharecropper and Muslim mother. Like most people in this southern Republic, Andre had come to detest the Soviet government after it absorbed his country in 1922. But he also believed Hitler was a bigger enemy and joined the army after Hitler's invasion of the USSR. It was during the war that Andre first made contact with American Intelligence. At the time he was a young idealistic lieutenant and one of the first Russian officers to enter Berlin. One day, he vowed, he would help liberate his country just as the Allies had freed Europe from the Nazis. After the war he moved to Moscow, where he contacted the newly formed CIA, or perhaps he was contacted. The files weren't clear on that. He disappeared for a while, then surfaced in December of 1956 weeks after the Soviets had invaded Hungary—this time as an officer of the KGB.

Andre was a widower with no children and lived alone. Baxter didn't know where he lived or even how old Andre was, which was for Andre's protection. The only photograph Baxter had was a faded black-and-white snapshot taken in 1972 that showed Andre standing behind Leonid Brezhnev while he and members of the Central Committee were greeting a delegation from North Vietnam. Andre was nondescript—medium height, black framed glasses, dark hair, plain and simple features. Since that time he had contacted the CIA on very few occasions, but each time the information he provided was of considerable importance. As in the past, Andre's current position in the government gave him access to many of his country's most guarded secrets. He was the assistant to the General Secretary of the Soviet Union.

Baxter looked up from his desk just in time to see Marshall Dixon flash past his door, gathered the transmissions and followed the tall gray-haired Ambassador into his office.

At sixty-two, Ambassador Dixon kept himself in excellent physical condition with early morning workouts and a strict diet. Tonight, however, he looked weary.

"Victor," the Ambassador said, "I expected you to be in your quarters." He took off his coat and threw it over the desk chair.

"How did it go?" Baxter stood just inside the doorway.

"Better than I thought it would, I think. I pushed hard on the fact they started shooting first and the General Secretary just sat there."

Baxter walked over to the Ambassador's desk and placed the current messages in the center of it. "Nothing important, they can wait till morning. Sounds like we got the same sort of treatment from the Sovs in Washington."

"You know, their response doesn't really add up. They didn't put a single one of their aircraft, ships or anything else on alert. We had additional fighters in the air within two minutes of the dogfight. The Air Force and Navy were ready to mix it up. And I'll tell you what, if Admiral Alton hadn't been on the bridge of that carrier there would be one heavy Soviet cruiser on the bottom of the ocean."

Baxter walked over and closed the Ambassador's office door. "Were you able to make contact with Andre?" Baxter asked.

"He was there in the room with the General Secretary when I arrived. They were talking about something, I didn't overhear.

He stayed for about half the meeting, then left. I thought he looked tired . . . I think he understood but I can't be sure. Of course he couldn't acknowledge me."

"Are you sure he saw your tie," Baxter said, referring to the Ambassador's plain burgundy necktie.

"I'm sure. I left my jacket open and even made a point to adjust it twice. The Ambassador moved his tie back and forth at the collar, indicating how he had made the signals. The American Ambassador wearing a plain dark red tie had been agreed on as a signal before Baxter had been stationed at the embassy. It seemed archaic to him but if it worked and kept Andre free from suspicion . . .

"Okay, the contact package is in place," Baxter said, "I made clear what Brady wanted on this super radar, or whatever it is. Now we'll wait and see."

MOSCOW, NOVODYEVICHII CONVENT

Andre stood in the cold air on the southern edge of a bend in the Moscow River. A distant glow in the east was the first hint of a new day. His breath lingered for a second before drifting off and disappearing into the night. Andre walked with a steady, determined pace toward the cemetery of the convent.

The convent was one of the oldest buildings in Moscow. Peter the Great's oldest sister, Princess Sophia, had been exiled there for supporting revolts against the czar in the seventeenth century. Napoleon had ordered its destruction during the final days of his occupation of Moscow in 1812. It was saved only at the last moment. Currently the newer cemetery of the convent was a place reserved for senior party officials, famous folk and government bureaucrats. The older part of the cemetery was used for aviators, scholars, scientists and writers. Andre had several friends buried here, he knew his way even in the dark.

Andre approached a gray headstone slowly, surveying the shadows and surroundings ahead of him. He stood in place for over a minute turning slowly in a small circle. All was quiet. When he felt comfortable, Andre knelt down and blessed himself, as if in preparation for prayer. He leaned over the grave slightly and pulled a small two-by-four-inch dark brown envelope from between the frozen ground and headstone, then swiftly placed it in his breast pocket. He would wait until he reached the safety of his apartment before reading the message.

10

PAST MISTAKES

RICHMOND, VIRGINIA

Koiser's face was somber as he looked at the small girl sitting at the table next to him. Her short light brown hair, large brown eyes and quick smile reminded him, inevitably, of his own daughter. The prospect of not seeing his child again was the part of his defection he deeply regretted, and knew he always would.

"Well, what do you think?" Tyransky asked, not aware of Koiser's thoughts. "We call it an Egg McMuffin."

Koiser nodded politely and took a bite. His eyes went to the newspaper in front of him that showed a picture of a Tomcat and a SU-27 just under the headlines. Tyransky had told him what had happened, and both had listened to radio reports. Koiser was still amazed at how much the American people were allowed to know.

It was a slightly higher risk moving Koiser by car, but Tyransky believed the man deserved at least some of the freedom he'd jeopardized his life for. Grigori would have his work cut out for him when he got to the CIA. Charles only hoped he could keep the media wolves at a distance.

"Grigori, I want you to know and be prepared for what it might be like there . . . where we're going a lot of people will want to ask you questions." Tyransky took a sip of coffee. "Everyone will think their questions are the most important and some may get aggressive. I'm going to try to keep these situations to a minimum but . . . well, tell me if you feel uncomfortable with anything or anyone. I'll try to be with you but realistically there will be some meetings I'll miss. You can trust me. If you don't trust me I can't help you. Do you understand what I am trying to say?" Tyransky looked up and across the aisle . . . an elderly couple was staring at them. Obviously they'd never heard anyone talking half-Russian and half-English.

"I will be fine, Charles," Koiser said in English. "I will be *okay*."

Maybe so, Tyransky thought. Maybe . . .

CIA HEADQUARTERS

A few hours later Koiser and Tyransky arrived at the CIA.

"Normally we don't keep people in this building. The Agency operates a safe house only three miles from here and that was where they had you scheduled to stay. I think it would be better to keep you close until we're surer of what . . . the Soviets are up to. You could be exposed and—" Charles stopped short. The guards had high-security clearance but he wasn't going to put anyone above suspicion. "Let's just say I want you here for now."

They stopped at a plain white metal door. The guard unlocked it and handed the key to Tyransky.

Koiser and Tyransky entered and Tyransky flipped on the light. The room wasn't what Tyransky had expected. The twenty by twenty-foot single room had a smooth concrete floor painted a flat gray with a small rug in the middle. The bare walls were light yellow. A bed was at the far wall. The bathroom on the right side had a sink, a toilet and a shower. A cardtable and chairs were in the far corner opposite the bed. The room was finished off with a couch and small television on the left side.

Tyransky tried not to show his surprise and closed the door behind them. "Well . . . you won't be spending much time here. Just to sleep."

Koiser tossed his duffel bag on the couch, then sat on the bed.

He looked at Tyransky and for the first time realized that the
man was old enough to be his father. His large round head and
white sideburns reminded him of his father, although the re-
semblance ended there. Tyransky's short round frame and baby
blue eyes made him look like an affable grandfather rather than
a CIA agent.

"I'm going to have to leave you alone for a while. Staffer
asked me to contact him when we got here. I'd like to find out
what they have planned. See you soon." He turned and left the
room, locking the door.

Mark Collins was just returning from an afternoon briefing. On
his desk was a stack of telephone message slips. Maddie had
asked and gotten the afternoon off. Mark picked up the messages. The first was from Christine.

"Christine Boyle. May I help you?"

"I hope so, you see I just got back from this meeting and—"

"And?"

"And now that I'm talking to you I'm sure that's what I
needed to get me through the rest of the day."

"Glad I could help. We still on for tonight?"

"Of course."

"See you at seven-thirty then, okay?"

"Okay." Mark hung up, stared at the picture of Amy. He still
felt the loss deeply. As if he were missing or had forgotten
something. *Something?* Had he made a mistake? Was it too soon
to see someone else? Only a year since Amy died . . .

He turned to his computer keyboard and began feeding the
last of the day's information into the ADABAS. He watched the
screen fill with data and then disappear with a push of a button.
The ADABAS was running behind again. Late afternoon crunch
time. He finished and closed out the system, signing off. He
pushed the two newspapers sitting on the corner of his desk
over the edge and into the waste basket. The rest of his phone
messages were underneath the papers and fell to the floor.
Mark had forgotten about them after talking with Christine. He
picked them up and read through each one.

"Damn, this one's from the FBI." He checked his watch, 5:15

P.M. Eastern. Let's see . . . 2:15 in California. How could he have missed this? He dialed the phone, listening to the tones as he punched the buttons.

"Andrew Carlsen, FBI."

"I need to speak with Brice . . . I believe it's Kroutromer?"

A moment later, "Kroutromer here."

"Mark Collins. I'm returning your call."

"Mark Collins . . . oh yeah, CIA. Look, I got word earlier today from contacts in Mexico City. The Mexican police found the guy they believe is the one you were looking for. Ken Welsh, he works for Euratech."

"I'd like to talk with him." Collins hoped this could be the break he needed on his 8224-chip case.

"No can do. Mr. Welsh is dead. Found him in a downtown dumpster. Had a single bullet wound in the head."

"Are you sure? When will you have a positive I.D.?"

"Forensics is working on it. I should have an answer within twenty-four hours. There was nothing on him, but he fits the description."

Collins's mind went blank. He didn't expect this. "I need to know right away. Fingerprints, photos, the works." Collins almost forgot he was talking to the FBI, and not a subordinate in the department.

"Hey, I *said* you'll have it as soon as we have it. That's the best I can do," Kroutromer snapped.

"I'm sorry, it's been a long day and I just wasn't expecting this kind of information."

"Like I said, you'll have it as soon as I have it." The FBI agent hung up.

Damn it. I hope that we learn something from that warehouse in New Zealand, Collins thought.

11

UNWELCOME GUEST

VOYSKA PVO HEADQUARTERS, MOSCOW

"Come with me, colonel," the young, well-dressed man said, entering the room.

Colonel Igor Belikov didn't know the name or title of the man. For all he knew he was being led to his court-martial. He had been ordered to leave the Sevastopol air base less than twelve hours ago, was put aboard a Tupolev VIP transport and flown directly to Moscow. It had to be something about the defection of Captain Koiser . . . The PVO wanted a scapegoat and he would be it.

"This way." The man turned to the left.

Belikov glanced over his shoulder as he passed through the doorway and entered the hall. He couldn't see anyone else in the long corridor ahead of him. No surprise there. The time was 6:55 A.M. and most of the staff wouldn't show up for another hour. He wasn't familiar with this section of the PVO headquarters . . . the other times he had been here to debrief his commanders and discuss proposed air defenses for a NATO attack had all been at the opposite wing of the building. This section was newer, more modern.

The escort had not said a word the entire length of the walk. Now he pushed open the door and let the colonel pass in front of him. The cold outdoor air of the early morning felt good, a

161

welcome change from the recycled air of Air Force headquarters. The feeling, though, only lasted a few moments as a chill came over him and the colonel knew the temperature was below freezing.

"Where are you taking me?" Belikov asked, putting his large hands in his pockets and continuing to walk at a steady pace on the sidewalk.

"It's not much farther," the man said, dropping his head in the breeze. The overcast gray sky gave a hint of heavy snow as small flakes swirled in the air above them. The man walked rapidly past Belikov and led him to a black staff car parked on the curve. Belikov could see its white exhaust pouring into the air.

"Please get in," the man said, pointing the way with his hand.

Belikov looked right and left at the guards on each side of him. He decided not to ask any questions. Ducking his head he entered the warm dark interior of the car. The door slammed behind him.

"Good morning, colonel," Nikolai Tomskiy said from the left side of the bench seat. "I trust you had a pleasant trip from Sevastopol. I apologize for not giving you more warning but security . . ."

"I understand." Belikov's mind was racing. Was all this pleasantness a prelude to the axe falling because one of his pilots defected?

"Colonel," the Minister of Defense went on, "you have an impressive record. I wish we had more men of your quality."

"I thank you, Minister," Belikov said, allowing himself to feel the man might actually mean it.

"Colonel, I have personally chosen you for a very special assignment," Tomskiy continued, realizing and enjoying Belikov's nervousness. "I am now going to take you into my confidence as I would few men . . . For the last ten years the PVO has been working on a top-secret defensive-radar network that will shield this country from any surprise attack. We were forced into developing this when it was realized that the Americans did in fact have the technology to build and deploy an aircraft that could evade our current air defenses . . . they call them stealth fighters and bombers. Our scientists have known how to build a radar system to detect their new aircraft but lacked the computers to run it. That lack was overcome with the special help of the KGB . . . they were able to, let us say, acquire, sufficient necessary components to build such a system. Five years ago construction and testing began at Ramenskoye. And five days ago we downed an American stealth F-117 over Sakhalin Island. It is now on the way to Moscow for examination and analysis. That is why the trouble occurred over the Sea of Okhotsk. The Americans didn't want us to have the wreckage and weren't about to give it up so easily." Tomskiy was enjoying this briefing. "Originally, colonel, we hadn't planned to reveal the presence of the network to the West until we had perfected it in all respects and secured the Arms Reduction Treaty with the U.S. Unfortunately, a traitor, Captain Koiser, flew his MiG at Ramenskoye before being assigned to fly with you. He helped develop the tracking system, knows its capabilities. When Koiser defected I was persuaded into deploying the system. Now I am afraid the West is also aware of our network and the element of surprise is lost."

Tomskiy paused. "Colonel, my colleagues at the Kremlin believe the Americans may still be pressured to sign the treaty because of domestic and world opinion. They also believe there is some question about them actually believing the defector. I am less hopeful. The Americans aren't stupid. It is my responsibility to protect this country, which brings me to the reason you are here. You have flown combat against the Americans. You have built your life around strategies for defending this country against them. I need your knowledge and leadership to defend the radar network's command center. To be specific, I am putting you in charge of a squadron of MiG-29s, and of the SAM and antiaircraft artillery sites surrounding the center. I want you to find and correct any weaknesses you find in our defense system. And, colonel, I want you to report directly to me."

Belikov nodded. "I am honored, sir." And relieved, he added silently. "But I must point out there are many generals who are more qualified than I am."

"Colonel, most of the generals on my staff are bureaucrats that don't have the skill or the guts to fight in combat. You've proved yourself in combat, I repeat. I'm confident you are the man I want . . . Do you remember General Yefimov?"

"Yes, I flew with him in Vietnam. I was a lieutenant and he was a captain. We lost touch about five years ago. He just dropped out of sight." As the last words left his lips he put it together. Yefimov was now a general, and was working on the secret project. "I didn't know he made general."

"Few people do. He has been stationed at Ramenskoye since his promotion. You will be working beside him. Not under him. He understands that."

Belikov's curiosity was overflowing. "Sir, could you tell me something of how this new system works?"

Tomskiy looked at his wristwatch. "We will be there in twenty minutes, colonel. Do you think you can wait that long?" Tomskiy forgot to smile when he said it.

HAHN AIR FORCE BASE, GERMANY

A dark green C-130H Hercules Compass Call "Herky-Bird" sat on the taxiway only fifty feet from its hangar. Its number two and three engines hummed smoothly at half-power. The other two engines were quiet. The pilot and copilot went over their check lists and weather reports one more time. The copilot hit a set of switches on the lower center of his instrument panel just below the yoke. The internal cockpit lights flickered off. In a few minutes the sun would rise.

Sitting inside the cargo bay, just before the ramp hinge line, a Pave Cricket stealth drone was also getting a review of its pre-flight checks. The little Pave Cricket would be at the heart of the mission this early morning. The C-130 would fly along the West German border and launch the drone in mid-flight so it could slip undetected into Soviet airspace. It would then fly straight at one of the Soviet Union's most advanced air-defense sites located in Leipzig, East Germany. The Pave Cricket was packed with electronics powerful enough to broadcast a radio signal that would make it appear on a radar screen as big as a B-52. After a few minutes it would shut down, disappearing off the Soviet's radarscopes. The idea was that if the plan worked the Soviets would have to call up their new radar system in order to find the drone, and the C-130H Compass Call would be there to monitor its electronic signals. The information learned would then be analyzed by Air Force radar experts in preparation for an attack on the complex itself.

"Nicad batteries fully charged and operating, sir," Sergeant Whittaker said.

"Got it," replied Lieutenant Colonel Mel Dramit. "Double check that fuel cap?"

"It's okay, sir. All it needed was a new washer." Whittaker made sure it was on and tightened it again. The small graphite fuel cap on the bottom of the right wing had been leaking the 122-octane fuel used to power the pilotless reconnaissance drone. If the mission failed Dramit didn't want it to be from a leaking fuel cap.

"All right, get to your station and go through your procedures," the colonel said, and knelt down next to the eight-foot-long bat-shaped drone.

Sergeant Whittaker sat down at his air control station located just behind the cockpit wall that separated it from the cargo bay area, adjusted his chair and took hold of the joy sticks of the control panel.

"Right aileron," Whittaker shouted.

The colonel watched the right-side aileron move up and down, signaled the sergeant with a thumbs up that it checked out.

"Left aileron." Whittaker moved the stick right to left, then went through the same procedure for the round stabilizer that shrouded the small thirty-inch propeller with the other stick in his right hand.

"Good, that's it," Colonel Dramit said, walking around the dark gray drone one last time.

The Pave Cricket weighed only 300 pounds fully loaded. Its uniquely shaped flying wing had been designed by computer. Its fuselage was dominated by smooth curves and flattened wing-root extensions. The frame and outer skin was constructed from preimpregnated Kevlar and epoxy, which made the craft transparent to radar emissions. It was powered by a small gas-burning engine. The exhaust was muffled to reduce infrared heat and to make it quiet. Such features, combined with the drone's nonreflective radar-absorbing paint, made the craft invisible on radar and difficult to see with the naked eye. The Pave Cricket also employed a massive night-vision system for operation even on overcast, starless nights; a target-location memory microprocessor allowing the drone to return to a high-interest point; a television-tracking unit for viewing moving targets and an imaging processor computer for real-time analysis of priority intelligence material.

But this drone had been modified for its special mission. Tucked away inside its small cargo bay, designed for add-ons, was an A1Q-126 ECM airborne jammer set and an ALQ-118 tactical decoy transmitter. The A1Q-126 gave the drone a broadband jamming capability and its on-board processor could choose priority targets when multiple threats were present. The ALQ-118 tactical decoy transmitter was designed to distract radar operators by making them track its transmissions as though it were a hostile aircraft; the TDT was computer-driven and programmed to mimic the radar signature profile of a penetrating B-52 bomber. A radar operator looking at his scope saw a "picture" of a B-52 coming at him that in reality was only the Pave Cricket.

Sitting at his station, Sergeant Whittaker put on his headset. It was his job to fly the drone into enemy air space once the Hercules dropped it from its cargo bay. The drone was controlled by watching a CRT console that sat above the sergeant's joy stick control panel. A map of the overflight area was pictured on the console once the flight began. Speed, altitude, angle of attack and fuel status were continually updated on the far right side of the screen. Whittaker really was the pilot, except his cockpit was a hundred miles away.

Colonel Dramit's job was more complicated. His side of the control station, the right, contained an assortment of information-collection and imaging-sensors. From his seat he operated the Texas Instruments' IR line-scan camera for restricted visibility, the radar jammer and navigational equipment. He was responsible for analyzing the data intercepted by the drone, then for instructing Whittaker where to fly. Dramit had been involved in the development of the Pave Cricket's systems, and so was the obvious man for the mission—one small detail; he suffered from acute air sickness. You just didn't talk about that in the Air Force.

Dramit took his seat just as the sound of the two remaining engines coming to life filled the bay.

"I think it's a go, sir," Whittaker shouted over the noise.

Dramit adjusted his lap belt and tried to swallow, his throat and mouth were dry—a side-effect of the double-dose of Dramamine he had taken two hours before. He gripped the armrests of his chair with both hands and leaned his head back.

"You okay, sir?" Whittaker asked, looking at the colonel's white knuckles. The big plane swung around and started to move down the taxiway. Dramit was quiet, trying to concentrate on one stationary spot. He ignored the sergeant.

RAMENSKOYE TEST CENTER

Belikov and Tomskiy passed the second security checkpoint and turned north on a two-lane gravel road. A high chain-link fence with rolls of barbed wire on top ran along each side of the road. In the distance Belikov could barely make out a rock ridge over 350 meters high rising out of the ground. It was shrouded in snow, and the cloud ceiling that hung over half of it covered the two large gray radar radomes. As they moved closer Belikov could see more details: The entire area was covered with a brown-and-white camouflage netting suspended twenty feet above the ground on about a five-inch plastic pipe. The netting was made of a special graphite-impregnated cloth that absorbed and deflected radar signals from space. The Americans could not get a clear picture of what was happening under the net even with their advanced synthetic aperture radar of the KH-12 spy satellite.

The car disappeared now under the protective netting, then swung around into an empty reserved-parking spot. The two security guards stood by a heavy steel windowless door waiting for them. Tomskiy presented several documents, and they were waved on. The LED light on the door's display panel switched from red to green and with a snapping noise the thick, heavy steel door opened with hydraulic assistance and they proceeded down a long steel tunnel to the command center, where Tomskiy said General Yefimov would be waiting for them. "I will show you then what is about to turn the balance of power in favor of our country," he told Belikov.

Lieutenant General Yefimov waited patiently on the opposite side of the last security door. This was unexpected, Minister of Defense Tomskiy was not a man of surprises. The general wondered if possibly this had something to do with his inability to complete the full deployment of the system, although the General Secretary had been told the system was ready and fully operational. The new radar network worked without a problem, but tying it into the PVO's extensive SAM and radar-control antiaircraft artillery was proving to be more difficult than he'd expected.

The door opened now and Tomskiy with Colonel Belikov entered the command center, and General Yefimov led them down to the main floor of the complex.

The observation center sat fifty feet above the command center, its front and side walls made of one-inch thick glass. Belikov moved to the glass wall, stopped only inches away, and stared into the amphitheater below. Projected on the two-story wall in front of him was a sixty-by-eighty-foot computer-generated color map of the world. The land mass was outlined in a dark blue. American, Japanese and NATO military bases along with surface ships and submarines were arranged on the map and coded green. Soviet bases and ships were shown in red. Thin white lines crisscrossed both countries showing what aircraft were in the air. Commercial flights were easy to locate; their lines were straight and even. The military flights swirled and constantly changed. On the right side of the main map screen were two smaller displays, one on top of the other, that showed coded information with numbers that changed on the farthest side—data on the movements of American submarines. On the left side of the map were four smaller displays updating weather, Soviet and American tank movements, satellite tracking, attack-warning and the status of the command center's communications.

Sitting below the displays in a semicircle were ten computer work stations, each equipped with a telephone, keyboard and its own monitor. The video displays cast an ominous glow on the faces of the men operating the systems. Everything seemed quiet and in control. Belikov's question was "how did this tie into the new radar network?" The Soviet Union already operated a system similar to the United States NORAD. He had toured the center at Tyuratam. He had no idea this place even existed.

"Let me give you some background on what you will be protecting, colonel," the general said. "Five years ago we started to build this project. You are standing fifty meters below the surface. Over 450,000 kilotons of solid rock had to be blasted and removed before construction could begin. The entire complex is just over 5000 square meters. We have enough food and water in storage for the sixty-two people who work here to live for seventy days. We are completely self-sufficient.

"The sensors you are watching below are real time . . . as it happens, we see it. The center is fed information from our worldwide surveillance and communications network. The incoming data is fed directly into our high-speed supercomputer, which processes, analyzes and translates it into what we see here. Our mission is to defend this country from attack."

"Minister Tomskiy has also told me something about a computer that makes this system possible," Belikov said. "My question is, how does this system work?"

"The technologies behind the system are top secret, but I will explain the principles behind it." Yefimov walked over and hit a set of switches on his desk as Belikov continued to look out over the control center. A flash of light caught Belikov's attention as what he thought to be the right-side wall of the control center below lit up and the supercomputer became visible through a row of blue-tinted windows.

It sat there on a clean black floor. The main structure was as big as three freight-train engines placed side by side. Circling it were ten small car-size black boxes that connected the main frame with six-inch-diameter cables. A series of small red, green and yellow dimly lit lights blinked on the side of the ten boxes —control and circuit warning indicators.

"We call it Zashchita, our shield," the general said. "It is the fastest, most powerful computer in the world. We had to build a separate nuclear reactor for it that is located on the other side of the computer room's far wall. The computer contains 240 microprocessors. It can take a problem, break it into small pieces, solve the pieces and put it back together again in seconds. Complicated military battle plans that take our biggest and best computers days to analyze, Zashchita can do in a fraction of a second. Colonel Belikov, this computer makes over five hundred billion calculations a second."

"How does this affect the new American bombers?" Belikov had been in the military too long and seen too many "super" weapons fail when put on the battlefield. He still had his doubts, and reminded himself one downed aircraft did not necessarily make a system.

The general turned off the switch and the computer room became dark again. "This computer is tied directly into nearly every one of our command-and-control radar stations. Each of our SAM and antiaircraft artillery sites, the backbone of our air defenses, can be fed current data instantaneously on where to find, track, lock-on and fire on American stealth aircraft. Because of this computer we no longer need to fear their technology."

Belikov was still not convinced of the so-called supercomputer's capabilities.

"The system allows us to scan on all radar bands at the same time, and with multiple-scanning the computer can then analyze the returns and find the aircraft," Tomskiy put in.

Belikov turned to face the two men. He had had access to and had reviewed the PVO's top-secret reports on the capability of the new American bomber's ability to enter Soviet airspace undetected. He knew the American B-2 was designed not to reflect any radar . . . "I don't understand. The stealth bomber is engineered so that it does not give a radar-return and the radar that does strike it is absorbed. How can this system find it?"

General Yefimov was pleased to tell him. "It doesn't find where it is, it finds where it *isn't*." He waited, letting his last statement hang in the air. "When a radar is sweeping the sky there is always a certain amount of clutter that appears on the operator's scope, caused by the radar reflecting off the clouds, rain, snow or just the air moving through the atmosphere. For years our scientists have been trying to eliminate this clutter from our radarscopes so a clearer picture can be presented from the target returning the signals. Now we can take a different approach. With this system, when radar waves are sent into the sky we no longer look for returning signals. Rather the computer can show us where there is no signal at all. A hole in the sky, you might say. That *hole* is our target. An area on the radarscope where there is nothing. The stealth aircraft deflects or absorbs the radar waves from the incoming signal and the same for the returning signal being reflected off the background clutter. From that information we know where the bomber is and this command center can direct SAM and artillery fire and vector your MiGs to get a visual. Once you see the target it can be destroyed. The system works, colonel, we have an F-117 en route to Moscow to prove it."

"How are the SAM sites linked into the system?" Belikov asked.

"We use the same secure microwave data link that is part of our standard command operations. The SAM radar emitters transmit their readings to us here, the computer breaks apart the signals, processes them and then relays them back to the SAM site with the altitude, heading and speed of the target. The operators will be able to see the aircraft on their scopes. We can use most of our older SAMs along with our newest and most advanced. The same applies for our antiaircraft artillery . . . their fire-control radars work the same as the SAMs."

"And the MiGs, are they tied into the system?"

"No, the radars on the MiGs are too small to be linked to the network. We will have to guide them to the bombers. They will have to be sighted before our pilots will be able to engage them."

Belikov nodded, a skeptic convinced.

C-130 HERCULES COMPASS CALL

"Here we go, gents, make sure you're strapped in," the pilot's warning was drowned out by the noise of the electric motors starting to open the cargo ramp. At 10,000 feet it was no easy maneuver . . . the pilot had to adjust the trim to maximum nose-up to compensate for the added drag of the ramp door being extended.

"Launch in thirty seconds, we have a go," the pilot shouted over the intercom.

Whittaker and Dramit were blasted with cold air as the rear of the C-130 slowly opened.

"Five, four, three, two, one . . . launch," from the C-130 pilot.

The Hercules nosed up sharply. The colonel felt his stomach turn and fought the bile from moving up his throat. Sergeant Whittaker punched the launch button on his control panel, releasing the restraints that had kept the drone in place. The drone slid out the back of the plane and floated lifelessly in the air until Whittaker started the drone's engine, watching the RPM meter fluctuate back and forth.

"Contact sir, she's up and operating." Whittaker focused on the red dot on his video screen that showed the location of the drone seven miles from the East German border.

"I copy, take her down to two hundred feet and head one zero niner." Dramit double-checked the instruments. The drone would fly silent until crossing over the border, then Dramit would send the coded signal to the tactical decoy transmitter, telling it to start.

Three minutes later Dramit called out. "What do you have, sergeant?" He also closed his eyes and tried not to lose his breakfast.

"Five minutes to the border. Altitude two hundred feet, speed constant at ninety knots."

"Take her up and increase speed," Dramit said, and fine-tuned the controls on the panel in front of him. He sucked in a long breath, trying to clear his spinning head. According to his instruments the drone was flying undetected. Dramit turned on the sensors and the IR line-sight camera. His color video display came on-line along with the computerized comsight equipment used to store the intelligence photos, IR images and other objects on-disk. Everything checked out.

"Altitude 1000 feet and steady, speed now 260 knots. Sir, I can take her up to 275 but after that she gets real squirrely on me." Whittaker, Dramit noted, manipulated his controls like a surgeon with his instruments.

"Hold at two sixty and turn heading one five eight," Dramit said, and watched the brown-and-green countryside flash below on his video display, then a row of large trees. His instruments indicated the drone was just north of and heading straight for the city of Gotha. He waited, not wanting it to pass directly over the populated area. "Now turn zero seven four."

The drone banked quickly, came around to its new setting, and now was heading due east, and southwest of the city of Leipzig. The East German air force operated a large SAM fire-control radar station there and it would be easy for them to pickup the signals from the drone.

As Dramit turned the knob and started the Tactical Decoy Transmitter, a round gauge swung up to full power on the upper right side of his control panel, showing that the TDT was running at full power. Instantly a surge of J-Band radar emissions streamed from the drone, making it appear to be as big as a B-52 on a radar screen. In seconds the Pave Cricket would be swept by a dozen radars from various SAM sites.

Whatever's going to happen, let it be quick, thought Dramit, figuring he was either going to get sick or die at any moment.

LEIPZIG, EAST GERMANY, AIR DEFENSE CENTER

The master sergeant came closer to the radarscope and resisted the urge to blurt out what he was seeing. He adjusted the sensitivity, but it didn't make any difference, the signal on his scope remained strong and even.

"Major . . . I show an unidentified target due west. Heading zero seven five, altitude three hundred five meters, speed two hundred sixty-two knots. It's big, either civilian, a transport . . . or a bomber."

"I need a *positive* identification, sergeant."

"Referencing now, major," the sergeant said as he swung around to the computer keyboard next to him and punched in instructions for the station's computer to identify the radar returns of the target. In seconds he had the information.

"The computer shows it to be a B-52 bomber." He was careful to let the major know it was the computer and not he saying it was a B-52.

"Can you lock on?"

"Yes—"

"Then do it. Contact PVO headquarters. I want two MiGs in the air. *Now . . .*"

C-130 HERCULES COMPASS CALL

"They got us, I/J Band. Probably an SA-6's," Dramit said. "Take her down to five hundred. We'll see if they can stay with us."

Whittaker nosed the tiny drone down fifteen degrees and slowly descended. The drone could have dived for the deck much faster but he wanted the radar operators to believe they were looking at a B-52, not a harmless recon vehicle.

Radar Cross Section, radar energy an aircraft reflected back to a radar's emitter, was measured by determining the size of a sphere capable of returning the same amount of energy; the aircraft's RCS value was the size of the sphere, which was then translated into square meters. The RCS of a B-52, head-on, was as much as 1000 square meters, so it was important for Whittaker to keep the drone pointed directly at the radio emitter so that it looked like a B-52.

"Turn right heading zero eight one, we got another SAM looking at us from the south. Make sure it picks up a signal," Dramit ordered.

Whittaker moved the control stick down. The left aileron moved up, causing the drone to turn south a few degrees. "Five hundred feet, sir, she's handling like a dream."

Two strong search-and-track radars were now sweeping the drone. The first on I/J-Band, the new one on K-Band.

The K-Band was probably a ZSU-23-4 antiaircraft artillery site, it normally uses a 2–0.75 cm. wavelength, Dramit knew. A red warning light that appeared on the panel told him the I/J-Band had just locked up on the drone's signal. "Take her back up to a thousand, we've played their game long enough," and he turned the TDT off, watching the signal die.

Dramit sat back and envisioned the Soviet operators wondering where the B-52 they'd been looking at had gone. After all, a 450,000 pound aircraft doesn't disappear.

"Come on, baby, bring up that new radar." Dramit muttered. "Take the bait."

LEIPZIG, EAST GERMANY, AIR DEFENSE CENTER

"It's gone . . . it just vanished."

The major, bending over the operator's shoulders, also saw it blink off the screen. "Try to find it, now."

"Major, I've got headquarters on the line."

The major took the phone from his assistant and told what he had just seen on the scope . . ."I need two interceptors in the air at once, colonel. The bomber is still out there somewhere. Our last contact showed it climbing." He kept his eyes on the radar screen as he listened to the orders from the colonel. "Yes, I understand," the major said, and hung up. "Damn it, where is it? Contact Ramenskoye Test Center now . . ."

RAMENSKOYE TEST CENTER

The phone on the general's desk rang, breaking into his conversation with Tomskiy and Belikov. General Yefimov listened, then said: "Patch him in to me immediately." He put his hand over the receiver. "We have a problem in sector sixteen . . . major, if you pick it up again inform me at once," and Yefimov hung up. "Well, you get to see this operation in action. It seems we have a mystery aircraft in one of our defense sectors." The general hit the intercom connecting him to the men working the controls on the floor. "Zoom in on sector sixteen," he ordered.

The large display on the wall split in half and a detailed color map of southwestern East Germany appeared. The location of the SAMs and triple-A sites could be seen as well as the location of each command-and-control center for each subsector.

"Our radar station at Leipzig was tracking what they identified as a B-52 but it disappeared. We'll locate it again for a more positive I.D." He turned and looked back to the large display below them. "If it's out there, we will find it," he said with confidence.

C-130 HERCULES COMPASS CALL

Drone was now only nine miles south of Leipzig. The K-Band radar had not painted it for the last two minutes. However, the stronger I/J-Band of the Leipzig Air Defense Center continued its search, the radar sweeping the drone every two seconds as it rotated in a large circle.

"Bring it around to two three five, make it slow and long," Dramit said, instructing Whittaker to turn the drone around slowly and fly back through the same air space. Dramit turned the TDT back on to full power, thinking that maybe the other side didn't believe their eyes. "Let's see what you think about this," he said as he hit the switch to the A1Q-126 ECM jammer. "If a B-52 isn't enough to get your attention, how about a B-52 that's trying to jam your ass?"

LEIPZIG, EAST GERMANY, AIR DEFENSE CENTER

"Contact . . . heading two zero four, turning west . . . it's jamming now, major, my scope is gone." The sergeant sat there, staring at a scope full of long wavy lines.

"Can you burn through?"

"I think so, it's not very powerful." The sergeant boosted the power of his emitter to maximum, sending a narrow radar beam directly at the drone. The scope slowly cleared with each pass of the beam. "There, I have it again. Heading two one nine, speed 257 knots, altitude 203 meters."

"Signal Ramenskoye, now," the major ordered.

RAMENSKOYE TEST CENTER

General Yefimov gave the order to bring the system up and ready. "Stand by for computer power," he ordered throughout the command center.

Belikov and Tomskiy watched in silence as the center came to a dead calm. The information screen constantly changed before them.

"There," the general said, pointing to a small orange triangle moving slowly to the southwest of Leipzig. The display on the far right side was showing the target's altitude, speed and heading.

Belikov also studied the information, "It seems slow for a B-52. Are they sure?"

"Yes, we double-checked it with our current data base on B-52 radar cross sections," Yefimov told him. He picked up his phone to contact the air defense-command center in Leipzig. "Major, lock-on to it and bring it down." And he slammed down the receiver hard, the way he wanted that B-52 brought to earth.

C-130 HERCULES COMPASS CALL

The red warning light flickered on and off before turning solid red, indicating the I/J-Band radar had just locked on the drone.

Dramit didn't notice it at first as he had several other things on his mind. Such as where would the best place be to throw up. It seemed they didn't know what to make of his little spy in the sky. He had been listening to the ground air-controller giving instructions to two intercepting MiGs on the general area of the radar emissions. According to Dramit's instruments the MiGs would not be near the drone for another five minutes.

But then Dramit noted the upper half of his panel and the red indicator light. They've got me, he thought, but not for long. "Sergeant, drop her down to 200 feet." He switched off the TDT and the jammer at the same time. "Now you see me, now you don't," he said quietly.

RAMENSKOYE TEST CENTER

"It's gone, general," the radar control officer said from the floor of the command center.

"I can *see* that," Yefimov snapped. He squinted, looking at the screen where the target had been. Two red triangles slowly moved toward the last known position. I have no choice, he decided, and hit the communications button on his desk. "Bring up the system and locate the target."

Below, the major in charge relayed the order to the men on the floor. In a flash a surge of power was transmitted to the radar station at Leipzig, and Belikov watched in astonishment as the computer did exactly what he had been told it would do.

"Give the order to fire when ready," Yefimov said, looking away from the screen as he spoke. "Now we wait and see. Our MiGs are almost in range. We are seconds away from engagement."

C-130 HERCULES COMPASS CALL

Dramit was amazed at what he was seeing. His radar-warning indicator-lights were lit up on all radar bands, all originating from the SAM sites around Leipzig, although only two of the bands, I/J and G/H, had locked up on the drone.

He started his recording instruments. He and his boys back in research would have one hell of a time trying to cope with this one, he thought.

RAMENSKOYE TEST CENTER

Belikov watched the orange symbol start to move to the west. "They're testing us, looking for any weaknesses in the system," Belikov said, a note of admiration in his voice. "I would have done the same thing."

"What the hell are you saying, colonel?" Tomskiy demanded.

"I have seen hundreds of B-52s on a radar screen. This is not a B-52. My guess it is some kind of intelligence drone."

Tomskiy studied the map. The amount of information on the screen was confusing to the untrained eye and it took the Defense Minister a few moments to make out the symbol.

"The Americans are trying to figure out how this system actually works, and looking for defects at the same time . . . I would say they are learning—"

"They can try to learn all they want. It will do them no good. Our MiGs are in the area, it's just a matter of time," Yefimov said, watching the red computer-generated images. The MiGs were, indeed, only a few thousand meters from the drone. "What will the Americans learn from their aircraft after we blow it out of the sky, Colonel Belikov?"

You underestimate the Americans, the colonel thought as his attention went back to the screen.

C-130 HERCULES COMPASS CALL

"Get the hell out of there. I can't *believe* this. How are they tracking it?" Dramit was yelling at Whittaker.

The sergeant turned the drone to full power. It was flying now through a narrow valley at treetop level sixty feet above ground. It was still twenty-five miles inside the border, heading due west out of enemy airspace. Whittaker could *feel* Dramit's anger that the Soviets were tracking and had locked onto the little spy plane.

"What's your ETA for making it over the border, sergeant?"

"At least twelve minutes, sir."

"That's not good enough . . . those MiGs are breathing down my neck. Get it on the deck, I don't want those bastards to get my drone . . ."

RAMENSKOYE TEST CENTER

"Turn right to three zero one . . . you should be right over the top of it," the communications officer called to the intercepting MiGs.

"A child could see a B-52 at that distance. Why can't they see it?" General Yefimov's face was so close to the glass wall of the command center that his breath was fogging his view.

"As I said, sir, it is *not* a B-52," Belikov replied quietly.

Tomskiy was standing slightly behind Yefimov and Belikov. There was now absolutely no doubt in his mind that Colonel Belikov was the right man for the job. The colonel had the ability to project himself into the mindset of the enemy. He could read and anticipate what the other side was up to. Rare qualities.

"General, you are right that a child could see a B-52 at that distance," Belikov pressed. "The MiGs flew over the top of it and did not see it . . . look, they are turning around now to make another pass. I suggest you tell the pilots to drop down to only thirty meters and look for anything in the air . . . or better yet fire a SAM at it."

"Suppose you are wrong? We might even shoot down a friendly aircraft."

"But what if you let the intruder escape?" Belikov responded, unshaken by the general's obvious annoyance.

Tomskiy spoke up then. He was, after all, the Defense Minister.

"Colonel Belikov's insights are worth considering, general."

"Minister, I have worked with this system for five years. With all respect, I believe I know what is best at this time," Yefimov said, and turned back toward the screen.

Spoken like a true general, Belikov thought.

C-130 HERCULES COMPASS CALL

"Three minutes, sir, she's only six miles out," Whittaker said, not taking his eyes off the red dot representing the drone. He continued to move the control sticks back and forth, making the camouflaged pilotless plane jink up and down, slide right to left and back again. He could tell by the look on Dramit's face it was still in trouble. The radar was still locked onto it.

By now the lieutenant colonel had forgotten about his air sickness. The situation developing in front of him on the instruments took all the concentration he could manage. The MiGs were turning away and heading back toward the drone. Dramit could hear the pulsating ring of their look-down shoot-down radars in his headset as they tried to find the drone.

"Turn left to three one seven. If I give the order I want you ready to fly that thing right into the ground, understood?" Dramit called out.

"Yes, sir, only three miles to go. She's just crossing over the border," Whittaker said, smiling. "They didn't find her."

"Take her up to a thousand and land her back at the base soon as possible." Dramit let out a long breath as he slouched in his chair, listening as Whittaker told the crew the mission was over and to head for home. The cargo plane now started a slow banking turn to the east and nosed up a few degrees to start its climb to 18,000 feet.

Dramit felt drained and tired. His head and stomach were still swirling but he was glad all he had to worry about now was whether or not he was going to throw up. The mission had been a success, the electronics on the Compass Call recorded everything as it had happened. The information gathered would now be analyzed by the radar and intelligence people.

RAMENSKOYE TEST CENTER

"Instruct the MiGs to return to base," General Yefimov said as the image of the drone crossed the East German border. The big screen showed the two MiGs turning away in the opposite direction just short of crossing. The general shut off the internal intercom with a push of his thumb. "That's all we need is a pair of Twenty-nines chasing a ghost into West Germany." The general's anger had subsided some with relief that the threat was gone.

Belikov felt he should emphasize that it was not a B-52, but "an American drone, probably not too different from the ones our own air force uses. I would like, general, permission to debrief the pilots. That should give us more clues—"

Defense Minister Tomskiy cut in. "Colonel Belikov, you do not need permission. I remind you that I have put you in charge of the defense of this center. If you feel it is necessary to talk with the pilots of the MiGs, then do it." All said while looking directly at the general.

12

PUTTING IT TOGETHER

THE PENTAGON, GENERAL JACK DAWSON'S OFFICE

"Who else has seen this?" Secretary of Defense John Turner asked, referring to the report on the Pave Cricket's flight into Soviet territory.

"The engineers who put it together and General Zaranka at Ramstein. It arrived via the general's special assistant."

"Jack, I know this is just the preliminary report but I need to know if there are any holes in it. I want to set up a meeting with the President tomorrow."

"I've read through it twice and can't find anything that doesn't fit. I don't know what more he would need. There's no question now that they've somehow come up with a defense system that we figured was maybe thirty years away." Dawson took a deep breath. "The question I have is what in the hell is he going to do about it?"

"The President authorized me to draw up a plan. We already have gone ahead with the drone. What's the next step, he'll want to know. You and I both know what Robinson will say. Do nothing. I want to recommend an action that will make the Soviets know we aren't afraid to act. What do *you* have in mind, Jack?"

"The way I look at it we have few if any options. We can tell the Kremlin we know about their new secret system and that if they want the arms reduction treaty signed they'll have to dismantle the radar network first. Fat chance. Seriously, we can send in a surgical-strike force and take the mother out. That will allow the President to sign the treaty safely and buy a few years to develop a counterdefense in case they ever rebuild.''

"Captain Koiser has told us their command center is located at Ramenskoye. If he's right it's located in the middle of their heaviest defenses. What kind of operation do you have in mind, Jack?''

Dawson looked at Turner, realizing he was under the gun, yet this was his great opportunity. Take it slow and careful, he told himself. "Going nuclear is out of the question. A cruise missile is a possibility but I doubt it's accurate enough and we must be sure it's destroyed the first time. I'm sure by this time they have figured that we have some knowledge of it from Captain Koiser and are preparing for possible attack by us . . . The way I see it, John, the only way that makes sense is a manned bomber flight.'' Jack Dawson's twenty-five-year Air Force career included seven years in the left seat of a B-52G. As a lieutenant colonel he had been one of the primary planners in Vietnam for the Linebacker II missions into the North. He knew the capabilities of U.S. air power as well as anyone in the Pentagon.

Turner sat quietly and looked through the report on his lap. "Jack, if they can find a stealth *fighter* and shoot it down, what makes you think a B-1B can do the job? Its radar signature is four times the RF-117C. Wouldn't that be like sending our pilots on a suicide mission?'' He hoped Dawson had a good answer, since he'd already indicated to the President he favored an attack.

"I wasn't thinking of the B-1B for the mission . . . The only plane that can complete this mission is a B-2. The very one some people want to do away with.''

"The B-2 won't be operational for . . . what? Six years?''

"Mr. Secretary, the B-2 stealth Bomber program is the highest priority of our strategic modernization. There hasn't been a program so secret since the Manhattan Project back in the forties. What I'm going to tell you is deep black, only the President and a handful of others know about it. I'm breaking security by telling you without specific authorization from the President.''

Turner looked ready to explode as Dawson hurried on. "John, when I was Secretary of the Air Force I approved the funding of two full-scale, proof-of-concept demonstrator prototypes. They are preproduction aircraft and designated YB-2. They have been in flight-test since 1981. They're located at Groom Lake Proving Grounds just north of Las Vegas." Dawson stopped and pointed at the area on the map.

Turner sat speechless, not taking his eyes off Dawson.

"John, the Air Force isn't about to spend five hundred million dollars a copy on a plane that doesn't work."

"And why don't I know about it?" Turner finally got it out. Here he was authorized to develop a plan and he wasn't even told the B-2 was operational. "What else goes on in that desert proving grounds of yours that I don't know about?"

"It's part of the President's need-to-know policy. He decides who knows what, not me."

"Okay, it doesn't matter," Turner said, deciding this wasn't the time to put ego in the way of the main objective. "So you're saying send in the B-2 prototypes to take out the command center."

"Basically, yes, the bombers are fully capable. All we have to do is remove the test equipment and prep them for the mission."

"How soon can a plan be worked up?"

"I'll have a preliminary by the end of today. That's why I'm meeting with General Westcott . . . he knows how to get into and out of Soviet air space. I flew with him in Nam."

"Does he know about the B-2s, too?"

"Yes, but that's only one of the reasons that I want to talk with him. He doesn't sit around and polish a seat. He's on the flight line, he knows the best bomber crews in the Air Force and he'll give us honest answers. I need your permission to brief him."

"You got it," Turner said, still trying to shake off the sting of not knowing about the status of the secret bombers. "Call me when you have things worked out, I want a complete briefing on the mission's profile. And if there's anything else I should know before the NSC meeting I'm going to ask the President to call for, by God you had better tell me."

THE KREMLIN, MOSCOW

"Your trip was productive?" the General Secretary asked Defense Minister Tomskiy.

"Yes, sir. And disturbing. The Americans know of our system and are actively trying to find ways to defeat it."

"How do you know this?"

Tomskiy briefed him on what had happened while he was at Ramenskoye with Belikov and Yefimov.

"I know what your concerns are, minister. We did not anticipate the incident over the Sea of Okhotsk. Fortunately, it seems to have turned world opinion more in our favor. And the defense network is now in place and operating. We have the upper hand."

"Sir, the shield is operating, but there are still problem areas. The north-central region is not altogether tied into the system and it may take some three weeks before it's fully operational." Tomskiy paused, trying to read the Secretary's reaction. "There are over 4000 SAM and antiaircraft artillery sites in this theater, many of them located in remote mountain ridges."

"Then I suggest you tell your people to work around the clock until the system is *complete*."

"I have already given those orders, it is all detailed in my report," Tomskiy said, setting the report on the table between them.

"Then I gather there is nothing more to worry about."

"No, sir." Tomskiy stood, knowing that it would do no good to tell the General Secretary that he was wrong. How wrong might well decide whether he or his Defense Secretary survived.

CIA HEADQUARTERS

Turner entered, carrying his standard black briefcase.

"Gentlemen," he said, seating himself and sounding energized.

Brady and Staffer noted this quickly.

"You sound better, John," Brady said.

"Let's put it this way, at least I know beyond a doubt what we're apparently up against." Which was as far as he wanted to go at this point. He handed the report to Brady. "And you, Tony?"

"Well, as I said on the phone," the DCI began, "I've good news and bad news. The command center is located right where Captain Koiser said it was, that's the good news, we know exactly where it is. The bad news is, it's right on the edge of Ramenskoye, which is very heavily defended, of course. SAM sixes, threes and their latest triple-A stuff. Damn, I don't know how they did it but they did."

Staffer said, "Mr. Secretary, we showed Captain Koiser some real-time satellite photos of the area this morning. He told us the complex is under some two hundred feet of solid rock. I cross-checked his info with the data we've collected independently. It all checks out. I can have a written report for you by mid-afternoon."

"I'll take it."

"What do you have in mind, John?" Brady asked.

The next hour was spent with the three of them discussing the possibilities of a surprise attack against the computer complex. They would meet, they agreed, once more before the NSC meeting to coordinate strategy.

THE PENTAGON, GENERAL JACK DAWSON'S OFFICE

General Lamar Westcott shook his head. Being a twenty-six-year-veteran of SAC he fully appreciated the ramifications of what he was reading. As a young captain he had flown in the B-52 Arc Light operations against the North Vietnamese. He and his crew had been based in Guam, where the average mission lasted over eighteen hours. The experience he'd gained on those long missions with the Eighth Air Force 486th Bomb Squadron gave him the special insight to become SAC's leading expert on intercontinental-bombing missions. He looked at Dawson now, not wanting to believe what he had just read.

"When they downed an RF-117C some real hell broke loose. As you know they're trying to make us look like aggressors in the world, and they're doing a pretty good job of it . . . I called you in because I need your expertise. I'm going to propose to the President that we strike and take out the command center. Actually, I've already proposed it, but without a specific plan . . .''

He then proceeded to fill Westcott in on the location of the command center in Ramenskoye thirty miles south of Moscow.

"What's on your mind?" Westcott said.

"The way I see it, there's only one system that might have a chance to make it in and out. A manned bomber."

"I can have a dozen B-1Bs ready to go at a minute's notice—"

"Lamar, the radar cross section of a B-1B is too large. They'll find it easily. The B-2 has a head-on RCS of one millionth of a meter, less than a humming bird. We have two operational prototypes. How long would it take your boys at Groom Lake to bring them up and ready for a mission into the Soviet Union?"

"How much time would I have, Jack?"

"I don't now know, not much. Can you do it?"

"It's got to be good . . . we don't want those prototypes to end up in Soviet hands. You get me the details and I'll put together a mission."

"What about the crew?"

"We'll pull from the best B-1B crews we have, transport them to Nellis and start the process."

"How long will it take you to work up a mission profile?"

"I'll start right now."

General Lamar Westcott suddenly looked ten years younger. To use the vernacular, he was turned on.

CIA HEADQUARTERS

"Grigory, I've told you, they are keeping you under heavy security for good reasons," Tyransky was saying.

Koiser set down his fork. "It has to do with the radar network, they think I am lying, they think I am a KGB plant—"

"NO," Tyransky said loudly for emphasis, then quickly looked around the cafeteria. "That's not true. They *do* trust you." He had lowered his voice. "It is just that, well, there are unanswered questions, and until they are resolved you will have to put up with living like this."

"What questions are unanswered, I have told them everything I know."

"The questions have nothing to do with you. They have to do
with"—Charles sighed, not wanting to get in any deeper than
he already was—"damn it, captain, you told us the radar network was untested. Well, they tested it on one of our stealth
fighters that was on a mission over Sakhalin Island. It was shot
down and the pilot was killed. When the two SU-27s were shot
down it was because we wanted to know how much of the
wreckage was still intact. The Soviets didn't want us that close
and you know what happened. It was not an innocent misunderstanding."

"So it does work . . ."

"It works, and what I just told you is top-secret." Tyransky
felt better for telling him the truth. "Now you know why you
are being treated this way."

"This is even more serious than I'd thought," Koiser said,
trying to fit the pieces together. "But I can help, I can show you
how the system can perhaps be defeated. I do know and understand how it works."

"Captain, you have already done more than your share."
Tyransky did not add that from here on the CIA would not be
likely to confide in Koiser.

Collins' desk was covered with stacks of computer papers that
had arrived from the CIA's office in New Zealand. His hunch
had been right. New Zealand customs agents and CIA agents
had traced the Euratech shipment from Germany to an airport
warehouse in Auckland. They had uncovered a major Soviet
computer-smuggling operation. The documents recovered in
that raid were now on his desk to be analyzed.

Some of the information he quickly saw made no sense,
other data was useless. The best he could tell was that the KGB
had been using the Auckland warehouse for more than five
years to transfer illegal shipments of high-tech computers and
computer components. Now he wanted to find out just what
they had stolen and who they had gotten it from.

13

PRESSURE POINT

TSENTRALNY RESTAURANT, DOWNTOWN MOSCOW

The breakfast rush ended almost as quickly as it had begun two hours earlier. Most of the customers, government employees and city officials, had to be at work by 8:00 A.M., so the restaurant was only half-full by the time Andre arrived. He enjoyed coming here once or twice a week, getting away from the pressures of the Kremlin. The atmosphere was Old World with dark stained wood and brocaded cloth-covered chairs. Each table had a single burning candle on it. Morning sun streamed in through the large stained-glass windows. He liked the background sounds of people talking and laughing. Not like the Kremlin. Damn little laughter there these days.

With the morning edition of *Pravda* tucked under his arm he seated himself at a table for two along the far wall in a corner. He had been waiting for thirty minutes for that particular table to open up. An older man and young girl—maybe secret lovers? —had been occupying it.

"Will anyone be joining you this morning?" the waiter asked. Before answering, Andre studied the waiter's face, making sure their eyes met.

"No, I am alone. However, someone may be stopping by later. We have not seen each other for a long time. I may have a hard time recognizing him."

189

"If I see someone who seems to be looking for you I will tell him you are here," the waiter replied, handing him a menu.

"That would be kind of you." He took the menu and glanced at it. "I will take toast with coffee and sugar."

"I am sorry, but we are out of sugar today, unless you would like brown sugar." The waiter did not look up from his note pad as he spoke.

"That would be fine," Andre said, and took the paper from his lap, laying it on the empty plate across from him.

"Would you like some more coffee?" The waiter smiled slightly.

"No, just the check please," he said after eating the last of his food.

The waiter pulled the check out of his apron and handed it to Andre. "It seems your friend isn't going to show up."

"No, I'm afraid not. I was looking forward to seeing him. We haven't spoken for five years and I do have a lot to talk about."

"I am sorry," the waiter said, clearing the dishes and stacking them carefully in one hand. "May I get you anything else this morning?"

"No, I should be going. I've spent too much time reading the paper this morning," he said, and gestured toward the paper on the opposite side of the table. "Thank you." He wiped his lips with his napkin and pushed himself away from the table.

The waiter, with his free hand, casually picked up the newspaper and carried it and the dirty dishes toward the kitchen.

After paying for his meal Andre exited the restaurant and started the long walk back to the Kremlin. The cold fresh air hitting his wrinkled skin felt good. A fine fall day, he thought. Cold air, bright sun with no clouds and not a breath of wind. Quickening his pace, he walked along the Garden Ring street that circled central Moscow, watching the busy traffic along Gorky Street just ahead . . .

ANNANDALE, VIRGINIA

"Clayton, it's for you . . . wake up," Beverly Boyle said, exasperatedly, giving him a shove.

"Uh . . . yeah, I got it. This is Clayton Boyle."

"Hello, Clayton . . . sorry about this but I need to see you right away. I think I'm onto something and I need your help."

"Who is this, do you know what time it is?"

"Clayton, this is Mark Collins. I know it's late but this is important." Collins was clearly excited.

"Where are you?"

"I'm at work."

"Can't this wait until morning? For pete's sake, I was sound asleep . . ."

"No, it can't. I just finished putting a ton of information into the ADABAS and the stuff it's spitting out doesn't make a whole lot of sense to me."

Clayton's specialty was computers, and unless someone was trying to take over the world, why in hell couldn't it wait until the morning . . ." Mark, just what is this all about?"

Collins was hoping to avoid a lengthy explanation over the phone.

"Do you remember when I talked to you about why the Soviets might be interested in importing Intell 8224 chips . . . the time you invited me over to meet Christine?"

"I remember."

"Well, I tracked down the export company . . . damn it, Clayton to make a long story short we busted what looks like it could be a major computer-smuggling ring. It seems the KGB has been funneling parts and equipment through a warehouse in New Zealand. What I'm trying to figure out is if they were just getting anything and everything or were they after specific material. That's why I need you."

"All *right*, give me forty-five minutes," he said and hung up.

Thirty minutes later he was in Collins's office.

"Well they didn't leave anyone out . . . NEC, Toshiba, Hitachi, Fujitsu, and IBM," Clayton Boyle said, flipping through the paperwork. "Some of this stuff goes back four, maybe five years. And you're sure none of them broke any export laws?"

"From the looks of it, each company thought they were selling to a legitimate electronics firm," Collins said. "It all checks out. I never would have caught it if I hadn't checked the financials of Euratech in Germany. The amount of chips they were importing just didn't add up to their production. They were the ones that led us to the warehouse in New Zealand."

"How did you come up with this information?" Boyle was referring to the ten-foot computer printout still attached to the printer, which he reached over and ripped off.

"I took each item, from all the different companies that had been shipping into the warehouse and entered them into the computer. I had just hit the print button when I called you. It took about thirty minutes for it to spit it all out."

Clayton slowly studied the printout. "Do you have a high-lighter?" he finally asked.

Collins opened the center drawer of his desk and handed him a yellow marker.

The ADABAS had organized the shipment by date from the oldest to newest. Clayton didn't start highlighting until the fourth page, then made three lines through the center of the page and went on. At first what he was seeing didn't bother him, but the deeper he got into it the more intense he became. The Soviets were filling what appeared to be a shopping list, not stealing random items.

"Well, what do you think?" Collins asked, standing over him.

"I think this was no small operation. Whoever was ordering this material knew exactly what they wanted . . . or needed. Digital-analog-converters from Fujitsu, and not just the standard ones that would go into your home PC. They got the top-of-the-line models, the 3000 series." He turned back a few pages. "On one shipment they received about four hundred 18459 NEC microprocessors. We use those in our fastest military computers, mostly in F-18 and F-15 fire-control radars. And that's just one shipment. Here's another one for 300 more."

Clayton was clearly getting angry the more he studied the list of components and parts. "Whatever they want this for is big and fast." He put the data back on Collins' desk.

Collins waited.

"They've got themselves enough gallium arsenide memory chips to operate fifty mainframes. Those chips are five times faster than standard silicon-based technology. They're used in only our fastest machines—" Clayton stopped then, as if a light went on in his head. He picked up the data sheet again, staring at the last half of it.

UNITED STATES EMBASSY, MOSCOW

"Andre is still working with us!" Baxter said. "How did you receive this?"

"Just like we'd instructed, table six, Tsentralny restaurant, about nine o'clock. He wrapped it up in the morning edition of *Pravda*," the special agent answered.

Baxter nodded. "Anything else?"

"No, sir, that's it. If he makes any further contact I'll let you know," the agent said, buttoning his coat. "I'll be on my way."

Baxter took the elevator to the ninth floor. He didn't want to waste time. The CIA had been wanting just this sort of information for days.

"I need this transmitted to Langley. Send it HOT FLASH PRIORITY ONE." He looked at his watch. "It's four A.M. in the States, this should get them hopping."

CIA HEADQUARTERS

"Look at this. I wonder who sold them these. I didn't know anyone could be that stupid." Clayton Boyle pointed to the computer readout.

"What is it?" Collins, who had done all the work, felt like an outsider.

"I'm seeing a pattern. These are the product numbers for five cryogenic cooling systems. They are used in supercomputers to keep them from melting. *Literally* melting. In a supercomputer the circuitry is packed so tight that the electricity flow causes a tremendous amount of heat. In some cases a computer can melt and become a million-dollar pile of junk. IBM solved the problem by using supercooled liquid-helium to bathe the circuits. It keeps the microprocessors close to a temperature of four hundred and twenty degrees below zero. The machine then runs cooler and keeps the electricity flowing through the circuitry loops with little or no resistance . . . superconductivity. The closer to zero the machine gets, the faster it can operate because there is less resistance."

"Our agents must have caught them off guard, they didn't have time to destroy anything—"

Clayton put a hand in the air, stopping Collins. "I don't know what this is, it looks like part-numbers, Japanese part-numbers. They're in a sequence."

"What do you think they're doing with all this?" Collins asked, already suspecting the answer.

"I think it's a good possibility they've built themselves some sort of a supercomputer."

"Just from all this?"

"No, not from all this. A supercomputer takes a lot more than the items on this sheet, but it's a hell of a good start. If they know what they're doing and incorporate some of their own technology, they could do it."

He cross-referenced the different sets of Hitachi parts, and was surprised to learn that some of what he assumed were just ordinary internal pieces of a mainframe computer were actually larger parts of an entire operating system. The Japanese had learned from American mistakes. If an American computer broke down it could take days to bring it back up on line because only the damaged part could be removed and replaced. With the latest Japanese systems the damaged part or parts could be removed and replaced in seconds by reinstalling the entire section—the defective part as well as the good one. The section could then be repaired, allowing the computer to continue to operate.

"I don't *believe* this," he said out loud.

"What?" Collins was standing over him.

"Looks like they got themselves a couple of S-820/80s. One of Hitachi's top end-units. They got them in over a year's time, part by part. Someone has the specs, they knew exactly what they needed."

"How good is the computer?"

"It's *good*. We tested it against an experimental two-processor Cray, the X-MP. The S-820 is only a single processing machine . . . it beat the Cray ten to one. We have better computers like the IBM GF-11 and RP-3, but by Soviet standards the Hitachi is better than anything they have or can make on their own."

"Parallel processing, that's why they need chips." Collins went to his file and took out his notes. "Remember when I asked you about the Intell chip, the 8224, and why the Soviets would be wanting to get them from us again when they have the machines to make them?" Collins scanned his notes. "I have it right here, in '82 they stole two Digital VAX 11/782 computers. They used them to make the 8224 chip . . . Now they're having to steal that chip again. It makes me think they're using those computers for something else . . . the cooling system, the other new faster chip . . ." Collins was trying to recall the name of the other chip.

"Gallium arsenide."

"Yeah, and now you're telling me they have some hot-shot computer from Japan. The Soviets pulled this off right under our nose. With this stuff, just how big and fast a computer could they build?"

"With this stuff, the know-how and the right software I'd say they could build themselves one hell of a supercomputer."

"I want to take this to Tom Staffer. Will you put what you just told me in writing?"

"Don't you think we should look at it a little longer?"

"We know what they have, we know how they got it. You just told me what they could build with it. I'm no genius, but if they've built a supercomputer I'll bet a million they're not using it to study the dynamics of peacemaking."

THE PENTAGON, SECRETARY TURNER'S OFFICE

The stress could be seen on Turner's face as he sat at his desk waiting for Dawson and Westcott to get settled in the chairs in front of him.

"I don't anticipate any problems with the planning, training and practice runs," Westcott began. "I'll say it'll be at least three, maybe four days before we'd be ready. Ramenskoye is a Soviet strategic-bomber base so we already have attack plans in the computer. I can have the bomber crews pulled and transferred to Groom Lake field in twenty-four hours. I talked with the chief of the flight-test operation last night. He said the bombers could be ready in two days. Both B-2s are in flight condition . . ."

"What do you think, Jack?" Turner asked.

"Do I think it will work, or do I think the old man will buy it? Well, let's start with the plan. The only thing we don't know for sure is if the B-2 can get in and out. As far as the President is concerned, John, I feel it's our job to convince him."

Turner inwardly winced. He already knew that. What he didn't know, would it work?

CIA HEADQUARTERS

"This came in from Moscow station about an hour ago, sir. It's marked HOT, your attention," the messenger said, handing DCI Brady the large brown envelope.

Brady read over the ten-page message, EYES ONLY in big red letters on its cover, then hit his intercom. "Get me Turner." Within seconds his secretary had John Turner on the phone.

"John, I need to talk with you," and hung up without waiting for Turner's reply.

"Mr. Staffer has been expecting you," the secretary said, leading Mark Collins into the Deputy Director's office.

Staffer burst through the door, startling Collins.

"Mark Collins, how are you doing?" Staffer didn't offer to shake his hand. "You wanted to see me . . . ?"

Collins took a deep breath and handed Staffer his rough report and proceeded to give a verbal synopsis, including details from how the investigation began to finding Welsh dead, and the warehouse in New Zealand.

". . . I thought it was important, that's why I'm here," Collins said.

Staffer looked at him. "You were right. How long did it take you to find this?"

"About two and a half weeks . . . I had some breaks—"

"Mark," Staffer cut him off, "there's a meeting of the NSC at the White House. Seven-thirty in the Situation Room. I want you to tell the President what you've just told me."

Collins wasn't quite sure he'd heard Staffer right. "The President?"

"That's right."

"May I ask what this is about?"

"You'll find out tonight."

THE WHITE HOUSE, SITUATION ROOM

The President was the last to enter the room. Wearing a dark blue sweater with Levi blue jeans and a pair of brown leather handsewn shoes. He looked more like a late-blooming college student than the chief executive of the U.S. of A. His tall body, tanned face, graying hair and blue eyes gave him a presence.

"Good evening, gentlemen. John, you called this meeting. You have the floor."

Secretary Turner leaned forward, handing him a half-inch-thick report with a deep-purple cover.

Everyone else already had a copy. He didn't open it, keeping his eyes on Turner.

"As you know, sir, we have discovered that the Soviets are operating a new type of radar system." Turner opened his book, and the President followed his lead. "First, the information gathered from the downing of the RF-117C over Sakhalin. Multiband radar scanning followed by a lock-on with one or more radar bands and then the aircraft is fired on with SAMs or anti-aircraft artillery." Turner flipped to the next page of the report. "Here is a KH-12 satellite photo of what we know is the command and control center of the network. It's located thirty-two miles south of Moscow on the edge of Ramenskoye test center. From the information we have gotten from the defecting Soviet pilot, Captain Koiser, the Soviets have a large supercomputer in operation along with a 500-megawatt nuclear reactor. From there the Soviets are able to link up their air-defense sites around the country. They communicate via secure microwave relay transmissions. We believe the SAM and triple-A sites are the eyes and ears of the command center. Their radar emitters scan the target, relay the electronic signals to the computer at

Ramenskoye, where it is broken down and analyzed. The data is then automatically transmitted back to the sites and fed into the fire-control computers. That's how they were able to shoot down the RF-117C.

"The command center is 200 feet underground in a hardened bunker fortified with steel and concrete. As you can see, they have it surrounded with a network of SAM and triple-A sites. We believe the two large radomes on the top of the mountain are part of their relay system. Also we think they've tied the system into their ABM defense and are using the large phased-array radar at Krasnoyarsk in Seberai, Mukachevo, Baranovichi and Skrunda north of Moscow, and Pechora to the northeast. There is a diagram on the next page showing these. We are sure that the system can work with their over-the-horizon-back-scatter network for long-range detection."

The President studied the photograph, not saying a word.

"The next section has a detailed account of our intrusion flight into the Soviet Union with the Pave Cricket stealth drone—"

"What intrusion flight? Why wasn't I notified?" Secretary of State Robinson interrupted.

"I authorized the flight and I didn't find it necessary to inform you," the President said, not taking his eyes off the report. "Continue, John."

"The data is conclusive, again they were able to track something that should be invisible. The drone has a radar cross section that is comparable to a stealth fighter. When we entered their airspace the Soviets brought up the system just as we thought they would."

"Why didn't they just shoot down the drone?" the President asked.

"They tried, several SA-6 sites locked-on, but they didn't fire. We recorded the conversations between the MiG-29 pilots and their air-command centers. The PVO vectored two MiGs to the drone's position. The MiGs got within half a mile but didn't shoot. We think they couldn't see it. Otherwise there's no question they would have downed it . . . They had to know for sure if the system worked. Captain Koiser has said they had no way of really testing the system because they don't have any stealth-type aircraft. It's my belief that's why they shot down the RF-117C, their air force needed to test the system on one of our aircraft."

Robinson had to challenge. "Let me ask you this, if their radar system works like you have said, they have to activate it, correct?" He didn't wait for an answer. "How do they know when to turn it on? How did they even know an RF-117C was in their airspace? According to this report of yours the system is turned off until it's needed."

Jack Dawson moved in before Turner. "The RF-117C is designed to take out SAM and mobile antiaircraft artillery that operate on a different frequency than the radar that first picked up the RF-117C. The Soviet's long-range search-radar that was sweeping the Black Ghost the night it went down was built in the sixties. It operates on one of two bands, A/B or B/C, those bands are very long wave . . . slow in comparison to the short-wave search-and-track radars the Soviets now use on their SAMs. Those operate on I/J through K, they're short wave and don't stay on the target very long. The longer waves of the A/B and B/C stay on the aircraft longer and the radar waves don't disperse as easily. If the radar operator is a good one he may get a ghostlike picture on his screen. Obviously the Soviets knew something was out there before they activated their system."

"So you're saying they knew it was out there all the time?"

"No, that's not what I'm saying. We have flown that same mission-profile over thirty times and they never knew we were there. Or if they did they couldn't do anything about it. Damn it, look at the facts. The Soviets have a super radar system," Dawson said, his voice rising.

"I think we have *established* that," said the President. "Now, can anyone tell me how they came up with this thing without us knowing about it?"

Collins could feel the palms of his hands getting wet. He now knew why Staffer wanted him at the meeting. He was the only man in the room who knew how the Soviets got the computer.

"They stole it, sir," Collins said abruptly.

Staffer jumped in. "This is Mark Collins, Mr. President. He works in the Strategic Research Department at the CIA."

"Mr. President, I've uncovered evidence that over the last five years the KGB has been stealing and buying computers and components from Japanese, European and American computer firms. They were routing them through a phony company in New Zealand that has allowed them to bypass our export laws controlling the transfer of sensitive high-tech equipment to the Eastern block. We know for sure they have two Hitachi S-820/80 supercomputers. They have also been able to acquire several thousand top-of-the-line gallium arsenide chips that are now used in only a few of our fastest machines," Collins said, glancing back down at his notes. His voice had steadied as he talked. "Only eight months ago five IBM cryogenic liquid-helium cooling systems were transferred to Poland. This is one of IBM's best computer-cooling systems and was developed for gallium arsenide chips and the high heat they generate. Because they are five to ten times faster than standard silicon chips they generate a tremendous amount of heat. Without these coolers, the computer may melt."

"So the KGB was able to steal enough parts for a computer capable of operating this radar network?"

"I don't believe they stole all the parts they needed, sir, but certainly the ones they couldn't make themselves. For example, they also acquired over seven hundred 18459 NEC microprocessors. And that leads us to believe they are using parallel-processing techniques. We know for a fact that without our technology the Soviets wouldn't be able to manufacture a parallel-processing computer for at least ten years. I repeat, though, to some extent I'm sure Soviet engineers did build part of the supercomputer. But the machine *using* these components is on the cutting edge and they just don't have that sort of technology. Their entire semiconductor industry only produces three percent of the world's silicon chips and they make no gallium arsenide chips at all. Their economy just isn't geared up for computers."

"Just because they don't have personal computers doesn't mean a damned thing," Robinson put in.

Director Brady's face showed his anger. "We monitor their telecommunications. They don't have the technology. Larry, you know as well as I do they can build a hydrogen bomb but can't supply their doctors with sufficient medical supplies."

"Look at the facts." Turner spoke up now. "They operate the only mobile strategic-missile force. They're developing and testing antimissile lasers at Sary Shagan in Central Asia. Their navy operates the only titanium-hulled submarine in the world. Where have they cut military spending to increase consumer goods to help their own people? And why in hell do you think they're still stealing our high technology?" Turner was getting on a roll. "They talk about making sweeping cuts in their forces in Europe but even a fifty-percent reduction would still leave them with an advantage—"

The President held up his hand. Enough. "Leo, what about you?" he asked the National Security Advisor.

"I think there is enough evidence for us to be damned worried. There is strong evidence their generals and KGB are pulling the strings. Most of all, I think this radar network is a threat to our nation."

"We need to react to it by showing the world that America really does want peace. My advice is to sign the treaty," Robinson said.

"Mr. President, if you sign the treaty and let them keep that system we would be at an enormous disadvantage, to put it mildly," said Turner. "Leo is absolutely right, it is a threat—"

"What if we don't sign, Larry?"

"The Soviets will negotiate a separate treaty with Western Europe. We will have a renewed arms race . . . you may not be reelected."

"Let's forget my personal or political agenda. At the risk of sounding stuffy, what counts here is what's best for this country. The number one responsibility of this government is to protect our people from any outside threat. Right now the Soviets are that threat. If I don't sign the treaty our allies may get real unhappy with me. I don't like that but I can live with it. Therefore . . ." He looked directly at Turner, as though cueing him.

". . . Therefore," Turner said, "we should move to destroy the computer complex."

"Go on . . ." the President said, knowing what Turner was going to say.

"I've been proposing a covert air strike. Penetrate Soviet air space with two operational stealth bombers."

Robinson tried to cut in and was waved silent by the President.

"We can have our two prototypes operational in a few days. General Dawson, Brady and I have already spoken with General Westcott at SAC. The mission is in the planning stage right now. Westcott was involved in the Israeli mission to take out the Iraqi reactor."

The President took a deep breath, released it slowly, tapping an index finger. "John, if they can shoot down an RF-117C, what makes you so sure a B-2 can get the job done?"

"The B-2 is fourth-generation stealth technology. Its radar signature is one one-thousandth of the RF-117C. It is the only weapons system that makes sense. Once the B-2s enter Soviet airspace the pilots will know if the mission can be pulled off. If they're detected they can turn and run. If not, then they can proceed."

"Do you honestly think the Kremlin would just sit back after something like this happened?" Robinson said.

"Yes, I do. What option would they have? Tell the world we blew up their stolen supercomputer complex that was their last line of defense? They wouldn't say a word."

"Brady, what do you think?" asked the President, turning away from Turner.

"I think we should do it."

"And its chances?"

"I would have said fifty-fifty a few days ago but I just received this from a deep-cover mole this morning." Brady started to hand the President the top-secret report.

"Tell me what's in it, I'm sick of reports."

"Sir, it's a copy of a memo from their Minister of Defense, Nikolai Tomskiy. It describes the capabilities of the radar system, its weaknesses and where they are having problems. It seems because of the number of SAM sites in their northern defense theater, they haven't been able to tie everything together. However, we believe it will take the PVO only ten days to two weeks before their network is completely operational. If we are going to act I suggest we do it fast." Brady turned to General Dawson.

"Jack here feels he can have his crews ready to go in two or three days."

"That's right, Mr. President. Remember, we already have Ramenskoye targeted. The mission should be completed in less than eighteen hours with recovery of the bombers in Turkey. I've already asked the CIA to transfer Captain Koiser to our test center in Nevada, where he can help in the planning."

"Are you sure two bombers are all that are needed? I don't want another Iran disaster on my hands."

"That's all we have," Dawson said. "The mission-profile we're working on calls for one B-2 to fly interference, a decoy. And the other to destroy the center. They can then cover for each other on the way out. Once the center is destroyed the Soviets will be blind again, the B-2s should have clear sailing."

The President looked down at the table for a full minute, the only sound that of the slowly circling overhead fan.

"Let's do it," he finally said.

14

THE CREW

CIA HEADQUARTERS

"He's been turned inside out the last few days," Tyransky was saying to Staffer. "Leave him alone. It's time he began to start his life over. You and everyone else around here have squeezed every ounce of information out of him. There *isn't* anymore."

"I've done everything you've asked, Charles. I got you clearance to see every memo that had anything to do with Koiser and a few you probably shouldn't have seen. You've had control over him from the beginning. I'm asking for one last thing—"

"Why does he have to be at some air base? He spent eight hours with SAC today, what more do they want?"

"All right, I'll *tell* you, but if a word of this leaks I'll bust your ass . . . We need his input on the best way to attack the computer command-center that controls their radar network. Last night, Charles, at an NSC meeting we recommended to the President that a covert operation be undertaken to destroy it."

"And?"

"And *what*?" Staffer knew he had to take Tyransky into his confidence to get him to line up on the side of Koiser going along. Or at least not oppose it. The two were so tight, Tyransky could probably stop Koiser even if the Soviet wanted to help.

"If he wants to help I want your word this is the last time."

"Charles, admit it, what you're really worried about is that he may want to stay involved, just like Falcon did. That really should be his decision . . . But we'd like you on board too, obviously."

Tyransky said nothing, and Staffer decided he had won this round.

RAPID CITY, SOUTH DAKOTA

Lieutenant Colonel "Duke" James, considered by his superiors the best B-1B bomber pilot in the Air Force, heard the sharp raps on the door, rolled out of bed and fumbled around in the darkness before finding his dark green running shorts.

"What's wrong, honey?" his wife Katie asked as she sat up and looked at the clock. "It's almost midnight, who could it be at this hour?"

"I'm going to find out," he said, and moved down in the darkness, turned the outer porch light on and cracked the door ajar.

"Colonel James?"

"Yes."

"My name is Joseph Banks. I'm with the special office of the Secretary of the Air Force." A young man wearing a light gray business suit and wire framed glasses flashed an I.D. at him. Behind him were two Air Force MPs.

"So?"

"May I have a word with you please, sir?" Banks reached inside his coat pocket and pulled out a set of orders that he handed to Duke through the crack in the door.

Duke James glanced over them. "Come on in," he said quietly.

The three men entered the house and stood in the entryway as Duke sat and carefully read over the orders.

"There's a storm, sir. We need to leave immediately." Banks' tone was somber. Duke James nodded.

"Is everything all right?" Katie appeared at the top of the stairs wrapped in a bright red robe.

"Yes, honey." He moved quickly up the stairs and she followed him back into the bedroom.

"I've got to go," Duke said quietly. He reached into their closet and pulled out a clean shirt and a pair of Levi's.

"Where are you going? No . . . you can't tell me, it's a secret . . ."

"I don't know, Katie." And that was the truth.

"Duke James, what the hell do you mean you don't know? Three strange men show up at our house in the middle of the night and you don't know where they're taking you?"

"Katie . . . this is *all* I know. The man said 'There is a storm.' That's code for a crisis situation. I won't kid you. We've been at this too long. I won't know more until they decide to tell me." He reached into the closet, pulled out his prepacked flight bag and leather flight jacket. She waited on the landing separating the master bedroom from the kids' room as he entered the room and stood there looking at his two children asleep in their bunk beds. He leaned over and kissed Pamela and pulled the soft wool blanket up around her shoulders, then did the same to Matt.

Downstairs, Duke asked, for Katie's sake, knowing what the answer would be, where they were going.

"Sorry, sir."

"Yeah, right."

After they had left, Katie made her way upstairs and back to bed, knowing that sleep would not come the rest of this night.

The ride back to the air base was a quiet one. Duke James didn't bother to ask any questions that wouldn't have any answers. As they pulled into the base he could see an old white Lockheed C-140 JetStar with USAF markings sitting at the end of the far runway. Its directional lights burned brightly against the black night sky.

"That's it," Banks said to the MP driving the car, "just pull up next to it."

As they got closer James could hear the low humming of the jet's four Pratt and Whitney turbofans. They pulled up and parked on the right side of the aircraft.

"When was this built—1960?" Duke asked.

"It's all we could get on such short notice . . ." from Banks.

"I just hope it stays up long enough to get us where we're going."

"I'm not going, sir."

Duke James threw his duffel bag through the door of the plane and then walked three steps into the jet, seated himself in the first seat across from the window and watched Banks strain to close the heavy door.

"Good evening, colonel," one of the pilots said, emerging from the cockpit.

"So what's the story?"

The young pilot gave him a look. "Sir, if you would fasten your seatbelt please we'll be taking off."

James rested his head between the cold window and the worn leather seat. He was alone with his thoughts and the noise of the four jet engines spooling up for takeoff. He closed his eyes and let his mind fill with thoughts of Katie and his family. No use speculating about where or what he was going to.

15

BLACK MAGIC

WATERTOWN STRIP, GROOM LAKE, NEVADA

General Westcott stood motionless in the morning sun as it warmed his back. It felt good to be back where the action was instead of staring at four office walls at SAC headquarters in Omaha. He looked out over the barren dry desert to where it touched the bright blue morning sky. In the distance he could see two Soviet-made MiG-23s flown by two pilots from the 4477th test-and-elevation squadron based at Tonopah near Mud Lake in Nevada.

The 4477th went by the name of "Red Eagles" or "Mig Squadron." The various MiG 17s, 19s, 21s and 23s were Soviet aircraft that had been acquired over the years and were now used to fly against U.S. aircraft in mock combat. Along with the MiGs, the squadron operated simulated SAM and triple-A sites that electronically engaged the American fighters.

Watertown Strip, Area 51 officially, was located 130 miles north of Las Vegas. Next to it was an old dry lake named after the prospector who discovered it, Groom Lake. The lake bed, about the size of Switzerland and dry most of the year, made an ideal emergency strip for the aircraft being tested. The small base lay in a valley surrounded by sagebrush-covered mountains away from any roads.

The Air Force used the base to test and develop its most sensitive and top-secret projects. The 12,000-foot runway paralleled the line of mountains to the north. The base was invisible to any person looking at it from the ground. The control tower, hangars, crew headquarters and a few garages to park the jeeps and security equipment were the only buildings on the surface and those were camouflaged. The rest of the buildings were buried in the side of the mountain or covered by sand and rock.

The Nellis test range was ringed by a comprehensive radar network used to monitor all air traffic. Private and commercial pilots had been advised not to enter the Groom Lake airspace, the official line being that it was for "safety precautions," the actual reason was that anything flying into the controlled airspace would result in what could end up a fatal confrontation.

General Westcott walked the 300 yards to the senior officers' barracks, then up the pathway to the door of the small rock-and-sand-covered building. He knocked twice before entering.

"Good morning, Duke," he said.

Duke James, sitting at a small table rose, was startled by the sudden entrance of the general. "Hello, general." Duke raised his right hand to salute.

Westcott stopped him. "Hey, forget it, this isn't SAC. Damn, it's good to see you again. When was the last time?"

"I think it was our last squadron reunion in Atlanta five years ago."

The general nodded, surveying Duke's quarters.

"Yes, right . . . well, I hope you've had time to get some rest. I'm sorry about all this hush-hush and rush."

"General, I figure we crossed one, maybe two, time zones last night."

"Just one. You're at Groom Lake Test Field north of Nellis."

"So that was Vegas I saw last night on the way in. And I guess it explains why we were escorted down by two armed F-4s."

"I have a briefing scheduled in about an hour with the other members of the team, but I wanted to touch base with you first. Duke, you've been picked for a highly classified mission. I recommended you because of your skills and experience as a pilot . . . and your knowledge of Soviet air defenses." He hesitated a moment. "The team leader is Mike Fullerton . . . I know how you feel but I want you to put that behind you. He was chosen because he has the same qualifications as you. I need you to work with him as if nothing ever happened that night . . . This mission is too damned important, and dangerous, for the two of you to be at each other's throats and I want to know upfront whether or not you're capable of working with him."

Duke could feel the blood rush to his face, and waited.

"Don't think I'm attacking your professionalism. I'm not. Hell, I'm not sure I could handle it either if it had been *my* brother I saw going up in flames. It was a screw-up. You never should have been flying with your brother in the first place. But the fact is I need both of you if this thing is going to work."

"General, I have served under you before. You can believe I'll do my part in the mission . . . what is it?"

"You'll hear it all at the briefing, but I have something special to show you before that."

Duke's eyes were just starting to adjust from the bright sunlight to the shadows of the interior when the general opened the door to the main hangar.

"There she is," Westcott said, "the most advanced airplane in the world." He smiled. "We call her the Nightstalker Zero Two Five . . . and you'll be flying her."

Duke didn't hear that last statement, he was mesmerized at the sight of the aircraft. He hadn't imagined it would be such an ominous-looking machine. He walked toward the front of it.

It looked like no other plane he had ever seen. Unlike conventional aircraft, the bomber's all-wing design did not incorporate a tail or fuselage and it had virtually no edges or straight lines. The wingtips were cut off at a near-right-angle and were not parallel to the airflow. The black bottom and gray top blended continuously into three-dimensional curving surfaces, and the inner trailing edges gave it a boomeranglike shape. The raised cockpit merged smoothly into the center section of the wing with two rounded engine pods on either side concealing four engines. There were no abrupt changes on the bomber's surface, rather the contours were slight and gradual, producing a bizarre shape.

General Westcott walked a few steps behind the colonel. "Five years of R & D and over twenty-two-point-nine billion dollars. She's quite a bird."

"Have you flown her?" Duke asked.

"A couple of times. She's like no other plane."

"I never imagined . . ."

"The B-2 is the first aircraft ever to be completely designed by computer. To reduce the radar cross-section to the levels needed to penetrate Soviet air defenses we had to redesign the entire airplane. The engineers couldn't have done it without the computer. You can play around with aerodynamics, but electromagnetics are a different story." Westcott pointed to the curving shape of the bomber. "Ninety-nine percent of the radar energy that hits her either rolls off or is reflected off at an angle away from the emitter. The other one percent is absorbed into the airframe and turned into heat. The entire airframe is filled with irregular-shaped radar baffling, porous honeycomb chambers with composites of carbon, boron and silicon. The radar energy is absorbed by bouncing around inside the chamber, where it's dissipated. It's painted with a specially developed retinyl Schiff base-salt coating that absorbs the full radar energy spectrum from short-wavelength to long-wavelength and high-power search-and-track radars. The coating reduces the radar cross section by ninety percent and helps dissipate infrared radiation. You can fly right down their throats and they may never know you're there until it's too late."

"You sound like you're in love, general," Duke said, hoping he wasn't out of line.

Westcott smiled. "I guess I do. Maybe I am."

"How tough is she, can she take a hit?" Duke asked.

Westcott looked at the ground, grinding a small pebble into the concrete with the toe of his boot. "I know there's been a lot of shit flying around SAC about the B-2 being a plastic airplane. Some say she will go down with a near-hit from a SAM. Bull. The B-2's internal structure is titanium, covered with a microwave absorbent superplastic with a name I can't pronounce. We've also developed a new alloy, aluminum-lithium 7050 that's twenty percent stronger and lighter than anything before. It's used in the critical load areas of the wing and weapon bays. It's also in areas where the temperature rises above 290 degrees. The inner-structure of the airframe is reinforced with Kevlar and spectra one hundred. Fibaloy is used for the internal and external skin and the fuel tanks . . . it's stronger than aluminum and doesn't reflect radar. Around the engines we're using carbon-carbon composites and fiberglass and graphite-strengthened ceramics. Believe me, Duke, this bird is tough . . . its damage tolerance is fifty percent greater than a B-52's and tests indicate it can lose three of its four engines and still function."

Duke put his hands on his hips, still studying the bomber. As a pilot his first instinct was to believe only half of what the engineers told him. Ditto generals.

"We've also made breakthroughs in infrared and visual detection. This is a complete system . . . and you're going to need it, all of it," Westcott said, thinking of the mission.

"What's her range?"

"Because of her large wingspan . . . 172 feet . . . and her ability to cruise above 50,000 feet for part of a mission she can fly over 8000 miles unrefueled." Westcott pointed to the windows. "The large cockpit windows act as load-bearing parts of the fuselage and allow for the big-picture HUD that you've already worked with in the simulator. The digital-flight-control-systems are backed with a quadruple redundant computer system that drives the fly-by-wire control systems. They run along four different channels so if one of them gets knocked out, three keep operating. The fly-by-wire uses its high-speed electronics to control eight trailing-edge flaps that maneuver you in flight." Westcott knelt down to show Duke the control surfaces. "Trailing-edge exhaust deflectors are well behind the over-fuselage exhausts. They control the B-2's pitch by vectoring the exhaust up or down. They also operate in the left and right differential to roll the aircraft. At low speeds, Duke, when you're right next to a stall, thrust vectoring can save your ass. Our test pilots have put this plane into the tightest situations and so far she's always come through. As I think you know, the flight engineers developed an artificial system that can take part of the work load off you and your copilot during combat. That's why only a crew of two are needed to fly her. This is aircraft number one. The one you'll be flying . . ."

"General, I've never flown this thing. Why did you choose me, and why can't the B-1B do the job?"

"You *have* flown this thing, you have how many . . . five–, six-hundred hours in the simulator? You've made over a hundred takeoffs and landings in there. You're *combat* ready, my test pilots aren't."

Duke looked back at the plane. "So where am I going?"

The General looked at his watch. "You'll know soon enough."

VOYSKA PVO HEADQUARTERS, MOSCOW

Belikov sat at the head of the table in the small conference room that adjoined Minister of Defense Nikolai Tomskiy's office. Rolled out on the table in front of him was a map detailing the area around the computer complex on the southern edge of Ramenskoye. Tomskiy and KGB chairman Volstad sat on either side of him.

"I need at least fifteen ZSU-23s and twenty ZSU-57 antiaircraft artillery guns to be placed in these positions here," Belikov pointed to the yellow dots on the map. "I also need twenty more mobile SA-6s and ten SA-10s," this time pointing to the red dots. "I've given orders to start construction of hardened bunkers to protect these new SAM and artillery sites. The command-and-control center radars for each system will be placed on the highest ground so we can have a true look-down, shoot-down capability. This will ensure the greatest defense against any high-speed low-altitude aircraft and cruise missiles. Here and here"—Belikov pointed to the north and south of the large control radomes on top of the computer command center—"will be a mix of antiaircraft artillery and SAMs. Along with the MiG-29 squadron I will be commanding."

Tomskiy nodded. "I have already approved your requests for the additional equipment and men. You will have those no later than tomorrow. I am pulling them and their crews from operational field systems around Moscow and Leningrad."

"The ABM system that surrounds Moscow will give us protection against nuclear attack," Belikov went on. "From the command center we operate over thirty long-range and low-atmospheric silo-based interceptor missiles." Belikov looked directly at Tomskiy and Volstad. "The computer complex, gentlemen, will be impossible to knock out."

KGB Chairman Volstad reviewed the locations of the new air-defense sites, then looked at Belikov. The deep lines in the man's skin showed his age and the tensions of years of combat training and flying. "Are you positive you have covered all the weaknesses? As you know, the CIA has moved their KH-12 twelve degrees west and lowered its orbit to zoom in on the computer center. I don't like it that so many gaps were found in our present system." He was testing the colonel.

"Chairman Volstad, the present defenses are set up according to the doctrine of the PVO. I found nothing out of place. The improvements I have proposed will give us *additional* backup and fire power. I understand the importance of this complex."

"Colonel, I suggest you make sure the new defenses are operational quickly or not at all," Volstad said.

"The new defenses will go in speedily," Tomskiy said, and then to Belikov: "Instruct your men to camouflage and conceal their work. I want those sites combat-ready. Now."

GROOM LAKE TEST CENTER, NEVADA

Duke closed the door to the large briefing room and followed General Westcott up the center aisle to the front of the room. His attention focused on a map different from those he had seen in the past. It included a section extending into Utah that he hadn't even flown. As he studied it the general disappeared into the adjoining room.

"Colonel . . . Colonel James," a familiar voice sounded from the back of the room.

Duke turned around and saw his young copilot Tucker Stevens, walking quickly up the aisle toward him.

"Damn, it's good to see you," Tucker said. "I thought I was the only normal in this place. Last night Lisa and I were ready to head to her place when these two MPs told me I was going with them. No explanation . . . nothing. Three hours later, I'm here. Locked up in a room and no one will tell me anything. Then this morning some major picks me up in a car with blacked-out windows and drops me off here . . . Do you know what's going down?''

"I have an idea."

"I wish I did, I feel like I'm in never-never land."

"Tuck, it seems we've been volunteered for a mission . . . in a B-2. Where and what it's about I don't know. That's what this briefing is for."

"A B-2?" Tucker looked at the colonel. "They haven't even finished building one yet."

"That's what I thought. It seems we've been testing two full-scale protos since '81. General Westcott *showed* me one this morning."

"So we're at Edwards."

"No, Tuck, we're at Groom Lake . . . the Ranch. About a hundred miles north of Nellis." Duke watched the expression change on his copilot's face. "I know what you're thinking, it's crossed my mind too. But you and I have six hundred hours on the B-2 simulator. We fly a minimum of ten combat training missions a month in the B-1B . . ."

"They want us to fly the B-2? Flying a sim isn't flying the real bird . . ."

Just then the door opened to the side room and General Westcott emerged followed by four Air Force officers. Duke recognized the last man—Mike Fullerton. Neither man said a word to the other.

"Please have a seat, gentlemen," Westcott said, and took his place behind the podium. "First of all, I know you have a lot of questions on what's going on. I'll do my best to answer as many of them as possible, but remember, anything you see, do or hear at this base stays at this base. You are at Groom Lake Test Field in Nevada. Officially this place doesn't exist. We test our latest and most secret aircraft and weapons systems here. I can't tell you how long you're going to be here because I don't know. Your families have been notified that you are on an extended training mission.

"We have chosen the two best bomber crews in SAC to prepare for a covert mission into the Soviet Union. You will be flying two B-2 stealth aircraft. Each crew has been flying the stealth in the sim for over a year. All that's needed is to check you out in the real bomber before the mission. I have scheduled your first sortie for the next gap in Soviet satellite coverage . . . 1300 hours today. The training mission will take you through simulated Soviet airspace." Westcott traced the flight plan with his fingers along the map. "Our test range runs for 570 miles along this route into Dugway Proving Grounds in Utah. Located at the base of Baller Mountain is a large concrete bunker. Your mission will be to take out that bunker with live weapons. You'll have to evade the Soviet SAMs and triple-A threats. There will also be MiG-29 simulators, F-16s painted in Soviet camo trying to hunt you down. Colonel Fullerton, you will be flying lead. Lieutenant Colonel James, you will fly backup. Because of security, your flights will not involve instructor pilots. You are already past that stage in the sim so you shouldn't need any help."

They have a hell of a lot of faith in their simulators, Duke thought.

Westcott looked around the room. "Any questions?"

"Yes, sir." Fullerton raised the pencil in his hand. "Just what are we practicing to take out?"

"A new Soviet command-and-control center south of Moscow. When we break for planning I will give you the details of the threat it represents."

"Why the B-2, sir?" Duke said. "I would think letting us fly the B-1B would make more sense." Duke's question caught the attention of the three other pilots.

"We believe, colonel, the B-1B would only have a ten percent chance of completing the mission, maybe less."

"And what are the B-2's chances?"

"A lot better than anything else we've got to fly against them."

"What about the *mission*?" Duke asked, pressing the point.

"Believe me, Duke, you'll have all the details you need, nothing will be held back. Meanwhile, here's an important detail . . . you'll be flying the most closely guarded secret we have. This bird will only land back at her nest. If you run into problems and can't bring her home, then you auger in . . . even if you have to go in with her. If there's water, put her down in it if possible. The B-2 program will not be compromised. Okay, let's get to work."

"I really didn't expect to see you here, Duke," Fullerton said.

"I don't like it any more than you do, but it's not my decision. Let's just set it aside and get the job done."

"Fine, just remember who's flying lead," Fullerton said as he started to cut in front of Duke, making his way to the conference table next to the podium.

"Is there a problem?" asked Westcott, still standing at the podium.

"No problem, general," Fullerton answered.

The general looked at Duke.

"No problem, sir." Except the little ferret hasn't changed, Duke silently added.

"I was told we were to be flown to Nellis Air Force Base, not some test center in the middle of nowhere," Tyransky was saying to the sergeant who had just delivered food to Koiser and himself.

The door opened abruptly. "Hi . . . Mr. Tyransky, Captain Koiser. Sergeant Gunderson tells me there's some sort of misunderstanding, I apologize for any mix—" General Westcott began.

"General Dawson said we would be flown to Nellis, Captain Koiser would be debriefed one last time and that was to be that," Tyransky said, still protecting. "Last night we landed out here in the desert somewhere, we're locked up and this sure as hell is not Nellis."

"Captain, do you feel you have been treated unfairly since your defection?"

Koiser looked over at Tyransky and back to Westcott. "No, I have been treated fairly."

"Have you been pressured in any way to give us information against your free will?"

"No."

"Captain, I have respect for you and the courage you've shown. I'm sure you've been through a difficult ordeal, but right now the United States needs even more of your help. If you feel you're not able to give it I will understand. You are under no obligation to do anything further. I suggest, though, it's up to you, not Mr. Tyransky. If you want to leave here, just say so."

"What do you need?" Koiser asked quickly, wanting to speak for himself.

"Please sit down. I'll get right to the point. Captain, we need your help in planning a mission. I want you to advise my pilots. The information you have already supplied us is *very* valuable and will help us very much. Think it over, captain." And with that he turned and left the room.

Koiser was quiet.

"You fought your war, Grigori, now you're free. It's enough," Tyransky said.

"I am not so sure, what about all the others . . . ?"

"What others?"

"The people in my country. My little girl . . . this country is her only hope. If the United States is forced to back down to the Soviet leaders there will never be any real changes in my country."

Tyransky understood but was still opposed to it, realizing the danger it would put Koiser in . . . like Falcon, the last defector whose safety had been entrusted to him. Falcon had died at the hands of KGB agents in the U.S.

Koiser could feel the conflict building inside of him. Americans would be flying into his country to destroy a system he had helped create. Yet did it not need to be destroyed? Why, after all, had he defected . . . ? He closed his eyes and leaned his head back against the wall. It would be seven hours until darkness fell over the base. He had much to think about before he would sleep.

GROOM LAKE, THE STRIP

Duke James sucked a long breath of oxygen in through his mask, not taking his eyes off the runway. Long waves of heat radiated off its black surface. The distant mountains came in and out of focus as the heat waves rose toward the bright blue cloudless sky. To his left he could barely see the second B-2 piloted by Fullerton, its nose just a few feet ahead of his bomber. His copilot Tucker Stevens continued reading the preflight checklist off the color display above his computer keyboard.

The cockpit of the B-2 looked almost identical to the simulator they flew back at Ellsworth. The color of the B-2's interior was light gray where the Link simulator was a puke military-green. The hundreds of single-purpose lights, switches and gauges Duke was accustomed to seeing in the B-52 simulator and to a lesser extent in the B-1B had been replaced. The engine and conventional flight instruments were integrated into five computer-driven CRT displays. If he or Tucker turned off an electrical system, the system turned off on the display. In combat the B-2's information-management computer would supply them with maps showing the latest data acquired from satellite pictures of the target area and changes in electronic and tangible threats. The Threat Warning Panel located on the upper section of the instrument panel between the two pilots supplied the crew with additional data such as frequency of fire-control radars, SAM launches and enemy aircraft positions. The B-2's cockpit was so automated even the printed preflight manual was replaced by computer graphics.

"That's it, Duke, she's ready to roll." Tucker Stevens snapped his face mask in place after he completed the last check.

Duke brought his attention to the data displayed on the big picture HUD. The multicolored display that covered ninety percent of the large cockpit windows not only gave him and Tucker vital flight information—speed, altitude, heading and angle of attack through sight—it also interacted with them by sound and fingertip controls.

The flight information was focused at infinity and moved with the pilot's head. A sensor located on each man's helmet instructed the on-board computers to move the data either left, right, up or down, following the pilot's line of sight. Tucker could look out the right side of the cockpit and Duke the left and both would see the same information. When entering a combat zone the HUD automatically projected a safe flight path for the pilots to follow by showing them where the SAM and antiaircraft artillery radars were located and where they were looking. The combination of computer-generated images floating out in front of the pilots and the large windows of the B-2 gave the pilots a situational awareness. They could see any threats and, in theory, react to them before the enemy was aware of their presence.

Duke punched in radio numbers and brought the bomber's communication equipment in line with coded transmissions that would be used for this flight. He unsnapped his mask and sat back, waiting.

"Royal lead . . . clear for takeoff," the voice of the controller broke the silence of the cockpit.

"Roger, control . . . Royal lead rolling," Fullerton radioed back.

Duke snapped his mask back into place and put his right hand on the center stick control, his left on the throttle. His eyes scanned the instrument panel below the gray cockpit sill. Tucker set his hands on his knees; his job at the moment was to watch the instruments and advise Duke of any trouble during takeoff.

"You set, Tuck?"

"Yeah."

"You don't sound too sure."

"Piece of cake. Ha."

They watched as Fullerton's B-2 emerged out of the silvery mirage of the runway less than 6000 feet away. The dirty dull gray B-2 started its turn to the north before its camouflage blended in with the afternoon sky.

"Royal two . . . cleared for takeoff."

"Roger, control." Duke pushed the throttles slowly forward.

The four General Electric F118-GE-100 engines spooled up quickly. Duke steered the B-2 onto the center of the runway, lining its nose up with the center line.

"Royal two rolling," Duke radioed.

For the next few minutes Duke and Tucker climbed toward their cruising altitude of 15,000 feet. Duke then leveled the bomber and throttled back, decreasing airspeed to 450 knots. Royal lead was now in sight 500 yards ahead and about the same distance to the right.

"ETA to hostile territory, twenty-two minutes," Fullerton said, "follow me down on my lead and stay high. I don't want any hot dogging and don't deviate from the plan."

"Roger, Royal one, understood," Duke answered in a flat tone, releasing the microphone switch on his stick. "You prick," he said under his breath.

Tucker looked at Duke out of the corner of his eye. Don't lose it, buddy, he thought.

Duke steadied the B-2, then pressed the button activating the autopilot. After that the two pilots were silent as they monitored the bomber's instruments. Now they were over the practice range.

"Royal two, break high and right . . . starting our descent," Fullerton's voice broke the sullen mood in the cockpit.

"Roger, breaking right now, heading due east," Duke radioed back as he disengaged the autopilot and banked the B-2 to the right, gaining altitude, and trying to stuff his personal grievance.

F-16 NORTHBOUND, EIGHTY MILES FROM TARGET

Major Kenneth Wilbur liked everything about the 64th Aggressor Squadron. He liked the hot dry desert air. He liked the red star he wore on his shoulder, got a kick out of it. Most of all he liked the tactics and the flying time. He flew at least two combat training sorties a day, sometimes three.

This day his mission was to catch the B-2s before they made their bombing run.

The major banked his three-tone blue F-16, a MiG-29 simulator, to a new heading of 035, maintaining his current altitude of 14,000 feet. His wingman followed.

In the distance, to his left, he could clearly see Cedar Peak reaching up out of the desert floor like an ancient castle. In thirty seconds they would pass over the Utah border and into a new section of Dugway Proving Grounds. Once there, they would patrol the airspace above Baller Mountain, waiting to jump an unsuspecting B-2.

"Heads up . . . two minutes from descent, maintain current heading," Wilbur radioed his wingman.

"Roger, Baron, I copy."

"Be ready, they'll be coming in between the rocks. If you see one before I do it's yours, don't wait for me," Wilbur responded. "Those guys are too hard to find and too hard to track for one of us to get in the way of the other."

"Roger, I'll save you the leftovers."

ROYAL FLIGHT, THREE MINUTES FROM TARGET

Duke banked his aircraft slowly to the left to get a better view of the landscape rushing up to meet them. He and Tucker were still 2000 feet above Fullerton. If they spotted the target before Royal lead, Duke was to guide Fullerton to it.

"You got anything, Tucker?" Duke asked.

"Nothing, sir, it must be the camouflage. I'm not picking up a thing on IR or radar."

"We'll eyeball it." Duke throttled back to 300 knots. "We don't have enough time, Royal lead. We'll have to do a fly-by to I.D. the target."

"That's a negative, you're up there, you find it and find it now. I want to do this in one pass," Fullerton radioed back. "I'm going right to the base of the tallest peak, chances are it will be there."

"Roger," and Duke clicked his mike off. "He should be up here with us." He brought the nose up a few degrees, quickly gained 1000 feet as he took her up to 4300, then nosed over and put her into a shallow dive and headed for the base of the mountain, the large front windows of the bomber filling with the ground below.

"There he is," Tucker said, referring to Royal lead about 3000 feet below them, hugging the deck. Its dark gray camouflage did not entirely blend in with the browns of the desert.

"I think I got something . . . three o'clock, two-thirds the way down that far gully on the south slope," Duke called out. "See it?"

Tucker studied the rocky terrain for a few seconds. "Yeah, just left of those two large boulders with camo netting hanging on it."

Both pilots could see what appeared to be a small square

concrete block the size of a school bus. In twenty-five seconds they would be on top of it.

"We got a visual, Royal lead, turn right fifteen degrees. Your target is south, located in a gully one third up the mountain. ETA twenty seconds," Duke radioed.

Fullerton watched the mountainside fast approaching. He and his copilot had seen nothing. He would have to trust Duke's word. "Roger, I copy." Fullerton applied pressure on his stick, banking the big bomber south. At only 1000 feet above the ground and traveling at 350 knots reaction times had to be quick. "Open bomb-bay doors," he ordered his copilot.

"Weapons bay open."

"Tallyho, I see it." Fullerton was relieved to finally see the bunker. He glanced at his HUD, it was showing he only had fifteen seconds to drop his weapons and clear the mountain. "Here we go, hold on . . ."

Fullerton skillfully guided his B-2 into position, lining up the computer-controlled target-sight on his HUD. Within seconds the fire-and-control computer had made all the adjustments and a fire signal flashed in the center of his display. Ten seconds until impact.

"Now," Fullerton said, and squeezed the trigger on his stick, releasing two dark green 2000-pound MK-84 slick bombs. The nose of the B-2 pulled up sharply, changing the pilot's view from cactus, rocks and sand to the deep blue afternoon sky as they started to follow the steep contour of the mountain. The big bomber shot straight up, banking a few degrees to the north away from the target.

Major Wilbur didn't have to ride wild horses to know what one felt like. Just strap into an F-16, take her down to 500 feet, pour on the coals and hold on. The heatwaves rolling off the desert were enough to loosen anyone's fillings.

The major and his wingman were now heading due west. They had circled around and were speeding straight at Baller Mountain from the opposite side from which the two bombers were approaching.

The two F-16s, Baron one and Baron two, were a thousand feet apart, Wilbur slightly ahead of his wingman.

"Baron two, this is Baron lead. Remember, one quick pass, turn, burn and nail their ass," Wilbur said as he reached up and lowered his dark blue helmet-visor over his eyes.

"Roger, lead, let's do it."

The major leaned back on his stick and brought his nose up to start his climb over Baller, sighting his wingman out of the corner of his right eye banking right and climbing up the mountain. Speeding at 450 knots, the ground was just a blur 500 feet below. Both F-16s would cross over the top of the mountain in six seconds.

Duke held his breath as he watched the two 2000-pound slick bombs crash into the bunker and penetrate several yards before they exploded.

"Bullseye," Tucker yelled.

Duke banked his B-2 to the north, trying to follow Fullerton off the target. His altitude was 4800 feet and climbing slightly. He had a perfect view of everything happening around him as he and Tucker watched Fullerton's B-2 top the mountain—

Just then Duke caught sight of an F-16 streaking below from the opposite side of Baller less than 100 feet away.

"Holy shit, what was that?" Tucker's voice was shaky.

Duke didn't hear him, his mind only half-accepting what he saw out of the left side of the cockpit.

The second F-16 desperately tried to avoid the collision by banking hard right and dropping its nose. There just wasn't enough time. The fighter's left wing caught the leading edge of the B-2, ripping it apart. The F-16 spun end-over-end in a quick blur before exploding less than two seconds after impact. The pilot didn't have time to eject.

Duke could only watch as Fullerton tried to keep his crippled bomber in the air, watch its right-wing tank spew fuel as smoke started to pour out of its two right engines.

"GET OUT, GET OUT!" Duke heard himself scream.

The crew of Royal lead never had a chance. The F-16 had come up beneath them, they didn't know what hit them.

Suddenly the wing collapsed and the B-2 folded like a giant bat closing its wings. It hung in the air a split-second, then exploded in a ball of orange fire and dark black smoke. The main fuselage spun over upside down before hitting the ground.

"Mid-air, mid-air," Duke radioed air control. "Rescue equipment needed in sector KILO ZERO NOVEMBER. This is Royal two, I'm declaring an emergency . . ."

"Roger, Royal two, state your situation."

"One bomber and one fighter down."

"Royal two . . . can you maintain present position to aid in S & R?"

"Roger, control, Royal two will maintain until help arrives." Suddenly Duke felt his body go limp as the initial shock wore off. He applied power and started to climb up and away from the mountain. "Keep an eye out for that other Sixteen, Tuck."

Tucker couldn't answer, his throat was clogged.

Duke unsnapped his mask and wiped the sweat from around his eyes. He felt queasy, lightheaded. It wasn't as bad as when he had watched his brother die, but to witness the abrupt death of other human beings . . . He wanted to be on the ground, wanted to be with his wife and family . . .

He kept the Nightstalker flying in a slow wide circle above the crash site. He and Tucker stayed quiet, neither able to get any thoughts together to speak out loud. Instead they fixed on the rescue helicopter as it appeared in the distance.

Neither was thinking that now there was only one . . . one precious B-2 left.

16

OPERATION LAREDO TRAIL

THE PENTAGON

John Turner set the receiver back on his phone after ending his conversation with General Westcott. Over an hour had passed since the word had come in from Groom Lake. Two aircraft gone . . . three pilots dead, a four billion dollar hole burning in the ground. He rubbed his face with his right hand trying to relieve some of the tension. Jack Dawson had called him right after he had been notified of the accident, and Turner expected him at any moment . . .

"Mr. Turner, General Dawson is here to see you."

The Joint Chiefs Chairman entered and closed the door.

"You want a drink?" Turner asked.

"Bourbon on the rocks."

Turner made it for him.

"Talk to me, Jack, what the hell are we going to do now? Half of our B-2 operational force is gone."

"Well, we still have one . . ."

"Can *one* bomber do it?" Turner asked.

"Maybe . . . we're talking about a precision strike, not an

invasion . . . With the right planning why couldn't we do it with just a single—?"

"But you said we couldn't. One B-2 was supposed to attack while the other flew decoy." Turner searched Dawson's face, looking for an answer.

"One bomber could pull it off. I know in Nam there were times I would have preferred to send a single in on an important mission. The rules said no, but a single is harder for them to find and track. With the B-2's range . . . we could change its weapons mix, rethink tactics—"

"Wait a minute, Jack, slow down. If . . . if we did, who would fly the mission?"

"Colonel Duke James and Captain Tucker Stevens. They were slotted to fly the decoy B-2 on the original mission."

"You know we still have an ace in the hole . . ." Turner's voice trailed off.

Dawson got up to pour himself another drink. "What would that be?"

"The defector . . . Koiser. He knows more about the secret system than anyone else on our side."

"No question about that . . ." Dawson said.

"He's passed every psych test we've thrown at him . . . sodium pentothal, everything. Whatever he's given us has checked out . . . all of it."

Turner's face was set. "Give me a timetable when your men would be ready to go. I'll take it to the President. I still have to fill him in personally on the accident."

GROOM LAKE TEST CENTER

They were in Duke James's room, Duke and his copilot Tucker Stevens.

"I just can't get it out of my head . . . those two aircraft buying it," Tucker was saying.

"Tuck, you're one hell of a pilot. The mid-air was a fuck-up. Don't let this screw with your guts. A lot has happened in the last twenty-four hours, reminds me of Nam, stuff happening so fast you don't have time to sort it out . . ."

Tucker looked up, realizing Duke was lost somewhere in the past.

"Fullerton and me, we were in the same squadron at Anderson in Guam during the final days of '72," Duke went on, lost in a mood. "At the time he was a captain flying left seat and I was a first lieutenant flying right seat with a Major Callahan. It was December twentieth and we were three days into Linebacker Two. We'd just come off our worst night. We had over two hundred SAMs fired at us and lost six birds over Hanoi. Command had worked out a plan for us to break down their defenses by using ECM packages like the ones fighter-bombers carried on their flights into downtown Hanoi. The ECM equipment was supposed to be most effective when used in a three-plane integrated cell. You know, the three B-52s had to stay in tight formation for the full strength of the electronic counter-measures to focus on breaking the SAMs' fire-control radar. If one bomber broke formation, the shielding effect of the ECM system was shattered and our bombers suddenly became quick easy targets. The number-one thing you needed to fly those missions was . . . self-discipline, you had to stay in your three-cell group even when you were surrounded and all hell was breaking loose."

Duke's voice was becoming curiously flat, lifeless . . . "We took off that afternoon and flew eight hours to get to our target area. Our cell's callsign was Peach Two and we were coming in north of Haiphong. Our target was the Gia Lam railyards. Everything was okay, then fifty miles off their coast we picked up their radar. It followed us all the way in. Charlie had set up a few new SAMs, trying to guess what our flight path would be. They guessed right. We started picking up SAMs while we were still five minutes out from bombs-away and it got worse each mile closer. That's when the trouble started." Duke seemed to wince, as though reliving it. "Each time a SAM would light up, Fullerton broke left. Before long he was three hundred yards out. Major Callahan ordered him to come back into range. We had to keep a tight formation if we were going to survive. Fullerton never responded, just kept breaking left until he was almost a quarter mile away from the rest of the flight. We were only sixty seconds from bombs-away when there was an explosion off our starboard wing. Then a huge fireball lit up the cock-pit. I remember being scared shitless and thinking it was us that got hit. It was the third aircraft that took a direct hit in the belly, they never had a chance. Everyone bought it. Including my older brother. He was the pilot."

"Hey, Duke I didn't know—"

"Callahan tried to get an investigation but they didn't want any more bad press than they already had. The official report said that on account of the new SAM implacements it was un-derstandable that he could have become disoriented and wan-dered off course. Sweet, huh? He fucked up, Tuck, just like he did today. I'm sorry for his family that he's dead but you can't keep screwing up. Sooner or later it happens. He should have pulled up sooner . . ." Duke cleared his throat. "You remem-ber that, Tuck, you only have to screw up once and you or someone else can end up dead. Okay?"

"Sure, colonel, I'll remember. But there's this . . . we show up here in the middle of the night, I'm told about some super-radar system that can shoot down stealth planes. They give us three days to plan and train to fly into the USSR in some high-tech piece of unproven machinery and blow up some moun-tainside thirty miles south of Moscow. We may get blown out of the sky the second we enter Soviet airspace. Just how in hell can I *not* make a mistake? I feel like I just walked into the Twilight Zone."

Duke nodded. He understood. "Tuck, fact is that they can hold us hostage if their new radar works as advertised. We don't know for sure if they can detect the B-2 or not. It's the most advanced plane in the world and if there's any one system that can pull off the job it's the stealth. Remember, this is what we've been training for and you and I do it better than most anyone else. Fuck false modesty. In case you've forgotten, it's been me flying next to you the last two years. I know what you're capable of. If you weren't the best you wouldn't be here . . . I flew under Westcott in Nam. It didn't matter what mis-sion we were assigned to, he always let us call the shots. If this is a suicide run you and I will know and there isn't a general in SAC that would order us in." He wondered if he really believed that.

THE WHITE HOUSE, OVAL OFFICE

"John," the President said, "the mission was tough enough with two B-2s and now you tell me you want to do it with one?"

"Mr. President, there are advantages to a single bomber. And with Captain Koiser's help, well, I know we can do it." He hoped he sounded more confident than he felt. "From the data we've already collected we know if the B-2 is going to be detected it will be within the first hundred or so miles inside their border. If it runs into problems, escape routes will be planned to abort the mission."

Turner studied the President sitting across from him. Was he convinced?

GROOM LAKE TEST CENTER

Staffer was talking to Koiser. "The reason you've been brought here is because we were planning to destroy the computer center by flying two prototype B-2 bombers into the Soviet Union. That was up to about seven hours ago when we lost a B-2 and an F-16. They collided over the northeastern part of the test range. The pilots of both aircraft are dead and the aircraft destroyed."

Tyransky was getting edgy, knowing what was coming.

"Captain," Staffer pressed on, "we are now down to a single B-2 and we need your help, more than ever."

"I want to go," Koiser said quietly, getting right to it. "I can help you get in and out."

Staffer was stunned. He hadn't actually thought of this, but . . .

"That would be impossible," General Westcott said, speaking up for the first time. "A Soviet on the B-2?"

"Why not?" Staffer said. "The B-2 has provisions for a third crewmember. Koiser could help guide them through . . ."

Before Tyransky could say anything, Koiser spoke up and said it was his decision and he wanted to go.

"Let me know if you need anything," Staffer said, and he and General Westcott left the room.

"You're serious about this," Westcott said as both men made their way through the cold night desert air to their waiting car.

"Damn right I am," Staffer said.

"My God, he's a Soviet—"

"He's a Soviet *defector*, the President has granted him asylum. I've watched him, checked him out . . . Tyransky has tried to overprotect him in my view, and it turns out Koiser *wants* to help us. After all, he expected it when he defected."

Westcott looked skeptical.

Duke looked at Koiser sitting across the table from him. Spread between them was a detailed map of the northern United States, the Arctic Ocean, including Greenland and Iceland and the western half of the USSR. Stacked in various places around the maps were the latest satellite reconnaissance photos for different proposed routes into the Soviet Union.

Duke had known the Soviet less than five hours, but he liked him. Answering endless questions on Soviet defenses, Koiser kept polite and to the point. Sometimes he said he didn't know.

Duke leaned back in his chair and glanced at the large round black-and-white clock above the door—2:47 A.M. Damn, I'm beat, he thought. To his right was a Mission Support System II computer. The MSS II was a black box the size of a twenty-inch television set. SAC had developed it to help pilots in mission planning. The MSS II had the capability to link up a network of satellite photos, color graphics and color prints into a 3-D picture to help the pilot plot a course into and out of the target area. Duke and Westcott had been working on attack routes the B-2 could take.

Koiser was laying out where the Soviet defenses were the weakest. "General Westcott, the PVO has high-power long- and short-range radars along the Ural Mountains. They scan thousands of square kilometers. Penetrating from the east and having to cross them would be very dangerous. With some holes in the system north of Moscow it would be best to fly the valleys and rivers east of Petrozavodsk." Koiser traced the route with a forefinger. "Enter here . . . across the Kola Peninsula. Their radar is not good over water and we can use the cover of darkness to move down the coast of the White Sea. From there we can detect weaknesses in the system until we reach the heavy defense around Moscow. That area is one I fear very much." Koiser looked up at Duke keeping his finger on Moscow.

"Ramenskoye is on the southern edge. The SAMs and triple-A's will be murder," Westcott put in. "I don't like the idea of penetrating the northern defenses around Moscow. I still think it would be better to cross the Urals and come in from the south."

"General, you are correct. The air defenses between Leningrad and Moscow are the heaviest in the world, but they are also some of the oldest, and if your secret PVO report is factual the northern region shows the most confusion." Koiser was sticking to his plan.

"I have to agree with Captain Koiser," Duke said, feeling the general was mostly trying to bait the Soviet. "If we come in from the south we waste time and fuel. Get in, get the job done and get the hell out fast as you can. If we get as far as Moscow and hit the target there will be so much shit in the air it won't matter where it came from." He looked at Tucker. "Tuck you'll be the navigator, what do you think?"

"I think the least amount of time in their airspace the better. In and out fast, like you say. And I'm a believer . . . that B-2 bird should make it tough to find us." Hell, he *had* to believe . . .

Westcott turned to Koiser. "Captain, we are installing a computer terminal next to your seat in the B-2. The screen will show you the same information as on Captain Stevens's tactical display screen . . . the locations of SAMs, MiGs and antiaircraft artillery along with the radar frequency their control radars are using. All the symbols on the screen will be in both Russian and English. That suit you okay?"

Koiser looked over to Staffer and Tyransky sitting at the next table. "Yes, sir, that suits me okay."

"Your main job will be to help Captain Stevens. He'll need to know what radars will be threats and the tactics the MiGs might use to hunt you down."

Westcott then asked Duke if he agreed on the mix of weapons.

"Yes, sir. Six AGM-131C SRAMs, all armed with metastable-helium warheads in the number one weapons bay; eight AGM-136S supersonic Tacit Rainbow antiradiation drone missiles along with a dozen Tactical Air Launched Decoys. That's as many as we can cram into the rest of the area. I still want double the chaff and flares we would carry on a normal mission." Duke paused for a moment. "Anything else R & D have they haven't told us about?"

Westcott shook his head. "All the cards are on the table. Any questions? All right, the defensive weapons will be loaded here at Groom. We'll wait and load the offensive at Minot, just before the mission. Now I want you guys to get some sleep. We're going to fly to Minot tonight. It will take operations that long to get your bird ready to fly. Our target time to launch will be twenty-hundred hours two days from now."

THE WHITE HOUSE, OVAL OFFICE

"Mr. President, since I spoke to you last night I've received the revised updated plans for an attack on the computer center. General Westcott and his staff worked through the night to prepare them." Turner handed the President and Brady each a copy. Dawson already had one.

"We believe a single B-2 could complete the mission, sir," Dawson said, breaking into the conversation. "The only support needed would be a single KC-10 tanker to top off her tanks right before entering Soviet airspace, and a B-52 used as a cover until the B-2 reaches the Soviet border. The B-2 has the range to make the trip, take out the computer center and be recovered in Turkey within three to four hours."

The President's attention shifted to the first page of the mission outline. The top read, OPERATION: LAREDO TRAIL.

"Escape routes are marked in red," Turner said. "If the B-2 is detected by their system it can fly into Norway. A squadron of F-15s will be on alert to fly support if needed . . ."

The President said nothing, studying the map as Turner talked.

"With information we've learned from our Kremlin connection the pilot will have alternate attack routes. The weakest areas are marked in blue. It will depend on the air defenses and which flight path Captain Koiser thinks is safest—"

"Captain Koiser? The Soviet defector will be communicating with the B-2?" the President broke in.

This was the tough part, and Dawson spoke up first: "Mr. President, communications with the stealth will be kept at a minimum." Dawson stopped, waiting for Turner to lay it out about Koiser.

"Sir," Turner began, trying to low key what he was about to say, "the Soviet, Captain Koiser, we've decided it's to our advantage, the mission's advantage, to have him fly as a third crewmember and help navigate . . ."

"This seems pretty extreme, are you sure?"

"Sir, he helped develop the system. He knows Soviet air defenses." Turner looked to Brady for help. "Tony . . ."

"He's safe, Mr. President, he's been checked out over and over," Brady said. "Koiser, in fact, could be our trump card. With his help we have a better chance to take them by surprise. And General Westcott and the B-2 crew feel they can pull it off flying without a second B-2."

"What's the time-frame until you're ready?"

"Two days, Mr. President. All we need is your approval," Turner said, holding his breath.

The President was quiet, then: "John, what else?"

Turner took in a deep breath. "These latest KH-12 photos show the Soviets are increasing the amount of SAM and triple-A sites around the complex by at least twofold." He handed two photographs to the President. "The new sites are circled in white and can easily be seen around the command center. They're trying to camouflage them with netting but the construction is happening too fast."

"What are you saying? They may know we're planning something?"

"Not likely sir," Dawson broke in. "I believe since they've proved their new defense system works, at least on our stealth fighter, it's more important to them than ever. They're just following natural procedure."

"It also means the longer we wait, the harder it's going to be to get the job done," Turner said, which, of course, was the main point to get across.

The President let out a long sigh. "Gentlemen, the ball's in your court, to coin a phrase. I would like to be able to stand before the American people and tell them we will be signing the treaty and not have any reservations about it. If you're successful, I suspect the Soviets will be anxious to sign and then some." He looked to each man. "This had damn well better work, gentlemen."

GROOM LAKE TEST CENTER

They were walking to the hangar housing the B-2, Capt. Grigori Koiser, Soviet defector, and Col. Duke James, a U.S. top gun. Quite a combo, Duke thought. No question, he still felt uncomfortable with the Soviet. He had read the man's file, and wondered about him. After all, he had been a top officer and pilot, someone trusted with deeply held secrets. Yet he had turned against them and now wanted to help the old enemy on a mission to destroy the secret project that could change U.S.–Soviet relations for all time. Because without this supercomputer-driven enhanced radar, they'd be really vulnerable. And a vulnerable enemy could change his spots real quick . . . He wished he knew the man better.

For his part, Koiser could tell the colonel was doing his best to make him feel at ease but wasn't comfortable with it. The man still had reservations about bringing him along. Koiser couldn't blame him. They had known each other less than twenty-four hours. He would just have to let Colonel James work it out in his own way. He couldn't force acceptance on him.

"You flew MiG-29s," Duke said.

"Yes, and before that MiG-23s."

"Why did you defect?" Duke decided to be blunt. No time for chitchat now. True, he'd been told what Koiser had already said about his motives, but he wanted to hear some of it direct for himself.

Koiser turned and stopped, waited for Duke to do the same. When they were facing each other Koiser spoke up. "I defected

for personal and other reasons. Freedom is no empty word to
me or the people in my country. You are willing to die for it. So,
colonel, am I . . . Colonel, do you have a family?''

"Yes . . .''

"I left my little girl back in Moscow. I have not seen her for
two months. I don't know if I will ever see her again. I do know
that if I am ever to see her again my country has got to change.
But they never will if they feel strong. If this secret project is
knocked out, they will have to change. It is the last hope for the
leadership. Its destruction is our last hope . . . more, my
daughter's . . . As far as the mission, I understand my position, colonel. You are in command, I will be along only to assist
you and Captain Stevens.''

As Koiser finished, they arrived at the B-2 hangar. Duke decided he'd gotten as much as he was going to get from Koiser.
The man was convincing.

The doors of the hangar were open slightly allowing a stream
of sunlight to penetrate the darkness inside. Members of the
ground crew were working around the bomber, getting her
ready for the mission. Two twelve-inch-diameter orange-and-
red-striped hoses were connected to the underside of the Nightstalker feeding cool air into her interior. The doors of the bomb
bays were open, and Duke could make out weapon racks sitting
empty. Everyone in the hangar seemed to be in an organized
hurry. Duke could barely make out the outline of the B-2's
upper fuselage, its gray color blending with the low light of the
hangar.

"Captain, if there's a warplane in the world capable of flying
this mission, it's this aircraft. My superiors know you better
than I do, and they feel you can help tilt the odds in our favor to
pull this off and come back alive. Let me just say this, up there
we're a team. I can't have any questions about a man's loyalty.
When we enter Soviet airspace I expect all hell to break loose.''
Duke didn't take his eyes off the B-2.

"Colonel, I'll be blunt too. I know you don't want me on
board your bomber. I would feel the same way if I were you. I
can only tell you I will not betray you or this country. Beyond
that . . . I am afraid you will have to trust my word.'' Koiser's

tone was firm. He looked straight at Duke James when he spoke.

Duke James looked back at him. "I hear you, Captain Koiser. So be it."

RAMENSKOYE TEST CENTER

The computer generated multicolored lights from the large billboard-size display, casting an array of colors over the computer command center. Colonel Belikov and General Yefimov studied the screen from their glass-encased control station above the floor. Each technician sat in his place monitoring the computer screen in front of him. All was quiet.

"We tied in four more SAM sites today, general," Belikov said. "That makes eleven in the last five days. At the rate we are proceeding the crews will finish three days ahead of schedule."

General Yefimov's expression did not change. "The CIA is keeping a close watch on your progress. Their KH-12 has not changed orbit, it continues to photograph the area around this computer center with each pass."

"Tomorrow I will be making an inspection of the base's MiG-29 squadron," Belikov went on, ignoring Yefimov's not so subtle dig. "With that in order every air-defense system will be combat-ready."

"Are you expecting trouble, colonel?"

"General Yefimov, I do not have to expect trouble to be ready for it."

GROOM LAKE TEST CENTER

"Try to get some rest in Minot, you'll only have twenty-four hours before takeoff," General Westcott was saying to Duke. "General Preston is in charge there. Moscow is his sector of command and control if SAC ever flies into Russian territory. You have any more questions, he's your man."

Duke nodded, not taking his eyes off the Nightstalker.

Westcott went on: "Your survival gear includes maps of Russian territory, two thousand rubles, instruction cards written in five languages if you're shot down. You'll have a loaded 9 mm.

Tokarev, except for Koiser. One other thing. I've left a second Tokarev taped to the ejection seat next to your left leg. It's in easy reach in case you need it."

"I understand, general, but I don't think—"

"Never mind what you think. If we're wrong about that guy, don't hesitate to blow his head off. Keep an eye on him at all times. Do you follow me?"

Duke nodded, wanting to get away from Westcott, who only reinforced some of his own reservations.

Tucker appeared now at the entrance of the hangar. Koiser walked directly behind him, followed by Staffer.

"Time, Duke. Good luck." Westcott gave Duke a quick salute followed by a handshake.

17

INFILTRATION

MINOT AIR FORCE BASE, NORTH DAKOTA

A heavy haze hung in the night air as Duke James taxied his B-2 into position on the edge of the runway. The bright lights of the distant city reflected off the low clouds and cast a silvery glow on the B-52H in front and to the left of him. He studied the dark silhouette of the long bomber that was to be his cover as a few snowflakes shot past the windshield.

Duke felt somewhat relieved as he sat at the high-tech controls of the big B-2. At least the waiting was over. The six-hundred hours he had had in simulator flight training were his preparation for his assignment. Their flight in from Groom Lake had been uneventful, and his ability to pilot the stealth no longer concerned him. Arriving at Minot Air Force Base the night before at 10:53 P.M. Duke, Tucker and Koiser were hustled off to meet with General Preston, and their B-2 was placed in a secure hangar for final mission preparation. At 1:00 P.M. the word came from Washington: OPERATION LAREDO TRAIL was a go. From that moment and for the next five hours Duke had not slowed down.

As he repositioned himself now in his ejection seat he pictured the events in the B-52's cockpit as its crew lifted her into the sky. He had not flown a B-52 for over nine years and yet he remembered each procedure as if it were yesterday. And just then the feeling this could be the last time he would ever see America came over him. A SAC bomber had never before attempted to penetrate Soviet airspace. All the planning and training in the world could not totally prepare him for that. If he and his crew were to survive it would take guts, skill, and one helluva lot of luck.

"Nightstalker . . . cleared to taxi," the tower radioed, snapping Duke back.

"Roger, Nightstalker." Duke pushed the throttles forward slightly and the bat-shaped bomber slowly turned and filled the void left on the runway by the B-52.

"All set, Tuck?"

"All set."

"Koiser?"

"Ready, colonel."

"Nightstalker, cleared for takeoff. Maintain runway heading to two thousand, turn left zero two niner. Wind zero two five at one four."

"Roger, Nightstalker rolling." Duke released the button on the stick and advanced the throttles to full power. The bright white-and-blue lights on each side of the runway started to fly past in a blur. Duke concentrated on the center line, not allowing himself to be pulled to either side by the bright border lights. As soon as the fully loaded B-2 hit 172 knots Duke pulled back on the stick and nosed the B-2 up eight degrees. The nose wheel lifted into the air only a split second before the main gear. He watched the airspeed climb rapidly through 205 knots.

"Gear up."

"Gear up." Tucker hit the switch with his left hand, sending a sudden whine through the plane.

"Spoilers?"

"Thirty percent."

"Inboard flaps?"

"Coming up."

Duke watched the altimeter increase on the left side of the large HUD. The weather briefing reported they should break out of the clouds at 3500 feet and have clear skies across the southern part of Manitoba as they headed north over Lake Winnipeg. From there they would follow the Hayes River north to Hudson

Bay, continue on a separate course and link up with the B-52 and KC-10 over Baffin Island at approximately 1:00 A.M.

Now the B-2 broke through the clouds at 3700 feet to the sight of a mass of stars. Visibility seemed unlimited. Duke eased back on the center control stick, pushing the B-2's nose up two more degrees, watched the airspeed fall back and cracked the throttles forward half an inch to increase their rate of climb to 1500 feet per minute.

"Tucker, run a diagnostic systems check again. Koiser, you might as well relax. It's going to be a few hours before we're in range of Soviet search radars."

B-52H CRYSTAL FLIGHT, TWENTY-FIVE MILES NORTH OF WINNIPEG

From the right seat of the heavy bomber, General Preston replied to Winnipeg control's request for his position: "Ah, Roger, Winnipeg control. Heading zero three four at flight level three two zero. Will maintain current heading and altitude for remainder of your control area."

"Roger . . . Winnipeg control." The response was cold, official.

Preston moved the oxygen mask away from his mouth. "Damn, they sure get fussy when we don't file flight plans," he said, to the smile of his pilot, Maj. Bobby Martin.

Preston glanced across the instrument panel checking the gauges, which showed they had a little less than three hours flying time before rendezvousing with the KC-10 tanker and refueling.

NIGHTSTALKER, SOUTHERN COAST OF BAFFIN ISLAND

At 30,000 feet Duke could easily make out the contour of the land below them. The three-quarter moon cast enough light into the coal black night to show the small valleys and hills on the snow-covered land below. The almost oval shape of Prince Charles Island was far off to his left, surrounded by the darker ice of Foxe Basin. The landmark indicated they were right on course, two hours thirty-seven minutes into the flight. It wasn't that Duke mistrusted the navigational computer, it was just nice to back it up now and again with visual references.

"The heat exchanger on number two and three is running a little warm," Tucker reported as he pointed to the electronic dial on the panel. "Compared to one and two it's up over fifty degrees."

"Keep an eye on it. Chances are it will fall off as soon as we increase the RPMs and go low-level. All right, let's catch up with our friends," Duke said, and advanced the throttles.

Within twenty seconds the Nightstalker had accelerated to 460 knots, quickly closing the gap between itself and the B-52 Crystal Flight.

THE *SOVREMENNYY*, BAFFIN BAY

Captain Nazaroff stood in the command center of the 6500 ton destroyer and observed the actions of his crew. The bitter cold no longer bothered him. Five months at sea feeling the bite of the north wind every day had made him hard and lean. The young captain knew that in order to advance his career in the navy several tours above the Arctic Circle would be needed.

Cruising at twelve knots up the western coast of Greenland the *Sovremennyy* sliced through the black icy water with little resistance. Her dual automated steam-propulsion power plants could scarcely be heard in the background. Designed as a fast, heavily armed destroyer, the *Sovremennyy* was crammed with the latest long-range surveillance and eavesdropping equipment. Captain Nazaroff and his crew's assignment was to collect data on American and British surface vessels, submarines, and air movements.

"Status, lieutenant," Nazaroff requested.

"Nothing new, captain," the lieutenant said, his eyes on the radarscope in front of him. "I still show an American P-3 continuing west 600 kilometers south. No other surface or air activity."

Nazaroff took a few steps forward and looked over the nervous lieutenant's shoulder. The Americans were obviously searching for him. His dash north at flank speed after the sunset had put off American surveillance. They were looking for him in the wrong place.

"I'm picking up a new target, captain." The lieutenant hesitated. "Heading zero seven two, speed 380 knots at 10,000 meters."

"I see it." The captain was feeling less exuberant as he noted a single faint oblong dot in the upper left side of the radar screen. "Can you identify it?"

"It will take some time, captain. It is at the edge of our range." The lieutenant paused again. "It is traveling slower than a commercial airliner . . ."

B-52H CRYSTAL FLIGHT

General Preston's eyes shifted back and forth from the dot representing the KC-10 tanker on the radar display grid to the red flashing light of the refueling boom only seven yards ahead. His air-to-air Tacan slowly read off the distance between the B-52 and the tanker as they approached.

A slip-up at this close range could easily mean instant disaster. Once the B-52 connected with the tanker it would suck in 20,000 pounds of fuel in eight to ten minutes, topping off its tanks for the run at the border.

"Ten . . . eight . . . five . . . two . . . contact," Major Bobby Martin counted down. "Damn, you can do that a thousand times and it's never the same."

"One miss and it's never the same either," Preston said, underscoring the obvious.

NIGHTSTALKER

"Yeah, I see it," Duke said. A weak D/E-Band radar was sweeping them from the southeast.

Tucker and Duke watched the faint red beam of the Soviet long-range search-radar come and go as a computer-generated image on their HUD. Their Texas Instruments AN/FSM-17 analyzer and Quick Reaction Contact IBM computer instantly identified the antenna pattern as a D-Band, 23cm, and E-Band, 18cm radar frequencies.

Tucker turned to the computer on his left. "I have a computer confirmation showing it as a naval Top Sail . . . 3D search radar only. Probably operating off that destroyer naval intelligence was trying to keep track of off Greenland. Navy intelligence said it would be a hundred miles south of here."

"Koiser, any input?"

"No, colonel, it is naval, I am not familiar with it."

Duke figured a naval Top Sail operating in the D/E-Band shouldn't be a threat to the stealth. Its radar waves painting the B-2 should either roll over its smooth edges and disperse or be absorbed. "Take down this message, Tuck, and blast it to Crystal. They shouldn't have been able to pick us up at all for another hundred fifty miles. Not even as a blur."

B-52H CRYSTAL FLIGHT

Their UHF receiver had picked up a high-speed blast of coded electronics from the B-2.

"Damn, they're looking for us already?" Preston said. "The B-2's sensors are picking up a Soviet long-range naval-surveillance radar. In a few minutes we'll be close enough for them at least to know there's two of us up here." Preston meant his B-52 and the KC-10 tanker. The Soviets shouldn't be able to see the B-2 on their radar scopes. In theory anyway . . .

"Sir, how are they tracking us?" Major Martin asked.

"With a Top Sail about 300 miles out."

Martin looked over his instruments. The older B-52's radar sensors didn't show any warning of a radar sweeping in their direction.

Preston looked again at the message from Nightstalker. "How long before we're finished refueling?"

"About a minute, the left wing tanks are already full."

"Okay, break off and slip in under the Extender. Get as close as you can. If we stay right underneath the tanker it may confuse them." SAC's latest intelligence, Preston knew, had reported a D/E-Band radar wasn't sophisticated enough to distinguish targets less than thirty feet apart. "We've got to convince those Soviet operators we're one aircraft," Preston added. "Just stay in close trail . . ."

THE *SOVREMENNYY*, BAFFIN BAY

Nazaroff watched the young lieutenant slouch over the computer keyboard as he entered a new set of instructions to the computer-controlled radar.

"I want confirmation now. What type of aircraft is it?" he demanded.

"I'm not able to confirm, sir. It is big, possibly an American 747 or DC-10. Or possibly two large aircraft flying in very tight formation. I cannot be sure, it is very difficult—"

"Two aircraft?" Nazaroff said.

"Perhaps, sir. At times the target almost appears to break in two . . . then joins together again."

Nazaroff didn't believe it. American commercial airlines never traveled in this sector. If they were flying 300 miles to the south he could understand it . . . He watched as the target, now in the upper center of the scope, moved steadily to the east. In ten minutes it would be less than fifty miles away to the north. Their best chance to identify it would come then.

NIGHTSTALKER

Duke heard the distinct double click in his headset as General Preston squeezed his mike trigger twice to confirm his message. Moments later Duke watched the dark outline of the B-52 gently edge away from the refueling boom and begin drifting under the KC-10 until the two aircraft blended into the darkness and became one.

Duke checked his airspeed, 380 knots. The B-2 was 200 yards behind the tanker.

"All right, Tucker, it's our turn."

With fingertips on the control stick Duke inched the Nightstalker up into the refueling boom of the tanker. Tucker reached over and turned on the switch. Now their half-empty tanks began to fill, and Nightstalker's flight computers automatically channeled the fuel to various areas of the bomber to keep its center of gravity perfectly balanced.

STRATEGIC AIR COMMAND, OFFUTT AIR FORCE BASE, OMAHA, NEBRASKA

The few lights that could be seen burning on the top floor of the three-story brick building gave no clue to events unfolding in SAC Central Building 500.

Below the ground-level buildings and basement was a building slightly larger than the structure above ground. Fortified under twenty-eight feet of rock and dirt, the self-contained building occupied over three acres of floor space. Its ceilings and walls were made of thirty inches of stainless steel reinforced concrete slabs with twelve-inch-thick steel layers between each floor and the outer walls. The roof of the center varied from two to four feet in thickness and was designed to take a direct hit from a twenty-kiloton nuclear warhead. It was home to SAC's Command Post. The information displayed simultaneously on the four center-screens gave the status and current location of SAC units worldwide as well as the movement of enemy aircraft.

Tonight the command center was relatively quiet. Technicians sat at their stations and viewed the massive video-display terminals along the far wall. The center screen showed the islands of Greenland and Iceland with the Arctic Circle running through the lower center portion of the screen.

It was just past midnight when General Lamar Westcott watched the three small bright green triangles slowly merge into two blips and move toward the western edge of Greenland. He watched the three aircraft make their way east, their altitude, speed and heading appearing in the upper right corner. At any time during the B-2's flight he could communicate with Colonel James directly, all made possible by the strategic and top secret tactical relay system, known as Milstar. The system was used in conjunction with 18 Navstar constellation satellites in semisynchronous orbit, which could transit instantaneous global positioning data to the pilots of the B-2 via high-speed computer. With the system Duke and his crew could find any target, anytime, even under the worst weather conditions and without turning on Nightstalker's active radar or other electronic position-finding equipment. As a result it was less likely Soviet air-traffic monitoring systems would be able to pick up and track the stealth through self-emitting electronics. Actually, the only signals the B-2 gave off were constant bursts of mixed 300,000 megahertz EHF radio beams lasting a ten-thousandth of a second—a transmission that informed SAC of the bomber's location.

"What the hell is going on?" Westcott wondered out loud. The display showed the two green symbols flying right behind one another. He glanced over at the flight data and noted the KC-10 tanker and B-52 showed the same altitude and speed.

He keyed the intercom on his desk. "Major Allen, I need a status report. Anything unusual in the flight area?"

"Satellite surveillance shows the Soviet destroyer *Sovremennyy* sixty miles to their south."

"That ship shouldn't even be in the area. It should have moved south. How far has it gone since the last flyover?" Westcott didn't take his eyes off the display screen. "And why wasn't I notified?"

The major keyed in a set of instructions and a moment later a map of Baffin Bay appeared on his screen—Baffin Island on the west and Greenland to the east. A thin red line arced north along the coast of Greenland showing the *Sovremennyy*'s latest course.

"It's moved seventy miles north, sir."

"North? How old is that data?"

"Only minutes, it just came in."

The general took a deep breath. The plan called for only *one* radar identifiable aircraft, the B-52, to fly out of Greenland's airspace. If the Soviets tracked two going into Greenland and only one coming out it might well make them curious. Or worse.

NIGHTSTALKER

Duke watched the green refueling-indicator light on the lower right side of the instrument panel flicker off, telling him they were no longer connected to the Extender.

Duke checked the CRTs in front of him. All seemed okay. He

gently moved the throttles back to decrease the B-2's airspeed by three knots. The stealth slowly floated away from the big tanker and lost a hundred feet of altitude before he stopped the descent.

"We'll be over Greenland in five minutes, sir," Tucker said.

"You got any idea when we'll lose contact with that Top Sail?"

Tucker tapped his computer keyboard. "The QRC shows less than twelve minutes. After that we'll be too far inland, they won't be able to track anything of us over the coastal mountains. Their radar waves will be broken up by the mountain ridges." He hoped.

"Any indication they know about us?"

"No. Their attention has been on the Fifty-two and the tanker. Like we figured."

"Tuck, tell SAC I need confirmation before continuing. I need to know how many aircraft that Soviet surveillance ship tracked entering Greenland."

THE *SOVREMENNYY*, TURNING NORTHWEST

The lieutenant didn't dare blink. The new image on the scope looked oblong and unusual. However, his attention wasn't focused on the bright blip. With the target at its closest point to the ship he concentrated on a small, soft, fuzzy image directly behind the strong clear blip on the radar scope.

"It will be out of range in ten minutes, lieutenant, I need an identification now," the captain said, impatience and worry on his face.

"I've never seen anything like this before," the lieutenant said, and pointed to the image fading in and out behind the bright blue dot.

"Of course you've never seen anything like it, there's nothing there, it's magnetic interference. Your job is to tell me what sort of aircraft is crossing to the north. I am not interested in ghosts on your screen." He turned to the radio intercept officer. "Anything on the communications channels?"

"No, captain, I have not picked up a single radio transmission."

The captain swiveled back around and faced the radarscope. The lieutenant sat beneath him. "Well, lieutenant, I am waiting."

This was the radar operator's first tour. Over the last few months at sea each aircraft he had tracked was easily identified. Once again now he tried to get the computer to identify. No luck.

"I am still waiting, lieutenant."

"It's an American . . . C-5 . . . their largest cargo aircraft." The panicked lieutenant was reaching for an answer—which he didn't really believe.

"I know what a C-5 looks like, that's nonsense—"

"Sir . . . normally they don't operate in this sector. I believe that explains its unusual shape on the scope and why it appears so large." The young operator held his breath, hoping the captain believed him.

The captain stood quietly, not saying a word for seconds that seemed like an hour to the lieutenant. "Bring her around to two five zero. Inform the VMF we have been tracking an American C-5. It will be entering Greenland airspace in seven minutes."

Moments later an electronic signal was entered in the ship's communication computer, where it was coded and transferred onto a U.S.-made 3.5 inch Kodak magnetic disk. The ship's two-meter dish rotated eighty degrees above the horizon, and the communication officer waited until the SIGINT satellite would be in position . . .

Three-hundred-seventy-two miles above the earth in a circular orbit with an inclination of 79.3 degrees the cylindrical-shaped, twenty-nine-metric-ton platform called Cosmos 1836 hurtled through space at over 18,000 miles an hour. The U.S. had code-named the satellite Proton II, and it had been carried into space only nine months earlier on a smaller version of the A-2 Soyuz booster. The satellite was designed to enhance the Kremlin's space-signal intelligence on telemetry interception, ferreting radar, ocean reconnaissance and communications . . .

With the push of a button the ship's coded signal was fired at Cosmos 1836. Traveling at the speed of light, the message was transmitted via ultra-high radio frequencies to the satellite, where it was relayed to the satellite-to-ground facilities at Viksjofjell.

VIKSJOFJELL GROUND STATION, USSR

Hidden under a large geodesic dome on top of a seventy-foot concrete tower two sophisticated UHF antennas, pointing in opposite directions, sat motionless in the cold Soviet night.

The signals from the *Sovremennyy* were recorded, decoded and logged by computer, then transmitted via a copper landline cable to naval headquarters in Moscow.

REYKJAVIK, ICELAND, NSA LISTENING POST

Two hundred miles to the east and three hundred miles higher than the Soviet Proton II relay satellite an older U.S. KH-11 moved its fifty-foot antenna two degrees to stay in line with the Soviet Cosmos. The quick blast of electronics sent to the Soviet satellite from the *Sovremennyy* had not stopped after being picked up by the Proton's receiving antennae. Its signal scattered in all directions like a beam of light reflecting off a polished cut-diamond. The KH-11 easily picked up the signal and stored it in its computer memory. Twelve seconds later it was transmitted to the ground station in Reykjavik, Iceland.

Master Sergeant Robby Neuman heard the sharp computer tone ring out from his console but did not look up. He continued to loosen the laces of his felt-lined packs.

"You got something coming in Robby," his partner said.

"Yeah, yeah I hear it," Neuman said under his breath. He looked up in time to see the words PRIORITY SIGNAL flashing on the upper part of his screen.

A KH-11 intercept.

The station's NEC 15GX-2200 series digital computer started to sort through the newly transmitted data. The four microprocessors converted the KH-11 information into a code the computer could manipulate. If the Soviet code was a familiar one it could be broken by the computer at the station level. If the code was unfamiliar it would be transmitted to the NSA computer bank in Fort Meade, Maryland. Neuman waited to see if his NEC computer knew the code to break the transmission.

Three minutes later he had his answer. "Bingo, we got it," he said.

He pulled his chair across the floor by his heels, the left rear wheel making a squeaking sound as he moved. "Got a hot one, sir," Neuman said to his lieutenant.

Lieutenant Philip "Woody" Woodward didn't respond. As senior officer on the floor, the lieutenant saw all his intercepts before they were retransmitted.

"It's off a KH-11, sir."

That caught the lieutenant's attention.

"A transmission from the Sovremennyy. They're tracking an unknown aircraft. Possibly a C-5, sir."

"Let me see that."

The lieutenant skimmed the message. "You show any scheduled comair or military flights in that area, sergeant?"

Neuman punched the information up on his screen. "None, sir."

Lieutenant Woodward studied the document for another minute, swiveled around in his chair to face the unoccupied communications center, then called the system up. A moment later he began to type the encrypted message that would be transmitted to the Pentagon.

STRATEGIC AIR COMMAND, OFFUTT AIR FORCE BASE

General Westcott read the message fresh in from the Pentagon via an NSA satellite downlink listening post in Reykjavik. The Soviet destroyer *Sovremennyy* had tracked only one large aircraft flying into Greenland and had wrongly identified it as a C-5A heavy transport.

"Hot *damn*," Westcott said out loud. He understood what was going on and why Duke was requesting permission to proceed. Duke's plan had worked, only Duke didn't know it.

"Major, contact the Nightstalker. Inform them OPERATION: LAREDO TRAIL is still a go. One aircraft in, one aircraft out."

NIGHTSTALKER, OVER CENTRAL GREENLAND

Tucker cocked his head to the right as he heard the hum of the computer printer. The B-2's communication equipment was receiving an EHF radio signal relayed via the Air Force's Milstar satellite-communication system. By using the stealth's ultrahigh-speed computers and the multiple array of available channels, communications to and from the bomber could be hidden and made near-impossible to jam or intercept. By typing up the messages and using computers rather than voice relay, the data could be sent in less than a fraction of a second.

When a low-pitch tone told him the message was complete, Tucker ripped it off the printer and held it low on his lap. The glowing red mix from the bomber's instruments supplied just enough light for him to read by.

"Command reports that a Soviet reconnaissance ship only tracked one aircraft into Greenland. We still have a green light." Tucker moved the paper back and forth to get the best angle on the available light. "They still don't know we're up here."

"What do you figure is their next move, captain?" Duke asked Koiser, who had been very unobtrusive up to this point.

"Standard procedure is to contact both the PVO and naval command centers. Remember though, they believe the *Sovremennyy* was tracking a C-5A transport. And right now it is so far out they probably won't worry about a single aircraft . . . at least not immediately. They will expect it to turn south and head for Greenland."

"And when it doesn't?"

"The long-range search radars at Pechenga will be waiting."

"All right, Tuck, tell SAC message received. We are on schedule and will proceed. Contact Crystal and that Extender. We're on our way." . . .

Fifteen minutes later Duke watched the green-and-red wingtip navigational lights of the KC-10 bank slowly to the south on its way to Reykjavik. The Extender quickly dropped down to 1000 feet and slowed to 230 knots on its way to Iceland.

"Okay, baby it's just you and me now," Duke said under his breath. He glanced over and checked his airspeed and altitude,

382 knots at 32,000 feet. Fifteen-hundred feet straight ahead was the B-52 Crystal Flight. In seven minutes they would be over the eastern coast of Greenland, and if intelligence was right, five minutes later they should pick up the first weak sweeps of a Soviet long-range Tall King early warning radar.

PECHENGA, PVO EARLY WARNING RADAR STATION, USSR

Located on the rocky north shore of the Kola Peninsula less than a kilometer away from the Norwegian border sat the weathered and rust-stained buildings that housed one of the PVO's front-line early warning air-defense radars. Built soon after World War II the station had undergone several upgrades. The latest was the installation of the P-14 and P-12 radars in the late sixties. Their single mission was to give the PVO sufficient warning of an American bomber attack and pass on the data to fire-and-control radars that directed the fire of eighty-nine SA-2 and SA-3 surface-to-air missiles.

The control center was dead silent with only a single officer on duty to oversee the three technicians operating the equipment. This night was like all others, long, boring and uneventful.

B-52H CRYSTAL FLIGHT

General Preston hit the switch and turned the rear anticollision lights on and off three times to signal the B-2 of his intentions.

The General drew a deep breath. "All systems up and running?"

"Now or never, sir." Major Martin reached over and advanced the eight throttles on the center console of the B-52 to full power.

Both men watched as their airspeed increased through 450 knots. The deafening sound of the eight engines at full power filled the cockpit. Martin pushed the yoke forward to drop the nose of the big bomber seven degrees and start their descent from 32,000 to 5000 feet.

NIGHTSTALKER

Duke followed the B-52's lead, staying 1000 yards behind. As they approached the Soviet coast he slowly decreased the distance between the two aircraft until they were less than 300 feet apart. At that point Crystal Flight planned its breakaway, which would leave him alone to penetrate Soviet airspace.

"You got anything, Tuck?" Duke asked, referring to the stealth's electronic and radar sensors.

"Nothing, Duke. We should be in range at any time." Tucker watched his center CRT, waiting for the analyzer and IBM computer to pick up and identify the Soviet long-range radar as soon as its signal was strong enough to detect. He did not have to wait long.

"I got it, I show one . . . no, two search radars to the southeast . . . sweeping at one five six degrees." Tucker read off the information as if it were routine. He did not feel routine. The IBM computer instantly identified both radars operating on an A-Band frequency.

Grigori Koiser watched the same information appear on the computer screen in front of him—two radars, one with a sweep rate of 2–6 RPMs on a frequency of 147–161 MHz, the other with a sweep rate of 2–4 RPMs on a frequency of 153–167 MHz. The NATO code names of Spoon Rest and Tall King appeared on the upper part of Koiser's screen.

"They should acquire Crystal in less than two minutes," Tucker said.

Duke's eyes shifted to the TWP on the center of his console just as a single yellow light flickered on, showing an A-Band threat to the southeast. If and when the radar achieved a lock-on the warning light would change to a flashing red. His attention moved back to the HUD. The B-2's rate of descent was 2500 feet a minute, speed 462 knots.

PECHENGA, PVO EARLY WARNING RADAR STATION, USSR

The senior sergeant on watch rubbed his eyes, trying to remove the sleep. A pulsating buzz from the right side of his scope brought him to life. He reached over and turned off the warning. Before saying a word he quickly double-checked his equipment to make sure it wasn't a false alarm. After that he flipped through his current data, checking the scheduled traffic in his sector.

"I show an unidentified target bearing three one two." He waited, not sure if the major had heard him. "Altitude 5000 meters and descending, speed 456 knots."

The major walked over behind the sergeant.

"Three hundred ten kilometers out, it's running parallel to our coast, sir."

"How long before it will enter our airspace?"

The sergeant thought for a second, he had been doing this too long, no need to reference the computer. "Approximately thirty-five minutes, sir."

The major watched the single luminescent green dot slowly moving across the scope. "Is it one of ours?"

"Not likely, sir. Its flight pattern, west to east, suggests it is flying out of Greenland. I have already checked current reported flight plans and they show no aircraft should be in the area." The sergeant adjusted the gray knobs on his control panel, trying to focus the radar blip.

"Speed increasing . . . 516 knots, altitude now 4200 meters. It's still heading toward the east and descending."

"I'll contact regimental headquarters. It's possible one of our bombers is off-course and having radio problems."

B-52H CRYSTAL FLIGHT

Major Martin listened to the faint pinging sound of the Tall King radar in his headset as it swept across the right side of the B-52. His eyes went from the altimeter to his Tactical Mission Computer showing only forty-five seconds to break-point Delta.

"Eleven thousand five hundred," General Preston called out. "Airspeed 552 knots and climbing."

"Throttle back . . . eighty-five percent," Martin cautioned.

Preston responded by pulling the throttles back slowly with the palm of his hand as he scanned the tachometer for each of the eight engines. "Ten thousand, eight, seven, five, three, two, one. Break now, major."

Martin used all his strength to turn the hard black metal yoke of his bomber to the right. The B-52 shuddered as it banked hard right, dipping its right wing at a forty-five degree angle and continued to dive toward 5000 feet. Martin kept steady pressure on the yoke for twenty seconds, bringing the B-52 to a new heading of 197. With his nose still pointing seven degrees down, Martin brought the bomber out of its steep turn as quickly as it had begun.

The Gs fell off and the pilots felt the biting pressure of their restraint harnesses ease up. They were closing at the radar site at over 500 knots. The B-52 was pointed straight at the radar center, to allow . . . to ensure . . . the Soviets a strong radar-return signal.

NIGHTSTALKER, TURNING SOUTH

Duke dropped the right wing of the stealth and slammed each man into his seat with the sudden force of 3.5 Gs. He watched the distant stars move across his windscreen as he forced the B-2 to follow the B-52 ahead of them.

The strobe of the two early-warning radars loomed in the distance. Duke and Tucker were aware the older, by U.S. standards outdated, Tall King and Spoon Rest radars were nonetheless real dangers. Because of the A-Band frequency, which operated on the long end of the radar spectrum, it was *possible* for the Soviets to pick them up in some fashion. The B-2's design made it less likely to be picked up by the shorter and faster pulsing frequencies of Soviet fire-control radars used by SAMs and triple-A's; I/J, I, J, J/K and K-Bands.

"I see no change," Tucker said. Only the single yellow radar-warning light remained on. "They're still only painting us with an A-Band and I'm showing no increase in power level."

The B-2 shook up and down slightly as Duke brought the bomber wings level and slipped in the stealth directly behind the B-52. With the two bombers only a hundred yards apart the air turbulence from the B-52 caused the B-2 to be tossed around.

Duke backed off the throttles and nosed the Nightstalker up slightly, decreasing his airspeed.

"One hundred twenty seven miles to the border. Nineteen minutes," Tucker said.

"Captain Koiser . . ." Duke hesitated. "How long before they'll be able to acquire us, you figure?"

"With the P-12 and P-14 A-Band systems . . . it depends on the operator. If he is very good they may do it as soon as the B-52 breaks to the west."

"I guess we'll know soon enough," Duke muttered. "Make sure you're strapped in tight. When the Fifty-two makes her break we're going downtown fast and hard."

He tugged on each of his shoulder straps, then snapped his oxygen mask in place.

PECHENGA, PVO EARLY WARNING RADAR STATION, USSR

The open-frame wire antenna slowly rotated in the darkness.

The major set the telephone back on the receiver. "Command reports no Soviet aircraft currently in that sector." He hurried back to the sergeant. "Status?"

"The target has turned, sir. New heading one nine five . . . straight for us. Speed 518 knots, altitude 1600 meters."

"Can you identify?"

"No, sir. However, the signal is much stronger and it is no longer decreasing in altitude. I show it 210 kilometers out . . . twelve minutes before it enters our airspace."

"I need more information."

"I have seen this before, sir . . . normally it suggests a big aircraft with large wing-mounted turbofans."

The major watched the scope. With each minute he liked the situation less. Finally he turned to the radio operator. "Open up all radio frequencies, broadcast the warning message."

B-52H CRYSTAL FLIGHT

General Preston thought about how two years ago a squadron of MiGs would already have been on their way, ready to fire at anything that moved. Now the Soviets were broadcasting a message. They didn't need another KAL 007 disaster.

"Ignore it, major," the general said. "I want them to sweat this out a few more minutes. Go to full power."

Martin advanced the throttles forward.

"Hold on, baby, hold on." The general watched the airspeed indicator climb through 585 knots. In six minutes they would break to the west and the B-2 would be on her own.

NIGHTSTALKER

Tucker focused his eyes on the computer data in front of him.

"Radar-power output shows 350 Kilowatts, Duke. They're taking a hard look."

"That's the P-14 radars' strongest output," Koiser added. "They are trying to identify us."

"Us or the B-52?" Duke asked. He watched the B-52's black outline against the dark gray background half a mile ahead of them, moving away fast . . .

PECHENGA, PVO EARLY WARNING RADAR STATION, USSR

"Eighty-five kilometers out," the sergeant announced, "speed now 620 knots."

The major picked up the phone that tied him directly to Murmansk air base. "This is Major Kashin . . . we are tracking an unknown target now eighty-five kilometers out. Heading one nine four, altitude 1600 meters . . . speed 600 knots. I am requesting an interception."

"Stand by."

The major felt blood rush to his face. "Stand by? I have an unknown target about to enter our airspace. I need two MiGs up there to give us a visual and—"

The sergeant broke in: "Major, the target is breaking to the west."

The major watched as the radar blip located in the lower center of the scope made a quick turn to the left.

"It's gaining altitude . . . 1700 meters and climbing."

The major started to report to Murmansk, then stopped. He had no idea what to say.

B-52H CRYSTAL FLIGHT

Martin kept steady pressure on the yoke, holding it back as the big bomber climbed through 8000 feet on its way to 35,000. Their new heading would take them due west back over the Greenland Sea.

"One more mile and we can tell the boys back home we've been to the Soviet Union and back," Martin said.

Preston wasn't amused but continued to look at that radar-warning panel, hoping its signal stayed strong and clear.

"Do you think they'll make it, sir?" Martin asked the general.

"By the time we land stateside we should have the answer."

PECHENGA, PVO EARLY WARNING RADAR STATION, USSR

"I am sorry to wake you, colonel, but the target is now turning to the west," the major reported uneasily. "I do not believe it to be a threat at this time and am no longer requesting MiGs to intercept it . . ."

One did not need to be on the phone to imagine the annoyance of the regimental commander being awakened to be told about a false alarm.

"Yes, sir I understand . . . you will have my report in the morning . . . yes, sir. Good night." The major hung up, not looking forward to the morning.

Meanwhile the sergeant's eyes moved from the blip representing the B-52 and swept the rest of the screen. About an inch from the bottom he noticed a long thin fuzzy-shaped object rapidly leaving the scope. He quickly adjusted the controls, trying to get a clearer picture.

"Major . . . I believe I have something else. I'm not sure, its return is very weak, almost as if it—"

"Sergeant, what the hell are you telling me now? *Do* you or do you *not* have a target?"

"I think I do . . . heading one nine two, speed 480 knots, altitude 1000 meters. It should be over our coast in three minutes." He bent closer to the screen.

"Show me," the major ordered.

"It's, it's . . . right here, sir." The sergeant pointed to the faint, almost transparent line on the scope. His lack of confidence was obvious.

"That is not a target, sergeant. I suggest you keep your concentration here." And he pointed to the bright green blip that represented the B-52. "This is your target. Now don't disturb me unless it comes back and heads for our airspace."

The sergeant watched the faint line grow closer to the very bottom of his scope until it disappeared, then, as ordered, shifted his attention back to the left side of his scope and the B-52.

NIGHTSTALKER

Duke banked the B-2 slowly to the west. Ahead he could make out the broken coastline of the Soviet Union only a few miles away. The foaming waves of the Barents Sea struck the rocks in the moonlight and marked the way. To the south was the town of Murmansk, the largest city on the Kola Peninsula. Updated intelligence showed a squadron of MiG-29 Fulcrums had recently been transferred there.

Duke banked back to the east and dropped the Nightstalker slowly to 2500 feet above the frozen ground. The plan called for them to skirt the Finnish border for 150 miles before turning east across the White Sea. If they encountered any danger they could break for Finland and hightail it to a recovery base in Norway.

The Threat Warning Panel was now clear. The stealth's sensors were not picking up any hostile radars sweeping the area.

"Holding steady at 2500 feet," Duke said.

18

DECEPTION

SAC HEADQUARTERS, OFFUTT AIR FORCE BASE

"They're over the fence." General Westcott watched the blue blip of the Nightstalker move south across the Soviet Kola Peninsula. It showed the stealth only a few miles from the Finnish border, snaking its way deeper into enemy territory.

The general reached over and picked up the phone, punched a five-digit code that put him in direct contact with the Joint Chiefs of Staff Chairman, General Jack Dawson.

"General Dawson here."

"Jack, this is Lamar. They just crossed the coast."

"What's their status?"

"About ten miles inland."

"Any trouble?"

"No, so far it's gone as planned. They followed the B-52 all the way in. Our listening posts in Norway haven't picked up anything. I'll keep you posted."

Westcott rubbed the side of his head as a hundred images of the air war in Vietnam played out in his mind. He had almost forgotten the feeling of ordering men into combat. Of sitting back safe and helpless, watching, waiting.

RAMENSKOYE TEST CENTER

It was 5:30 a.m. when Belikov emerged from the officers' quarters in the back of the center.

He was now in total command of the computer center. General Yefimov had been recalled to PVO Headquarters in Moscow to report to the General Secretary on the progress of tying the super radar into the SAM network. Belikov did not envy the general.

He walked up now to the desk in the center of the overhanging control room and looked over the edge, pleased to see the computer center running smoothly under the command of Major Slikuna. Belikov hit the intercom on the desk.

"Major . . . report."

Slikuna swallowed hard, turned and looked up at the glass control room.

"Everything is normal, sir." He wanted to start positive. "Earlier the station at Pechenga was tracking an unidentified target coming in from the north, it turned west before entering our airspace—"

"Why didn't you wake me!"

The major was glad he had rehearsed his speech before the colonel woke up. "Sir, the aircraft didn't violate our airspace. With the information I received from Pechenga I believed there was no danger so I didn't disturb you." He paused to see if the colonel would react. He didn't. "I believe it was an American reconnaissance aircraft."

Belikov considered it. True, it was not unusual for NATO RC-135 electronic spy planes to prowl off the northern coast of Norway.

"Where is the target now?"

Major Slikuna referenced his computer screen. "Distance one hundred nineteen kilometers out, heading west."

Belikov took his finger off the intercom button ending the conversation. An uneasy feeling came over him. Why would an American aircraft run at their border without trying to collect any data? No MiGs were in the area. It didn't add up.

NIGHTSTALKER

"Company," Tucker said, pointing to two red triangles representing the unknown targets in the upper right corner of the HUD.

"I see them," Duke said.

Underneath the triangles red letters spelled out their heading and altitude. Duke's attention stayed on the HUD. The B-2's large focal-plane infrared imaging sensors, located along each of the wings' leading edges, had picked up the low infrared signature of two aircraft over thirty miles away, heading south, high and away from the bomber.

"Can you I.D. them?"

"They're too far out," Tucker told him.

"They are probably MiG-23s out of Kirovsk. This is their sector to patrol," Koiser put in.

Duke looked at his copilot. "Punch it up, Tuck."

Tucker tapped on the computer keyboard a couple of times. A moment later an outline of a MiG-23 appeared in the lower center of the HUD. To the left, the model numbers appeared— A, B, BN, MF, U—as well as its performance data, range and weapons system.

"Keep an eye on them." Duke unhinged his oxygen mask, letting it hang from his helmet, then rolled the B-2 left to take it a little further away from the Finnish border.

So far, so good. Or so it seemed. The PVO wasn't painting his aircraft with any radar waves and there was no sign of the impact of any super-radar system. So why didn't he feel secure? Mostly, because in twelve minutes it would be decision time. He could either turn west and end the mission by landing in Norway, or he could turn east and head inland to the target. He liked to think he could make the decision at the right time on the evidence. But inside he knew himself too well . . . he had already made up his mind to take the Nightstalker east.

"I'm picking up a weak A-Band to the south." Tucker was glued to his computer screen.

"Here we go," Duke said under his breath as he snapped his mask back into place. He nosed the bomber up one degree until they were at 3000 feet, heading 203. As he scanned the stealth's instruments the yellow A-Band warning light on the TWP came on. The radar signal was strong enough for the Nightstalker's sensors to pick it up and analyze it.

"Looks like we also have an F-Band further to the south." Tucker was quiet for a while as he tried to get his equipment to lock in on the beam-width and pulse-repetition of each radar. He turned to Duke. "The A-Band is a Back Trap Frequency 2815 to 2835 Megahertz. Looks like the F-Band is a Big Bird."

Duke didn't waver from his course, feeling his way down the border.

BELOMORSK, PVO EARLY WARNING STATION

On a high rock cliff three kilometers from the White Sea the P-16 Back Trap antenna rotated in a circle covering a range out to 360 kilometers with each pass. The Belomorsk station had originally been built for the P-14 Tall King radar and was updated to the P-16 system in the early 1970s. At that time the threat of the United States Air Force XB-70, U-2 and SR-71 was fresh in the PVO's mind. The current system was being constantly updated and was equipped with the most advanced SA-5 SAMs the Soviets could field. Along with the station's air defense role it was responsible for early-warning and ground-control along the central section of Norway.

A young roundfaced sergeant watched the two MiG-23s move down the eastern edge of the Finnish border. To his right sat the station senior radar operator, a first lieutenant five years senior. Tonight, however, it was the sergeant's turn to guide the fighters through the clear night sky.

"Hetman Flight, turn left to one three seven. Maintain 3000." He watched the aircraft move slightly on the scope coming around to their new heading.

The lieutenant took a drink of tea and leaned back in his chair, glad to share the responsibility.

"One hour and I will be home with my pretty bride," the sergeant said.

"Your pretty bride? How long have you been married?"

"About four months now . . ."

"No wonder you still think she is pretty. Wait a few years . . . like me."

The sergeant's face turned red, but he said nothing more to this unhappy cynic.

The lieutenant laughed and focused back on the amber-colored scope in front of him. To the far right of the center screen he watched a Soviet transport move slowly south, probably on its way to Gorky or Moscow. On the lower third of the scope he watched another aircraft move to the east, this one was a little faster. Underneath the blip were the symbols BNZ-12 and DCR. A commercial airliner broadcasting an Identify Friend or Foe signal.

The rest of the screen looked clear except for an occasional dense cloud or mountain ridge.

Then something caught his eye, a narrow oblong-shaped blip. It appeared out of focus, fuzzy. Then suddenly it faded out altogether, only to reappear again in a few seconds. The lieutenant watched it without saying a word. The out-of-focus image was heading southwest.

The sergeant also saw it. "Maybe it's a large flight of birds?"

The lieutenant dismissed the idea, he had never picked up birds on his screen, unless it was an extremely large flock and this did not appear to be that large.

Suddenly it swung due south and went out of sight. But then it appeared again a few seconds later, only this time it was heading south*east*, right behind the MiGs.

The lieutenant froze, something was out there shadowing the fighters. "I am taking control of the MiGs," he said.

The sergeant did not protest. If something was wrong, let the old cynic take the responsibility.

"Hetman leader . . . Belomorsk control. Take a new heading of two seven four. I am tracking a possible target at your six." Controlling fighters was not new to him. His last remark would get under their skin. No fighter pilot would ever knowingly let anyone approach from their six o'clock. "Target speed 320 knots heading one seven three, altitude 1000 meters."

"Confirmed, Belomorsk . . . making our turn." The two MiGs turned together.

The lieutenant watched the two interceptors make a slow

arcing turn to the west. They passed high and south of the target.

He keyed his mike. "Hetman leader, take a new heading . . . one seven five. Target should be below and to the north. Get a visual and advise."

The lieutenant turned to the station's communications center located in the front part of the room. "Monitor all channels," he called out.

MIG-23MF HETMAN LEAD, TURNING SOUTHEAST

The captain continued his turn, watching his compass swing around to the new heading. The ground controller had turned him almost completely around. Now he was being ordered to get a visual sighting of something when it was still too dark to see.

"I would like to get one of those idiots up here with me sometime. Maybe then they would understand," the MiG pilot thought aloud. This was not the first time a ground controller had sent him chasing after thin air. As far as he was concerned ground controllers were little more than people who couldn't fly, who sat their fat butts in their warm chairs and talked to men that could. Someday, he thought, he would be in command of a flight center and would put only pilots in charge of guiding aircraft.

The captain brought his fighter out of its steep banking turn and came wings level at 3000 meters, heading one seven five. He throttled to match the speed of the alleged target as he reached under his HUD and flipped on the MiG's High Lark look-down, shoot-down radar. He adjusted its power to ninety percent and positioned the five-square-meter radar antenna to forty-five-downward degrees. Within seconds the J-Band radar was up and running, filling the airwaves with bursts of electronic energy.

NIGHTSTALKER

Duke watched the artificial horizon come level as he completed the left turn. He pushed the throttles forward a half inch, increasing the bomber's speed to 480 knots. The altimeter read 3000 feet. The Nightstalker was heading east away from Finland, and a safe haven.

"They're coming around, colonel . . . high and behind us," Tucker warned.

Duke watched the two red symbols in the upper right side of the HUD.

The A-Band indicator light flashed from yellow to red and back to yellow, telling him the big Soviet Back Trap was sending a steady, powerful beam of radio waves at his aircraft. It had yet to achieve a lock-on.

Duke envisioned what was happening. The Back Trap radar operator wasn't sure what he had. He only knew something was out there. The B-2's shape and radar-absorbing skin were not designed to dissipate and scatter the long A-Band radio waves. The operator could see *something* on his scope, so in order to identify it he was vectoring the fighters into the area to get a visual on the unknown target.

Duke's mind raced. At 3000 feet the Back Trap radar had plenty of time to look at him. He banked the B-2 southwest and dropped its nose.

Let's see what you can do at low level, he thought, and gave the order to engage the TFR, the terrain following radar.

Tucker hit the button on the center console. Instantly the heavy bomber lurched forward and headed for the deck.

"Set maximum clearance for two hundred fifty feet . . . I want us in the dirt until we're over the water," Duke ordered.

Tucker felt the Gs build as they forced him back into his hard plastic seat. He strained as he reached for the flight-control computer to feed in the new information. He looked over at Duke, who was now resting his hands, one on each knee, as he monitored the stealth's controls.

The large bat-shaped aircraft headed for the frozen earth below at a thirty-degree angle, gaining speed with each second. At 600 feet the computerized flight system automatically reduced power to all four engines. A millisecond later the computer gave the command to bring the nose up. The two outboard elevators, located in the outmost back edge of each wing, worked in unison with the two trailing-edge exhaust nozzles to force the back of the bomber down and the nose up. Suddenly the B-2 began to level out. A steady four-G pull pinned each man tightly in place. The blackness of the ground gave way to the gray dawn sky behind the horizon as the stealth pointed up and away from the earth.

Duke felt his heart skip a beat. *It doesn't matter how many times I do it,* he thought. *Handing over the controls to a machine scares the hell out of me . . .*

"Targets now heading one eight three, colonel. Altitude 9000 feet and they're matching our speed . . . 420 knots . . . I show two pulse-Dopplers to the south. From the way they're flying I'd say they're in a search pattern. They're looking for us."

"Have you got an I.D. yet? I need to know what's hunting us."

"Info coming up now . . ." Tucker watched it flash on the CRT. "Combat identification shows it to be a J-Band air-to-air radar. Probably a High Lark." He looked over at Duke, catching the light of the instruments in his eyes. "It has a look-down shoot-down capability."

Koiser heard the concern in Tucker's voice. He keyed his mike. "Once we are over the White Sea we should be safe from the MiGs," he said. "The radar and computers on the twenty-threes are not good enough to define targets flying at one hundred fifty meters or lower over water. The pilots will not be able to lock onto anything . . ."

"Great, we only have another eighty-five miles to play hide and seek before we get to the White Sea," Duke said unhappily.

The Threat Warning Panel now showed the A-Band fifteen degrees to the east. The yellow F-Band light was out, for the moment it was no longer a threat. He took a deep breath and tried to settle down.

Now he felt a surge of power as the B-2 started to gain altitude. In the distance he could see a high hill. As the bomber crested the top, the F-Band warning light flashed back on . . . yellow . . . red . . . yellow. The cycle repeated. The B-2 was just high enough for the radar to paint it.

BELOMORSK, PVO EARLY WARNING STATION

"There it is again, major," the lieutenant put his finger on the glass, leaving a greasy smudge. "One hundred twelve kilometers out and still heading for the sea."

"Any input from the MiGs?" the major in charge of the station asked.

"No, sir, they have not found a thing, they are only able to search with radar. However, in fifteen minutes it should be light enough for them to get a visual."

Major Melekin nodded. He had never seen anything like this before. "Continue, lieutenant, inform me of any change." He walked back to his desk and picked up the phone. "Get me PVO regimental headquarters . . . Leningrad five six nine . . ."

RAMENSKOYE TEST CENTER

Colonel Belikov was no longer in the glass command post above the main control center. He felt more in control being on the floor next to the big display screen, the men and equipment.

The uneasy feeling he'd first had when Major Slikuna briefed him about the night's activities had not left him. He continued to wonder why the Americans would fly straight at an early warning center and then veer off at the last moment just because they knew they were being watched? Why not penetrate Soviet airspace and wait for a reaction? That was the standard method of checking a country's response time. And the fact there were no electronic signals being picked up ate at him. The ringing phone broke into his thoughts.

"Colonel, I have General Vishenkov on the telephone."

General Vishenkov was the first PVO Deputy Commander in charge of air security in the northwest region in Leningrad. Before Belikov picked up the phone he studied the area around the city. The display showed nothing unusual.

"General, this is Colonel Belikov."

"Colonel, I have received word our station at Belomorsk is attempting to track a target in the airspace west of the White Sea. They are unable to identify the target. Is the network oper-

ational in that area?" The general did not like having to ask a
colonel about the status of the Kremlin's most secret project. He
had been briefed on the capabilities of the radar network only
days before.

"General, please explain . . . 'attempting to track'?"

"That is *correct*, colonel. It seems the return fades in and out.
Two MiGs are trying to intercept, but we cannot pass off con-
trol. Do you understand me?" The general's fuse was short. The
MiGs could not pick up the target on their radar screens.

Belikov stared up at the screen. "We only have two radars in
that sector tied into the network, sir. The P-14 at Pechenga in
the north overlooking the Arctic and the P-29L at Petrozavodsk,
which also controls the SA-10 sites north of Leningrad."

Which meant to the general that he would have to find the
target using standard PVO tactics. The super radar was not yet
operational in that particular sector. His next question especially pained him to ask . . ." On that information, do I have a
go-ahead to engage the target? I believe it is hostile."

Belikov allowed himself a tight-lipped smile. Secretary Tomskiy had not lied, he truly was in command.

"You have permission to engage target, sir."

The line went dead. Belikov looked back up at the Kola Peninsula. Was the general too cautious or had something, indeed,
entered the Soviet Union? Colonel Belikov decided he was
about to find out.

NIGHTSTALKER

The strong *pang pang pang* of the MiG-23's powerful Pulse-
Doppler search-radar sent a chill through Duke James as he
listened to it in his helmet. The lead Soviet fighter was less than
a quarter of a mile away to the north, on a parallel course. The
second MiG angled away to the south, its radar fading in the
distance, about a mile away.

Duke was waiting for the warning tone to sound in his helmet that indicated a radar locked onto Nightstalker. With
enough time to search, the MiGs would, eventually, probably
find them. The large surface area of the top of the B-2 could
absorb ninety-six percent of the J-Band radar hitting it. Not one

hundred. If the MiG pilots were sufficiently well-trained on their radar equipment they just might be able to distinguish the stealth from the ground clutter on their scope.

"This is pissing me off," Tucker said. "No matter which way we turn those bastards are on us like flies on shit. Each time we pull up over a hill that Back Trap is able to get a new fix on us."

The TWP continued to show the Back Trap as it painted the stealth at a fifteen-degree angle. They continued to head east, the sea only fifty-seven miles away.

Duke reached over and took hold of the control stick, which at the same time automatically disengaged the B-2's terrain following radar.

"*Now* let's see if you can find us," he muttered.

He smashed the throttles forward and moved the stick back and to the right. The B-2 went into a steep climbing turn to the southeast. The sudden maneuver put the stealth almost on its side. The horizon intersected the cockpit window at a right angle as the massive aircraft climbed away from the ground in a slicing turn. Duke waited for the airspeed indicator to read 500 knots with an altitude of 800 feet before he pulled out of the turn and came level. The threat warning panel showed the strong A-Band dead ahead.

"What the hell . . . ?" Tucker wasn't following Duke's line of thought.

"We don't have a choice, Tuck. If we maintain our current heading, running TFR, chances are those MiGs will find us. That Back Trap is guiding them. Pretty soon it will be light . . . light enough for them maybe to get a visual on us. Our least exposed radar cross section is when we run straight at a target, and that's an older A-Band."

The Nightstalker continued on its level course.

"I'll bet you a cold beer at Nick's Bar that if we run straight at them at maximum speed that A-Band will have a hell of a time tracking us," Duke said, and nosed up a few degrees, letting the B-2 climb through 1000 feet. The HUD showed the two MiGs fading away behind them.

"You're on, colonel," Tucker said, figuring he could only win by losing.

BELOMORSK PVO EARLY WARNING STATION

"I understand, sir." Commanding officer Major Melekin hung up, completing his conversation with regimental headquarters. He turned to the lieutenant.

"Status?"

The lieutenant squinted hard as he felt the strain of the last ten hours in the dark control center. "Target turning . . ." The faint transparent blip disappeared off the scope. He kept his eyes focused on the same area and waited for it to reappear. Twenty seconds later it did, except not where he expected.

"Now heading . . . oh nine three. Speed increasing." He swiveled around to face the major. "It is heading right at us."

The major's voice boomed through to the command center. "Recall the MiGs. Bring the SAMs to combat ready."

NIGHTSTALKER

The stealth streaked over a small rock-ridge, clearing it by less than 100 feet. Traveling at Mach .95, the air vortices streaming off the wingtips caused enough force to disturb fist-size rocks resting loosely on the ground.

At full power the B-2's four engines sucked in over 500 cubic meters of air a second, compressing, heating and blasting them out the rear of the aircraft. The stealth's especially designed S-shaped inlet ducts on the upper part of each wing were a maze of triangles . . . an extraordinary shape that broke up incoming radar waves as they traveled over the bomber. The radio waves entered the ducts and were channeled back and forth into the radar absorbent material that lined the inlet until the energy dissipated. Since the incoming radar waves never hit the whirling metal parts of the turbofan energy could not be reflected back. The airflow was split before it entered the main duct, which allowed a constant flow of undisturbed air into the engines.

Duke banked the bomber three degrees right and watched the needle on the Threat Warning Panel, the TWP, roll to zero. The lower center CRT, which contained a 3-D picture of the terrain ahead, showed uneven and broken hills. He nosed the Nightstalker up to 800 feet, a safer altitude. The Back Trap was now straight ahead. He pushed the throttles forward.

Tucker watched the MiGs disappear off the edge of the HUD. "We're clear of the MiGs, colonel."

"A-Band operating at peak power," Koiser reported.

Duke was starting to have doubts. He'd hoped they wouldn't run into this much trouble until they were deep inside the Soviet Union. The HUD showed only forty-six miles to the early-warning station. A little less than five minutes. Still, after that they would be over the White Sea and he could drop the stealth down to two hundred feet and use the background clutter of the water to hide in.

He noted the airspeed display to the right of the heading symbol, 619 knots and climbing. The Mach meter read 1.02. They had slipped into the supersonic zone without even noticing.

"You got to hand it to the engineers, she's a dream to fly," Duke said to no one in particular.

SA-5 SITE, NORTH OF BELOMORSK

The order couldn't have come at a worse time. The SAM site, located approximately twenty-two kilometers from the Belomorsk PVO Early Warning Station, was in a transition state. The night crew had just shut down all the systems as the day shift was coming on board. This happened every twelve hours, once in the morning and then again that evening for the night crew.

The Back Trap radar station was surrounded by three SA-5 emplacements—one to the south, one to the north and the largest one directly west of the radar. Located at the rear of the west site was a mid-frequency H-Band fire-control radar—NATO code name, Square Pair. Scattered out randomly in front of the H-Band were ten missile launchers, each loaded with a single 1500-pound surface-to-air missile.

The gray-haired master sergeant slipped into the cold metal seat of the command trailer. A thick white frost, he noted, covered the inside of the windows. As he affixed his headset the loud shouts of an angry ground controller rang in his ears.

"Confirm launch order at once, confirm launch order . . ."

"Ah . . . Sergeant Masashina here. Repeat order."

Major Melekin cut in. "We are tracking an unknown target. Now heading zero nine six. It will pass to the northeast of your position in four minutes. Engage and fire. Do you understand me, sergeant? Engage and fire."

"Confirmed, sir. Engage and fire." Masashina hit a set of switches, getting his radar up and running.

Four minutes, he thought, not enough time. From the sound of the major's voice he didn't have a choice. Fire at *something* . . .

NIGHTSTALKER

Duke was not surprised. The HUD display showed an SA-5 Square Pair H-Band radar operating at 6.62–6.99 GHz sweeping in front of them. Its target-acquisition radar was moving from the south across the front of the stealth.

"SA-5 . . . a bad choice," Tucker said. "I think we're in luck, colonel."

"I'll take it." Duke jinked the B-2 right and then left to try to break up the signal from the Back Trap. The seductive yellow A-Band warning light continued to pulse back and forth to red. Six inches away, on the Threat Warning Panel, the H-Band Square Pair warning light jumped to life.

Duke had been well-enough briefed to know the more powerful early warning radar would be handing off its information to the smaller fire-control radar at the SAM site as they drew closer. If he could delay the handoff, say, for a minute, he could blast past the SAM site without a scratch. What he couldn't figure out was why the PVO was trying to attack them with an SA-5, a long-range high-altitude missile designed to counter high-flying Mach-3 aircraft the U.S. had canceled some years ago. His B-2 was coming in at only 800 feet and Mach 1.

"Two minutes thirty seconds to the coast," Tucker said.

"I don't like this. Intel has fucked us up once already tonight. Didn't warn us about that destroyer off the coast of Greenland. Koiser . . . you have anything to add?" Duke said.

Koiser continued to study the new radar data on his screen.

He too was confused. Obviously this area wasn't yet tied into the major system yet. Only two radars were painting them and none had achieved a lock-on.

"What is the danger of the H-Band?" Koiser asked Duke.

"An H-Band can't pick us up. The operator will never see us."

"Why the SA-5?" Koiser asked, thinking out loud what Duke had wondered about. "It can easily be tied into the search-and-control radar. Possibly it is the only missile in the area. The PVO can't give every early-warning center overlapping SAM coverage with multiple systems." But he knew that waiting to the south there were areas where the PVO had overlapping SAM coverage, each different SAM defending at the same time. He didn't look forward to them.

Duke brought the Nightstalker back to the left and held steady, the outboard drag-rudders splitting on each wingtip to prevent the bomber from sliding back and forth. Speed was 690 knots, altitude 900 feet.

"How about the treetop approach," Duke muttered as he pushed the stick forward, and with the agility of a fighter the stealth headed for the deck.

BELOMORSK PVO EARLY WARNING STATION

"Find it . . . now!" The major straightened up, his shoulders aching from stooping over the radarscope.

The operator tried to boost the power. No luck. "It's gone, sir." He felt panicky. The target had dropped off the scope some thirty seconds ago and had not reappeared.

"It must have dropped down," he said. The closer the target got to his antenna the easier it was for it to slide in under the radar beam. He dropped the search angle of the antenna ten degrees, and the upper fourth of his scope filled with ground clutter. He studied the middle portion of the screen for a few seconds.

"Contact, major," the lieutenant said as he watched the ever changing smudge move quickly toward the center of his scope.

"Altitude?"

"I'm not able to define, sir. Too much ground interference."
The major swore. "Fire when ready."

SA-5 SITE, NORTH OF BELOMORSK

The sergeant hurried through the last of his prelaunch check
list.

"Target . . . eighteen kilometers north, fourteen east. Heading one nine five." Short pause. "Fire when ready," the order
came again.

At what? the operator wondered to himself. His radarscope
was clear. No blip, no static, nothing.

He keyed the radio mike. "Control, unable to engage. Unable
to find target."

The faster pulsating radar waves of the H-Band had been absorbed by the stealth's outer skin. Without the site being linked
up to the master computer in Ramenskoye it would not be able
to acquire the B-2 as it approached head on.

"Transfer command at once," the major ordered.

The sergeant set his power output to one-hundred percent
and turned on the data relay switch. By way of two redundant
underground data relay cables the Early Warning Radar then
did take command of the SAMs.

NIGHTSTALKER

Black had slowly turned to gray as the eastern sky grew pale. As
long shadows filled the interior of the B-2's cockpit Duke got his
first glimpse of the Russian landscape. Snow, rocks and scrub
brush covered the gently curving hills. To his left he could make
out a single-lane gravel road. In the sky ahead a few purple
clouds hung low over the horizon.

Duke looked straight ahead, using peripheral vision and instinct to fly the bomber. Traveling at 1000 feet per second only

200 feet above ground the slightest mistake could be fatal. No more so, he decided, than the alternative that faced them.

"Power level increasing," Tucker observed. The B-2's radar sensor recorded the H-Band Square Pair as it went to a full eighteen kilohertz.

Duke did not acknowledge. The color display on the HUD showed him the best possible path through the airspace in front of them.

"It's gone, colonel, disappeared. H-Band is gone," Tucker announced as the yellow warning light on the TWP flickered out.

"They're using the A-Band to control the missiles," Koiser said, "they can't pick us up with the smaller fire-control unit—"

"Can they do that?" Tucker's relief quickly dissipated.

"It can be done. I've seen it tested on high-altitude aircraft." Koiser kept his eyes on his display.

"I show a launch . . . ten o'clock," Tucker yelled. "TWP shows one . . . no, make that two . . ."

The Threat Warning Panel lit up. Two launch-warning lights began to flash red. A fluorescent orange SAM LAUNCH symbol appeared in the lower left corner of the HUD.

Ten kilometers to the north the SA-5's four wraparound solid-fuel boosters ignited, spewing a streamer of white smoke behind the launcher. A split-second later the dual-thrust first stage of the thirty-four-foot-long missile roared to life and lifted into the air. Moments later a second missile 100 meters away streaked off its transloader.

Duke broke hard left and came across the beam of the accelerating missiles at a forty-five-degree angle. Within seconds he and Tucker could see the white vapor of the SAMs exhaust streaking toward them from the south.

Duke pulled back on the stick to gain more altitude to maneuver, broke through 600 feet and banked hard right in the opposite direction, bringing the B-2 wings levels and back in line with the hostile radar. He pulled the nose back and put the bomber into a shallow climb.

"Keep your eyes on those SAMs."

"I got 'em, I got 'em." Tucker turned his head halfway around and looked straight out the top of the cockpit windows. The SA-5s rocketed above and away from the bomber at 2500 feet a second on their way to Mach 3.9. At 10,000 feet both missiles exploded in a brilliant yellow ball when the warheads detonated and the resulting explosion ignited the remaining solid-rocket fuel in each missile.

The launch-warning lights were now off, the TWP was clear. Only the nagging yellow A-Band warning remained on.

Duke steadied the stealth at 1500 feet. "What the hell are they trying to do?"

Koiser knew the answer. "The PVO cannot attack us with this system. We are too low and moving too fast. And we are now in the SAMs' minimum range. They cannot track us so they are trying to hit something . . . anything."

"Thirty seconds to the coast," Tucker said.

Duke was quiet. He could see the charcoal gray water of the White Sea only three miles ahead. To the left he saw a group of lights in a small cluster that he guessed to be the Back Trap early-warning station. He didn't have time to look for the antenna.

As the B-2 flashed over the coast, Duke turned to Tucker. "They want something to shoot at. Let's give them something. Punch up a TALD."

Tucker nodded as he moved to activate the Tactical Air Launch Decoy.

"Decoy guidance programmed and ready, colonel. Set to start transmitting at 500 feet."

"How far away from the site do we need to be, captain?"

"A minimum of thirty kilometers, forty would be better," Koiser told him.

They were only seven miles east of the Back Trap, heading away. Its signal was already growing weak. Koiser was right. The A-Band was having trouble finding them over the water, they would have to wait another three minutes before launching. The B-2's forward-looking sensors showed nothing. No other radars were in the area.

Duke eased Nightstalker down through 1200 feet, still worried that Back Trap might acquire them again. He throttled back and decreased speed to 450 knots, feeling uneasy about the prospect of being fired at. It had been over twenty years, after all, since he'd last faced death in the air. But they had not been picked up by the new Soviet radar, and he had never thought for a minute it would be easy penetrating the northern coast. Now, if the decoy worked as advertised they could pull a disappearing act. He readjusted his grip on the stick and sucked in a long breath as Nightstalker continued its slow descent.

Stacked away in the left interior weapons bay a single nine-foot-long, 400 pound light gray Sanders ALQ-316 tactical missile-decoy ran through its final computerized self-checks. The high-speed flight computers aboard the B-2 programmed the decoy's main microprocessor with speed, heading and false target data. The concept, originally designed by the navy to defeat semiactive air-to-air-missiles, transmitted a false frequency greater than the illuminating radar's reflected echo. The idea was that the decoy's signal strength was high enough to make it a more attractive target than the stealth. Once launched, the decoy deployed a transmission antenna, flew along its programmed path at speeds up to Mach 0.95 as it transmitted false data by mimicking the radar return. It could cover over fifty miles of territory, and the miniature receiver-transmitter could be updated while in flight. The decoy's course could be changed and the frequency-power boosted along with increasing or decreasing its speed and altitude. On an enemy radar operator's scope it would look, act and fly like a real aircraft.

As they passed through twenty-five miles east, Duke keyed his mike. "Let's do it."

Tucker flipped open the power supply for the weapons-bay doors. Duke felt the computer trim-up the bomber, the drag of the open weapons-bay doors causing a slight yaw to the left. Duke then gave the order to launch.

The missile-decoy jettisoned from the bomber, its ten-inch forward-folding control fins deployed as it hit the cold air. It descended fifty feet, which allowed its turbojet to spool up, then started to fly under its own power.

Duke counted slowly to three, then banked the bomber hard, high and to the right. He waited to make sure the decoy was clear before he brought the stealth back left, leveling out and dropping the nose. Without taking his eyes off the HUD, he pointed Nightstalker to the water and traded altitude for airspeed.

"I got it . . . nine o'clock and climbing," Tucker said, and turned back to his computer screen. "Looks okay, engine coming to full power, control surfaces deployed."

Duke caught sight of the decoy-missile as it angled upward at forty-five degrees, even with the stealth and only 200 yards away. He banked toward the decoy, slid in underneath and leveled-out at 500 feet. If the Back Trap was looking at them when the decoy started to transmit Duke didn't want the operators to see two different returns. He waited for the signal from Tucker that the decoy had started to broadcast its false radar-return.

"Contact, I show an A-Band return signal," Tucker said. He double-checked the decoy's readings. "That little sweetheart is running perfect. Keep it up, baby, keep it up."

Duke put forward pressure on the stick and dropped down to 100 feet over the water. A light haze made it difficult to see more than a couple of miles out, but Duke also knew that should make it harder for anyone to spot them from above.

RAMENSKOYE TEST CENTER

Colonel Belikov watched the screen out of the corner of his eye. The Kola Peninsula was quiet. His hand gripped the telephone, hard. "Are you still tracking the target?"

"No, colonel, it is now somewhere out over the White Sea but we are not able to find it." Major Melekin flinched as the words left his lips.

Belikov hung up and swung around to face the display screen. Why couldn't the fire-control radar track the target . . . if there really was one? And Belomorsk, of all places to enter the Soviet Union . . . only two long-range early-warning radars on the northern coast had not been tied into the network —Belomorsk in the northwest and Amderma in the northern part of the Urals. How could an enemy know that? If the enemy *was* there . . .

He went over to the nearest computer station. "Lieutenant, where are the AWACs closest to the Kola Peninsula based?"

The lieutenant keyed the question into the computer. "I show one at Vologda air base, 420 kilometers south of the White Sea. It's scheduled to leave this morning to return to its home base at Arkhangelsk."

"Good." Belikov swung back around to the communications officer. "Put me through to Vologda air base . . ."

BELOMORSK, PVO EARLY WARNING STATION

The operator watched the smudge appear again. Only this time the signal was sharper and clearer.

Of course, he thought, unaware he was watching a decoy, I'm getting a stronger return because the target is now traveling away. He turned to the major. "Sir, target now heading zero one three, speed 440 knots and climbing."

"Can you lock-up and fire?"

The lieutenant manipulated the controls, trying to focus a narrow beam at the target. "It's still climbing, breaking through 1000 meters. Speed and heading constant." He turned to his commanding officer. "The higher it climbs, the better shot we will have."

They waited, neither man taking his eyes off the small dot. Two minutes later the target had climbed to over 5000 meters and was ninety kilometers east of the radar site, its return signal strong.

"I have radar lock, major. The target is in optimum range—"

"Fire."

OVER THE WHITE SEA

The cold, dense morning air provided additional lift as two SA-5s accelerated toward the strong A-Band return signal. The missile's radar-seeker head would not activate for another few minutes, when the SA-5 was sixty kilometers from the radar and its rocket booster would separate to allow the missile to be controlled from the ground or internally. Correction data would then be sent to the SAM's guidance system for final approach and interception.

The stealth's infrared sensors picked up the fiery 2000-degree exhaust of the SA-5s as they broke through 5000 feet and headed east. Tucker was the first to notice. "I show a launch . . . two SAMs six o'clock. They're tracking the decoy. Breaking through 7000." The two red triangular symbols moved quickly across the HUD.

"Steady . . . steady . . ." Tucker said under his breath as he watched.

Traveling at Mach 3.7, 14,000 feet, fifty kilometers from launch site, the four wraparound boosters and main engines simultaneously shut off and the boosters fell away from the main body of the SAMs. At the same time the radar dish buried inside the nose cone started to transmit and instantly acquired the decoy drone.

The two SA-5s, propelled by momentum left from the boosters and main engine, started to glide toward their target.

BELOMORSK, PVO EARLY WARNING STATION

Sixty kilometers to the west, Major Melekin watched the scope over the lieutenant's shoulder. He concentrated on the blip representing the target on the far left side. Less than an inch away and closing fast were two more blips, indicating the position of the missiles.

"One minute to contact . . ." The lieutenant did not look up. "Booster separation complete. Each missile is active."

Suddenly the blip turned south and started to drop in altitude. It picked up airspeed, then nosed up as it turned to the east.

"The target is trying to evade."

The blips, which represented the SA-5s, separated slightly as they continued to track the target.

"Thirty seconds." The lieutenant's hands stayed off the missile controls. The SAMs were having no trouble tracking the target independently.

The decoy's internal-guidance computer, misreading the speed of the attacking SAMs, instructed the decoy to break hard to the north and dive, but the decoy could not react fast enough.

The first SA-5 streaked past the drone within ten meters, its internal radar activating its proximity fuse and exploding the warhead. The force of the explosion turned the missile into a ball of fiery shrapnel a hundred feet in diameter. The second SAM entered the fireball seconds later, its sixty kg. warhead exploding and adding more power to the first explosion.

Pieces of flying metal impacted the decoy and tore it apart, the main body of the fuselage going end-over-end to the water below.

The three blips on the screen disappeared.

"Target is destroyed," the lieutenant announced.

The major straightened up. "Get two MiGs back out there right away. I want visual confirmation."

NIGHTSTALKER

"They got it, colonel. It's gone."

"And so are we." Duke leveled at 150 feet above the water. The A-Band warning was flashing on and off as the radar's signal faded. He backed off on the throttles until the stealth was cruising at 450 knots. The B-2's ride was steady.

Koiser reviewed his computer. It too was clear. They shouldn't pick up another radar for the next fifteen to twenty minutes, he figured as he sat back, took a deep breath and tried to relax.

RAMENSKOYE TEST CENTER

Ten minutes later the report from the major was given to Colonel Belikov.

"What do you mean they're finding nothing? Tell them to make another pass."

The lieutenant repeated the colonel's request.

Belikov double-checked the time. The MiGs could only have been over the area where the target went down for a few minutes. He wanted a more thorough search, then some quick passes.

Two minutes later the same report came in. The MiGs had found nothing in the water around the crash site.

19

CONTACT

PVO HEADQUARTERS, MOSCOW

Defense Minister Tomskiy looked at General Yefimov over his half-moon glasses. "Colonel Belikov says there's been a violation of our airspace in the northwest theater?"

"Correct, sir. The station at Belomorsk tracked, engaged and, Colonel Belikov believes, downed an apparently unidentified target—"

"What do you mean 'apparently unidentified target'? It's either one or the other."

"MiGs were vectored to the area but were unable to find—"

Tomskiy's face grew hard. "Stop sounding like a damned diplomat, general. Give me a clear answer. Tell me exactly what you know."

The general repeated what he had learned from Belikov, simply and directly, and finished by saying Belikov had ordered a search of the area.

"I agree with the colonel, we need proof." Tomskiy took off his glasses and laid them on his desk as he rubbed the bridge of his nose. "What did he mean, the early warning station had never seen a radar return like this?"

"It was very weak and hard to track. It was there one minute and gone the next . . ." As soon as the words left his mouth

Yefimov realized he could be describing a contact with an American stealth aircraft. Was it possible?

Tomskiy sat down at his desk. The early morning sun cut through his window shades and cast long thin lines of light on the far wall that he stared at, as though the better to concentrate. "Why do you find this so strange? This isn't the first time early warning stations have observed strange types of radar returns in and out of our airspace. The Americans are always trying to test us."

"Sir, do you believe we downed another American stealth aircraft violating our territory?"

Tomskiy shook his head. "Until I have proof I don't consider any unknown aircraft shot down. General Yefimov, I want you to go to the PVO command center and open up a coded direct line with Colonel Belikov. Instruct him that I, too, want positive proof of that downed aircraft. It could have been a decoy. And until I get that proof I want him to consider us in a high state of readiness. He should continue monitoring the aircraft's last known flight path."

The general turned and exited the Minister's office, happy to be out of there.

Tomskiy's thoughts went back to his recent meeting with KGB Director Volstad and the warnings he had given about a new American interest in Ramenskoye. The change in the KH-12 orbit and the President not reacting to the pressure being put on him from Western European leaders to sign the treaty. Or, more important, to complain about the downed U.S. stealth fighter. What bigger fish were they frying?

Il-76 MAINSTAY, NORTHWEST OF VOLOGDA

The pilot continued his climb through 5000 meters, halfway to a cruising altitude of 10,000. He banked the big four-engine pale blue-and-white T-tail converted transport to the northeast. Its large saucer-shaped gray radome, mounted high above the main fuselage just behind the wings, rotating slowly right to left.

Similar in concept to the Lockheed C-141 Starlifter, the Il-76 was originally designed as a strategic and tactical freighter, with a reputation for being tough, reliable and easy to maintain. It was a logical choice when the PVO decided to replace its aging fleet of TU-126 Moss airborne early-warning aircraft with a more advanced look-down radar system.

In the strategic role, the Mainstay was required to detect medium and high-speed low-flying bombers such as the B-52 and B-1B, as well as small ground-hugging targets like the AGM-86 ALCM cruise missiles. It was also used in tactical fighter control, transferring its early-warning data to PVO interceptor squadrons, early warning radars and SAM sites.

The pilot nudged the yoke forward and leveled the Il-76 out at twenty-five meters below 10,000. He allowed the aircraft to slowly drift upwards to cruising altitude, then trimmed it for level flight.

"Scope is clear, major. I show nothing unusual," a radar operator radioed from the interior of the aircraft. All he saw was the southern coast of the White Sea and the contour of the land.

"Continue searching, we will be on the outermost area of last contact in twenty minutes."

The operator readjusted his headset and wondered what this was all about. As usual he had just been told to find a target, only this time he could tell by the major's voice *something* was very different.

RAMENSKOYE TEST CENTER

"I agree, Minister." Belikov hung up. Tomskiy was right, too much was at stake not to react.

He moved to the lieutenant responsible for monitoring the large display screen. "Lieutenant, focus in on the northwestern theater defense network. Show me where each early-warning radar is located and the SAM sites under their control."

The main screen flickered and showed the outline of the Kola Peninsula and surrounding area, which included Leningrad to the south and the Ural Mountains to the east. A thin blue line running down the center of the screen represented the Northern Dvina River. "Early-warning radars are colored red, colonel, the SAMs green." Each red symbol showed the location of an early-warning and acquisition radar, four green dots, SAM sites, encircled each station. Additional sites were also strategically placed. In the northwestern theater alone Belikov was looking at over fifty-seven different SAM locations.

"Now call up the ones in that sector that aren't tied into the computer system," Belikov told the lieutenant.

A flashing asterisk appeared next to only one radar station, Arkhangelsk at the mouth of the Dvina River. Belikov studied the screen, his intense blue eyes squinting as he took in details. "What was the last radar site to be tied in, lieutenant?"

"Vologda air base. General Yefimov personally completed the linkup only yesterday . . . before he left, sir." The lieutenant wasn't following the colonel's line of thought.

"And the radar at Vologda . . . what is it and what SAMs are under its control?"

"A P-15 mobile operating on a C-Band with one in reserve. It controls eight batteries of SA-6s and twelve SA-8s. Vologda also operates a number of ZSU-23-4 antiaircraft artillery as a point-defense."

The colonel let out a long controlled breath.

Basic military strategy, he thought, attack on the narrowest front possible. The Americans, it seems, know . . . well, I'll draw them in close, right into the heart of our defenses. "Contact the Il-76, order the pilot to take up station 100 kilometers north of Vologda. Maintain an altitude of 12,000 meters. I want his surveillance radar turned off . . . no emissions."

The lieutenant gave him a look.

"That's right, lieutenant, I want it shut down, turned off. I also want the station at Arkhangelsk to shut down. And contact Vologda, tell them to set up their second P-15. I want that one to operate on the lowest C-Band frequency possible. Understood?"

The communications officer hesitated.

"Do it *now*."

The lieutenant brought his full attention to contacting the Il-76 and the station at Arkhangelsk.

Belikov picked up the phone. "Put me through to Arkhangelsk air base. I want four MiG-31s on alert."

THE WHITE HOUSE SITUATION ROOM

Jack Dawson had just hung up the phone. "That was General Westcott in Omaha, Mr. President. The B-2 is in Soviet airspace. No major problems, so far."

The President nodded, loosened his tie and unbuttoned the top of his shirt. He looked at the display John Turner had provided.

"The pulsating red dot is the bomber?"

"Correct, sir. It's broadcasting on two high-frequency coded radio bands. The signal is bounced off one of our satellites, decoded by the computers in Omaha and transmitted to us. We know where the B-2 is at all times, there's no way the Soviets can intercept or decode the signal. We also set up a communication relay linked through SAC, so if you want, you can talk directly with the pilot."

"They have *no* idea we've violated their airspace?"

Dawson moved in. "Not exactly, sir. They know something is out there that they can't track or find. NORAD reports that three, maybe four SAMs have been fired in the direction of the bomber." He glanced over at the screen, "but as you can see they missed."

"They're *shooting* at them? And you tell me there are no major problems?"

"We don't know for certain. The stealth is armed with an advanced tactical decoy system designed to target and direct SAMs away from the aircraft." Turner looked to Brady to take over.

"Our team is in place. Any changing intelligence will be transmitted to the bomber as we get it. They should be receiving the latest KH-12 data as we speak."

So far, not too bad, the President thought. But the inevitable cover-your-ass going on from his people didn't exactly reassure him.

NIGHTSTALKER

The stealth had been flying unobserved for the last fifteen minutes. No radar was painting the bomber and the computer sensors showed no other aircraft in the area.

Tucker continued his checks of the B-2's offensive and defensive systems. Duke monitored the flight controls as the flying wing cut through the heavy morning air at only 100 feet above the sea. Captain Koiser, studying his screen, expected at any minute the long-range search radar at Arkhangelsk to sweep over them.

The sound of the computer printer broke the silence. "Westcott says 'good job . . . you're dead.' I guess that means they bought it," Tucker said.

"Any other radar activity?" Duke asked, thinking Westcott sounded like a cheerleader on the sidelines.

"Just the usual . . . ground control. It's coming from Arkhangelsk. Weather looks good around the target. Some low broken clouds, wind out of the southwest at ten knots. To the east we have a cold front, moved through early last night and it looks like ground fog and low muck for a couple hundred clicks. If it holds we should have a thick layer of muck to duck into after we take out the computer."

Koiser's thoughts were elsewhere. According to his computer information the PVO early-warning station based at Arkhangelsk was only ninety kilometers away. The radar station, a P-12, was classified by NATO as a Spoon Rest—a large fixed or truck-mounted A-Band warning radar capable of tracking targets out to 200 kilometers, yet so far their sensors hadn't picked up a reading.

Koiser keyed his mike. "Colonel, we should be picking up the P-12 Spoon Rest based at Arkhangelsk. I show nothing."

Tucker referenced his own instruments. "He's right, we should have picked something up a few minutes ago."

Duke scanned the HUD. "What do you make of it, Koiser?"

"Possibly it is shut down for technical problems."

Duke studied his instruments trying to come up with a clue. The Threat Warning Panel was clear. All radar warning lights were off. Duke knew that even at an altitude of 100 feet above the water they should be picking up *some* residual back-scatter.

"Okay, let's take a look." Duke snapped his mask back into place and tugged at his shoulder straps. With a flick he disengaged the autopilot and at the same time pitched the nose up ten degrees, adding power. The Nightstalker climbed quickly as it sliced through 2000 feet in less than thirty seconds. Duke added forward pressure on the stick and commanded the center trailing edge "beaver tail" to push the nose downward to level the big bomber.

By now the sun was a glowing orange ball in the sky, and Duke could make out the gray haze of the horizon meeting the blue sky in the distance.

"If this one's a freebie we'll take it. Tuck, how much farther to the river?"

"Seven minutes. We're only sixty-two miles out."

"Intelligence says this is the last A-Band we should encounter. Everything else inland will be higher frequency, C or above. I'm going to take her up to 10,000 to give us some breathing room. If they really think we're dead they won't be looking for us at this or any altitude."

He put the stealth into a moderate climb, adding silently that the operative word was *if*.

ARKHANGELSK AIR BASE

The high-pitched buzzer pierced the silence of the officers' barracks, startling the sleeping MiG-31 pilots. The regimental commander shouted out their orders as the flight crews got dressed in the cold damp morning air.

The pilots and ground crew at Arkhangelsk were among the best trained in all the PVO air-defense regiments. They flew the fastest interceptor in the Soviet air force—the MiG-31 (code-named Foxhound by NATO) was a more advanced two-seat version of the single-seat MiG-25 Foxbat, the first Soviet fighter to incorporate a true look-down/shoot-down capability with a multiple-target engagement. The Foxhound was big and fast, its twin Tumansky turbojets rated at 30,865 pounds of thrust each in afterburner and could accelerate the forty-five-ton fighter to speeds over Mach 2.5 while covering a combat radius of 1,305 miles.

By the time they reached their fighters the APUs had been running for three minutes warming up the radar, navigational computers and weapons systems. The weapon safety pins had been pulled from the mix of AA-8 (Aphid) and AA-9 (Amos) air-to-air missiles under each wing. The sickening sweet smell of jet fuel and the low whine of the turbojets told the pilots their aircraft were ready to go.

Pilots and navigators, with canopies closed and internal heaters operating at full blast, taxied to the end of the runway to wait for takeoff clearance.

"Stand by," the first instructions came from the tower.

NIGHTSTALKER

Arkhangelsk air base loomed fifteen miles to the east, and the instruments still showed no radar sweeping the area. Which did not make Duke feel any better as he banked the gray-and-black bomber right at a forty-five degree angle, pointing its black nose almost due south to a new heading of one seven five. They were now heading inland, straight into the heart of the Soviet Union—Moscow.

They had passed the point of no return.

In five minutes they would drop back down and pick up the Dvina River.

Duke did not feel like he was supposed to. Rather than attacking with the full force of SAC's bomber fleet he was sneaking into enemy airspace alone. No bombers were fighting their way in beside him. Knowing he was flying the most advanced aircraft in the world made things better, but not all that much. Concentrate, he ordered himself, on the mission.

"Pull up the data we have on Vologda," he told Tucker.

A map of the area showed the location of the large early warning station and the SAM sites. Directly east of the base it showed the PVO's heaviest concentration of air defenses north and west of the cities of Kirov and Gorky. The SAM fields were to protect the ICBM fields from American attack. The fewest surface-to-air missiles lay in a thin ten-mile strip twenty miles east of Vologda.

Duke traced a probable route through the SAM belt with his finger on the screen. "This area looks pretty good," he said to Tucker. "Feed it into the attack simulator."

Also shown were the locations of each SAM site, and they waited for the computer to verify a safe course through the SAM belt.

UNKNOWN suddenly flashed on the bottom half of the display, telling them that lack of adequate intelligence made it impossible to plot an evasive course. Only when they were in range of the hostile radar station could the B-2's offensive and defensive computers help to track at least a probable safe course.

"It's too far inland," Duke said. "We'll have to wait until we're in sensor range."

They were close enough that Duke could make out a wall of thick white clouds to the east, and he keyed his mike and disengaged the autopilot at the same time.

"I'm taking her down."

He dropped the left wing and put the B-2 into a twenty degree dive, the steering symbol on the HUD showing their nose pointed well below the horizon ahead.

"I see a weak radar sweeping from the south," Tucker reported.

Vologda, Duke thought as he glanced over and saw the yellow C-Band warning light flash on.

"Strobe indicator shows it's hitting us fifteen degrees to starboard." Which told Duke Nightstalker was not pointed straight at the radar, when the stealth would offer the least amount of radar cross section.

Duke swung the bomber right fifteen degrees and nosed down slightly and continued the descent until he was pointed straight at the radar.

"Flat Face Band," Tucker reported.

The altimeter showed 1000 feet. Duke pulled steadily back on the stick and brought the B-2 out of its dive, then watched the G meter climb to 3.5, hang there and then trail off to 1.0 as he came level at 300 feet.

"Engaging TFR . . . now." Duke hit the button on the console.

They blasted over the west bank of the Dvina River at 480 knots, turned right and came back in line with the river at the lowest point in the valley away from the searching radar. Duke felt the computer overcorrect and swing the stealth left and then right. Duke advanced the throttles until they broke through 500 knots. To anyone on the ground the B-2 would be little more than a blur of gray and black.

MIG-31 FOXHOUND

Lead pilot Lieutenant Colonel Viktor Anatoly caught sight of his wingman out of the corner of his left eye as they broke through 500 meters and banked to the south. Their powerful search radars were turned off and two other MiGs pulled in on their six, slightly below them.

The tower had instructed them to use only infrared search-and-track sensors. The target was unknown. The cold background of the frozen earth gave their IR sensors a few more kilometers in range than usual. The IRST, combined with the laser range-finder system, could find, track and engage low-flying targets less than thirty meters above ground with twenty-five percent more accuracy than an angular side-view tracking radar.

"Stay with me," the colonel ordered. "Maintain formation, break only on my order. And keep your radars off."

Why the hell do the engineers put radars in our planes if they don't let us use them, the Lithuanian-born colonel thought. He was not at all happy at having to follow the directions of a junior flight-control officer. Just give me a vector and I'll kill your target . . . He trimmed up his big MiG and continued his climb at 500 meters a minute with the four other fighters tucked in neatly behind him.

NIGHTSTALKER

The yellow C-Band warning flashed back on just as Tucker took his eyes off the computer screen.

Koiser watched the radar data change as the B-2's computer analyzed the latest readings. "I show two C-Band radars sweeping from the south. Both Flat Face . . . the second is operating on a lower frequency."

Tucker confirmed the information.

"It's not unusual to have two early-warning radar operating out of the same base," Koiser said. "But I have never seen two of the same type."

Duke had flown against the Flat Face before in North Vietnam. The B-52 crews all knew if a Flat Face was looking at them a volley of SA-2s weren't far behind.

A flash of orange high in the right corner of the HUD caught his attention just as Tucker relayed the same new information. "IR showing one or two targets forty miles northwest. They're right on the edge of our sensor range."

"More company," Duke moaned.

"C-Band signal growing stronger," Koiser reported.

"Unknown targets 20,000 feet . . . speed 450 knots, heading 179 and steady. That's almost parallel to us. I still can't tell what they are, but by the speed I'd say they're military," Tucker said.

"Ready another TALD and program a Tacit Rainbow for C-Band intercept." Duke felt his palms getting sweaty.

VOLOGDA AIR BASE, CREW TWO

At first the sergeant didn't take notice of the tiny blur on the upper left part of his screen. A weather disturbance or a surveillance balloon, he thought.

Actually he was more concerned with trying to warm his feet with the small electric heater beneath his equipment. His orders were simple, operate the radar at the lowest possible frequency and report any indication a target was approaching. The regimental commander had emphasized that he should be looking for anything, no matter how insignificant it might appear.

To his left was the latest addition to his mobile radar. Two large black boxes he had helped install only twenty-four hours ago. The boxes contained coded electronics that tied him directly into the fancy new command center at Ramenskoye. The data collected by his station could be fed directly into the main computer command center and each SAM could be fired independently from Ramenskoye.

He looked more closely at the scope, the better to see the out-of-focus transparent image. This was all just a test of the new equipment, he thought. As the object faded away for the second time he motioned to the other technician to come closer.

"What do you see?" the sergeant asked.

"I see nothing."

"No, look here," and the sergeant pointed to the image. It could even be mistaken for a tiny flaw in the scope.

"Can you track it?"

"No. From its position on the scope it is still 200 kilometers out. I can't get speed or altitude, the return is much too weak. I don't know if it is anything or nothing . . ."

"It must be something," his fellow-technician said. "After all, we would not be able to see it if it was just thin air. Thin air does not change position." He smiled at that last thought.

The image reappeared, and this time it stayed on the scope for all of fifteen seconds before fading away. Now there was no doubt in either man's mind.

"Our orders are to report anything. I suggest we do that," the technician said.

The sergeant agreed and picked up the phone to contact regimental headquarters.

RAMENSKOYE TEST CENTER

Belikov watched the position of the MiGs and the Il-76 north of Vologda. The Ilyushin was on the backside of its orbit and the MiGs were fast approaching from the east 250 kilometers away. Again, he wondered if he had made a mistake. The area was clean, no one had reported any activity in the last thirty minutes. Possibly the aircraft was down over the White Sea. Or he had misjudged and it was now out of Soviet airspace. He paced back and forth as he watched the screen. He kept asking himself: if he were to attack the command center how would he do it. . . ?

"Colonel, Vologda Air Base is reporting a strange return on their scope. Unable to identify or track."

"Which station reports contact?"

"Station two, sir. The one you ordered into place," the communications officer said.

Good, Belikov thought. It's in the same location as the MiGs. "Everyone to your stations, I want this center operational in one minute."

A faint hum could be heard building in the background as the computer started to pull power from the nuclear reactor.

"Bring up the radar," Belikov ordered.

The large display screen did not change as the super radar came up to power. Belikov concentrated on the area north of Vologda, east of the MiGs. He saw nothing new.

"They are out there," he said softly, "hiding below our radar, following the terrain." Soon the target would be forced to show itself. The farther south it flew, the flatter and gentler the ground. Yes, sooner or later a radar would acquire them. And when it did, Colonel Belikov had control of every MiG, SAM and AAA site in the country.

"Contact the Ilyushin. I want the MiGs to start their search *now*," he ordered.

NIGHTSTALKER

The instant the stealth crested the hill it happened.

"Son of a bitch," Tucker yelled as almost all the yellow warning lights blinked on at the same time. They were being swept on seven of the nine radar bands simultaneously.

"It is the PVO defense radar," Koiser interpreted quickly.

"Can they see us?" Duke asked him.

"I don't know . . ."

The Nightstalker dipped back down into a shallow valley and the warning lights turned off.

"Tucker, pull up an aerial map of this area. They can't see us if we stay low between the rocks." Again Duke felt the TRF pull the nose up as the B-2 came over another hill. As they reached the top, the yellow warning lights flashed on for a second, then turned off as the bomber started down the other side of the hill.

"There it is," Tucker called out. On the computer-generated satellite map, ten miles to the west, Duke could see a maze of canyons and deep valleys winding their way to the south following the west fork of the Dvina River.

"That's what I want," he said.

He disengaged the TFR and brought the B-2 up to 1000 feet, cut the throttles back and hit the air brakes to slow the stealth to 360 knots.

"I'm picking up a strong I-Band to the north. One . . . maybe two radars." Tucker turned his head in the direction of the signal as he listened to the pulsating tone in his headset. "Those are big Pulse-Dopplers, Duke . . . MiGs."

Duke swung the bomber into a steep left turn, crossing over the Dvina River and heading southeast. His map showed the Dvina River forked in about another seven miles—two minutes. The river flowed out of a steep canyon that ran for almost fifty miles to the southwest. If he could hide from the radar and MiGs by using the canyon and a decoy to pull the MiGs off their course, he could buy some time. Then he would have a chance to catch them off guard and sneak in from the east.

Barely coming into view now were the steep 300 foot walls of the Western Dvina River canyon that cut through the rocky hillside in the distance. Duke leveled the B-2 and headed straight for the gorge.

"Just like the Middle Fork canyon of the Powder River back in Wyoming," he said, turning to Tucker. "Only a lot bigger. Tuck, right before we enter that canyon launch the TALD. Program it to head two four-five, altitude 2500 feet. Send it back over the White Sea. Set it to transmit on C- and I-Bands."

Tucker quickly fed the coordinates into the computer, which then programmed the decoy.

"Ready."

"Stand by . . ." Duke waited as the mouth of the canyon grew closer, the yellow radar warning lights ever present.

A mile out Duke gave the order: "Launch!"

He banked the bomber into a hard right turn as the decoy fell away and headed for the ground 100 feet below. Seconds later the TALD's guidance system kicked in and it started to gain altitude and climb to the west heading up and over the barren landscape.

Duke chopped the throttles further to cut his speed to 230 knots and flared the air brakes again to hold the B-2 in check. He pushed the stick forward and forced the bomber's nose down. Suddenly the stealth headed for the ground. Thin lines of white vapor trailed off each wingtip as the aircraft gained speed. At 300 feet and still descending Duke put the bomber into a slow, graceful turn and lined the stealth up with the entrance to the canyon. Now he eased it down until he was fifty feet below the top of the rocky canyon walls. The slow-running river beneath them and the low morning sun cast long shadows over the rocks and shrubs.

The radar warning lights were off. The radar waves were passing over them, not able to penetrate below the top of the high rock walls. Duke double-checked the satellite map. The first thirty-five miles of the fifty-mile-long canyon looked navigable . . . after that the canyon progressively turned into a series of tighter and tighter angles. The last ten miles would literally be hit or miss, he figured.

On the HUD the IR images of the MiGs were also gone. The canyon walls not only blocked enemy radar but also limited the B-2's own infrared detection system. But in his headset he could hear the constant pinging of the I-Band radar searching in the distance.

"Can you tell how far away the MiGs are?" Duke asked.

"No, and I can't tell if they're taking the bait," Tucker said, anticipating Duke's next question.

Duke did not answer, he needed all his concentration to fly the Nightstalker through the winding rock corridor. He drew in a long breath of oxygen and banked the stealth right to follow the tortuous winding river.

RAMENSKOYE TEST CENTER

The target had just disappeared. The captain who ran the computer felt the pressure mounting. Three times he had tracked the unknown target and three times he had lost it. He could feel Colonel Belikov's presence behind him, watching his every move as he walked back and forth. The colonel's stare seemed to burn into his back. The captain fully understood the consequences of failing the colonel now.

"Contact again . . . target now heading 278, speed 300 knots, altitude 750 meters," the captain reported.

"Identify," Belikov ordered.

The captain swallowed hard. He fed in a new command and waited for the computer to answer. His eyes now met Belikov's. "Computer not able to identify target. Radar return is only strong enough to track it, sir. It is a very small aircraft . . ."

Belikov, trying to contain his frustration, watched the radar image move northwest toward the White Sea. The nearest SAM was more than 300 kilometers to the south. Interception would have to be made by the MiGs. Damn it, was more than one target flying in his airspace? One going south and the other trying to pull his fighters away from it. Make a decision, he ordered himself.

"Contact the Il-76, give them a vector. I want those MiGs on top of that target. I want to know what is out there."

The order went out to the Ilyushin, and almost at once the MiGs broke into pairs—one turned right and the other left as they moved to the north.

MIG-31 FOXHOUND

Colonel Anatoly keyed his mike, "Heading . . . heading." He looked over his shoulder at his back-seat radar operator, his head buried in the radarscope.

"Turn right heading three five five. Radar contact . . . target twenty kilometers out. Lock-on in ten seconds . . . you should be able to see the target." The radar operator did not look up from the powerful radar that swept the area 200 kilometers in front of them.

Anatoly rolled the big interceptor right and then left, trying to better his view of the ground below. The MiG-31 had poor downward visibility, originally designed to attack high-altitude strategic bombers with the support of ground-control radar, not low-flying aircraft. It only took on the role of low-level interception after the KGB managed to steal the technical plans for an advanced digital radar of the U.S. Navy's F/A-18 Hornet and installed it in the MiG.

"I can see nothing, nothing in that direction," Colonel Anatoly said as he rolled back to the right to scan the brown countryside and look for a small movement, a flash of light, *anything* that signaled the position of the target. He knew he should have requested a new back-seater, someone with more than 200 hours of experience. Too late for that now.

The young radar operator continued to watch his scope. He could see the aircraft on his *screen*, less than seventeen kilometers out and closing fast. He manipulated the narrow I-Band beam closer to the target.

"It's out there . . . find it," he muttered quietly, angry at the colonel for not being able to eyeball the enemy.

Eight miles to the west the decoy continued on its course toward the White Sea while constantly varying its direction, its microprocessor sending back an exact duplication of the MiGs I-Band radar frequency. The signal on the back-seat MiG pilots' radarscope—unknown to them—was not their own radar reflecting off the target but rather the signal their instruments were recording of the decoy's own transmitter. The MiGs would have to get within five kilometers before their radar could pick up the small radar cross-section of the decoy, and only then could they lock on and bring their weapons on line to fire.

"Speed three-hundred-ninety knots, altitude seven-hundred-forty meters, heading three four seven. Turn right five degrees."

Colonel Anatoly turned his MiG to the right and chopped his airspeed for a split second, then dropped his nose to regain it and watched his altimeter click off the meters and leveled out at 1000.

"Heading . . . heading," Anatoly shouted again.

"The target is straight ahead," his back-seater fairly screamed back. Suddenly his yellow radar-tracking symbol turned red to indicate that the secondary I-Band beam was hitting the target.

The reflected energy enabled his radar finally to lock on the target below. They were twelve kilometers from the coast.

"Lock-on," the operator reported. "I have radar lock-on, AA-9s locked and ready. Fire . . . fire."

"Hold fire," came the colonel's reply. "Hold fire. We must have a visual sighting. Do you see the target?" Anatoly's voice was strained with frustration.

"I can see it on my scope, it is there."

Anatoly opened his communication channel with Ramenskoye and keyed his mike. "Unable visually to verify target. Have radar lock-on. Request permission to fire." He waited. In three minutes they would be over the water and his radar would lose most of its tracking capability. Either he destroyed the target now or very possibly would lose it over the sea.

His headset crackled with the response: fire.

The colonel was still searching the sky for the target when he ordered "Fire . . . two missiles away." At the same time he squeezed the launch button on the stick.

Two white, thirteen-foot long AA-9 air-to-air missiles rocketed away from under each wing, leaving a trail of gray smoke. Anatoly held his MiG steady and kept the radar pointed straight at the target.

Fifteen seconds later both pilots saw a bright flash against the dark ground as the first missile passed within lethal distance of the target. The AA-9's proximity fuse ignited the thirty pound warhead, hitting the decoy with a volley of supersonic shrapnel that caused the second missile to veer off course and tumble to the ground.

Their radar was clear, the target was gone. Anatoly keyed his mike, banked the big interceptor to the south and picked up speed and altitude. "Control . . . target is destroyed."

NIGHTSTALKER

Although the Soviets had not achieved a radar lock-on on the B-2, Koiser was still surprised. The system swept the stealth on seven bands at the same time and was working just like the engineers back at Ramenskoye said it would. The only unknown was if the new radar worked well enough to pick up the

B-2 and track it as it moved across Soviet airspace at high speed using the terrain to mask its presence. The Americans were counting on him to guide them through to the target, but he wondered if it could be done, knowing as he did the heavy air-defense systems that lay ahead—SAMs, MiGs and the PVO's most vicious point-defense, the radar-controlled antiaircraft artillery gun. So far they had escaped. What lay ahead gave him little confidence.

Koiser felt the bomber roll to the left as Colonel Duke James maneuvered through the canyon. He had only known the colonel for a very short time, but it had been quality time. The colonel could understandably have denied his request to go on the mission, a Soviet defector as a third member of the crew . . . Duke understood he was the only man in the West who knew in detail about the system and any of its weaknesses they might encounter on the way. He respected the colonel and felt a deep responsibility not to fail him.

Tucker's voice brought him back. "The MiGs must have followed the decoy, I don't hear a thing."

Duke swung the Nightstalker left and climbed up level with the top of the canyon. The walls were now much closer together, and each turn was increasingly risky. Duke kept his airspeed as low as possible, right above a stall.

"It's time to move," he said. "This decoying and dodging won't work forever." He advanced the throttles and let the stealth build airspeed slowly, then eased the B-2 up and out of the canyon and crossed a high-level plateau to the right. He brought the bomber up to 500 feet, leveled off and took a southwesterly heading. The radar warning lights all came on again the moment he broke into the open. He corrected a few degrees and brought the stealth into a head-on course with the C-Band search radar.

The HUD showed no evidence of the MiGs. Duke focused back on the horizon. The land ahead held little cover, mostly flat with only a few hills and valleys to hide from the searching radars. What he had to do was get past the SAMs at Vologda, after that they could head east, where the terrain changed again into high rolling hills and broken bluffs for fifty miles. They could hide there, away from the long-range radars surrounding

Moscow before their run west at the command center at Ramenskoye. But Duke's first and most immediate concern was the SAMs. The latest satellite recon photos showed they would enter the control area of the first missile SA-6 site within some seven minutes.

Duke had moved the throttles forward, stopping just short of full power. The eight injection ports poured fuel into the B-2's engines at a rate of a gallon a second, the added thrust pushing the stealth into a steep climb. The Threat Warning Panel was still clear, and none of the yellow warning lights had turned red indicating a lock-up. They broke through 8000 feet and Duke continued to climb, speed now 450 knots and increasing.

"Where are we going?" Tucker asked.

"Up," was Duke's only reply. With the SAMs ahead, speed and maneuverability were the best friends a pilot could have, and maneuverability meant altitude.

RAMENSKOYE TEST CENTER

"Nothing, colonel. The search team is on top of the crash site now. They report no debris." The major held one end of his headset to his ear and repeated the information as he heard it in the other ear.

"If it was an aircraft the impact of the water would break the fuselage into a thousand pieces . . . there should be something," he added.

"And the other—"

"MiGs also report no debris, colonel. They have passed over the presumed crash site a dozen times and have spotted nothing."

Belikov was understandably angry. He looked almost foolish, although he now knew he had made the right decision in ordering the MiG-31 to engage the unknown target without first seeing it.

"Colonel, possible target, heading two seven three . . ." The captain did not sound very confident.

Belikov bore in on the screen. "Where is the target?"

"One hundred eighty kilometers northeast of Vologda. It is very faint, sir." The captain wondered if he should have waited.

He tapped another command into his computer and tried to sharpen the image. It did not work.

The colonel was quiet, and then, sure enough, a faint pale speck could just barely be seen crossing from right to left. "Identify," he ordered.

"Unable, the computer shows no record. The radar return is so small . . . I can barely track it," the captain said.

"Should I order the MiGs into the area?" the major asked.

"No, let it come closer . . . let it enter the SAM belt. If we can track it so can the SAMs." Belikov turned back to the captain. "Distance before they are in range of the first SA-6?"

"Less than twenty-five kilometers, sir. About two minutes."

"Good. Contact the SAM sites . . ."

NIGHTSTALKER

Fifteen miles to the southwest the first Kub SSNR engagement radar and command center started its dual antennae rotating in opposite directions a full 360 degrees. Its antenna had been shut off so as to not give away the radar's position until the target was in range.

The two-crew mobile truck mounted-command shelter was equipped with two radar antennae. The larger upper antenna was used for missile guidance and tracking the target; the lower antenna was for surveillance and target acquisition. The engagement radar was located in the center of a neat square. A launch battery of SA-6s was on each corner, and each launch site contained three missiles.

As soon as both members of the crew heard the launch order come in from Ramenskoye they switched the search radar to full power. Their system was already linked into the main computer for target acquisition.

They waited. Thirty seconds later the G/H-Band acquisition radar picked up the target.

"They got us . . . lock-on on G/H-Band, Straight Flush, two o'clock," Tucker warned as he gave the NATO code name for the radar.

"Not yet," Duke said.

"What?"

"I'm not ready, damn it." Duke watched the altimeter run through 20,000 feet, then smashed the stick forward to bring the bomber level. "That will have to do," he said, and banked hard left to come in line with the SA-6 acquisition radar. He hoped that would be enough to defeat it—no luck. The red radar-warning light stayed on. A slight glimmer caught his eye followed by two more flashes. He waited for the Threat Warning Panel to I.D. the launch.

Tucker called out: "Three up . . . accelerating . . . dead ahead . . ."

Duke jinked the bomber right and left while varying his altitude. Sweat beaded his forehead. No one said a word. The Threat Warning Panel lit up. It showed a launch ten miles out and to the southwest, three o'clock. He watched three missiles, one at a time, appear on the HUD. The computer automatically prioritized them.

Tucker noted that the stealth was within the missile's maximum range.

"Ready the chaff," Duke said.

Tuck instructed the computer to ready the proper-frequency chaff into the stealth's dispensers.

Duke watched the white smoke from the booster rocket grow closer. How many times had he been through this in the simulator, a hundred maybe two hundred . . . It didn't matter, he could feel his guts tighten into a palpable knot. He waited for the last moment before he broke left and rolled. "Chaff *now*."

Tucker hit the chaff button and threw an eight-foot-diameter bundle of Fiberglas-impregnated aluminum foil behind the stealth.

Duke rolled the bomber over so as not to lose sight of the SAMs.

The first missile headed straight for the chaff; it would miss by a half-mile. The second arced toward them, Duke didn't look for the third.

He completed the roll, forced the nose down and turned left again as he watched the missile follow. Airspeed 500 knots . . .

increasing, altitude 19,000 feet. The second missile was now seconds away.

"Break *now*." Tucker pumped the chaff button again.

Duke changed direction and banked back to the right, shoved the throttle forward and continued his dive as they came across the front of the SAM. The radar-seeker head was not able to follow the stealth through the turn, its design limited it to a 15-G turn.

"One more," Duke said as he searched the HUD.

"Low, two o'clock."

Duke caught sight of the last missile. Its white smoky exhaust gave away its position. While outturning the second SAM he had inadvertently put the Nightstalker in perfect position to be engaged by the third.

He brought the nose up, veered back left and leveled at 16,000 feet. He placed the SAM in the center of the HUD . . . and waited. The missile's closing speed was over 2800 miles an hour, so close that he could make out its white control surfaces. He had a split second to react.

"Hold it, hold it . . ." anticipating Tucker's next move.

"Again, *now*." He smashed the stick forward. The B-2 dove, its fly-by-wire controls seeming to be a part of Duke, an extension.

Tucker hit the chaff button and did not take his eyes off the HUD as the cockpit windows filled with ground 15,000 feet below. The B-2's speed increased . . . 470, 480, 500.

They watched the twenty-foot-long missile race overhead at Mach 3, scarcely 200 feet away. It tracked straight for the stronger radar return of the chaff. The moment it hit the chaff cloud it exploded, sending a ball of steel and hot aluminum through the air. Pieces also hit the back left-side of the stealth, pitting and denting the skin.

Duke steadied the bomber, brought the nose up fifteen degrees. They were still heading southwest at 525 knots. The Threat Warning Panel showed the radar at a forty-five degree angle to the stealth. The launch warning indicator was clear. The Straight Flush was still below them, now at its closest point.

Duke's mouth was dry as he asked Tucker, "What's next?"

Tucker was too busy with his instrument checks and looking for evidence of serious damage.

Duke checked the HUD. So far he had used two decoys, but still had a full load of radar-homing Tacit Rainbows and SRAMs.

"Colonel, we may have sustained some damage to the skin but nothing too major." Tucker kept a close eye on the fuel gauges . . . a leak in the main tanks could mean a quick end to the mission.

"Watch that warning panel, damn it."

Koiser was fixed on his computer screen. At first he didn't see the change. The G/H-Band was still painting them from the northeast, its beam hitting them every second along with some spillover from the SA-6's data-link I-Beam frequency. The pulsing from the G/H-Band was constant, not changing since they first came in contact with it. And then he noticed the change. Every third or fourth pulse the frequency would jump. Not a lot but enough for him to notice—as if for a split second the radar was out of sync or another radar was sweeping the area.

Koiser keyed his mike. "Colonel James . . . I believe there is a second H-Band search-radar sweeping us from the south. Its signal is weak but it is there."

"Tuck, what other SAMs are in this area?"

"Two SA-8s due south."

The J-Band warning light turned red. The closest SA-8 site had just turned on its target-tracking radar, its parabolic antenna sending out a heavy-pulsed beam of energy.

"Damn it, they're on us again," Tucker said.

"Second H-Band sweeping to the southwest," Koiser announced. "Sensors picking up another strong J-Band." He waited, knowing it was a matter of seconds before the other acquisition radar would lock onto them.

Duke readjusted his oxygen mask with a tug on the hose. The intelligence on the SA-8 was sketchy. It was a more advanced system than the SA-6, designed to be highly mobile. It had its own engagement radar mounted on a single vehicle, and since it didn't have to rely on a Straight Flush radar for its information it was able to engage more than one target at a time unlike the older SA-6. The only drawback Duke was aware of was that the SA-8's smaller tube-launched missiles had a shorter range and carried a less powerful warhead.

Koiser pictured the scenario. Straight ahead lay two SA-8 sites, one on each side of their flight path. Each site operated on the same radar bands, contained the same missiles and would attack the stealth the same way. Each was also sending out identical electrical impulses. The PVO, he decided, had made a mistake.

"Colonel, take the bomber down. Fly right between the two SAMs."

Duke didn't take his eyes off the HUD, which showed the area the engagement radars were sweeping. Each time he changed heading or varied his altitude, the radars followed.

He hit the mike. "Captain, explain—"

"One up three o'clock," Tucker warned. "Two up . . . this one's at ten."

Accelerating slower than the SA-6, the SA-8 still hit Mach 2 in less than sixteen seconds. Duke looked on as the threat panel prioritized the two missiles. The warning symbol on the HUD showed the second missile as the number-one threat—although it had launched second it would impact the Nightstalker first.

Duke saw Tucker ready the J-Band chaff dispenser out of the corner of his eye, snapped the B-2 into a ninety degree roll to the right and lowered the nose to gather speed and change the radar return of the stealth. An instant later he rolled the aircraft upright and continued the dive at 540 knots. The tactic didn't work, the SAM's radar seeker-head stayed locked onto its target.

On the HUD the smaller SA-8 looked farther away than it really was. Duke estimated it was two miles out, about 5.5 seconds. He didn't have a visual on the second missile but he knew it was out there.

"Three up, four, five . . ."

"Oh, shit, I don't need this . . . !" Duke slashed the stick left and back at the same time, G-forces smashing them against their ejection seats as the stealth turned on its side and climbed up, decelerating. Duke felt his G-suit fill with air, forcing the blood to stay in his upper body. He watched the G-meter climb to four before he shoved the stick forward, causing the B-2 to push over and pick up speed again. A bright flash told them the SAM had missed. It exploded only 200 yards to the north.

Duke pumped the stick back three quick times and brought the Nightstalker level at 15,000. He had used 4000 feet to outfly one missile.

"One o'clock . . . six miles," Tucker called out.

"Head for the ground, fly between the two sites . . . maximum speed." Koiser's tone was dry, flat. In the vernacular, cool.

"Explain," Duke said as he searched for the other SAM.

"They will track us. When the emitters cross beam they will jam each other." Koiser tried to give Duke the concept without going into detail.

Duke didn't have time to argue. He either trusted the man or he didn't. He pushed the throttles all the way to the stop and moved the stick forward until he felt resistance. The engines revved to full power. His eyes went back to the HUD. Speed 600 knots, the second missile was now arcing over, still tracking him. Duke wasn't surprised . . . the SA-8 could track and down a target as low as thirty feet. He would have to jink his way to the deck, structurally taxing the Nightstalker to its limits.

Tucker pushed the chaff button three quick times. "Five seconds to impact."

The worst part was waiting. The SAM was above and to the right. Duke couldn't see it, still having to rely on the computer image displayed on the HUD.

Duke broke right. "One . . . two . . . three, *now*." The B-2 banked hard back left, leaving a bundle of chaff churning in its vertices . . . The tumbling two-inch strips of J-Band reflecting-foil broke the radar lock of the missile.

Another SAM suddenly appeared starboard and streaked past the cockpit, failing to detonate. Duke winced. He rolled the bomber 180 degrees and watched as they passed 690 knots, Mach 1.06. More chaff, right . . . left . . . right, more chaff. More stick. He completed the roll. Altitude 4300, heading 172, the two SA-8 radars still pounding them from opposite sides.

"Two more coming around from the east, nine o'clock," Tucker called out.

Duke watched the altimeter hit 2500 feet and realized they

might not be able to pull out of their supersonic dive. He leaned back on the stick and watched the Gs climb. Four Gs . . . 1500 feet, airspeed 650 and dropping. He opened the air brakes. More aft pressure, five Gs . . . 800 feet . . . almost there. He watched the nose come up slowly. A little more six . . . six point five.

A disembodied voice warned, "Over G, over G."

"I *know*, damn it." More back pressure on the stick. "Come on, baby, hold together for me . . ."

At 100 feet above the frozen brown earth Duke steadied the bomber, retracted the air brakes and pulled the throttles back to ninety-five percent. The stealth was screaming along at 630 knots.

No room to maneuver, and two SAMs still on their tail.

"Fifteen seconds to impact . . . coming over the top," Tucker said, looking at the top part of the HUD that projected an image of the SAMs heading for the bomber.

The two radars followed the bomber as Duke maintained a steady course between the two antennae.

"Twelve seconds," Tucker again.

"We will pass between the emitters in ten seconds . . . hold steady," from Koiser, his eyes on the computer. The signals from the two H-Band and J-Band radars were growing stronger with each mile.

Duke climbed to 300 feet and pushed the B-2 for everything it had. The tachometers on all four engines were red-lined, giving him 645 knots. With the extra altitude he could break either way, giving the SAMs a mouthful of chaff and have a chance to evade. But if Koiser's plan didn't work he might be able to outturn the first SAM but not the second.

"Six seconds . . ." Tucker looked over at Duke.

Koiser took a deep breath and held it.

"Four . . . three . . ."

One thousand yards behind the bomber the nearest missile completed an 11-G turn after it followed the B-2 down from 13,000 feet. The dual-thrust solid-fuel rocket motor had burned out some ninety seconds earlier. The missile was now gliding,

using the earth's gravitational pull for velocity. Its forward ca-
nard-fin controls worked in coordination with one another to
keep the nose pointed straight at the stealth, homing in on the
14.5 GHz J-Band frequency return. The missile only had to pass
within thirty feet of its target to detonate the softball-size fragmentation warhead.

A high-pitched tone in Duke's headset replacing the pulsing of
the Soviet radar . . . the Head Up Display showing they were
directly between the two search radars—the radars in fact *looking* at each other . . .

The strong H-Band and J-Band energy that broadcast out of
each site's power-emitters flooded into the other's smaller receiver. The emissions had blocked the weaker returns of their
own signal . . . without realizing it the Soviets had, ironically,
blinded one another.

"Two . . . one . . ."

They waited. At 300 feet, 645 knots, it would not take much
to knock them out of the sky, Duke thought.

Tucker watched the missile start to weave back and forth. He
had seen it before, over Nellis when their B-1B's ECM equipment jammed a SAM; the jamming made it lose lock-up and go
into a search mode as it tried to pick up the signal again.

Duke watched the second missile head for the ground, then
hit the horizon to his left and disappear into a ball of dust.

"Break, break," Koiser shouted. "More chaff."

Duke thrust the stick back and cut the B-2's speed at the
same time. The aircraft leaped upward 500 feet before the air
brakes cut in enough to slow it down. He rolled right just as
Tucker hit the chaff button. He didn't think twice about his next
move. This time he twisted the B-2 to the left and pointed the
steering symbol toward the deck to pick up speed. The Gs fell off
as he added power and let the stealth plunge to 300 feet before
he leveled out.

All the while Tucker was sending out a stream of radar-foul-
ing chaff.

Duke studied the terrain to the south—level and even for at
least the next twenty miles. Gently, deliberately he dropped the

B-2 below 100 feet, let it gravitate to fifty. Now it was below both search radars, whose beams swept high to the southeast and southwest. The acquisition radars at each site had been off-target long enough for the operators to lose contact. The radar-warning lights were now out.

Duke relaxed his grip on the stick, barely touching it with his finger tips, trimmed up the stealth for low-level high-speed flight and pulled the throttles back until the Nightstalker slipped under 600 knots. Don't burn more fuel than necessary, he told himself.

He banked to a new heading of 182, kept focused on the furthest point ahead of them. The B-2 did not vary in altitude more than ten feet.

"Good job, captain," Duke said, purposely using Koiser's rank to show his respect. The man knew his stuff, and Duke wanted him to know he was glad to have him aboard.

Koiser sat quietly. They were safe for the moment, but he knew more advanced defenses lay to the south. They still had to fight their way more than 350 miles to the target and he, with reason, feared the PVO's overwhelming air defenses would eventually track them down. No question—the toughest part of the mission was ahead—

A warning tone in his headset instantly confirmed his feelings. "Strong H-Band to the east, colonel." Koiser watched the power level of the radar go to the end of the scale. The emitters were only a few miles away.

"I got it." Duke watched the warning lights jump and a moment later the H-Band and J-Band turned red.

"Where the hell did *they* come from?" Tucker said as he checked the HUD.

A third SA-8 site had just activated its search radar. It had moved into the area during the night and was not on the B-2's latest intelligence. The crew operating the site had chosen to keep silent until the stealth was on top of it, masking its presence from the bomber's sensors.

"I show a launch! Break—" the rest of the words never left Tucker's mouth.

A single SA-8 missile exploded thirty feet above the right side of the cockpit. In a flash of blinding-bright light the Nightstalker shook violently. The explosion cracked the right-window screen as pieces of the warhead tore into the skin of the warplane. The explosive thrust on the right of the aircraft forced its wingtip down, the edge of it missing the ground by only ten feet.

Duke felt his head snap back and hit the left side of the cockpit wall with the force of a sledgehammer. For a few seconds the bright light blinded him. On instinct, he pulled the stick back to force the B-2 to gain altitude. The aroma of burnt plastic filled the air.

"Tucker, damage . . . ?"

No response.

"Tucker, I need a damage report." This time he looked over at his copilot.

Tucker Stevens was slumped over, leaning against the right side of the cockpit. His face was out of Duke's view. Duke reached over and grabbed the front of his flight suit and pulled him toward him.

"Oh, God . . ."

The sudden force of the explosion had been enough to tear pieces of the stealth's equipment off the cockpit walls, throwing them around the interior like popcorn. From the look of Tucker's face something had hit him like a rifle bullet. His green camouflage helmet was cracked and his oxygen mask dangled at his side. Duke could see white skull bone through a broad gash in his forehead. His right eye was covered in blood and his cheek was purpled with cuts and lacerations.

Duke forced himself to look back at the HUD. His aircraft was at 3000 feet and still climbing fast.

"Son of a *bitch*." He meant it in more ways than one—for what had happened to Tucker, and for the bomber being too high. He lowered the nose to put the Nightstalker into a medium dive, the radar warning lights showed yellow but at least the TWP was clear.

"Koiser . . . you okay?" Duke turned and caught sight of the Soviet getting out of his ejection seat.

"Yes, colonel, I am okay." He moved up and knelt down between Duke and Tucker.

Duke waited for the B-2 to reach 300 feet before he hit the

Terrain Following Radar. Nothing happened. He hit the switch again and still nothing.

"TFR is out, I'll have to fly by hand." He looked over at Koiser, who was trying to help Tucker. "You'd better get back in your seat, if I have to dodge any more SAMs you'll be bouncing around like a ball." And worse, he'd have two casualties.

Koiser nodded toward the warning lights, off now. "Colonel, Captain Stevens is alive but badly hurt, I think . . . he would be better off in my seat." Koiser paused, waiting for a reaction. "You will need my help to fly to the target . . ."

Duke knew the man was right. With Tucker down, he didn't have a choice anyway. "Okay, but hurry. I've got to find out how much damage we've taken."

Koiser quickly started to unstrap Tucker Stevens's unconscious body from the ejection seat.

RAMENSKOYE TEST CENTER

This is no ordinary aircraft, Belikov thought. Otherwise we would have long since downed it. He studied the screen, tracing the path the aircraft had traveled. It had, remarkably, managed to penetrate more than 1300 kilometers into Soviet airspace, and so far the PVO had been unable to bring it down or even track it for more than a few hundred kilometers. Each time the same story . . . The SAM sites and search radars only had the target on their scope for a brief piece of time. When they did engage the aircraft with missiles it got away. He had watched the last SAM detonate above the current position of the target, right before the aircraft disappeared off the screen again. Colonel Belikov no longer believed for an instant the aircraft had been shot down.

He paced the floor. Look at the evidence, he told himself. Maybe intelligence wasn't as good as he'd been led to believe. Was it possible the Americans were actually flying an operational longer-range stealth aircraft into their airspace? The target did fit the computer-profile of how a stealth aircraft would look on a radarscope. How else could the Americans have gotten this far? The stealth bomber wasn't supposed to be operational. The evidence said it was . . .

He got on the direct line to PVO headquarters and the Kremlin.

"Minister Tomskiy, I still don't have confirmation the aircraft in our airspace has been shot down. I believe—"

"Colonel, this aircraft is not flying randomly. What is its position and heading?" The minister already had a good idea what Belikov's answer would be.

"When we are able to track the aircraft it is on a continuous heading south . . . toward Moscow. I have never seen a radar-return like this before—"

"*What* are you saying, colonel?"

"Sir, I strongly believe we are dealing with an American stealth aircraft. Possibly two or three. We have already downed one of them, at least. What I can be sure of is that they are heading here, to this complex . . ."

"Are you sure?"

"No, sir, I am not. But nothing else makes sense."

A pause, then Tomskiy said: "I agree. Ready your defenses for an attack. I am ordering General Yefimov to return. I will be in the Kremlin war room. Contact me there." And he hung up.

Belikov turned to the major. "Put ground forces protecting this center on full alert. Contact the SA-11 and SA-12 sites. Tell them to move out at once. Contact Kubinka air base, I want their full squadron of MiG-31s in the air. Instruct them to search the area between Gorky and Moscow. I want every long-range early-warning radar in the Moscow air-defense region to look north, east and west." He turned back to the screen, hoping the target would reappear. "Put my squadron on alert. If I have to, I will complete the assignment myself."

In fact, he was looking forward to it.

20

RUNNING THE GAP

NRO, THE PENTAGON

The SAMs were on the move. Bernard Simmons had already found and plotted the new locations of two other SA-11s that transferred out of their standard stations to hardened concrete sites on the highest hill in their sector. He suspected the three other SA-11s had just done the same thing. His question was, when would they move again and could he spot them in time to warn the B-2.

Simmons instructed the computer to pull up the disk containing the information on the only SA-12 in his sector—the SA-12, a large, less-mobile tactical SAM requiring three various radars to operate and developed to counter the American and NATO decision to deploy Pershing II missiles in Western Europe. The system was so good the PVO moved many of the SA-12s in and around Moscow to defend against high- and low-flying strategic aircraft.

Simmons zoomed in on the SA-12's position. It had not moved and SAC's intelligence officer Lt. Col. Paul Sullivan did not seem very concerned about the system.

"Anything new?" The southern accent told Simmons it was Sullivan asking the question as he leaned over his shoulder and stared at Simmons's computer.

"The SA-12 hasn't moved but five out of my eight SA-11s have."

Sullivan seemed surprised. "The word must have just gotten out."

"How can you tell?"

Sullivan pushed the reverse arrow key on the keyboard to move the screen to the first set of pictures.

"See here," he said, and pointed to a white bluish smear next to an SA-11 launch vehicle. "That's cold diesel exhaust. A cold start. That launcher has been sitting there for a long time. It's typical for the PVO to move their launchers around every two weeks or so." He called up the next set of photographs. "But when it's cold out, like the last few days, the crew running the SA-11s almost never takes off without first warming up their trucks. But you can see by the trail of white smoke they didn't have time to do that. Somebody high up has ordered them to move out. It also means we need to update SAC every fifteen minutes. Now let's get this info fed into the main data bank, I want to transmit it to Duke James fast as possible."

THE KREMLIN, MOSCOW

"Of course, I am speculating. I haven't received a visual telling me with one hundred percent certainty that it is an American stealth aircraft, but our interceptors have not been able to track or even find the aircraft. No other explanation makes sense." Tomskiy paced back and forth between the KGB chairman's conference table and the front of the room. "We have intercepted and shot down two targets but so far we have found nothing. Both targets disappeared off the scope and when we search for the downed aircraft we find no trace. No bodies, no debris . . . nothing."

"Then it is obvious your pilots are not capable," KGB Chairman Volstad said. "What are they shooting at? You tell me they shot down an aircraft but there is no aircraft? It is difficult to believe the Americans are in our airspace with a stealth plane. Their B-2 is not even operational and will not be for another six years." Volstad knew he was in trouble if he was wrong.

"Don't treat me like one of your deputies," Tomskiy snapped.

"If they destroy the computer at Ramenskoye, this country is naked."

"That's impossible . . . they'll never be able to get close enough. The system will find them and we will force them down—"

"The last time the target was acquired it was only 600 kilometers northeast of Moscow. We have not been able to track it with consistency. It may reach Moscow and we will never know it—"

"Then as Defense Minister I suggest you stop them."

"I intend to do that. And as Chairman of the KGB I suggest you inform the General Secretary of the circumstances."

SAC HEADQUARTERS, OFFUTT AIR FORCE BASE

"Reconnaissance reports SAM movements around the Ramenskoye area." The room was nearly quiet as the intelligence officer relayed the information. "NORAD is also reporting aircraft movement around Kubinka air base. Their IR signature suggests big turbofans. Our guess is they're MiG-31s."

General Westcott could feel the stress building inside him. The Nightstalker was in the middle of the Soviet Union and was being fired at. The Soviets were stacking the odds. With enough aircraft flying and enough time to look they could find the B-2. The concept on which the stealth was built, its ability to fly into hostile territory and remain unnoticed, was being compromised. If the B-2 couldn't do the job no other aircraft could.

"Those pilots need our help, damn it. You tell me you guess they're MiG-31s!" Westcott slammed his fist on the balcony. "You tell those people at the NRO and the Pentagon I need better information than that. And not just where the hell the SAMs are located and how many MiGs are in the air. I don't want the Soviets to guess what we'll do next. I want them off balance."

Westcott had enough combat experience to know what it meant when the enemy was forced to react rather than following standard procedure. If the PVO could be forced to change its tactics to find the intruder, they might make mistakes. Their air defenses had to operate under strict rules and the personnel operating the SAM sites and flying the MiGs were efficiently programmed. Westcott figured that no matter how well the Soviets might have planned for a situation like this everything was not going to go right. He was betting they would miss something.

He looked at the briefing officer. "You tell them there has got to be a weakness, something the PVO has overlooked. We need something we can exploit. I don't care how small or insignificant it may seem I want to know about it. Remind them we have an American aircraft with American pilots inside the Soviet Union who are relying on us for more than a guess. This mission will succeed only with quick and precise intelligence." Westcott paused, letting the sound of his voice echo throughout the command center. "Is that all clear, major?"

"Yes, sir."

"Now code what you have and get it ready to be transmitted to the crew." Westcott turned and looked back at the screen, watched the blue dot of the B-2 slowly move down the display.

NIGHTSTALKER

The radar-warning lights were still out. The search radars looked north and west of the B-2's position. Duke nursed the bomber east toward the safety of the broken terrain. The powerful signals of the radars surrounding Moscow were out there and they would meet up with them soon enough.

"Captain Stevens is still unconscious," Koiser said as he buckled himself into the copilot's seat. "I tried to bandage him . . ."

Duke looked over his shoulder. Tucker's body sat upright with his head resting against the interior wall. Koiser had ripped strips of material off Tucker's flight suit and used them to wrap his head and neck and face.

"His breathing is very shallow."

Duke could only nod and hope Tuck would last until they finished the mission and could get him home. Finish the mission . . . Tuck's life depended on it, never mind all the big deal international stuff. He looked at Koiser. "I need your help, Captain Koiser."

Koiser did not show what he felt inside. He looked at the

instrument controls. The cockpit design was clean and simple—
five separate large CRT's displayed the B-2's flight information,
three on top and two on the bottom near the center console.
The two CRTs on the top, nearest the fuselage, were out. Both
screens were filled with wavy gray-and-white lines. To his right
was the fly-by-wire control stick and on his left the throttles.
On his far right was the computer and the printer Tucker used
to communicate with SAC at Omaha. Koiser looked at the
cracked window screen and the broken pieces of graphite mold-
ing that had shattered after the explosion. The ones that
wounded Tucker.

Koiser looked out the right-side window to asses the damage.
He could see three large dents in the skin plus smaller holes and
scratches. He expected more damage. He looked closer, a tiny
string of white vapor was flowing out of one of the small holes
just above the leading edge of the wing. He watched it for several seconds until he was sure it was a fuel leak, then looked out
the front window at the HUD, which was still functioning, although, with all the damage, Koiser didn't know how.

Duke was now cruising over the flat terrain at 300 feet, 480
knots, heading 143 and fast approaching the broken terrain to
the southeast.

Koiser plugged in his helmet mike and keyed it. "Colonel,
there is a small fuel leak on the right wing—"

"Where?"

"Between the cockpit and the engine intake. About six centi-
meters above the black paint on the leading edge."

"That's the main right wing tank." Duke checked the fuel
gauges—rock solid, not moving, showing two-thirds of a tank.
"The fuel system isn't varying. How big is the hole?"

"It is small . . ."

"Keep your eye on it. I *need* your eyes. You've got to help me
fly. Watch out for SAMs and MiGs. I can handle the weapons
and communications. The CRT on your left"—Duke pointed to
it—"is the same as the one you were watching in the back. You
monitor the radars that are sweeping us and keep me informed."

Duke focused his attention back to the stealth. Its damage.

The terrain following radar and autopilot were out, along with the IR sensors on the right side of the aircraft. Which left them with only one set of instrument readings and nothing to compare them to. He wasn't sure if the communications computer was still working. It would have to wait. The right-side cockpit window screen was cracked in over a dozen places but seemed to be holding up. If there was any damage to the flight controls the computer had automatically rerouted the circuitry, which allowed the B-2 to continue to fly. All in all, not good, not terrible. Except for Tucker, of course. If a B-1B had taken that hit it would be a burning ball of metal.

"Now the engines," he said under his mask as he scanned the engine gauges. He pushed the throttles forward. The RPMs on all but the number-three engine moved ahead, slowly.

"Trouble," Duke thought as he throttled back.

Just then the number-three engine warning light flickered on.

"Fire in number three." Duke shut down the engine by stopping the fuel supply, then hit the fire-suppression button three times with his thumb. An instant later the engine compartment was flooded with Halon to smother the fire. Duke could only hope he had caught it in time . . . otherwise the number-four engine could also catch fire and the wing might well explode.

Number three's RPMs fell to zero. The stealth pitched up and yawed right. Duke put pressure on the stick just as the B-2's computerized flight controls adjusted for the loss of power on the right side of the plane. Now he and Koiser waited for the fire-warning light to go out.

"Can you see the fire?" Duke asked.

Koiser turned his head around until he was looking straight behind him out the corner of the broken window. "I don't see it, there is no smoke."

The warning light went out.

The stealth's airspeed now fell below 450 knots. "It must have sucked in some debris from the SAM and busted up the compressor blades," Duke said. "That's going to cut our top speed over the target to less than 600 knots."

Koiser sensed Duke's diminishing confidence. "We can still do it, colonel. I think I can show you where the air defenses are weakest. If we can get by the MiGs we should make it. We're almost there. And when the computer is destroyed they will not be able to find us."

Yeah . . . *when*, the colonel silently responded.

NRO, THE PENTAGON

The Jumpseat II eponymously named ferret satellite had been over the Soviet Union for three hours. Although its ground-speed was the same as any other satellite, its special elliptical orbit allowed it to remain over Soviet territory for eight hours.

Bernard Simmons watched as the information from the ferret appeared on his screen. At least a dozen different radars were sweeping the region where the B-2 was flying. Every two minutes the map changed, giving Simmons a different picture. The Jumpseat's mission was to ferret out and record the pulse width of every radar that looks more than one degree above the horizon. The data was then down-linked and analyzed to show any gaps in Soviet radar coverage. Simmons had adjusted the Jumpseat's orbit two days earlier to correspond with the B-2's flight and was glad he had. The PVO was changing their ground-radar surveillance patterns.

He gestured to Colonel Sullivan. "Hey, Paul take a look at this."

Sullivan came over, then asked, "Have you compared it to their standard pattern?"

"Yeah." Simmons instructed the computer to split its screen and show the PVO's radar-search pattern on the left side. "These two stations have obviously been ordered to look north and this one west." He pointed to the left screen. "Normally they would have this region covered."

"This should give Duke a radar-free shot at least to within 300 miles of Ramenskoye," Sullivan said. A narrow path, void of color, not more than a few miles wide could be seen on the screen. The gap separated an orange color-coded E/F-Band long-range radar and a green-colored shorter range G/H-Band. The corridor ran south between the cities of Dzerzhinsk and Kolomna.

"Put it together and I'll get it to Westcott in Omaha," Sullivan said.

MIG-31 FOXHOUND

1st Lieutenant Alexander Vorkato and his back-seater were the last members of the fifteen-plane squadron to take off. Radio problems had kept them grounded for over fifteen minutes. The lieutenant was the youngest, newest and least-experienced member of his squadron. He had recently been transferred from an East German fighter wing, Jagdfliegergeschwader 3, named after the Soviet cosmonaut Vladimir Komsrov. In Germany he was known for his toothy grin and sandy-colored mustache. In his new squadron he was known for nothing more than being the last man to qualify in the MiG-31. Lieutenant Vorkato was itching for the first opportunity to earn his squadron's respect. This was it.

Now he banked his MiG, Bitva zero nine, to the left and took a heading south, searching the sky for any sign of his fellow pilots. They had disappeared, leaving long lines of black smoke as the only hint of their presence.

"Take a heading of three-" The transmission from the control tower broke apart.

"Repeat heading," Vorkato radioed back, frustrated that the radio still did not work.

This time he heard the air-control officer.

"Confirmed tower . . . heading one three three." The lieutenant brought his interceptor up to 200 meters, leveled and added power. Because of his inexperience the commanding officer had given him the outer edge of the search pattern, 200 kilometers west of the target's last known position.

Vorkato understood . . . damn them, he would not make a mistake. He instructed his radar operator to turn the radar to standby, letting it warm up. Two minutes later he gave the order to bring the radar to full power and start to scan the area sixty kilometers out in front of him. He then activated the MiG's passive infrared search-track sensor, adjusting its sensitivity for a twenty-kilometer scan. He turned the MiG's autopilot on and ran through his weapons checks for a second time. He was feeling better, almost in control.

SAC HEADQUARTERS, OFFUTT AIR FORCE BASE

General Westcott's mood was growing sour. It was like he was revisiting December, 1972. This time though, a B-2 was alone in Soviet airspace and had to fight through its entire mission, not just the last twenty minutes of a flight. Which was why he wanted fast accurate information—the only kind that could help Duke and his B-2 make it.

General Westcott examined the color computer printout showing the latest radar coverage. No doubt about it, Simmons was the best.

He looked over to the communications officer. "I want this new information and the locations of the SAMs transmitted to the B-2 now."

RAMENSKOYE TEST CENTER

The general watched the ground grow closer as the rotor wash from his helicopter started to pick up dust and swirl it in a fast-moving curl. He buttoned the top of his coat and waited for it to touch down.

Yefimov stepped off the helicopter, ducking his head below the whirling rotator blades, and walked rapidly toward the front entrance of the complex. He felt a burst of icy air pour down his neck as he lowered his head and quickened his pace. The 100 meters to the computer center always seemed much longer when he was in a hurry. A minute later he passed through the last security checkpoint and headed for the control room.

In the glassed-off control room Belikov was nowhere in sight. Yefimov keyed the intercom and ordered Belikov to report to the command center. Almost at once he spotted Colonel Belikov walking up the metal stairs toward the command center.

As Belikov entered he got right to the point. "We still have not relocated the enemy aircraft—"

"I know that. And it's not acceptable."

Belikov tried mightily to control his temper. "The aircraft has dropped below our radar coverage. We have interceptors in position along its last known course." He pointed to the symbols on the screen representing the MiGs.

"Minister Tomskiy is meeting with the General Secretary within a half-hour. I want different news for him and it's up to you—"

"I'm using every resource I have, general," Belikov cut in, more and more resentful.

"I do not want your excuses, colonel—"

"I don't give excuses, general. By now you must know that if it has gotten this far it may get close enough to threaten this complex. I suggest we begin to face facts." When he said "we" he meant "you."

Yefimov seemed puzzled.

"The aircraft knows our weaknesses, it seems. The pilot knows which radar sites are tied into the network and which still aren't. It has managed to defeat each SAM system it has come up against, and our MiGs have not gotten to it. Don't you find that damn strange?"

"Are you saying—?"

"I am saying the Americans know more than they should. What about that defector? He or *someone* is—" Belikov didn't finish. A faint smudge had appeared again on the screen. Followed by Belikov's order:

"Vector the MiGs, vector the MiGs . . ."

NIGHTSTALKER

"MiG to the north, colonel. Strong I-Band . . . MiG-31," Koiser announced, hearing the pulse of the radar in his headset, the tone faint but steady.

Duke brought the Nightstalker up to 500 feet and banked sharply to the south, then back to the east and increased power. The wounded stealth didn't accelerate as quickly as before but it handled the turns. If the MiG was looking at them Duke wasn't going to make it easy. He brought the big bomber back around on its original course, heading through the radar-free zone shown on the HUD.

"Computer shows target now ten miles north and closing," Koiser reported.

"Hell, how fast is he moving?" Duke checked the radar warning lights—the I-Band light was yellow, which meant the MiG had not locked up on them. "That MiG must be cruising at over 650 knots," Duke said unhappily. He pushed the throttles forward a fraction from the throttle stop, and his airspeed climbed until it reached 602 knots, then stopped moving. He banked to the east, bringing the B-2 in line with the clear path on the HUD, and the radar lights turned off except for the I-Band. He lowered the nose and put the B-2 into a shallow dive, bottoming out at 300 feet.

The MiG was now in range of his IR sensors but he could see nothing on the HUD. It must be approaching from the northwest . . . he remembered that the SAM had damaged the IR sensors on the right side of the plane.

"Watch the right side, Koiser. Try for a visual. Try to make sure we see him first . . ." Duke looked in the opposite direction and saw a large wall of clouds hugging the ground about twenty miles away. It should be difficult for the MiG to acquire them on their I-Band radar. But if the Soviet got close enough to spot the Nightstalker from above Duke would fly the B-2 into the cloud cover. Except then he would be out of the radar-free zone and if a PVO radar got a fix on his location he would have more than one MiG to worry about.

The signal got stronger with each pulse of the radar. Koiser checked his computer. "It cannot be more than five miles out now, colonel . . . closing fast."

"How does he know where we are?"

"The pilot is following standard search pattern. He will fly in a straight line until a ground controller tells him to turn and cover another area." Koiser kept his eyes on the sky.

Duke had two choices. Take a chance the MiG really didn't know his position and maintain course, or head for the cloud cover, where this MiG could not find them. He didn't like either one.

A flash of light off of the MiG's nickel-steel frame caught Koiser's attention. "I *see* him, coming up on the right side. About seven, eight kilometers away."

Duke held the Nightstalker steady. He had waited too long. If he moved to the clouds now, chances were the MiG would see him. He would have to see what the MiG's next move was before he reacted. No pilot liked to be in that position.

MIG-31 FOXHOUND

The Pulse-Doppler radar on the MiG moved methodically, criss-crossing the landscape. Its computer software could distinguish a small hard target the size of a cruise missile flying only fifteen meters above the ground. Many times Lieutenant Vorkato had practiced finding a low-flying target and locking onto it. Now he told himself this was not any different. He also felt he would not find a thing, or worse yet he would find something and make a mistake engaging it. He went back to monitoring the search-track scope.

The back-seat radar operator hadn't looked up from his scope for the last fifteen minutes. Only greenish streaks of light showing the contour of the ground were visible. He concentrated on the images, looking for any fluctuations that might give a hint of the target. Nothing. If a target was flying out in front of them he would see a different return than what came from the ground . . . even when the ground changed, the image would stay the same.

Suddenly a burnt orange-colored spot appeared in the upper left hand side of Vorkato's IR-detection display. The color told him it was a very weak heat source, not strong enough to get a missile lock. Vorkato watched it for a few seconds before making a decision it really was time to act.

He keyed the MiG's internal mike. "I think I have a target bearing . . . one four four. What do you see?"

The radar operator seated directly behind him checked his scope again. He saw nothing. "There is nothing on my scope, are you sure?"

The spot on the screen was now more brown than orange. Whatever was out there was cooling off fast and Vorkato knew if he did not react immediately it would soon be off his screen. He disengaged the autopilot and pushed the stick forward, putting his MiG in a dive. The target was only five kilometers away, and closing steadily.

NIGHTSTALKER

The engine fire had generated a tremendous amount of heat that turned the inside of the engine compartment into a molten mess. Result was, the surface temperature of the stealth's upper skin was still hot enough to attract attention from the infrared-detection sensor on the MiG, but neither Duke nor Koiser were aware of it.

What Duke did know was that the MiG was breathing right down his neck. It was close enough for the sensors on the left side of the stealth to pick it up and display it on the HUD.

"Two kilometers, colonel, still no radar lock," Koiser said.

"I'm not so worried about the radar, the LDSD breaker should defeat it. I'm worried about him eyeballing us." He chopped the throttles and pulled the nose up, letting his speed fall below 580 knots. Duke could only hope the MiG would go over the top and not notice the gray boomerang-shaped stealth. He looked at the HUD, waiting for the LDSD breaker to turn on.

As the MiG grew closer its strong radar pounded the top of the bomber with more and more power, but the stealth's retinyl Schiff base-salt coating absorbed the radar's electric energy as it hit its skin, which in turn denied the operator a clear return on his scope. But Duke knew that if the signal got strong enough the special coating would not be able to absorb *all* the radar emissions and the radar operator would be able to see a hole on his scope revealing the position of the B-2. The LDSD breaker was designed to fool the enemy radar with an exact duplication of the ground return. The idea was the radar operator would think he was looking at ground clutter instead of the stealth.

"One and a half kilometers and closing, altitude decreasing." The sound of the radar hitting the bomber filled Koiser's headset.

And then the LDSD breaker did kick in, and the MiG's radar operator read the signals as if picking up the reflecting radar off the ground.

But for how long?

*   *   *

The MiG raced above the B-2 only half a mile away and 500 yards above. Close enough so that Duke could see the underside of the aircraft through the HUD, its white air-to-air missiles coming clearly into view as the MiG banked to the south away from them.

The LDSD breaker switched off.

"Watch him, where's he going?" Duke asked Koiser.

The MiG made a long arcing turn out in front of the stealth, gained altitude and was coming around for another pass.

"He knows we are here," Koiser said. He checked the radar-warning and Threat-Warning panels. Both were clear.

"The MiG has only two ways to find us, colonel—radar and infrared. It is not tracking us on radar . . . so the pilot's IR sensor must be picking us up."

Duke did not argue. He had to draw the MiG away from his aircraft.

"Tell me when it's heading toward us again. I'll give the son of a bitch something to track." He adjusted his grip on the stick, placing his index finger on the second trigger.

Lieutenant Vorkato brought his fighter around and out of its maximum 2.5 G turn until the brown blip on his scope was in front of him again. He swept the sky, trying to eyeball the target, but could see nothing as he passed over the brown, snow-spotted earth 400 meters below. He felt his jaw muscles grow tense to the point of paining him as he imagined the comment that would be going around the base if he didn't find this target. He squeezed the control stick as he tried to concentrate on the MiG's IR-detection screen and estimated he would only have time for one more pass before the target disappeared.

This time he would have to find it.

"Control . . . Bitva zero nine. Possible target heading one five seven." He heard his faulty radio cut out again before he finished. He keyed his mike, repeating the message. No reply. "I need authorization to engage," he mumbled.

He checked his airspeed, he was coming in too fast, he

needed more time to stay over the target . . . He pulled the throttles back and opened his air brakes. The nose of the MiG pitched up and the MiG fell below 400 knots. He pushed the stick forward, and the nose came down as he released the air brake. *This* time he would match the target's speed and follow it until his back-seater was able to get a lock-up.

"I can't see him, he's behind us," Koiser called out as he watched the computer screen show the position of the I-Band radar. "He is matching our airspeed."

Duke put the Nightstalker into a shallow climb of 500 feet. He wasn't sure if he was more angry or scared. Why wasn't the damn MiG attacking? Then he knew . . . the pilot must be waiting for the *rest* of the squadron.

"The chaff button is above your right knee. When I say, you punch it . . . understand?"

Koiser did not have time to answer.

"Hold on, here we go," Duke said as he smashed the stick to the right and went to full power. The B-2 shuddered in protest under the strain of an instant 5 G turn, rolled to the right and picked up speed as Duke lowered its nose.

"Where is he now?" Duke's voice sounded more like a series of snorts as he forced the air out of his lungs.

"East . . . east." Koiser's answer came back in the same strange language, the blood vessels popping in his neck as he struggled to turn his head.

"*Now* . . . chaff," Duke ordered at the same time he squeezed the trigger on the stick. This time the stealth's survival really depended on the diversion working.

As the chaff ballooned behind the bomber a magnesium infrared decoy flare also ejected from the stealth's bottom. Normally used to confuse heat-seeking missiles, the high-temperature flare floated along with the chaff until gravity took over, pulling it to the ground.

Follow this, Duke thought as he brought the B-2 out of its hard right turn on a heading of 004 due north. The Gs fell off and he leveled at 200 feet. Now the MiG was behind them, heading away, because the MiG was limited to a 2.5 G turn

Duke knew it would be some thirty seconds before the pilot could react.

"The IR flare and chaff combination *should* get his attention," Duke said, and tried to picture the MiG pilot. If the first part of his plan worked the enemy pilot should pick up on the two distractions and be drawn off long enough for Duke to maneuver the Nightstalker north.

"He is heading for the chaff," Koiser said quietly, holding his breath.

"Come on, baby, come *on*," Duke muttered.

The sudden radar-return on his scope surprised the back-seater. "Head zero one one," he intoned.

Vorkato also saw the "target" on his IR sensor screen. Unfortunately for him he did not look outside his cockpit . . . if he had he would have seen the bright white flare as it fell toward the earth. Instead he brought the MiG out of its turn and leveled out at 350 meters, then pushed the nose down to regain the airspeed lost in the turn.

He reached down and armed his missiles.

"Target three kilometers and closing."

"Lock-up, lock-up," Vorkato ordered.

"The signal is growing weak . . ."

The chaff was dispersing.

"Control . . . this is Bitva zero nine. We have radar contact on unidentified target. Permission to fire." Nothing came. He repeated the message.

The broken sound of static filled his headset but he understood enough of the controller's reply to know they didn't understand what he was requesting.

"Unable to lock-up weapons, lieutenant," from the back-seater.

Vorkato, angry and nervous all at once as the blip on his screen slowly disappeared, rolled his MiG right and left, hoping to see something below him . . .

* * *

Duke banked to the right, this time pulling half the Gs, took an easterly heading for twenty seconds, then turned left and headed north again.

"Ready the chaff . . . on three." Duke waited, hoped the MiG pilot was following his lead. If he were he should be about five miles south, heading north and toward them again.

"One, two, three . . . chaff." Duke pushed the stick hard left, this time putting the Nightstalker into a maximum G-turn. He hit the flare button and lightened up on the stick at the same time. The G-meter now fell back to 3 and his airspeed quickly fell off. At 200 feet he could not use gravity to accelerate his aircraft. He continued the turn until the stealth was pointing 180 degrees in the opposite direction—south. He brought it wings level, pushed the throttle forward and the airspeed climbed quickly and he nosed up, now gaining altitude.

Koiser stared out the right window and tried to catch sight of the MiG as it passed high to the west. His eyes did not stay there long. A thick white streak of fuel, pouring out of the hole in the right wing, caught his attention.

"Target now, eight kilometers to the northeast."

"I see it," Vorkato radioed, "I see it." He swung the fighter right until the hot IR signal was lined up perfectly on his screen. He would get the intruder this time, he told himself, with or without permission. He keyed his mike. "Radar lock-up, NOW."

As the chaff cloud slowed and grew larger its radar-return signal became increasingly less dense; it did not stay on the radio operator's screen for more than twenty seconds the first time before it disappeared. The signal from this radar-return behaved the same way. The computer software that drove the MiG's radar equipment was not sophisticated enough to tell the operator the target was not real. All it could tell by the returning Doppler signal was that *some* target was present and moving. The back-seater's missiles would not lock-up on the target.

"Unable to engage target, lieutenant," he said, waiting for his pilot to react with anger.

Lieutenant Vorkato said nothing. What the hell could he say? *Act*, he ordered himself. He switched his weapons system from radar-guided AA-9 missiles to AA-8 heat-seekers. It only took the cooled lead-sulphide seeker-head a few seconds to lock in on the 2000-degree flare. He hesitated, though, tightening his grip on the stick everywhere but the trigger.

Where *was* the damn target? Why couldn't he see it? Vorkato heard the high-pitched tone that told him the AA-8 Aphid had locked up on the heat source. *Now.* And he squeezed the trigger two times.

WHOOOSH . . . WHOOOSH. Two missiles accelerated a split-second apart, off the twin-rail mount under the left wing. Vorkato rolled right to get a view of the white exhaust curling toward the ground.

Then he saw it. A bright burning spot only ten meters off the ground. He pulled back the throttles and began to circle. The two Aphids tracked straight for it. Instantly then, the first missile exploded into a whitish blue ball of fire.

And Vorkato understood.

"A decoy flare," he said loud enough for his radar operator to hear. He rolled back left, trying to find the real target, but knew in his guts there would be nothing to see. Oh, yes, he had been deceived.

Duke let the B-2 gain altitude. The MiG had taken the bait, and he was back on course, south toward Moscow—and then, Ramenskoye.

Don't relax, he warned himself as he watched the fuel level on the right tank fall steadily.

"The stress of the turns must have increased the size of the hole," he told Koiser. "At the rate we're losing fuel that tank will be empty in fifteen, twenty minutes."

They heard the moan in the back. Tucker had turned his head, still unconscious. Koiser unbuckled himself and went to look at the injured copilot.

Ten minutes later Duke leveled the Nightstalker at 24,000 feet and reduced his airspeed to 380 knots. The slower speed would conserve fuel, and since twenty-five percent of it was being sucked out of the right tank, he needed to save all he could. He scanned the deep blue sky ahead of him. A few scattered clouds dotted the horizon to the west. The HUD showed a radar-free path for the next eighty miles. After that he would have to take the stealth back down to the deck and hide from the hundreds of search radars that surrounded Moscow. Okay, they'd escaped a MiG. But, he knew, the hardest part was yet to come . . .

He looked over his right shoulder and watched Koiser readjust Tucker in his seat. There was a fresh line of blood that slowly ran down the center of Tuck's face.

The bomber was not in what anybody could call a healthy condition. The SAM had done a lot of damage. The loss of one engine was restricting the B-2's performance. It didn't have the thrust to push it through the turns as rapidly as Duke wanted and needed. Choices . . . if he chose he could go low-level and head straight for Turkey without ever trying an attack. No shame in it, right? He had already proved the B-2 could penetrate Soviet air defenses even with their advanced radar system. The B-2 fleet could threaten the PVO and burn a SAM-free zone for the B-1Bs to follow. If war came SAC could still do its job— forget it. I'm rationalizing. The *mission* was clear from the beginning. Go in and destroy the computer at the Ramenskoye complex that had turned the Soviet's ordinary air defenses into a super-radar system. If the decision to terminate the mission came it would not be from the likes of Duke James. He was supposed to do a job. So *do* it.

"Captain Stevens needs medical attention," Koiser said as he buckled himself into place.

Duke nodded. And the sooner we complete this mission the sooner Tuck would get it.

THE WHITE HOUSE, SITUATION ROOM

Jack Dawson was standing. The rest of the room was quiet. All eyes were on the screen, watching the stealth continue its slow advance south. Every fifteen minutes General Westcott broke the silence and gave them a brief update on the B-2's progress.

"They know it's there, and they know it's ours. Why haven't they said anything?" Turner asked.

"They're probably still shocked we had the balls to try it," Staffer said with his usual subtlety.

"How long before they get to Ramenskoye?" the President asked.

"Less than an hour, sir. Depending on the strength of the defenses they run into." Dawson looked back to the screen. "And if I know Duke James—"

The speaker phone buzzed. Dawson reached over and opened up the channel with Westcott.

"General—" Before he could say another word Westcott cut him off.

"I have an open line to the bomber, Mr. President. The pilot, Colonel James, is reporting battle damage. One engine is out. His copilot is seriously injured and not able to fly. Multiple systems are out. He is asking permission to continue."

Turner looked at Dawson. "You said we could link up with the stealth."

Dawson spoke into the speaker. "General, tie us in directly with the B-2."

Staffer came in. "Even if they do intercept the transmission, Mr. President, they will have to decode it." Spoken, the President thought, like a true spook.

A loud static filled the room and then Dawson said, "Go ahead, Colonel James."

"Present location . . . two hundred fifty-three miles north, seventy-two miles west of the target. Soviet air defenses stronger than expected. Our aircraft is damaged. One engine is out, damage to flight instruments and loss of fuel. Captain Stevens is badly wounded. We are at seventy-percent strength." Short pause. "Possible loss of aircraft over the target. Requesting your permission, Mr. President, to continue." Duke's voice faded into the static.

Turner looked at the President. "He's asking if you're willing to trade a downed B-2 for the destruction of the computer complex."

"If I weren't, I wouldn't have authorized the mission in the first place. What are their chances to complete the mission and return safely?'' he asked Dawson.

''Not being there, sir, I would say they are the only ones who can make that judgment.''

''Put me through to the crew.''

Dawson pushed the button on the speaker.

''Colonel James, this is the President. With the damage to your aircraft, what are the chances of you completing the mission?''

''Unknown, sir, until we reach the target area.''

The President stared at the screen. ''You have authorization to proceed. But if at any time you feel you and your crew are unable to complete the mission you are to break off the attack and run for it.''

''Understood,'' said Duke. And to himself: Like hell, I will.

21

ON TARGET

THE KREMLIN, MOSCOW

"Once the American aircraft enters the defense zone that encircles Moscow we will be able to engage it with our best weapons," Defense Minister Tomskiy was saying to the General Secretary. "I believe the target is an advanced strategic stealth bomber. Maybe one we know nothing about or possibly they're using one from their test base in California—"

"There are *no* B-2 test planes at Edwards," KGB Director Volstad cut in. "My people monitor every test flight at the base—"

"Your people? We have been able to track the aircraft with the radar network. Its radar signature is not unlike that of their F-117 spy plane that we shot down. However, the enemy pilots have been flying through our weakest areas, areas that have not yet been tied into the computer." Tomskiy looked back at Volstad. "I believe this is not just a coincidence—"

"Comrade Volstad, this is not the time," the General Secretary said. "But please explain."

"I just got an update from General Yefimov and Colonel Belikov at Ramenskoye. The colonel believes the Americans know where our weak points are and are exploiting them. Those areas are being strengthened now, we will destroy this target."

The General Secretary was not so sure. "Minister Tomskiy, what else is being done to solve this problem?"

338

Tomskiy waited for the red-faced Volstad to sit down. "I have a squadron of MiG-31s in the air right now searching. The SAM and antiaircraft artillery sites around Moscow and Ramenskoye are on the alert. I have also ordered our search radars to sweep north, west and east. It is just a matter of time, we will find the intruder."

"I suggest the two of you work to solve this," the General Secretary said. "I want this aircraft shot down. Certain people are watching my every move. This could be all it takes for the so-called reformers to push me out of power. If this brings me down, I will make damned sure you all come down with me. Is that clear?" He turned and left the room.

SA-13 COMMAND SITE, 159 KILOMETERS NORTHWEST OF RAMENSKOYE TEST CENTER

The thirty-eight-year-old senior officer Captain Ilyich V. Chilin III stood in front of the armored transporter and scanned the skies to the north with a pair of German-made binoculars. A short, muscular Ukranian with dark brown hair and black eyes, he was liked and respected by his men and commanders.

In the chill air, the heat from the launch vehicle warmed his back. The order to move the four mobile launchers under his command to their new position had come only minutes before and it was taking a while to get everyone settled. From his experience on the Syrian border north of Israel he knew it was sometimes possible to see the enemy approach long before the radar picked it up.

Behind him mounted on the launcher were four infrared heat-seeking missiles secure in their canisters and ready to fire. Located between the missiles a small parabolic dish scanned the sky out to a range of twenty kilometers. Below it a large IR-seeker system looked north for any heat emissions from approaching aircraft. The site was also tied via radio-data link to a forward alerting G/H-Band Thin Skin surveillance-and-acquisition radar that operated twenty kilometers to the south. The two other members of the crew, the driver and missile-launch operator, stayed at their posts inside the launch truck.

As Captain Chilin lowered his binoculars he could hear the

low roar of jet engines to the northeast, and by the variation of sound he could tell there was more than one aircraft. He raised the binoculars in time to see a pair of MiG-31s kick into afterburner and head north as they climbed high into the sky.

He continued his search . . .

NIGHTSTALKER

Duke watched the right-side main fuel gauge go to empty. He made a quick calculation . . . they now had only enough fuel to remain over target for two minutes.

The Nightstalker was still in the radar-free zone 241 miles north of Ramenskoye traveling at 24,000 feet. Duke surveyed the landscape that stretched out before him. Directly ahead the land was light brown, showing the colors of fall. Traces of snow were tucked along the sides of the roads and on the shadowy side of hills where the sun could not reach it. Beneath him passed several black paved highways that connected the small towns and farms dotting the countryside. To the east he could see where the land had been carved into sections for farming and beyond that it broke into rolling hills. Their green color told him they were probably covered with pine trees. All in all the interior of the USSR didn't look much different from the interior of the United States. He wondered about the families he was flying over. Did they understand that life could be better than the life Koiser talked about . . . ?

Duke took a deep breath. Thinking about family, his family, now would drive him crazy. His mind went back to the mission. With only a few minutes left to study the stored satellite information appearing on his targeting CRT, he scrolled the screen as it showed the latest location of SAMs and triple A sites on the way to the target. The stealth's computer locked the locations of the threats into the HUD's memory so that when the B-2 came into range the pilot would be warned.

Since the new Soviet radar system—even with Koiser's input —represented so many unknowns it had been decided during mission planning that there was no one exact way to attack the center. Defenses were extremely strong no matter what direction they flew in. Duke and his crew would have to rely on the latest satellite intelligence and fight their way to the target. His CRT told him the ten remaining TALDs were still secure and ready for launch. Eight of the decoys had been programmed. Their job was to pull the PVO defenses away from the bomber. He checked the antiradiation drones, cycled their miniature computers to make sure each drone's electrical system was up and running. From there he called up the data on the SRAMs, the short range attack missiles located in the right weapons bay.

"I'm not getting a response on number five," he said. He looked over at Koiser. "We got a dead one."

"Dead one?"

"One of our SRAMs must have been knocked loose. I can't get it tied into the targeting computer. There's no other way to program it." Duke punched the recall button again hoping to get a different answer. He didn't get one. "The warhead's still active, we just can't launch the damned thing."

Duke referenced the HUD. In three minutes the free ride would be over and they would begin the most dangerous part of their mission. He looked behind him at Tucker. The dried blood around Tuck's face and eyes made him look thirty years older. Duke began to wonder if he would make it.

"Picking up a weak G/H-Band from the southwest, colonel," Koiser broke in.

It's starting, Duke thought, and pushed the stick forward to put the Nightstalker into a steep dive. He could feel the bomber vibrate slightly as the airspeed passed 550 knots, the uneven fuel distribution affecting the stealth's ability to cut through the air smoothly.

The G/H-Band warning light was now followed by five other yellow lights. Duke swung the bomber left as they sliced through 10,000 feet, speed 592 knots.

RAMENSKOYE TEST CENTER

"Contact . . . heading one seven four." The controller's voice filled the command room.

Belikov pointed to the screen. "They are ten kilometers west of the city of Vovrov. Do you *see* it?" His vehement panic was evident.

The two men stood there for a few seconds, eyes fixed on the screen as the shadowlike image of the bomber moved slowly to the south.

"How did it get this close?" Belikov turned to the general. "It's less than 400 kilometers from Moscow—"

"Target descending . . . altitude 3500 meters. Speed . . . 590 knots."

General Yefimov picked up the phone. "Major, vector the MiGs to the target. Order the SAMs to go on maximum alert. Tell them not to wait for orders. Engage the target. Now."

NIGHTSTALKER

They were now only 190 miles northwest of Moscow. Just a few miles more and they would enter the Moscow air-defense network that consisted of SAMs, fighters and antiaircraft artillery. The network was ringed with overlapping search-and-targeting radars. When attack plans were drawn up at Groom Lake, Duke estimated there could be some 200 different radars painting him at the same time. The SAMs would soon follow. One thing Duke had learned in Vietnam was that if the enemy threw enough junk in the air he would eventually hit something. The skies over Hanoi were bad, but Duke figured that he was about to enter a hell to make Hanoi look like a tea party.

He could see the industrial city of Dzerzhinsk in the distance to the east only thirty miles away, a brownish gray cloud of pollution hanging over it.

"Right on target," he said loud enough for Koiser to hear.

"IR sensors picking up two targets to the east . . . MiGs" Koiser said, "heading this way."

The HUD showed the two threats were still over thirty miles away. Duke was more concerned about the radars looking at them, radars that controlled the SAMs.

Duke pulled back on the control stick, and the Nightstalker came level at 8000 feet. The HUD showed two more radars had come up four miles ahead, sweeping in their direction. Fire-control radars trying to acquire a target.

"That G/H-Band must be tracking us," Duke said. But so far none of the radars had locked onto them. He rolled right to escape the first radar by only 150 yards, then cut through the second, staying in its beam for a few seconds but not long enough, he hoped, for the operators to achieve a lock-on.

"You got an I.D. on that search radar yet? It must be controlling every acquisition radar in this area," Duke said as he rolled left again to avoid a third and fourth radar that appeared on his HUD.

"Yes, computer shows it . . . a Thin Skin." Koiser couldn't help it, he felt uncomfortable using the NATO code name. "It controls SA-6 and SA-8 SAMs—"

The H- and I-Band warning lights turned red. The Threat Warning Panel lit up and Duke watched as two, three, four missiles lifted off and headed for the Nightstalker.

As the missiles broke through at 100 feet the B-2's sensors projected them on the HUD, angling toward them at two o'clock. Duke held steady at 8000. "Damn it, I wish I had more room to maneuver." The B-2 was a wondrously advanced if delicate aircraft, but she had to depend on deception and evasion more than he would have liked. Well, you can't have everything, he told himself as he gave the order once again to ready the chaff, then banked right and came across the front of the first missile, leveled and rolled a little right in order to see the speeding projectile and maintain a straight course.

"When I break, hit the chaff button."

Moments later Duke realized the first and second missiles would pass behind him and looked to the two other SAMs.

"Turn left five degrees," Koiser said.

Duke rolled the Nightstalker to the left, stopped dead on five degrees. The SAMs were only 3000 yards away and still heading straight for them.

"Hold," Koiser said. "Break hard *right*." He pushed the chaff button as the big bomber broke inside the lead missile. The SA-6 was traveling at three times the speed of sound and couldn't make the turn. It exploded 800 yards behind the B-2.

"I-Band to the east, I am picking up two of them," Koiser said. "They are moving this way fast, colonel."

At 1000 feet Duke added a steady back pressure on the stick and came level at 300 feet. Intelligence was reporting no triple-A threats in the area. He hoped they were right. Running into a wall of 57 mm. cannon fire would bring them down just as fast as a supersonic missile.

Koiser turned to him. "MiG-31s seven miles east and closing." The signal of the Thin Skin still pounded them.

"Open the right weapons bay," Duke ordered, and realized if he didn't take care of the Thin Skin there would be a hundred MiGs on them. "Come on, baby." Duke was waiting for the computer to tell him the homing drone was programmed and ready to fly. He pulled the bomber up to 600 feet to give the missile room to maneuver. "Launching." He pushed the button to release the nine-foot drone. Its two wings deployed, stabilizing its flight. Moments later two solid-fuel rocket boosters ignited, sending it speeding away from the stealth in the direction of the radar.

Duke looked to his HUD as the drone disappeared in the distance. The rocket boosters would soon burn out and the drone's small ramjet engine would kick in.

Duke refocused on the HUD symbols . . . the MiGs were close enough to be picked up by the B-2's IR sensors, the enemy fighters were less than three miles away on a direct intercept course.

RAMENSKOYE TEST CENTER

Belikov, back on the control-center floor, watched the two MiGs move closer to the image of the target. They should be on top of the bomber in less than thirty seconds.

"Order the fighters to shoot on sight." Major Slikuna relayed the message, and the room filled with tension as the two blips closed in on one another—and the MiGs passed over the target and continued on west.

The major hated to say it: "Pilots report their radars are unable to pick up a target—"

"Tell them to turn, drop down and find that aircraft," Belikov said, furious. "There's an enemy aircraft only two kilometers away from them!"

NIGHTSTALKER

Koiser looked out the top of the front cockpit window, waiting for the MiGs to make another pass. By their previous flight pattern he could tell they were being controlled by the ground.

Duke had dropped down to below 200 feet. The MiGs had passed over the B-2's nose minutes ago only 3000 feet away. The next time they made a pass, chances were they would be a lot closer.

He pulled the stick back as they crested over a long hill before dropping back into a small valley about a mile long. The terrain was becoming more rugged. He could not maintain such a low altitude much longer.

The Tacit Rainbow guidance system made one course adjustment on its climb to the target, pushed over at 1500 yards from the emitter and gained more speed as it headed for the radar's thirty-foot-wide wire-mesh antenna. Seconds later the drone slammed into the KraZ-214 truck, the speed of the missile causing its twenty-pound warhead to penetrate the quarter-inch armor before detonating into a fifty-foot ball of smoke and fire and turning the radar into a mess of twisted molten metal.

"It's gone," Koiser reported as the G/H-Band warning light went off. There was no exaltation in his voice. These were, after all, his people not so long ago.

Duke did not celebrate either. He brought the Nightstalker up to 500 feet and broke hard to the east. They needed to get away from the MiGs, and fast. He could hear their I-Band radars growing closer.

He swung the stealth north in a fast steady turn. The images on the HUD revealed the two interceptors were heading east only two miles away. Duke waited until he had put more than three miles between him and the enemy fighters before he turned left again and headed west. He was now parallel to them but going in the opposite direction.

Koiser put the image of the destroyed truck with until recently fellow-Soviets behind him and followed Duke's line of thought. Straining to see the dark outline of the big fighters against the light blue morning sky, he saw traces of their dark jet exhaust first and followed it until he saw two black dots moving away.

"I see the MiGs . . . south crossing to the east."

RAMENSKOYE TEST CENTER

General Yefimov watched the target disappear off the screen. The MiGs had shot it down, he assumed. He picked up the phone, dialed a code and an instant later Minister of Defense Tomskiy was on the line.

"The target has been destroyed, sir. It went off our scope—" Yefimov heard Belikov enter the room and slam the door.

"One of our radar stations has been destroyed, General."

"What?"

"The surveillance radar that was feeding us the data has been destroyed. The report just came in from one of the MiGs. The computer is no longer receiving data from it."

Yefimov took a deep breath and closed his eyes. "I am sorry, sir," he now said to the Minister. "I cannot confirm the kill. I have just learned our surveillance station at Rostov is no longer functioning, I will contact you when I have more information." He hung up before Tomskiy could blast him.

"General, I suggest you take stronger measures," Belikov said.

"And what do you suggest? You are just as much in charge here as I am—"

"We have only a single squadron of MiG-31s patrolling the area north of here. Not enough. The only way to find this target is to get enough fighters in the air to spot it." Belikov keyed the intercom mike to Major Slikuna.

"I want every interceptor based at Kubinka in the air. MiG-21s, 23s, 25s, 29s everything that will fly. I want them to sweep the sector to the northeast. Have my squadron at Ramenskoye fueled and in the air. Instruct Major Nikitov that *nothing* is to enter the sector around this complex."

He looked back at the general sitting hunched at his desk. A weak old man whose time had passed. His kind were a threat.

SA-13 COMMAND SITE

The launch sergeant threw open the heavy metal blast door leading to the interior of the launch truck.

"Captain Chilin, I have lost contact with the control radar."

"Check the system, find the problem."

"I have rechecked our equipment. It is not in our receivers. From what I can tell the control center is no longer broadcasting."

"Have you tried to reach them by radio?"

"No response."

"What are you telling me? The radar is no longer there?"

"I am not sure. My early warning and azimuth data suddenly went out." The sergeant didn't offer any conclusions, this was for his commander to figure out.

The captain put the glasses to his eyes and scrutinized the sky. In the distance a trace of black smoke curled into the air. He watched it grow into a large ball until it could be seen with the naked eye.

"Get back to your post," he ordered the sergeant. What else could he say . . . ?

NIGHTSTALKER, SOUTHBOUND

Duke steadied the bomber at 500 feet. His latest satellite data relayed that they would encounter their next radar threat in less than ten minutes. Koiser was right about the PVO not expecting an attack to come out of the east *toward* Moscow. They only had one early-warning radar looking to the east, all the others watched for an attack to come from the west, south and north.

Moscow was now 130 miles to the south and fifty-two miles to the west. At their present speed they would pass the city of Noginsk in eighteen minutes, and Noginsk was just thirty miles away from downtown Moscow. Duke's plan was to fly past Moscow and circle in from the southeast, heading straight for the computer center. If the decoys worked, the PVO would be busy tracking and destroying eight targets, including his bomber . . .

The chatter of the computer printer filled the cockpit. Koiser handed the sheet to Duke, who nosed the B-2 up to 800 feet to give himself some breathing room. He took the computer sheet.

"Westcott says SAC estimates forty to fifty fighters are airborne and headed our way."

Koiser watched his instruments, trying to picture how the PVO would react. He had been on the same sort of drill a hundred times himself. He turned to Duke. "We must stay very low and fly as fast as possible. With that many fighters in the air . . . we can hope there will be some confusion. I have never seen that many fighters preparing to attack." Koiser cocked his head to the right. "Radars . . . moving from the south." The radar warning light for an I-Band blinked on again.

Duke's eyes went to the TWP. Two targets had just appeared, accelerating toward them. No apparent confusion here.

MIG-25 FOXBAT

"Follow my lead," Lieutenant Colonel Dmitri Taskaev ordered his junior wingman. The colonel did not want to be held back by the inexperience of a younger pilot. At thirty-seven Taskaev was himself one of the youngest and also brightest lieutenant colonels in the PVO. He was single, he didn't drink and disciplined himself with a strict routine of physical exercise. He had an overwhelming desire in life—to fly and to fight. And just now there was no question what he had to do—find and destroy the enemy aircraft that had penetrated Soviet borders.

The colonel heard his orders crackle through his headset as he started his descent to 500 meters and continued to search visually along with his radar. To the west and east of him other MiG-25 teams were doing the same thing.

Taskaev could feel the energy pump through his muscular, compact body as he scanned the instruments of his fighter. He had been flying the twin-engine MiG for three years and was considered to be the best pilot in his squadron at high- and low-level interception. He was a master at using the high-thrust, fast-dash speed of his MiG, combined with its radar, to hunt and bring down enemy aircraft during mock engagements. Originally he had been trained to attack high-flying American B-52s and F-111s before they entered Soviet airspace. Recently he had been assigned a new mission—to find and kill American low-flying B-52s and the new B-1B Bomber. From what he had been able to piece together from the radio reports he was sure, at least hoped, it was a newly deployed B-1B that he was hunting . . . the difference now being that this time it was for real.

Taskaev keyed his mike. "Turn right ten degrees . . . radar twenty-degree search beam," he said, and increased the radar's search pattern.

SA-13 COMMAND SITE

Captain Chilin's attention turned back to the northern horizon. At first he thought it was one of the MiGs—a dark speck more than fifty kilometers out and heading his way. He noted the aircraft's location and continued to scan right and left. He could hear the sound of jet engines in the background fast approaching his position.

He came back to where the black spot should now be on the horizon—it wasn't there. The aircraft was moving much faster than he had first thought. It took him a while before he caught sight of it again, this time cresting the top of a distant hill, then immediately it dropped back down, disappearing into the background colors of the hillside.

"This is no MiG," the captain muttered to himself. He refocused his binoculars to refine the clarity of the image. He watched it grow closer and follow the contour of the terrain. As he watched the thought of it possibly being a TU-26 or SU-24, returning to Kubinka from a training mission crossed his mind.

He didn't take his eyes off it. As the distance shortened he could tell it definitely was not a SU-24—its wing span belonged to a large aircraft and it seemed to change shape as he caught different angles of it. He now estimated it was less than ten kilometers away, one minute. He reached behind him and pounded on the command vehicle three quick times.

The sergeant appeared from the interior.

"Do you see anything on the IR scope?"

"No, sir, nothing."

Chilin raised his binoculars. "I want your heat seeker set for maximum range. There's an unidentified aircraft approaching straight ahead."

"Yes, captain." He didn't tell his commanding officer he had already set his sensor for maximum range. He was, after all, not an idiot even if he was only a sergeant.

NIGHTSTALKER

"I got 'em eight miles out 3200 feet." Duke watched the images of the MiGs appear on the HUD in the upper left corner.

"These are not MiG-31s." Koiser watched his computer screen. "The signal is for an older type of radar."

Duke pushed the stealth's nose down as they came over a ridge covered with wiry pine trees. Even if Koiser was right and they were older aircraft he felt more comfortable below the 500 foot level.

"I have computer identification." Koiser read the data on the computer screen. "MiG-25M . . . limited look-down shoot-down capability. Six miles and closing at 900 miles an hour. Altitude 700 meters and decreasing."

Duke double-checked the chaff and flare dispensers. The pulsating sound of the radar was now filling his headset.

"Five miles," Koiser updated as he leaned forward and tried to see the interceptors.

Duke cracked the throttles forward a hair, trying to coax a few more knots out of the bomber.

SA-13 COMMAND SITE

"Still nothing, the scope is clear," the sergeant said as he sat at his post.

Captain Chilin said nothing. He looked inside the command launcher and pulled out his headset plugging it into the jack on the outside of the launcher. He was now tied into the command launcher as well as the other three missile sites.

He pressed the button on the side of his headset. "That is

impossible, the aircraft is within your range." He swung around and picked the target up with his glasses. He kept the button pushed, shutting off any reply from the sergeant. "We have a target bearing three seven six. I am instructing you to fire as soon as you have a lock-on."

The launchers confirmed his order. The launch sergeant behind him reached up and closed the armor-covered door. The target was thirty seconds away.

It was like nothing Captain Chilin had ever seen. The aircraft did not have a tail or fuselage. When it was pointed right at him all he could see was a thin black line. There wasn't any smoke spewing from the engines. For that matter he could not see *any* engines. He watched the strange looking plane vanish behind a hill. Moments later it topped it and banked slightly to his right. If it stayed on its course the target would pass a couple of kilometers to the east of the control launcher.

The clicking sound of cold metal gears coming together told him the massive IR seeker was turning side-to-side. Searching the northern sky, the crew had still not locked onto the target.

Lieutenant Colonel Taskaev caught a glimpse of his wingman's canopy flash in the sunlight. He was ten meters off his left wing and a meter behind him.

"Break five degrees south and stay 200 meters off my wing," Taskaev ordered. "Turn your radar to max and stay alert. If you sight the target before I do I want to hear about it. We will engage on my orders. Understood?"

"Yes," came the response from Taskaev's wingman.

Taskaev leveled his fighter at 500 meters and reduced his airspeed to 410 knots. At that altitude and airspeed he hoped he could *see* the target as well as pick it up on his radar. He lifted his head from the cockpit controls, watched his wingman bank away and surveyed the airspace around him. He felt his aircraft rock up and down as he climbed over a tree-covered hill and headed out across a long valley. Taskaev had studied American strategic-bomber tactics and knew they called for their warplanes to fly at low levels when attacking. He felt confident he would find the target below 500 meters, and probably heading south.

"Four miles and still closing," Koiser reported again. He was having a hard time seeing anything to the southeast . . . the bright morning sun had climbed high into the sky and made it increasingly difficult for him to spot a distant aircraft.

Duke noted the warning lights were clear as well as the TWP. "Let's get past these MiGs. I'm showing nothing else to the south."

"Left eleven o'clock, I see them, colonel—"

"All right, hold steady, tell me if they move."

One-and-a-half kilometers east of the SA-13 command launcher, site number two detected the first weak IR emission from the stealth—a very faint spot in the upper center of the operator's scope. The redheaded sergeant operating the system had noticed it several times before but had, not unreasonably, ignored it as a hot spot in the atmosphere. This time it was more than a blur. Something was there, it was fuzzy but it was there . . . He waited for the automated system to lock up on the target, swiveled around in his seat to the launch-control panel. When the system locked up on the target it would signal him with a low-pitch tone in his headset. Now he had to position the missiles for launch.

The turret moved the four missiles forty degrees to the left, lining them up in the right azimuth. The operator watched the red indicator light come on. Next he selected the number one and two missiles to be fired, depressed the right-side launch-button halfway down, which opened the canister front doors and exposed the lead-sulphide IR seeker head of the SA-13 missiles. He waited for the tone signaling that the missiles had achieved a lock. Then he would depress the launch-button fully and the two SAMs would be on their way.

* * *

The two MiG-25s passed to the north of the well-camouflaged SA-13 site at 500 meters, continuing on a course of 327 degrees. Taskaev's search radar showed only ground clutter and interference. He looked up from his radarscope and surveyed the sky ahead. Spotting a low-level high-speed target was a skill he had become very good at. The trick was to look for movement, a flash of light or a blur above the ground, anything out of the ordinary.

He and his wingman were now heading almost due north, their big twin-turbofans pointed to the south. The 1200-degree temperature of their exhaust nozzles gave the IR-seeking sensors of the SA-13 site an ideal target . . .

Unknown to the operator the tone he heard in his headset was not that of his sensors locking up on the infrared radiation of the intruder. His attention was not on the scope or he would have seen two new targets entering the picture. Rather, he watched the sky from a small plexiglass window directly above him.

A double-launch tone filled his ears. Each missile had locked onto a target. He now fully depressed the hard plastic launch button. The mobile-launch vehicle shook and the window above him filled with white smoke. The first missile was on its way. Quickly he released the button, resetting the launch sequence.

He waited for the tone to become even and constant again, pressed the button again, sending the second SA-13 missile into the sky. Next he readied number three and four missiles. The front door of their canisters opened and he waited for their seekers to also pick up the target.

Seconds later the first seven-foot missile impacted the closest MiG. A brilliant white flash engulfed the back of the aircraft. The SAM's fragmentation warhead exploded two meters under the left tail and below the rudder. The fragments of the exploding warhead instantly cut into the nickel-steel and aluminum structure of the fighter, slicing electrical cables and hydraulic lines. The huge MiG rolled to the left and pitched up . . .

The young pilot flying wingman to Colonel Taskaev reacted by trying to level his stricken fighter. He jammed the stick down and right at the same time. The controls were heavy and sluggish, his MiG didn't react. The instrument panel lit up with a half dozen red warning lights. He was losing hydraulic pressure and fuel. He turned his head around just in time to see the second SAM slam into the left side of his fighter.

This time his MiG rocked violently to the right. The force of the explosion ripped into the engine, throwing broken compressor and turbine blades into the main and aft fuel tanks. Instantaneously the entire left side of the fuselage was engulfed in flames. The MiG nosed over further and slowly rolled uncontrollably on its side.

The pilot tried desperately to regain control as the fire-warning light came on. Too late. He reached up over his head to grab the ejection handle. It was his last conscious thought. The middle section of the 77,000-pound aircraft exploded and tore into the cockpit.

The fighter rolled completely over and headed for the ground at a thirty-degree angle. Fifty feet before impact the second main tank exploded, causing the fuselage to break into two pieces. A moment later the two distinct sections hit the ground spewing fire and wreckage over a half mile. Two secondary explosions followed as the solid fuel from two of the MiG's four Aphids air-to-air-missiles ignited.

It took a few seconds before Colonel Taskaev realized what had happened. He looked over his left shoulder. His wingman was gone. Shot down. Instinctively he banked the MiG hard right and left to put his fighter into a steep climb. He squeezed the flare-dispenser button on his throttle three times, releasing a stream of IR decoys behind his aircraft, then snapped the MiG over 180 degrees so that he was flying inverted. He twisted his head around as he tried to see who was firing below or behind him.

"Our own *SAM* site," he muttered, outraged. Friendly Fire, they called it in Vietnam, but every pilot dreaded it.

Just then he saw a grayish black blur flash beneath him to the south. It was like nothing he had ever seen before. It wasn't a B-52, it wasn't a B-1B . . . what the hell was it?

SA-13 SITE

"HOLD FIRE, HOLD FIRE," Captain Chilin screamed into his microphone. The stricken MiG had crashed only 500 meters away. He could hear the sound of the fighter's 23-mm. cannon ammunition popping and snapping as it cooked-off from the intense heat of the fire.

He heard the high-pitch shrill of jet engines pass to the west . . . and looked up in time to catch a glimpse of what was the B-2 streak overhead less than a kilometer away. He watched it pass over the hill behind him and vanish.

"Sergeant, get me PVO headquarters, *fast*."

MIG-25 FOXBAT, TURNING SOUTH

"Damn it, I know better," Taskaev said under his breath as his anger built. He had hesitated just long enough to lose sight of the aircraft. Now he had to find it again. He banked his MiG left, bringing it around to a new heading of 175. He refocused his look-down shoot-down radar to its widest beam and increased his airspeed to 500 knots. He reached over and turned down the volume level of his radio switch. He didn't want help from the other MiGs and he didn't need their chatter interfering with his concentration. This was *his* chance.

NIGHTSTALKER

Koiser listened to the pulsing tone of the MiG-25's radar in his headset. One of the two I-Bands was gone, its signal had stopped. He and Duke had just seen one of the MiGs explode and break up. He was sure it was one of the MiG-25s that was flying at them from the southwest. Now what about the other MiG, it was still out there somewhere behind them . . .

"Do you hear it, its signal is growing stronger," Koiser said.

Duke didn't take his eyes off the horizon. They were flying over a series of broken hills and rocky ridges. "Do you think he saw us?" Duke wasn't worried about the Foxbat's radar picking them up, but at close range he could be picked up visually.

"Turn fifty degrees left and let's find out."

Taskaev rolled to the right while still maintaining his southerly course, the only way he could clearly see the air space below his MiG. He studied the sky, then banked left. He rested his helmet against the MiG's plexiglass canopy as he looked across the horizon. About halfway back he saw it—a gray triangular aircraft flying less than a hundred meters off the ground, banking to the east away from him.

He cut his airspeed and dropped the nose of the MiG, matching the turn-rate of the target, then switched his radar-homing missiles from standby to active and rested his thumb on the launch button. Three kilometers out, the kill should be quick and easy.

"He's following us . . ." Duke checked his airspeed and altitude as he banked the B-2 back to the south.

Koiser saw the MiG was turning with them. He caught a glimpse of the silver-and-black fighter as Duke leveled and added power. He knew there was no way they could outrun the Foxbat. Chances were the MiG was loaded with a mix of radar and infrared homing missiles. And at close range the heat-seekers could lock onto the bomber.

"He's directly behind us," Koiser warned.

Taskaev waited. His speed was now 480 knots and he could easily see the target below him. But he couldn't understand why his radar wasn't locking up. The target was in the center of his HUD. It was receiving a strong blast from his MiG's powerful Pulse-Doppler radar. He adjusted the sensitivity level, expecting the color-aim point on his HUD to change from green to yellow to indicate a lock-up. But it didn't, and his missiles wouldn't lock on.

The electronic emissions from his radar were, unknown to him, being absorbed by the B-2.

He cracked his throttles forward and watched his airspeed creep up. He was now two kilometers out. Enough of this, he thought, and switched from radar-homing missiles to his four heat-seekers. He listened for the tone in his headset to change from a hum to a high-pitched squeal.

"We're in deep shit, man . . . this guy's on my back. Any more ideas, captain?" Duke's forehead wrinkled with tension.

Koiser looked at the instruments before he spoke. He had experienced the Nightstalker's performance when outmaneuvering the SAMs and believed it could outturn the MiG, which fully loaded was fast but couldn't pull more than a 3.5-G turn. The B-2 could pull 6.5 or maybe 7. Anyway, it was their only chance.

"Damn . . . I should have lock-up," Taskaev muttered into his oxygen mask. Why weren't his AA-8 missiles locking onto the target?

The answer was the B-2's computer that controlled an exhaust cooling system designed to make it very difficult for heat-seeking missiles to target the bomber from behind unless an aircraft attacking from behind was extremely close. Only then could its heat-seeking missiles lock on.

Now, at only one kilometer out, Taskaev did finally hear the tone change in his headset . . . whatever was flying ahead of him had the smallest IR signature he had ever encountered.

"Now . . ." he murmured as he pressed the button on his stick two quick times, launching two AA-8 heat-seekers.

"Go vertical, colonel. Maximum power . . ."

"Vertical?" Duke questioned. There was no way they could outclimb a MiG.

"*Do it now.* Maximum power and go vertical."

Duke stopped questioning, smashed the throttles forward and yanked the stick back with all his strength, the Nightstalker responding with a force of 5 Gs.

Taskaev shook his head in frustration as he watched his target slice straight up and away from the ground. His heat-seeker wouldn't have time to adjust. Just then one of the AA-8's hit the exhaust from the B-2, exploding into a red-and-orange ball a hundred meters beneath the bomber.

Taskaev banked left to avoid the debris of the exploding missile and pulled his stick back at the same time.

The stealth shuddered from the force of the AA-8 exploding beneath it. Pieces of its warhead ripped into the underside of the left wing.

"Climb . . . climb," from Koiser.

Duke watched his airspeed fall as they climbed through 1000 feet and on upward. "Four hundred ten knots . . . fifteen hundred feet," he called out.

Koiser didn't react, his eyes stayed on the part of the HUD showing airspeed and altitude. At 2000 feet he started to scan the air space around the bomber, looking for the MiG.

"Three hundred eighty knots," Duke read out.

"Roll her. I have to find the MiG." Koiser motioned with his hand to show Duke he wanted him to roll the B-2 360 degrees.

Taskaev came even with the Nightstalker at 1100 meters above ground. Both his MiG and the bomber were climbing straight up, a half-kilometer apart. He watched as his target twisted around, the black bottom of the aircraft turning into dark gray. And for the first time he saw the cockpit, actually saw the white helmets of the pilots.

I won't make the same mistake twice, Taskaev told himself and moved his throttles forward, rocketing past the B-2.

* * *

"There he goes," Koiser said, his eyes following the Foxbat as it climbed away from them.

"Two hundred ninety knots . . . 4000 feet." Duke was worried, they would stall in less than thirty seconds.

Koiser knew what Duke was thinking. If they stalled they couldn't maneuver and the Nightstalker would be a sitting duck for the MiG.

"A few more seconds . . . a few more." Koiser didn't take his eyes off the MiG above them.

Taskaev pushed over upside down at 2000 meters, the shoulder straps of his ejection seat holding him in place. He reduced power, his airspeed fell off and he pushed the nose of the MiG toward the ground.

"Now," Koiser shouted. "Push over and head for the ground."

Duke chopped the throttles and forced the nose of the B-2 down.

"No . . . full power, we need speed."

No time to argue. Duke pushed the throttles forward and felt the Gs start to build.

Taskaev lined up the target on his HUD as his airspeed climbed. He knew what he had to do . . . get close enough to fire his missiles but not so close that they could not maneuver if the target turned away.

He also was well aware of the weakness of his MiG—in a steep dive he would have to be very careful and not wait too long. Otherwise he would not be able to pull up and would fly into the ground.

"Here he comes," Koiser said.

"Yeah . . . terrific." Duke watched the ground coming up

straight at them. The Nightstalker's airspeed was now 560 knots and building.

"At eight hundred feet pull up," Koiser said. "There will be no way he can follow us, he will fly into the ground."

Duke adjusted his grip on the stick and throttle. Koiser was pushing it—800 feet left no margin for error.

Colonel Taskaev cut his airspeed. His intent was to slow down so he could make the turn with the target. At lower speeds he could turn much easier. Then he would go to full power, catch the target and make one quick pass firing his remaining two missiles. If that didn't work he would ram the target and try to eject at the last moment.

He watched the target descending. They would have to pull up at any second. He opened his air brakes, slowing his fighter to an even 400 knots and started to pull back on his stick. He eased up at 3 Gs and watched the black nose of his MiG come up. If he timed it right he would only lose sight of the target for a few seconds.

"Here we go . . ." At 800 feet Duke popped the air brakes, brought the throttles back to half-power and hauled back on the stick. The Nightstalker seemed to resist, not responding as Duke would have liked.

Koiser's chest grew heavy as the increasing Gs smashed him into his seat. He called them out in short breaths. "Five . . . five point five . . . six . . . six point five . . ."

They were at 350 feet and still only halfway there. The horizon was in the center of the windscreen as their airspeed dropped and the nose slowly pushed up.

"Come *on*, baby" Duke grunted, and kept a solid 6.5 Gs pull on the bomber.

Taskaev caught sight of the target pulling up from the ground. He let his fighter continue to drop as he applied steady back-pressure to the stick.

At 4 Gs he gently nudged the stick forward, the MiG started to pull out of the dive and come level. He had practiced this maneuver hundreds of times. Experience told him he would bottom out at 100 meters, then he could let the aircraft drift down to forty or fifty meters and he would be directly behind the vulnerable target.

At seventy-eight feet the Nightstalker came level. Duke and Koiser felt the Gs bleed off as they streaked across the frozen ground at 560 knots. Three miles ahead was a high rock ridge.

Koiser focused on the IR sensor readouts of the HUD as they waited. If his plan worked the MiG's IR signature would be gone and the MiG would now be a hole in the ground. If . . .

In one motion Taskaev thrust the throttles forward, putting his fighter into afterburner. Its twin turbofans erupted with power, throwing him back in his seat. He was closing on the target at a rate of 1000 kilometers an hour. His full concentration was centered on keeping the target in the middle of his HUD and waiting for the tone to change in his headset.

He could feel it. In fifteen seconds the target should be destroyed.

Koiser looked at Duke. His eyes told the story. His plan had not worked, the fighter was still on their tail.

"He's still on us, colonel, closing fast," Koiser finally got out.

Duke nodded. "We're not done yet. Two can play this game. Watch our altitude." And so saying he jammed the throttles forward and rocked the bomber left to right, at the same time pushing the nose down. His eyes went to the horizon.

"Come on . . ." he yelled out in anger. "Come and get us."

"Ten seconds," Taskaev mumbled. "Lock up, lock up," he fairly crooned to his missiles.

The tone in his headset pulsated. He was almost in range, the target was squarely centered on his HUD. He rested his thumb on the launch button.

"Five seconds . . ." Taskaev did not blink. All he could see was the long thin profile of the strange bomber ahead of him.

"Four thousand feet and closing." At any moment Koiser expected the bomber to explode and break up.

"Give me more, sweetheart, give me more." Duke was nursing every ounce of power out of the Nightstalker.

The high rock ridge was only a mile away and rushing toward them. His timing had to be just right. If he broke too soon the MiG would follow . . .

"Three thousand feet behind us . . . two thousand eight hundred," Koiser called out.

Now Duke could clearly see large rocks and snow-covered pine trees at the base of a small mountain ahead of him. A few more seconds, he thought.

"Three . . . two . . . one." Taskaev waited until the tone was clear and even. Then, just as he started to put pressure on the launch button, he saw the bomber break to the right and start to climb straight up.

Duke had both hands on the stick. He watched the side of the ridge race by . . . rocks, trees, dirty gray boulders a mixed blur. His first thought was that he had waited too long, there was no way they would clear the top of the ridge. He held his breath as the Nightstalker strained for the sky.

Taskaev felt the blood rush from his head as his body was driven into his seat. He held the stick back, hoping to bring up the nose of his fighter. His airspeed was 1700 kilometers an hour and increasing as he headed straight for the side of the small jagged mountain. His head was pinned against the headrest as the G-meter climbed past 4, 4.5 and came to rest on 5. He was overstressing his aircraft and he knew it. He didn't have a choice.

"I can do it, I can do it," he muttered as the dome of his radar antenna started to inch up.

The Nightstalker flashed over the top of the ridge with less than twenty feet of clearance. A moment later Duke pushed the nose down and cut his airspeed, then banked hard left and came wings-level at 500 feet.

Taskaev had only seconds in which to react. Not enough. No way to avoid hitting the side of the mountain. His fighter, flying at a high rate of speed, could not turn as fast as the bat-shaped thing he was chasing.

He reached over his head with both hands and pulled the dual red-and-black ejection cords straight down with all his strength. Almost instantly he was blasted away from his doomed fighter as it sped toward the side of the ridge, then erupted in a cloud of flames and flying metal.

Colonel Taskaev's parachute opened fifty meters above the ground as a burst of heat from his exploding MiG passed over him, and he started to drift toward the ground. The fact that he would live was no consolation.

RAMENSKOYE TEST CENTER

Major Slikuna cupped his hand over the mouthpiece. "It's confirmed, colonel . . . we have lost a MiG-25."

Belikov did not take his eyes off the section of the display from which the aircraft had disappeared.

The major hung up the phone. "An SA-13 commander has just reported seeing a strange looking aircraft flying south . . . one hundred fifty-nine kilometers north of Moscow."

Belikov's eyes seemed to bore through him. It was clear he did not believe the major was telling him everything.

"He reported seeing what he calls a flying wing," Major

Slikuna said uneasily as he watched Belikov's jaw tighten with anger . . . and comprehension.

Belikov looked back at the screen. No use denying it . . . the Americans were flying a stealth bomber, a B-2. Which wasn't *supposed* to be fully tested and operational. Still, even with a B-2 they shouldn't have gotten this far. The strength of the PVO should still be able to shoot down a single bomber, even a stealth. It was almost as if the pilot somehow knew the system, knew its remaining weaknesses . . . Of course, only one man had such knowledge about the new radar system.

"Captain Koiser," he said quietly and bitterly to himself.

The major turned and looked at him.

"Contact the base, major. Tell them to ready my MiG."

22

SILENT DEATH

NIGHTSTALKER

Ramenskoye was now twenty minutes away. Duke watched four MiGs move across the sky to his left and swing south in front of him, the glow from the orange flames as the afterburners pushed them through the turn clearly visible. Two more came out of the west and also turned south, banking back and forth in a long S-shaped search pattern. The IR sensors on the HUD showed a half-dozen more farther south and converging into the area ahead of them. The satellite map displayed on the CRT to his left showed they would soon enter the radar-surveillance area of two early-warning radars. Their last known locations placed one a few miles north and the second just south of Moscow. The acquisition and fire control radar sites were scattered in various locations all the way to Ramenskoye. It was not possible to avoid all of them.

"That MiG must have radioed that he got a visual on us," Duke said as he pulled the throttles back and decreased his speed to 380 knots. The Nightstalker was cruising at 500 feet down a long valley.

"Open the left weapons-bay door," Duke said.

Koiser flipped the switch to the open position.

"When I say so, press that button on the left."

Duke waited until the HUD told him a decoy was programmed.

"Launch."

As Koiser sent the decoy on its southerly course, Duke banked the stealth high and to the left, taking the bomber east. To give the decoy time to pull the MiGs away he did not increase his airspeed.

As the B-2 came out of its turn and leveled, Koiser caught sight of the drone speeding away, and watched it for as long as possible before it climbed out of sight and disappeared into the blue sky at 3000 feet. He felt Duke bring the bomber up as they topped the nearest hill and started down the other side.

The Gs fell to zero at the same time the F-Band warning light came on. Koiser waited until the main computers had a chance to analyze the emissions. What it told him was no surprise . . . again they were being swept on all radar bands at the same time.

"How far away is it?" Duke asked.

"Ninety-three miles."

"And the second one?"

The screen showed only the one radar. "Unknown. We will have to wait until we cross into their overlapping coverage."

The HUD now showed the MiGs moving away, and Duke brought the bomber around and back onto its southbound course. They were still, he decided, too far away to launch a Tacit Rainbow to take out the Big Bird and he was reluctant to launch another decoy anyway . . . he needed them for the final assault on the computer complex. Their only option was to use their speed and stealth to get into range.

Gently Duke nosed the B-2 down to 200 feet and advanced the throttles. He watched the airspeed indicator climb past 500 knots before he eased them back enough to maintain speed.

Ninety more miles, he thought.

Abruptly the I/J-Band light turned red. Two SA-10 acquisition radars had just started to paint the Nightstalker.

Ah hell, Duke sighed.

RAMENSKOYE TEST CENTER

"FIRE, FIRE," General Yefimov ordered into the intercom, his voice reverberating throughout the control center.

All eyes were on the target as it moved down the display, and on six PVO interceptor aircraft, represented by red triangles, that were fast approaching the blip that showed the enemy aircraft. The General's eyes pierced the screen, he expected the target to fall off the display at any moment.

Suddenly, fifteen kilometers away, a *second* target appeared as it broke into the radar cover of the long-range search radar. This target was not as clear.

"Second target heading one seven two." The captain announcing he felt lucky the target had stayed on the screen long enough for him to get a fix on it. The return signal was too weak for him to compute its speed and height.

"Damn it, split the MiGs. Vector half to that new target," Yefimov said, and pointed to the new blip on the screen. The communications officer immediately radioed the lead aircraft, giving him the position of the new target.

Major Slikuna keyed his mike and looked up at the overhead command center. "General, the second target can be engaged with SAMs. I suggest you order the MiGs out of the area—"

"NO . . . order the MiGs to attack and tell the SAMs to fire. I want that target brought down." His eyes shifted back and forth between the two spots on the screen.

The American bomber will be brought down before you ever get into the air, Colonel Belikov, Yefimov silently promised as he made a fist and smashed it into the palm of his hand.

NIGHTSTALKER

Duke lined up the B-2 with the Big Bird. The HUD showed one I/J-Band two miles to the east and looking right at them. He wasn't worried about the other Flap Lid, it was six miles to the southwest. The launch warning on the HUD flashed on.

"One missile up," Koiser said. "Nine o'clock . . . accelerating." He waited. "Two missiles up."

Duke shoved the throttles forward and forced the stealth into a climb. The Nightstalker still not responding as fast as he'd hoped. He watched the RPM levels climb past ninety percent before he started to maneuver.

Koiser concentrated on the HUD, taking in the computer symbols and watching for the SAMs to appear on the left side. "3000 yards," he warned. The SA-10 was streaking toward them. "2000 yards . . . closing fast."

Duke barely had time to react. The SAM was seconds away. He cut right away from the accelerating missile and broke through 4000 feet, jammed the throttles to the wall and leveled the bomber.

"On my signal."

"1000 yards . . ."

"Now . . . chaff," Duke ordered.

Koiser hit the chaff button as Duke pulled the Nightstalker almost straight up, gaining 1000 feet. He chopped the throttles back and let the airspeed bleed off. Now the pilots felt the Gs go back to zero as they hung there almost weightless for a few moments. The HUD showed the first missile was heading for the chaff cloud some 300 yards beneath them.

Duke jammed the stick to the left and down as the B-2 started slowly to nose over and roll gently toward the ground.

"A mistake," Duke groaned.

The bomber was now a lifeless piece of plastic and metal hanging there a mile above the earth, without any airspeed or maneuverability.

"More chaff," Duke said as he squeezed the IR-flare trigger on his stick and the throttles went forward as he rolled the B-2 upside down and headed for the ground to pick up airspeed.

Koiser continued to fill the air behind the stealth with bundle after bundle of the radar-breaking material.

The second SAM was now speeding toward them at Mach 3.6 and still accelerating. Duke watched it on his side of the HUD, above them and heading for the long chaff cloud Koiser had laid down.

The search radar continued to sweep the B-2. Duke kept the nose pointed down and waited until the airspeed indicator hit 400 knots, then brought the stealth out of its dive by maintaining a steady 5-G nose-up pull. The I/J-Band radar was no longer locked up.

"That was close, too damned close. So much for the high-altitude stuff with that system."

"What was the flare for?" Koiser asked, not understanding why Duke would try to defeat a radar-guided SAM with a heat-seeking decoy flare.

"Hell . . . I had to do something." Duke almost allowed a smile. He banked the big bomber right in order to skirt the second Flap Lid acquisition radar, stabilized and came wings-level. He made sure they weren't above 200 feet, wanting at all costs to avoid any more encounters with SA-10s. Their acceleration was incredibly fast. Koiser had told him they needed to stay low and fast and he was right. Duke started to inch the throttles forward just as the TWP picked up the second I/J-Band starting to sweep the bomber. A moment later the yellow warning light turned red—lock-up.

Duke watched the needle on the TWP. The Flap Lid was looking at them from out of the southeast five miles away. If he could come in *under* the radar . . . he put forward pressure on the stick and took the stealth down to 100 feet. No change, the I/J-Band lock-up was still there.

"A launch . . . one . . . two . . . *three* missiles. Right, two o'clock . . ." Koiser turned to Duke when he didn't get a reaction.

Duke continued to force the bomber down, eighty feet, seventy feet. He turned seven degrees right until the stealth was flying directly at the radar.

"Twelve o'clock . . ." Koiser called out.

The Nightstalker was now only 50 feet above ground, speed 490 knots. Duke's peripheral vision watched the radar warning lights, no change. "Come *on*, baby, I'm running out of room." His insides rolled over.

The HUD told him the first SA-10 was 4800 yards away and closing fast. He didn't have a choice, he nudged the stick, forty feet, thirty-five feet—

Suddenly the I/J-Band warning light flickered rapidly. Was the Flap Lid losing its lock on the stealth?

Duke inhaled a long breath and held it. He took the B-2 down to only twenty-five feet above ground. At that altitude a tree or power line could rip through the aircraft. Duke held steady, didn't vary from course. The I/J-Band warning was still flashing red to yellow.

Koiser looked on as the HUD clicked off the distance of the SAM. At 1000 yards he caught sight of its glowing white exhaust 300 feet above the ground. The SAM was on an intercept course straight for them.

Five hundred yards straight out, the nearest SAM veered to the right and started to climb. Koiser glanced down at the radar warning lights, they were clear. Apparently, against the odds, they had slipped in under the Flap Lid. A distant hill blocked the emission from the Big Bird. The Soviet could see the missile streak 500 feet over the bomber. A half mile in the distance the other two SAMs exploded above the ground into a cloud of white vapor. The controllers had detonated the 90 kilogram high-explosive warhead by remote control after the radar had lost contact with the target.

But they were too low for safe flight. Duke brought the B-2 up slowly and banked five degrees left. He had no desire to fly directly over the SAM site. His attention was divided between the warning lights and the HUD. The closer he got to the acquisition-radar the higher he could fly.

Back to the HUD. He watched the altitude readout edge up past eighty . . . ninety . . . 100 feet. At 120 feet he got his answer. The warning lights flashed on. They were high enough again to be acquired by both radars. He had no choice, Duke knew, as he let the Nightstalker drift back down below 100 feet, and dangerous territory.

MIG-23 FLOGGER

"Lock-up, lock-up," 1st Lieutenant Valery Iachin said as he tried to coax his weapons into firing position. The high-pitch tone in his helmet told him the real story. It was uneven and inconsistent, his MiG's pair of AA-8 Aphids were not getting a strong enough IR emission from the target. He cracked the throttles to pick up a few extra knots of airspeed and dropped down to 2000 meters.

Lieutenant Iachin had over 600 hours of flying time logged in the five-year-old green-and-brown camouflaged MiG-23. It was the only fighter he had flown since graduating from flight school two years earlier. His hope was to move up to the new and faster MiG-29. Young, ambitious, he prided himself on knowing every inch of the sleek single-tail swing-wing fighter. He also did not have any delusions about his ability to fly . . . he knew he wasn't the best pilot in his squadron and he knew he wasn't the worst. His goal was to get better every day, to learn from every mission so he could be promoted to captain. Now here was his chance to prove himself.

The target he had been tracking for the last three minutes on his radar was three kilometers away. He was getting annoyed because he still hadn't gotten a visual I.D. If he was seeing the radar return of an American bomber, like the ground controllers were reporting, then why couldn't he *see* it.

The sound of two MiG-27 pilots to the south complaining to the ground authorities filled his headset. They had been ordered to break off their search and fly west to hunt for *another* target that had just been sighted. They too had been in radar contact with the American target.

Iachin watched the tracking symbol move on his heads-up display as the target changed course again. This time he didn't try to engage it with his AA-8s. At least he was learning with each mistake. He put his MiG into a ten-degree dive and headed straight for the monocolor holographic symbol that seemed to float out in space on his HUD. If he couldn't engage it with any of his missiles he was determined to find it and shoot it down with his MiG's pylon-wing-mounted GSh-23 air-to-air gun.

He adjusted the MiG's wings to a sweep-back of fifty-two degrees, which decreased drag and helped him pick up a few knots as he descended. Radar advised he was now less than a kilometer away from the target—he didn't believe it. He had learned during training not to trust everything his instruments told him. Equipment could vary from fighter to fighter and he had only been flying this one for a couple of weeks.

He blinked hard to clear his eyes. At 430 knots and 500 meters altitude the terrain flashed below so quickly he had a hard time focusing on anything in front of him. But his instruments reported the target should now be well within sight. Did a target even exist?

The silvery blur came into focus on the right side of his canopy, disappeared a split-second later, blending into the ground below.

The lieutenant froze, eyes on the same location in the sky. He tried refocusing to get greater depth perception. Seconds later he saw it again. And this time he didn't lose it.

Iachin squeezed the radio trigger on his stick: "Control, this is Volga two two. I have contact bearing two zero three. It is a . . . cruise missile . . ."

He banked to the right, coming in behind the small decoy missile.

He heard the ground controller authorize him to fire. Instantly he lined up his fighter behind the small missile and accelerated.

No wonder I couldn't see it, he thought, it's so damn small.

He waited until his MiG was 100 meters behind the "missile." Its course was straight and level. He lined up the gunsight on the back of the target and slowly squeezed the trigger, heard the muffled sound of his 23 mm. cannon explode under his right-wing root. Every sixth round glowed orange as he watched his first burst miss.

He continued to close on the target. At seventy-five meters he squeezed the trigger again. This time he did not let up. Black smoke poured from under his aircraft as the lethal projectiles cut through the air at 4200 feet a second, white vapor streaks showing the direction of the cannon rounds. A single shot struck the drone near its engine, tearing into the fuel supply, and the drone split in half and began to spin out of control. Iachin pulled back on the throttle to decrease his airspeed, rolled left to watch the missile twist and turn until it collided with the ground 400 meters below. It did not explode. Strange . . .

Iachin pulled up, increased his speed and turned southeast back to the base. "Control . . . Volga two two. Target is destroyed."

He was, of course, right. It just was the wrong target.

RAMENSKOYE TEST CENTER

The air space around Moscow and Ramenskoye was alive with military aircraft. All commercial flights had been ordered out of the area and the large main viewing screen showed only the MiGs in their search patterns. With the downing of the drone it was finally clear to the pilots and their commanders what the Americans were doing.

Major Slikuna turned toward General Yefimov as he hung up the phone. "All SAM and antiaircraft artillery sites reporting in position and ready, sir."

Yefimov didn't say a word. The major looked at the screen, which except for the MiGs was clear, the target was gone. "*Find* that enemy aircraft," he said.

Abruptly a smudge appeared thirty-one kilometers south from where it had last gone off the screen.

"Contact again." The captain said.

The target was skirting the town of Yamkino. The nearest fighter was more than twenty kilometers away and heading in the other direction.

"Vector the MiGs," Yefimov ordered.

"Faster," Belikov told his driver as they approached the hangar. He could see his MiG-29, complete with a standard mix of air-to-air missiles, being pulled from its storage area by a one-man truck.

As his driver pulled up next to his fighter, Belikov jumped from the car and ran to his aircraft, already dressed in his dark blue flight suit and carrying his helmet.

"Quickly, quickly," he said, gesturing to the crew to hurry with the ladder.

NIGHTSTALKER, TWELVE MINUTES NORTHEAST

The stealth's computer plotted the new SAM and triple-A locations on the CRT in front of Duke. It showed the bomber's position in relationship to the mobile SAM sites. The most immediate danger now, an SA-10 site east and an SA-13 west, was also projected. The radars were searching. A radar-free path was evident where the sites were spaced too far apart to provide overlapping coverage.

As Duke climbed to 500 feet the radar-warning lights were back on, the Big Bird was looking at them again. The data on the HUD suggested they would be clear of any fire-control radars for the next four or five minutes. After that they would break into the 100 kilometer defense radius around Moscow and Ramenskoye—and all hell would break loose.

He turned to Koiser. "Take the stick, captain,"

Koiser looked at him.

"Take the stick . . . just hold her steady. I got work to do," and Duke took his hand off the stick.

Captain Grigori Koiser, late of the Soviet air force, took control of the Nightstalker.

Duke now had to take over Tucker's job. He looked at his copilot still unconscious behind him. Ever since Tuck had been wounded, it had been tough for Duke to push his worry about Tuck into the back of his mind and keep focused on the mission. He hadn't been always successful, but it just wasn't something he could possibly take care of at this point. Tucker's head was resting against his chair and the fuselage, his face an unhealthy gray. Duke found himself staring at him, noting his shallow breathing, then shook his head, as though to pull himself back to the job at hand.

The first item to check were the SRAMs, the short-range-attack missiles. He turned to his right to the backup computer, and the keyboard swung out over the center console. He ran a weapons check and found all but one of the six AGM-131C supersonic SRAMs were still operational. Next he down-loaded the navigational data into each of the five SRAMs, and the Nightstalker's weapons computer programmed each missile with a TERCOM, a terrain-contour-matching-guidance program that compared the varying surface contours around Ramenskoye to the stored satellite ground-profiles. The SRAM could then compare its ground-hugging course to those of the satellite and make mid-course corrections along the way to the target. The upshot was that Duke should be capable of launching the missiles from any point in a 360-degree circle around the computer center.

Now the computer confirmed the seven remaining Tacit Rainbows were ready to fire, and Duke instructed the radar-homing missiles to attack only fire-control radars. This, he hoped, should take care of the highest-threat SAMs during Nightstalker's final assault on the secret computer center.

Lastly he called up the data on the TALDs, the decoys, and started by reprogramming eight of the nine to fly a simulated combat course into Ramenskoye and Moscow. The last rehearsal.

Koiser was looking over at the colonel as his gloved hand manipulated the rubber control-stick on his right side, his left hand on the throttles. The bomber seemed a live thing as he watched the ever-changing symbols on the HUD. He was *part* of the machine, he was its central nervous system . . . and yet it felt incredibly strange to be at the controls of America's most secret and advanced aircraft.

Moscow loomed now in the distance, the life he had left behind. The country of his father and his father's father. His daughter, his wife were only minutes away . . . it was impossible to stop the thoughts . . . had he made a mistake defecting? . . . did he really want to do this? . . . last chance, you could return a hero, the man who brought his country a stealth bomber, not a traitor—"*No*," he said aloud, startled by his own outburst, as was Duke, who looked up at him.

"You okay?"

"Yes." Koiser nodded to reinforce not only Duke but himself, then handed control of the stealth back to the colonel, who had finished his work on the keyboard.

Duke tugged at each of his shoulder restraints.

"Make sure you're strapped in tight, then. We're going in."

ZSU-23-4 SHILKA AIR DEFENSE GUN

The radar observer looked at his blank scope. He would not turn his acquisition radar on until he received orders from Ramenskoye. In the background he listened to his commander order the gunner to point the turret northwest. The driver locked the tracks of the light-armored PT-76 tank chassis into place in preparation for firing. The recoil produced from the four 23 mm. liquid-cooled guns, when fired at a rate of 1000 rounds a minute, was enough to push the fifteen-ton air-defense gun backward. The radar operator heard the whine of the motors as the gunner raised the gun up twenty degrees, then focused back on the screen and waited.

"Engage radar," the order came.

Instantly the radar operator turned his equipment to full power, the scope came on within a few seconds, and he could see a faint target moving toward them from the north.

He keyed his mike. "Target heading one eight two. Fire on my signal."

The gunner double-checked to make sure each of his four cannons was loaded and ready. He placed his face against the rubber shield around the optical sight and wrapped his fingers around the dual triggers. He believed if he could see it he could bring it down.

NIGHTSTALKER

Duke's attention was back on the landscape and sky. As they passed over roads and small towns he noted fields of machinery and farm workers gathering their fall harvest. He also reminded himself that at low level they could easily be seen. When he looked back to the HUD its readouts told him it was time.

He continued his gradual climb as the last decoys went out the weapons bay, then held steady until they were well clear of the stealth. At 2000 feet he rolled left and put the Nightstalker into a shallow dive, read his instruments that showed the TALDs were heading off on their preprogrammed course. At 400 feet he leveled off and advanced the throttles to take the B-2 past 500 knots.

The I-Band radar-warning light flashed on. Duke searched the HUD, a SAM site was not in the area.

Koiser's computer instantly identified the radar on the high end of the I-Band spectrum. "Shilka . . . antiaircraft gun."

Duke nodded, pulled the stick back and went to full power.

Just like damn Nam, he thought, between a rock and a hard place . . .

ZSU-23-4 SHILKA AIR DEFENSE GUN

The radar operator watched as the single target scattered into nine new targets. He readjusted his instrumentation to make sure he wasn't picking up electronic echoes. He wasn't.

The computer-guided radar locked up on the nearest target, and a narrow beam of radio waves reflected off the decoy passing two kilometers away.

Seconds later the moving crosshairs on his scope finally came to rest on the blip.

He keyed his mike and gave the order to fire.

NIGHTSTALKER

Three miles away the sky erupted in a blaze of red streaks coming from high on top of a pine-covered hill. The tracer rounds from the Shilka gun were unmistakable, bright fireballs turned into gray puffs of smoke as they dotted the horizon, and the explosive rounds detonated as they reached their programmed altitude.

Duke kept to a steady fifteen degree nose-up pitch, taking the B-2 past 2000 feet. And the decoy nearest the gunsight disappeared off the HUD as it fell prey to the fire power of the Shilka.

Duke banked away from the gun and out of the radar-free zone. Immediately the stealth was painted by two acquisition radars from the south ten to twelve miles out, or so he estimated. There was no lock-on, the operators were too busy trying to track and prioritize the new targets on their scopes.

"Two missiles up," Koiser reported.

Duke waited for the information to unfold on the HUD.

"Left . . . ten o'clock." The missiles arced up and away from the Nightstalker.

"I got 'em, so far so good." Duke didn't let up on the throttles. They were at 6000 feet and climbing 3000 feet a minute. The Soviets had their hands full for the moment and Duke was going to take as much advantage of it as he could.

In the distance three more SAMs streaked into the air. Duke watched the fire of their exhaust push them higher and faster. Suddenly they exploded only 3000 feet above ground, the fireballs brilliant even in the bright morning sky. The decoys were, no question, confusing the PVO. But not for much longer, Duke knew, as he heard the faint sound of two pulsating I-Bands.

"You hear that, Koiser?"

"Yes, MiGs. Too far out to see us."

At 12,000 feet Duke leveled out and jinked the B-2 right and then left. The I, I/J, J and K-Bands were all flashing on the TWP. The B-2 was being watched, but none of the sites had locked up on them. Yet.

Forty miles out. "Open the left-weapons bay."

Koiser did. Duke punched the launch-button releasing a volley of Tacit Rainbows. Four drones fell from the stealth.

"Lock-on, two up, straight ahead."

Duke saw the white smoke clouds as the two SA-13s left their launchers. Easy to see against dark brown earth below. A moment later two more SAMs rocketed into the air off the same launcher. He banked hard-right and nosed down to pick up airspeed. The missiles followed right on. He steadied and rolled right to get a look at the SAMs. Don't lose them, he thought. He waited, drawing the missiles closer.

"Ready . . . *now.*" Duke snapped the stealth into a tight left-hand rolling turn and dropped the nose, slicing in front of the two lead missiles only a thousand yards away. At the same time Koiser hit the chaff button as the tail of the Nightstalker broke out of the turn, two chaff bundles giving the active-seekers on the missiles a target five times bigger than the bomber's.

Duke eyed the other two white spears closing on them at Mach 2, the missiles curving toward the B-2 in an easy turn. He checked his altitude, 9500 feet, speed, 430 knots. He jammed the throttles forward and cut back to the right, and didn't have to say the word to Koiser, who instantly hit the chaff button.

Now the B-2 nosed up as the missiles flashed underneath, exploding. At 11,000 feet another launch warning broke into the brief silence.

"SA-10." Koiser said.

"Where, man, *where*?" Duke scanned the sky, looking for a trace of the deadly SAM.

"Seven miles . . . left . . . nine o'clock . . ." Koiser didn't sound too sure. "I show three . . ."

"Damn it, they'll be at Mach five by the time we see them," Duke said as he rolled left and headed straight for the acquisition radar. "Tell me when I'm heading . . ."

"Right two degrees," Koiser finished for him.

Duke nodded. The man was starting to think like him. He nosed over the Nightstalker and watched the airspeed build. Five miles out, he caught sight of the first missile shooting straight up for them, the smoky blue plume from its solid-rocket fuel making a serpentlike trail in the sky.

Duke watched it start to break over out of its climb and head toward him, gaining speed with the assist of gravity.

Duke rolled left, trying to break the lock of the I/J-Band radar. No good. He rolled right. Again, no luck. One choice: speed. He pushed the throttles to the stop and pitched over, putting the stealth in a thirty-degree dive, the bomber shuddering as the trim was adjusted.

At 8000 feet he keyed the mike: "I want a shit load of chaff when I break." He could now see the second missile coming toward them on a lower-flight profile, meaning it would reach them sooner than the first one.

Koiser's stomach did its own rollover. The huge SA-10s were intimidating enough just sitting on the ground. He never figured he would be dueling with them in the air. He watched the SAM approaching, his finger resting on the chaff button.

"*Now*," from Duke as he pulled the stick back, banked hard right, and the B-2 came out of its dive and nosed up. The G-force pinned him back into his seat, the airspeed dropped rapidly.

Duke snapped the stealth in the opposite direction and pitched the nose down. For a moment he lost sight of the second missile, then looked up to see in a blur as it passed just above them. "Down to 4000, give me more chaff." He tried to force the throttles forward. They wouldn't budge, he was already getting all the power he could out of the Nightstalker.

"Five seconds," Koiser warned.

"I know." What he knew was that he had to time it perfectly. He forced himself to hold back, counting "one thousand one, one thousand two, one thousand . . ." He couldn't wait any longer. *Do* it.

At 1200 feet he pulled up again and broke left, rolling into the missile. Koiser hit the chaff button before the Gs forced his arm back alongside his body. And each man watched as the missile veered just to the right and exploded in the chaff, sending a shock wave through the B-2 and the men inside it.

RAMENSKOYE TEST CENTER

"We are tracking eight targets, I recommend you and the General Secretary take shelter." General Yefimov spoke clearly and slowly.

Defense Minister Tomskiy was furious. "Where is the *nearest* target?"

"I am watching two," Yefimov said, eyes on the computer screen that was alive with MiGs moving toward each of the new radar blips. Two targets were on the outskirts of Moscow and moving toward the center of the city. "They are ten kilometers west of your position, we have MiGs in the area, they should be—"

Tomskiy cut him short. "Do *not* fire over Moscow." The thought of a hundred western reporters telling the world about MiGs shooting missiles over Red Square was not an acceptable prospect. "They won't attack the Kremlin, they're after the radar center. Don't you understand that! Defend the radar center, above all else . . ."

Suddenly five of the eight targets disappeared off the screen.

"Sir, we just lost our west-sweeping early-warning radar."

"General Yefimov . . . you find the *real* threat and *bring it down*." The line went dead after a loud click.

OVER RAMENSKOYE TEST CENTER

Duke didn't have time to react. No amount of training could have prepared him to fight against the lightning speed of the last SA-10 that was closing at over 2000 feet a second. He actually froze as he watched the twenty-one-foot missile make its final course adjustment, coming in perfect alignment with the cockpit, its gray nose looming larger and larger, its four white control fins giving it a starlike appearance.

Duke sucked in what he thought would be his last breath, let it out as the Nightstalker slashed through the smoke of the SAM's exhaust. He felt embarrassed for his moment of weakness, almost as though the Soviet had somehow caught him in it.

The missile had unaccountably shot straight down and missed the cockpit by only a hundred feet, headed for the ground and exploded seconds later.

"What the hell happened?" Duke asked, his voice tight.

Koiser nodded to the left side of the cockpit. "Look."

Half a mile away the wreckage of the Flap Lid engagement radar was burning, orange flames dancing beneath puffs of black smoke. The long trailer that carried the radar emitter was turned completely over, the center section was buckled and long strips of metal protruded from the burning center. A few hundred yards away Duke could see a launcher, its moss green missile canisters pointed up at a forty-five-degree angle ready to fire. But without the radar to guide them the SAMs had no eyes.

Duke tried to relax. His back ached with tension. He rolled his shoulders back and forth hoping to get some of the feeling back into his upper arms, then pulled the nose up and over a steep rock- and brush-covered ridge.

As the Nightstalker crested the hill and broke into the open, Koiser's heart jumped. "Ramenskoye," he whispered to himself, though loud enough for Duke to hear.

Duke forced the nose of the stealth over and headed down the 2000 foot drop of the opposite side.

Koiser had flown over the base and the land that encompassed it many times, but he was surprised they were, suddenly, *there*. Flying at low level and from the north had, if nothing else, changed his perspective. And that they had actually made it this far through the thicket of missiles, radar, MiGs . . .

A long flat valley stretched out before them. This was as he remembered it, nearly void of any living thing. The trees had been uprooted some forty years ago and each spring the valley was sprayed with a powerful defoliant. The Soviets had to build a safety zone around Ramenskoye for emergency landings, unlike Roger's dry lake bed at Edwards. Only a few roads crisscrossing at different angles and some large metal-roofed buildings scattered here and there broke up the smooth dry ground.

Twenty-five miles to the southwest, on the horizon, a long thin ridge was barely visible in the yellowish white haze that hung a thousand feet above ground. Koiser and Duke were looking at the backside of the computer center. Somehow it seemed out of place as it rose up out of the flat terrain. Its main entrance faced south, under thick layers of reinforced rock and concrete. The two large black radomes that covered the radar center's communication and data-relay equipment seen on top of the westernmost end looked, incongruously, like a pair of giant Mickey Mouse ears. Below, buried deep in the ground, was the computer complex itself.

Koiser scrutinized the landscape to his right. Fifteen miles to the west was the air base where he had spent five years of his life working on the system he was now helping to destroy. The long black runways were set up in a large triangle, their surfaces casting a silvery mirage. The main runway ran east-west and was 15,000 feet long. Koiser started searching the western sky for any MiGs in the area but lost sight as the Nightstalker banked left and headed east.

As the bomber came around Koiser saw why Duke was taking a new course. Three fast-rising pillars of black smoke could be seen coming off the valley floor. The high-threat acquisition SAM radars were now a pile of burning electronics. The Tacit Rainbows had done their job. For the next few minutes they should be able to follow a radar-free path at least up to the southern edge of the valley to the computer center before turning south again and making their first run.

Duke centered the control stick and throttled back. The B-2's airspeed dropped to 420 knots and drifted down to 400 feet. The TWP was clear. He looked around for MiGs, saw none.

"You picking anything up, Koiser?"

"No, colonel," Koiser went from his computer screen to the

HUD and back to the computer, repeated this check every fifteen or twenty seconds.

"Damn it . . . where are those interceptors?" Duke was properly suspicious. They were, after all, only miles away from the center, he had expected MiGs would be climbing all over their back by now.

He scanned his instruments, not wanting to break out into the open without knowing where the MiGs were. Running along the side of the ridge was the best bet—the B-2's upper camouflage blended into the greenish blue pine trees that dotted the hill side . . .

Ten miles to the northeast the decoys flew on, curving and changing direction every fifteen seconds to confuse the pursuing MiGs. One would streak up to 5000 feet, hang there a while, then dive for the ground, taking the pursuing MiGs with them. At the same time another one would be at 200 feet, snaking along the ground like a strategic bomber on its final run at a target. Two others made their way toward Moscow and Red Square.

Duke could now see the end of the ridge fast approaching. He double checked the electronic readouts—the SRAMs were ready to launch. Next he programmed the last TALD decoy for launch. Even though the Rainbows had taken out some of the SAMs' search-and-track radars Duke was sure the run at the center would hardly be free and clear.

The B-2 now flashed past the eastern end of the ridge and out into the open, nosed down to 1000 feet. As they cleared the last rock structure radar-warning lights flashed on. Duke continued on a straight course heading due east, waiting for Koiser to identify the radars.

The Terrain Warning Panel turned red. "Fire control radars . . . east, west and south. They haven't locked up on us yet," Koiser reported. "SA-10s, 11s and 13s. I am counting . . . twenty-three."

"*Twenty-three*? Where the hell did they come from?" Duke

looked at the center CRT that showed the location of the SAMs off the latest satellite photos. The data was sixteen minutes old and showed only nine in the area. The rest must have been camouflaged or buried deep in the ground where the satellites-detection equipment couldn't find them.

"MiGs?" Duke asked.

"Nothing in the area . . . yet."

Duke looked over his shoulder at Tucker. His copilot didn't look any better, ghost white. The last run-ins with the SA-10s had twisted him around in his seat so that his right shoulder was drooped and his head was pushed back on the left side of the seat.

Duke forced himself to turn back to the front, and as he did his eyes momentarily caught Koiser's, showing the same combination of fear and excitement he was feeling.

Five miles past the ridge Duke banked to the right, the Gs building as the airspeed climbed to 470 knots.

"Lock-up . . . I/J-Band," Koiser cautioned.

Duke held steady in the turn.

"Two missiles up. West two o'clock, eight miles out."

Duke leveled the B-2 at 1200 feet and pointed its nose toward the two large radomes twenty miles away, then jammed the throttles all the way forward and the speed jumped to over 500 knots.

"Open the left weapons bay," he ordered.

"Two minutes, twenty seconds out." Koiser toggled the button, the B-2 shuddered as the forty-foot bay door slowly opened.

Duke hit the launch button and the final decoy fell from the bomber. The small drone fell only 100 feet before it began operating and broadcasting on five different radar bands. Duke opened the air brakes, slowing the stealth to 450 knots while the decoy shot ahead and started its descent to 300 feet. Duke let the TALD get a half a mile ahead before nosing over to follow it down. He planned to stay behind the drone, letting it draw the fire from the SAMs and triple-A sites. When they were five miles out he figured he could fire the first SRAM and, he hoped, take out the radomes, which were the Soviets' eyes.

"Thirty seconds . . ."

Duke saw a flicker of light reflect off the lead missile, which was no longer heading toward them, the stronger radar signal coming from the decoy pulling it off. He banked north, grateful for the reprieve, then swung back south and let his speed continue to bleed off until he was at 430 knots, altitude 600 feet. He stopped his dive and leveled at 500 feet.

The drone was a mile ahead. Five seconds later he watched two SA-11s pass within 50 feet of the TALD. Each missile exploded, one right after the other, into a ball of yellow fire and gray smoke.

Duke nosed up to miss the debris, closed the air brakes and added power, pushed the nose down again to increase his speed more quickly. The decoy was, he noted, still on course for the computer center. Two MiGs now appeared on the HUD.

"Two MiGs . . . to the north. Computer shows I-Band Pulse-Doppler." Koiser's voice sounded tight.

This time Duke didn't vary his course. A mile ahead to the south the red tracer rounds of a ZSU-23-4 cut into the thick morning air, the shells exploding just below the drone.

"Thirteen miles to the target," Koiser intoned.

Duke tried to swallow as he sped past the Shilka 23 mm. gun, a hail of flying shrapnel erupting just behind. The operator was a millisecond late.

Duke brought the Nightstalker in behind the drone and leveled out, caught sight of three more SAMs lifting off in a fireball to the east four miles out and rocketing off in another direction after one of the other decoys.

The Nightstalker was at 450 feet.

"Air-defense guns ahead . . . lock-up. I see two," Koiser told Duke.

Duke instantly rolled right to avoid contact with the closest radar beam, but it followed him.

He swore at the operator under his breath, yanked the stick back, gaining altitude.

"Chaff . . . get him the hell off us."

Another warning, this one a K-Band, flickered on as they broke through 2000 feet.

"Two missiles up," Koiser said, and hit the chaff button as the space ahead of them was shattered by a dozen red fingers of twisted fire.

Duke rolled the bomber to a forty-five-degree angle and back to the right to change the radar return. After every shift in the B-2's direction Koiser filled air behind them with churning foil.

Duke leveled at 1100 feet and caught sight of the drone a mile ahead as the first of two SAMs slammed into it. The second missile entered the fireball moments later. The drone had done its job, but not for as long as Duke had hoped. He let the stealth float up to 1200 feet, banked to a heading of 187, keeping the bomber level. The radar was behind them, sweeping to the northeast.

They were back on target.

The canopy on Belikov's MiG-29 closed with a thud. His eyes didn't leave the cockpit instrumentation. He made sure each of his weapons systems checked out and his radar was ready to operate. He watched the instruments cycle and come in line with the fighter's computer. He didn't have time to run through his radio checks. He signaled with his hand to finish the fueling. His tanks only showed three-quarters full. That would have to be enough. The ground crew pulled the APU into position, the colonel heard the whine of the turbofans build into a roar. The red-flagged weapons pins were pulled from his missiles as he advanced the throttles, and his MiG quickly moved toward the end of the runway.

"Nine miles to weapons drop," Koiser called out. They were close enough to see the radomes were dark gray, not the black circles they had seen in the distance.

"Weapons bay open," Duke commanded as he down-loaded the final targeting data into the SRAMs' internal computer.

"Open, colonel."

Tracer rounds poured into the sky to the west half a mile away. Duke tried to ignore them, held steady at 1200 feet and inched the B-2's nose over two degrees to bring it into alignment with the target. With his other hand he pushed the throttles to the stop. He would have only one chance at the radomes.

One minute to weapons release, he estimated.

The TWP lit up again. The yellow H/I-Band lights turned red. "SA-11 . . . tracking," Koiser called out.

"I *see* it."

Four eighteen-foot-long missiles left the mobile launcher at the same time, their semiactive monopulse-seeker heads following the strong signal of the Fire Dome engagement radar.

"Radar lock . . . four up, eleven o'clock," from Koiser.

"Thirty seconds . . ."

Duke stayed fixed on the radomes. Out of the corner of his eye he saw the first flashes of red light. The B-2 quivered as half a dozen 23-mm. rounds poured into its left wing tip. Four of the projectiles exploded and tore holes in the thick graphite skin, exposing the internal structure of the wing. Two others punched holes in the left side of the spoiler panels.

He checked the instruments. No major damage. The Nightstalker rolled slowly right, the force of the cannon fire pushing it up.

"Fifteen seconds to launch," Duke called out.

"SAMs four miles out and accelerating."

"Twelve seconds."

"There's no time, colonel. Three miles."

"Bullshit." Another burst of pulsating tracer rounds flashed ahead of them.

"One mile, closing fast." The SA-11s were racing toward them at over Mach 1.

"Five seconds." A lifetime. Duke brushed his thumb over the top of the launch button on the stick, as if to make sure he knew where it was.

"Three . . . two . . ."

The SAMs were 1000 yards away.

He waited, the final second clicked off. "*Now*." Duke pickled the SRAM and pulled up hard and away from the target. The white-and-black-checkered attack missile fell from the B-2, its rocket motor exploded to life, sending it on its way toward the target.

Duke put the wounded bomber into a hard-right turn, not

wanting to pass over the target area after the explosion. The first SA-11 exploded under them less than 100 feet away and sent a shock wave through the cockpit that rocked Duke and Koiser. Fragments from the warhead ripped into the bottom outer skin of the aircraft. The B-2 vibrated violently and pitched nose down, but Duke somehow managed to stabilize enough to continue the climb. The three other missiles streaked beneath, all but one failing to explode, the B-2 too far away to activate the proximity fuses.

Meanwhile the SRAM from the Nightstalker headed for the surface and leveled out at fifty feet, its high speed and low-altitude flight path allowing it to blend into the background clutter so that it was nearly impossible to track on radar.

The 1800-pound SRAM, half-bomb, half-missile, did not vary more than a few degrees as it traveled the last miles to the target. Its forward-looking carbon-hydroxide-ringed laser internal-guidance system could not be jammed. Once launched the only way to defeat it was to shoot it out of the sky.

Ten seconds and two miles out the missile popped up to 500 feet, then at the apex of its arcing climb the computer instructed it to nose down in a twenty-G dive. The SRAM now headed straight between the two domes of the complex. The hardened chrome-nickel-steel nose dug into the ground thirty feet before exploding, the supercooled metasable-helium warhead detonating with the force of fifty 500-pound bombs. Fire, rocks and dirt flew hundreds of feet into the air. The impact of the blast ripped through the protective radomes and made the center section of each dome to cave in and collapse. The steel supports each dome rested on buckled and broke, and the whole area seemed to disappear in a cloud of smoke and dust as the hundred-foot-high balls tumbled to the ground.

General Yefimov, frozen with disbelief, watched the images vanish from the main-display screen as the control center shook violently, the destructive force of the explosion sending ripples through the walls and floor of the underground complex. The general jumped back just as the thick glass wall of the command room next to him crumbled and huge sheets of glass fell onto the floor below and shattered into a million pieces.

A hail of gold sparks danced around the electric cables that led from the reactor into the computer terminals. The small computer screens went dead, their silicon circuitry welded together as a powerful surge of electricity burned into each unit. Seconds later the far right ceiling fell with a deafening crash. Beams of steel reinforcement and concrete cascaded to the floor. A large crack appeared along the far wall of the room that contained the main computer as the ground shifted and the air filled with dust and smoke.

Then, as quickly as it started, the devastation stopped. The room went deathly quiet except for the sound of electrical circuits hissing and popping. People could be heard screaming. The smell of charred wiring and ozone burned Yefimov's nose. The lights went out, the red emergency lights came on, filling the center with an eerie glow as their beams cut through the dust-filled air.

Yefimov knew he had no alternative. He hit the intercom button: "This is General Yefimov. Evacuate the center. Evacuate the center."

Duke leveled at 2500 feet and rolled to the left to get a good look at the top of the ridge. As the Nightstalker flashed overhead two triple-A sites let loose with cannon fire. The B-2 was moving too fast at 570 knots, the gunners didn't have enough time to adjust their fire.

Duke tried to take in the damage. Through gaps in the black billowing smoke, the radomes were a pile of twisted metal and fire. He came wings-level for a moment, then dropped the right wing to put the Nightstalker into a gradual southwesterly turn away from the damaged computer complex. With the radomes down, radar couldn't find him, and so while the SAM and AAA sites could paint them, the operators couldn't lock onto the stealth.

It wasn't over, though, and Duke and Koiser knew it.

"Strong J-Bands to the north . . . four MiGs," Koiser said.

"How far away?"

"Eight, nine miles. I can't get a fix on their radar, it is sweeping with a very narrow band." And just then three more MiGs appeared out of the west.

Just one minute, give me one minute . . . Duke took the B-2 four miles out, altitude 2000 feet, throttled back and applied pressure on the right side of the stick. The stealth went into a 2.5-G turn. As the left wingtip dropped he felt a furious vibration. The damaged wing had cut through the air unevenly, making the big bomber unstable. He let off on the stick to drop to a G-load of 1.5. He could only hope the Nightstalker would somehow hold together.

Slowly the Nightstalker swung around to a new heading so that the front end of the complex came into view and he could see the top of it engulfed in smoke and fire.

It no longer looked anything like the satellite photos, that was for sure. At close range the camouflage netting was easy to distinguish from the landscape. Duke leveled the bomber and lined up the HUD's targeting cursor on the front of the computer complex . . .

Belikov pulled back on the center-mounted stick and brought the front landing gear of his MiG-29 off the runway. The rear gear lifted a moment later, and the colonel immediately put the MiG into a hard left hand turn, brought up the landing gear and jammed the throttles into afterburner. He reached down and fine-tuned his radio to the communication channel of the other MiGs.

Thirty-five kilometers to the southwest he saw the black smoke rising in the sky.

The computer-driven HUD was hard to see. The morning sun had just broken through the clouds and was glaring right where Duke had to point his SRAMs. He lowered his helmet visor over his eyes and squinted, trying to clear the bright spots out of his vision.

At two-and-a-half miles out he pressed the targeting button

and dumped the flight-path data into the remaining SRAMs again to make sure they were ready.

"Fifteen seconds to launch," Duke called out. "Weapons bay open."

Koiser gave him a funny look, he had forgotten to *close* it after the first launch.

"Weapons bay open. MiGs closing from the north."

Duke hadn't noticed, he was absorbed with keeping the stealth on target.

"MiG-29s, colonel . . . straight ahead, twelve o'clock."

"Ten seconds, stay on target."

"Five . . . four . . . three . . . two . . . one, launch." Duke squeezed the trigger and a single SRAM fell away. He squeezed the trigger four more times, two seconds apart, and the other SRAMs fell clear of the bomber and the B-2 jumped into the air with the weight of the SRAMs gone. But the final SRAM stayed locked up inside the bomber, its damaged electrical system not allowing the signal to reach its guidance computer.

Major Sergei Ivanovich, flying the lead MiG-29, flashed over the west side of the burning radomes at 500 meters and caught sight of the B-2 as it came off target eight kilometers ahead. The enemy aircraft was much bigger than he'd imagined, yet its thin silhouette made it hard to see against the broken backdrop of the ground. He checked his weapons systems—not a single missile was locked up. He didn't have time to figure it, he had to react . . .

Ivanovich brought up the nose of his MiG and pressed the trigger on his stick four quick times. Instantly a salvo of four seven-foot IR homing missiles streaked into the air. The advanced seeker head in each missile was just sensitive enough to engage a target head-on, picking up the heat signature radiating off the leading edge of an aircraft. As the missiles left their launchers their rocket motors filled the air with dense white smoke, which made Ivanovich lose sight of the B-2.

* * *

Duke and Koiser watched the last SRAM head toward the entrance of the computer center. The white smoke from its exhaust curled almost gracefully to the middle of the ridge, making the SRAM easy to follow.

"That's it, let's get out of here." Duke pulled back on the stick and put the Nightstalker into a steep climb as he added power. The bomber shook as the three remaining engines struggled to keep the stealth's airspeed above 500 knots.

"Come on, baby, come *on* . . ." The B-2 broke through 3000 feet and continued upward toward the clouds. Duke looked over at the radar-warning panel. It was clear. His only thought was to head for the thick clouds 18,000 feet above and hide out from the enemy fighters.

Neither Duke nor Koiser saw the missile until just before it exploded a few feet from the front of the aircraft.

Only one person was left in the computer control center. Everyone else had evacuated after the general had given the order.

General Yefimov picked up the phone and tried to contact the Kremlin to deliver his last report. The line was dead. He set the phone down on the table. Maybe there was still time to escape . . . As he reached the doorway the first SRAM from the Nightstalker hit and blew a hundred-foot hole in the side of the small mountain. The explosion knocked Yefimov back into the command room. The steel-reinforced tunnel leading to the outside collapsed, sealing him in. He struggled to his feet but was knocked down again.

The second explosion seemed more powerful. The right-side wall came crashing down and the large display fell away from its supports, crushing all the equipment below it.

When the third explosion came the general covered his face. The room was filled with a burning white fire, flying glass and steel. The interior of the complex became a mass of molten rock and metal, and the core of the reactor broke open exposing its deadly radiation.

The main room fell in on itself as the last SRAM hit, the final blast of explosives sealing the computer center—and the general—from the outside world.

23

PURSUIT

KART DAG STATION, TURKEY

10:20 A.M. General Sweeny had been in the Early Warning Station since 4:00 A.M. Tall, lanky, he shifted his weight from one leg to the other, tensing his muscles to get the blood flowing again. He walked down to the main floor of the radar room and stopped a few feet from the radarscope searching the skies to the north.

To his left sat Lieutenant Bowlings and Master Sergeant Roundtree monitoring the lime green radar screen as its brightly colored beam swept rhythmically back and forth. In the corner the third member of the team, Sergeant Roberts, sat, with his headphones on hunched over his communications equipment, trying to tie into coded Soviet military transmissions coming into and out of Sevastopol.

The priority phone rang and Sweeny grabbed it up.

"Sweeny, this is Westcott." Sweeny could hear the background noise of the SAC command center. "You picked anything up yet?"

"No, general."

Westcott sighed. "The bomber dropped off our display as it passed over the computer complex. We've been trying to reestablish contact ever since. I was hoping maybe you . . ." His voice trailed off.

Sweeny could hear the pain in Westcott's voice. He didn't envy Westcott's position.

"We're monitoring all the communication channels and the radar is still showing nothing."

"What about the Sixteens? Are they ready to go?"

This was the second time in the last two hours Westcott had asked him about the interceptors. "Yes, I have two sitting on the end of the runway at Incirlik. They're up and ready. If we pick something up they will be in the air in minutes."

"Okay . . . let me know if anything comes up," and the line went dead.

Sweeny could picture the chaos at SAC. "Damn, damn, pray to God we don't lose that bomber."

MIG-29 FULCRUM, SOUTHBOUND

Belikov was more convinced than ever that Grigory Koiser was involved with the destruction of the computer center. Only someone familiar with Soviet air defenses could have helped guide a single bomber into and out of the heart of the Soviet Union.

The colonel calculated his intercept plan. There was only one direction for the American stealth bomber to escape—south. Even with the radar network knocked out the bomber would not have the fuel or the defensive weapons to risk flying over Eastern Europe. They would have to make it to the nearest friendly country as fast as possible, and that was Turkey, the same country Koiser had defected to. The memory of the day Koiser defected was still too fresh in his mind.

The colonel kept steady forward pressure on the throttles as he tried to coax every bit of power out of the MiG's twin turbo-fans. His fighter now streaked through the sky at over 2000 kilometers per hour, Mach 2.02 at 10,000 meters. At that speed he would have just enough fuel to reach Sevastopol, he planned to land, refuel and take off again. If he was lucky the American would be crossing over the southern coast as he became airborne. The A-Band P-14, which looked south of Sevastopol, *should* be able to acquire the bomber as it flew high over the Black Sea. It would be his one final chance to even the score.

He was 180 kilometers out when he keyed his mike: "Sevastopol control, this is Colonel Belikov. I am inbound at zero three two. Estimated touchdown five minutes twenty seconds. I want priority clearance."

"This is Sevastopol control. You are cleared for priority landing."

"Sevastopol, put me through to General Smirov."

"Stand by, colonel." The controller's voice cracked through his helmet. "State your position, please."

"I am in pursuit of an enemy aircraft. I must talk with the general now." He released his mike button and added, "You asshole."

Moments later he heard the general's gruff voice. Belikov was surprised he was already in the ground-to-air command center at Sevastopol.

"General"—Belikov tried to keep an even tone—"the computer complex at Ramenskoye has been bombed by a single American stealth bomber. I believe the aircraft is trying to escape by heading toward the Black Sea and landing in Turkey. I need two more MiG-29s, have the pilots standing by to help me with the interception—"

"Minister Tomskiy informed me about the attack and that you were heading this way. Do you know for *sure* that the enemy aircraft is flying south?"

"I am convinced the American's only option is Turkey. I believe the P-14 early warning radar under your control has the capability to find the bomber. Please tell the radar operators to turn to full power and look north. Find the target and vector me to it." Belikov knew he was ordering a superior, but under the circumstances . . .

A long pause, then: "What is your ETA?"

"Five minutes. Have a fuel truck on runway three five right. There is *no* time."

Smirov didn't like Belikov's tone of voice, but this time he would have to take it. "You will have it, *colonel*. Sevastopol out."

NIGHTSTALKER

The badly damaged bomber barely responded. The cockpit was a disaster. Pieces of glass, graphite and plastic littered the floor. The stench of burnt insulation filled the air. The front windscreen was cracked in the bottom center corner and pieces of black steel could be seen stuck to the outside plexiglass.

Duke took in the controls. The only flight data available came from the main CRT display, but it was hard to read through the splintered outer glass. The other five displays along with the HUD were silent, black. Duke had to refer to his back up altitude-direction indicator by refocusing from the sky ahead to the center CRT.

The instruments on Koiser's side were also dead except for some static that sporadically would run through his CRTs, filling them with wavy white lines. Just under the cockpit window a six-inch hole in the fuselage let ice-cold air rush into the cockpit. Duke had shut down the environmental controls to prevent a fire, there was no way to counter the sting of the frigid air. The radio was gone as well as the satellite communications. The only other functioning displays were the radar and the Threat Warning Panel. How or why they were still working, Duke had no idea.

The outside of the Nightstalker wasn't in much better shape, the left side having sustained the most damage. The air intake over the number one and two engines was peeled away like the top of an aluminum pop can. Two large wing panels were broken and punched full of holes from the flying shrapnel. Large scraps and dents could be seen over the entire wing area, which caused the B-2 to vibrate because of uneven airflow. The Fibaloy outer skin on each side of the cockpit was cracked and broken.

Duke knew they were lucky to be in the air. If a B-52 or his old B-1B had been hit by two Aphids he and his crew would be dead and gone. His eyes kept going to the fuel gauges. The blast from the missiles hadn't torn off any upper sections of the left wing or punctured the main fuel tank. If *that* had happened the Nightstalker would have become totally uncontrollable.

Duke felt the strength leaving his body, his chest and arms fast becoming stained with blotches of his own blood. The knifelike puncture wounds from the shattered, multilayered radar-absorbing plexiglass of the windshield had cut him in dozens of places. Lowering his visor to shield his eyes from the sun was the only thing that had saved his eyesight. Some of the cuts along his arms and abdomen were more than an inch deep, and one thin piece of razor sharp plexiglass had pierced his ribs and lung. With each breath the pain became more intense.

He glanced at Tucker as Koiser came back to his seat.

"How is he?"

Koiser shook his head. "He has lost a lot of blood . . . he is not breathing very well."

"Damn it, hold on, Tuck, we're almost home . . ." He was talking to himself too.

As Koiser buckled himself back in his seat he swept the sky around them. His only injury had been a cut just above his knee . . . a hot piece of metal from the exploding warheads had punched a hole in the cockpit wall and hit him.

Koiser could see the blood on Duke's green flight suit. "How are you, colonel?"

"I'm okay, we'll be in friendly space soon. You look out for any trouble, our sensors are gone, we could have company and never know it—"

"I can fly this plane, colonel," Koiser said, surveying the sky. Fifty miles out in front of them he could see a wall of thick white clouds. Maybe they could hide there until they got to Turkish airspace.

Duke looked at him. "I know you can, thanks."

Suddenly the number one engine made a high-pitched whine, telling Duke it must have ingested some debris that damaged the turbine blades. The engine was running in the red, overheating and only putting out fifty-percent. He had to shut it down, he told himself, before it catches fire . . .

He nudged the stick forward, and as the stealth came level it started to yaw turbulently to the right. Duke corrected by applying left-side pressure to the stick and trimmed the B-2 as much as he could. At least the yawing stopped.

They watched the cloud bank grow closer, less than twenty

miles out. The Turkish border was thirty-five minutes away. Just a while longer, baby. Hang in there, damn it . . .

SEVASTOPOL EARLY WARNING CENTER

This was the first time the sergeant had ever been ordered to look for an enemy target trying to *leave* the Soviet Union.

He boosted the power level on the P-14CX to max. The massive thirteen-meter-high paraboloid mesh-reflector antennae turned at one revolution every thirty seconds, blasted the airwaves with a beam of electrons in the A-Band frequency range. In place since the mid-sixties, the radar station was responsible for early warning along the Soviet Union's entire southern border.

In the center of the scope the long bright radar reflection of the clouds cut across the screen. The operator, trying to concentrate, also wondered why he was looking north.

"Sergeant . . ." The major's voice startled him. "Have you found the target?"

"No, sir." He had not noticed a small white smudge moving on the screen that looked like the faint reflection of a cloud.

The major pushed the edge of his chair. "Move away." He took the sergeant's seat and started to work the controls, assuming rank not only had its privileges, it somehow also had superior sight.

Belikov cracked the stick back and let his MiG leap into the air using only 3000 feet of runway in his takeoff after hurried refueling. The two other Twenty-nines followed his lead as they powered into a sixty-degree nose-up climb, their exhaust nozzles emitting a fiery glow from the afterburners. At 1000 meters Belikov broke slowly to the north and keyed his mike.

"Activate your weapons systems. Follow my lead."

His two wingmen did as ordered.

KART DAG STATION, TURKEY

"I got two, three bogies breaking through 4000 feet, general." Bowlings waited for the computer to supply him with more detail. "Targets heading zero zero three . . . north. Computer shows ninety percent confidence they're MiG-29s. Looks like they're in a hurry . . . altitude 6000 feet and climbing, speed 500 knots and accelerating."

"Can you tell if they're trying to intercept anything?" Sweeny was now standing behind the two radar operators.

"I don't show anything," from Roundtree.

"Sir, I'm picking up some faint radio transmissions," Roberts said, hands over his earphones to get them tighter to his ears. "It's too weak, I can't define—"

"Increase your power."

"It's already on maximum."

"*I need to know if that bomber is out there,*" Sweeny said.

"Yes, sir—"

"Lieutenant, the B-2's radar image will look like nothing you've ever seen. It may appear to be just a faint smudge or a transparent cloudlike return. Don't ignore *anything*. If the Soviets are onto something I want those Sixteens airborne." Sweeny didn't sound too confident that American radar could pick up the B-2 . . . the U.S. Air Force had abandoned the older long-wave A-Band radar twenty years ago.

"Breaking through 9000 feet . . . still climbing," Bowlings called out.

Sweeny fought the urge to contact Westcott. He would have to wait and see to be sure . . .

NIGHTSTALKER

"It's a strong A-Band . . . either a P-14 or P-12."

"If I ever see another yellow light as long as I live," Duke muttered. He looked at Koiser. "What do you make of it?"

"I think they are using the early warning radar at Sevastopol to try to find us."

Duke agreed. With the powerful radar of the computer center

out, the only chance the PVO had was to find them on conventional radar. And since the SAM sites could not engage the B-2 without assistance from the super computer, their threat now came from MiGs.

SEVASTOPOL EARLY WARNING CENTER

"That's it," the major said so quietly no one else could hear. He had been manipulating the sensitivity relay system for the last few minutes, and finally it was paying off. The blip he was focused on was oblong and fuzzy and faded in and out, but he could also easily distinguish it, as opposed to what the general had said. But, of course, the major couldn't know that because of the B-2's battle damage it was giving off a radar return fifty times greater than normal. He toggled the IFF switch on the center of the display; he did not get a return signal telling him it was a Soviet aircraft.

"Contact, bearing one eight four. Speed 410 knots, altitude 8500 meters."

General Smirov turned sharply. "What do you have?"

"Unidentified target, general, coming in from the north."

Smirov stared at the screen. The blip was approaching the coastline and looked like it would fly into the cold front that was bearing down on the station from the west.

"Contact the MiGs. Order them to intercept."

NIGHTSTALKER

He never thought he would look forward to entering a cloud bank . . . the cockpit darkened as the bomber pierced the dense clouds and the B-2 started to bounce around from the uneven air. Duke put the stealth into a gradual left-hand turn and felt the aircraft out. If the Soviets were tracking them the radar operators should have trouble following them in the clouds.

He rolled right and leveled the Nightstalker, its two remaining engines producing only enough power to push it along at 425 knots. Instruments said they were over the water . . . twenty-five minutes from safety.

"J-Bands behind us, six o'clock. I count two, maybe three," Koiser said as the yellow radar warning lit up.

"I see it . . ."

Koiser didn't need the computer. The tone in his helmet sounded the frequency pulse width that alone let him know they were MiG-29s.

"What's their range?"

"Twelve miles and closing fast, altitude, 23,000 feet."

"They must be controlled out of Sevastopol, no way those MiGs could be tracking us on their fire-control radars." As Duke spoke they broke out of the clouds for a few seconds before being swallowed up again. As they flew away from the leading edge of the weather system the clouds were broken with areas of clear blue sky, and an instant later they blasted into a dense gray-colored fog to emerge out the other end into a clear spot.

Duke caught a glimpse of the gray blue ocean below. "I'm taking her down, we'll see if they follow." He nosed the crippled bomber down five degrees and backed off on the throttle. At 16,000 feet he leveled the stealth, and moments later they got their answer.

The steady pinging of the MiGs' radar told them they were only five miles away and had leveled out with them and followed them down from 23,000 feet. Duke jammed the throttles forward and rolled into a banking dive, the damaged Nightstalker vibrating in protest as it accelerated.

The only hope for escape, he knew, was to get under the A-Band radar.

KART DAG STATION, TURKEY

"Launch the Sixteens," Sweeny ordered. "Have them hold short of feet-wet until I say different." He hung up the phone. "Position, lieutenant?"

"Two hundred and eighty miles out. The targets are breaking through 10,000 feet—"

"I'm picking up new radio transmissions," Roberts broke in. This time he was able to lock the computer onto the set of UHF signals. "Gotcha." He boosted the power. "It's the MiGs, general, they're tracking a target. Sevastopol radar is guiding them."

Sweeny looked at Roberts. "They've got to be trying to intercept the B-2." He inspected the scope again. "Anything on your IFF readout?"

"No, sir, it's clean."

"See if you can contact Duke."

Bowlings punched up the predetermined radio frequency and keyed his mike: "Nightstalker . . . this is Watch Dog. Do you copy?"

No response.

He waited a few seconds and repeated the call. No response.

Bowlings turned to the general, his expression grim.

MIG-29 FULCRUMS

The three fighters were in a loose arrow-shaped sweep-formation, Colonel Belikov's Fulcrum the point aircraft, with the wingmen 500 meters behind him.

Belikov kept his MiG in a steady ten-degree dive toward the water. Ground control had advised him that at 2200 meters he would break out of the clouds and under the weather ceiling. By his own estimate they should break out of the clouds right about—now.

And they did. Soft cotton-candy clouds floated beneath the gray overcast. Belikov swept the sky and sea in front of him. If the controllers were right the B-2 should be only a few kilometers out in front. He checked to make sure the radar's power level was at one hundred percent . . . it was and he still could not distinguish a target.

He throttled back, realizing he had less than fifteen minutes to find the intruder that had destroyed the computer complex. Bringing it down was the only way he could hope to save himself. It was also his only revenge.

With over twenty-five years of combat flying Belikov was fortunate to still have perfect vision, which he now concentrated on the airspace between the ocean and the bottom of the clouds, trying to spot any dark or moving speck cutting across the light background of the sky. He saw nothing. The rolling waves with whitecaps breaking over them added to his frustration.

Actually the active gray saltwater helped camouflage the bomber, the stealth tending to blend into its curving bending surface. If Belikov was to pick up the bomber it would have to be with the MiG's infrared search-and-track receiver or its powerful electric-optical sensors.

Belikov now turned both systems to full power as his radio crackled with the news that the target had just dropped off the radar at Sevastopol, ". . . last heading 183, speed 425 knots, contact lost at 900 meters seven kilometers southeast of your position."

"Confirmed, turning to engage," Belikov answered, banked left, accelerated to 500 knots and listened to the faint warble of the IR-seeker scanning the air space to the south.

KART DAG STATION, TURKEY

Lieutenant Bowlings repeated the call to the Nightstalker one more time. Again nothing.

Roberts scribbled the last words of the message on his notepad: "General, the station at Sevastopol has just reported losing contact with the target. They lost it at about 2700 feet, three-and-a-half miles south of the lead MiG's position."

"Where is *that*?"

Bowlings pointed to the empty spot on the screen ahead of the MiGs.

"How long before those MiGs are in range of our interceptors?"

"They just broke a hundred thirteen miles south . . . peacetime orders say we can only intercept Soviet aircraft if they come within forty miles of the coast, sir."

"I'm fucking well aware of *peacetime* orders, lieutenant," Sweeny studied the radar screen. "Plot a course to those MiGs. Tell the Sixteens to get out there. I can't just sit here and wonder if our people are in trouble or not."

Bowlings felt his insides jump. "Timber Wolf lead, this is Watch Dog."

"Timber Wolf lead . . . we copy you Watch Dog, go ahead."

"Timber Wolf, you are cleared to go feet wet. Head northwest
. . . three two six. Three bandits . . . Fulcrums, heading one
eight five. We believe they are trying to intercept an American
reconnaissance aircraft exiting the Soviet Union. Altitude below
five thousand. Get a visual and advise."

"Roger, Watch Dog. Timber Wolf lead proceeding."

On the bottom of the scope Bowlings, Roundtree and Sweeny
watched the orbiting F-16s break to the north.

Sweeny folded his arms across his chest as the five blips on
the screen slowly made their way toward each other.

OVER THE BLACK SEA

The A-Band warning light had turned off when they hit 4000
feet above the water. Only the nagging J-Band warning of the
29s' Pulse-Dopplers was still on. Duke hadn't stopped when the
A-Band warning went out. He allowed the B-2 to float down to
500 feet, where he leveled out and pointed the nose straight for
Turkey. The gauges showed less than 5000 pounds of fuel left in
the stealth's undamaged tanks, enough for only twenty minutes
of flight at such a low altitude. By Duke's estimate, they would
fall short of Incirlik Air Base—but right now that was not the
worst of his worries.

"Lead MiG . . . four miles out and closing, 1200 meters
above us." Koiser was turned away from Duke looking up and
out his right-side window to get a visual on the 29s.

Duke felt the walls closing in on him. The control stick was
no longer solid, it quivered in a circular motion in his hand and
still pulled to the right. The aircraft felt sluggish, heavy, hard to
control. He took his left hand off the throttles. The B-2 was
going as fast as it could with the damage it had taken. Who
knew how much stress the bomber could take before it broke
apart from the G-forces? For sure Duke knew there was no way
he could beat a MiG-29 in a dogfight. And the prospect of staying low and trying to beat the MiGs to Turkish airspace didn't
sound too promising either.

What to do? How to pull them off us? He looked to the weap-
ons-control panel. It showed one SRAM left.

"Koiser, open the right side weapons bay door."

He pulled the stick back and nosed up seven degrees. Airspeed fell to 350 knots as the stealth struggled to climb. At 5300 feet he pushed the stick forward and leveled off.

"Weapons bay open," Koiser reported, and checked the computer. "Colonel, the MiGs are only two miles behind us—"

"I hope this works," Duke muttered. "Come on, baby, hold together, one more time . . ." And in one motion he jammed the stick forward and the throttles back. The B-2 nosed over, straight down, as its speed dropped off and the cockpit windows filled with the silvery color of the ocean.

He advanced the throttles, the two remaining engines spooled-up and pushed the Nightstalker past 450 knots in seconds.

The altimeter clicked off the altitude . . . 4500 . . . 4000 . . . 3700 . . . 3300. Airspeed was now 480 knots and building.

A stupid idea, Duke thought gloomily as he waited . . . the Nightstalker fell to 2800 . . . 2500 . . . 2000—"Okay, that's it," Duke said, and hit the emergency-jettison button for the right weapons bay. The fifteen two-inch-diameter stainless-steel bolts that held the rotary SRAM launcher in place exploded in a cloud of sparks and white smoke. And then the whole launch system fell away from the B-2, including the last missile.

With the instruments damaged Duke had no way of knowing if the launcher and missile had separated safely, he could only hear the sound of the explosion to confirm the plastic explosives had detonated.

He waited a moment, altitude 1400 feet, then pulled the stick back and watched the G-meter climb. Slowly the nose started to come up. The Nightstalker fought against the sudden change in direction. At 3.5 Gs Duke pushed the stick left and coaxed the B-2 into a rolling turn east, the big bomber rocking up and down as the left wingtip dropped.

"Nine hundred feet . . . come on," Duke grunted. The stick went back, the G-forces tore into the B-2's inner structure. The bomber popped and snapped as the graphite and epoxy joints stressed under the pull-up. Inside, pieces of the cockpit window shattered under the strain and exploded like firecrackers. Splinters landed on the floor and in the pilots' laps.

Duke sucked in a deep breath and held it. His damaged G-suit hissed as it labored to fill with air to keep his blood from leaving his upper body. Suddenly his head became light and his vision tunneled. The force of the Gs continued to thrust him into his seat with the energy of 900 pounds of dead weight. The pressure put more exertion on his already weakened body. His upper chest throbbed with pain, made it impossible for him to speak. He struggled to turn his head, but before he could warn Koiser his eyes rolled back into his head and he passed out.

The SRAM, still attached to the six-missile rotary, hit the water at 500 miles per hour. At that speed the density of the ocean's surface was like a twelve-inch-thick concrete highway's. Because the SRAM was designed to explode only after it had penetrated a solid object it didn't explode on impact. The missile's delay-system waited two seconds, which initially allowed the missile to dive more than 100 feet before it detonated. Only then did the warhead vaporize into a fifty-yard-diameter ball of fire and white-hot gases. The chemicals from the explosive charge reacted with the water and steam, turning the center of the explosion into a powerful acid.

A high-speed shock wave expanding out of the middle of the swelling underwater fireball sent up a foaming white tower of water 100 yards high.

Belikov caught sight of the wall of water and mist as it erupted into the air six kilometers to the west. Immediately he pulled his MiG into a hard right-hand turn, dropping its black nose for the water.

"Follow my lead . . . maintain five hundred," he ordered the other MiGs. He placed the center of his HUD on the water tower and allowed the energy of the dive to increase his airspeed. Because of the size of the explosion Belikov's first thought was the B-2 had crashed.

As Duke had hoped.

Moments later the colonel came wings-level at seventy-five meters and banked into a slow left-hand turn to orbit the large ball of churning foam. Carefully he studied the ocean below. If the American bomber had actually gone down the water should be littered with debris. With each pass he increased the size of his search pattern and looked for broken pieces of floating fuselage or the shiny reflection of a fuel slick.

It didn't take long for him to realize that whatever had exploded it wasn't the bomber. He saw nothing, just the green water boiling as the gaseous mixture from below continued to surface.

He put his fighter into a steep climb, thinking, the Americans must have known he was close. Why else would they have tried to pull him away? He joined up with his wingmen in a close three-man formation at 500 meters, and again they followed his lead as they turned south.

The MiGs were close enough so that Belikov could choose not to use his radio, thereby avoiding one of the few ways the Americans could know their location. But another way was the rhythm of their radar sweeping the bomber. He brought his fighter up and rolled to the other MiGs, whose pilots could clearly see him.

He made a fist, opened it quickly and ran his index finger across his lips—which told the pilots to turn off their search-radars and not use radio communications unless they came into contact with the enemy. He then held up one finger and pointed east, two fingers south, and three fingers west. The other pilots acknowledged by saluting. An instant later the MiGs broke formation. Number two flew straight ahead to the south. Number three broke right and flew west. Belikov banked to the east and jammed the throttles forward until the afterburners were engaged to make up for lost time.

Captain Morgan L. Cooper, flying Timber Wolf lead, leveled his F-16C at 8,000 feet and watched his airspeed creep up to 380 knots. His wingman stayed on the same heading 200 feet beneath him and 500 yards to the east. Cooper's heading was 326 degrees as they headed across the Turkish countryside toward the Black Sea.

Cooper couldn't have asked for a better assignment than being stationed at Incirlik, Turkey, and flying the F-16C. In his early thirties and single, he didn't mind at all living outside the States. Several of his flight-school buddies gave him a hard time for flying the single-engine fighter commonly referred to as the Fighting Falcon. His dream had always been to pilot the premier fighter in the U.S. Air Force, the F-15 Eagle. But after his first visit to Red Flag he found out at close range he could outturn and outshoot the larger F-15. The only thing the Eagle had on his F-16 was a more powerful radar and more speed. Other than that he could beat the F-15 almost every time in turning, which could be crucial in combat.

The captain kept a square bulletin board above his locker and pinned a red star on it for each time he had been scrambled to intercept Soviet bombers or help escort NATO reconnaissance aircraft flying near the Soviet border. Currently it had thirty-three stars. Cooper wondered what sort of recon bird he would be protecting this time. He had flown support for everything from sluggish C-130s to the super fast SR-71 Blackbird. Yet the tone in Watch Dog's radio message had him a little on edge. Was it that this would be the first time he would be facing MiG-29s?

Cooper scanned the broken line of clouds on the backside of the narrow cold front to the north. The light-colored background should make it easy to spot any approaching aircraft once they were over the water. Slowly he looked right to left. The airspace was clear of other aircraft. He focused on the cockpit's instruments, rolled the paint-chipped radar-receiver gain-knob clockwise with his left index finger. Without giving it much thought he moved his thumb to the antenna-elevator and clicked it half a dozen times. The clarity of the center-mounted CRT radarscope slowly changed, subtle adjustments he had just made tuning out most of the backscatter. Okay, he thought, coming, ready or not.

Koiser held the bomber steady at 2000 feet, heading due east. He reached over and grabbed a handful of the colonel's flight suit above his right shoulder.

"Colonel . . . *colonel*," Koiser shouted as he shook the pilot back and forth.

Duke moaned and his head rolled back onto the back of the ejection seat.

"Colonel . . ."

"Yeah . . ." Duke opened his eyes to see the blurred top of the cockpit. "What the hell . . . ?"

As his senses gradually cleared he realized what had happened, and sucked in long breaths of oxygen, each one making more intense the burning sensation in his side.

"Son-of-a-bitch it hurts," he muttered, but took control of the Nightstalker.

"How long was I out?"

"Not long. One . . . two minutes."

"Long enough. Let's get the hell out of here." Duke banked right, putting the stealth back on a southbound course, nosed over and dropped down to a 1000-foot cruising altitude. He watched the airspeed creep past 380 knots, stopped at 387. Losing the last SRAM and burning up fuel was at least making the B-2 lighter.

"Do you hear that?" Duke said, his voice lighter.

Koiser didn't answer. His helmet was empty of all sound.

"Silence . . . nothing . . . those damn J-Bands are gone. Our diversion must have pulled them off." At least temporarily, he silently added.

Belikov knew he didn't have much time—his estimate was the enemy bomber would be in NATO-controlled airspace in less than ten minutes. He pushed his MiG along as fast as he dared. His forward airspeed was over 650 knots, 1000 meters above water. He swung to the west and cut a large section out of the sky ten kilometers long before he turned east and flew the other way. He wanted to cover the maximum amount of airspace in the least amount of time.

With luck and skill, he would find the target . . .

He pushed the stick left and put the agile fighter into a hard 6.5-G turn. As the MiG came around and headed back to the east, Belikov rolled right and pointed the nose-mounted infrared search-and-track scanner to the south. He flew the MiG on its side to get the highest degree of resolution out of the heat-sensor.

Halfway across the ten-kilometer run Belikov noticed a small, hazy image on the IR scope, faint and transparent. He turned in the direction of the image and manipulated the stick until it was centered on the scope, then pushed the throttles forward again and felt the added thrust of the twin-afterburners kick in and press him back into his seat. As the MiG quickly accelerated to over 700 knots the image grew stronger while he closed the distance between it and himself.

Thirty seconds later the sensor showed the target was only three kilometers out and below him. He still couldn't *see* it. He opened his airbrakes, throttled back and decelerated. The size of the IR image indicated no more than a small single-engine plane.

Belikov dropped the nose of his MiG and slowed to 400 knots, concentrating on the sky in front of him. He expected to see the white T-shaped top of a single-engine aircraft slowly moving below him. What he saw filled him with a mixture of awe and anger.

The grayish outline of the B-2 passed beneath him, and shaking his head, he moved his MiG in closer so that the strange bat-shape of the aircraft became clearer.

At 300 meters above and behind it, Belikov could make out the battle damage along the left side of the aircraft. At 200 meters, the low-visibility insignia identifying it as a U.S. Air Force warplane were easy to see.

He studied the weird-looking aircraft, and decided that by the way it was flying its crew didn't know he was behind them.

He keyed his radio transmitter, holding the trigger down for several seconds. His thought was to contact the other MiGs, use them for backups—then released the trigger.

"*No,*" he said, "you belong to me."

He activated his four wing-mounted heat-seeking missiles. The weapons-armed indicator-light flashed on. He banked to the right and brought his fighter directly in back of the Americans, waited for one of the supercooled germanium seeker-heads to lock onto the IR signature of the bomber. His headset filled with a varying low-pitched tone as the missiles tried to home in on the target ahead.

Belikov became impatient. He was in ideal firing position but his missiles weren't locking up. If he turned his radar on and tried to engage the target with the MiG's four radar-homing AA-9s he would lose his advantage of surprise.

"Damn," he said under his breath as a faint tone in his headset finally became even and clear. Only one of the four heat-seekers had locked up and he could tell by the sound that it wasn't a solid lock. It would take more precious seconds for the two-dozen homing pixels, located in the tip of each AA-8C missile, to instruct the guidance system how to compensate for the minimal amount of heat coming off the back of the B-2. Belikov didn't wait. He dropped the nose of the MiG a few degrees and pointed it right at the B-2. He squeezed the trigger on his stick. A split-second later a single AA-8 streaked from the wing-mounted rail-launcher in a cloud of white smoke.

"Watch Dog, Timber Wolf lead . . . feet wet," came the call from Cooper as he and his wingman in their F-16Cs flashed over the white sandy coast and climbed out over the Black Sea.

"Do you have a visual?" Cooper radioed his wingman. During the last few minutes both pilots had been tracking a single target on their radar, not, of course, knowing the target in front of them was attacking a B-2 bomber.

"No sir, nothing yet."

"We're almost on top of it. Break left, I'll go right," Cooper said as he banked to the east and added power.

"Four minutes to land," Koiser said, still not daring to sound too encouraged.

The overcast and heavy moist air prevented Duke from seeing the Turkish coast.

"What the hell . . . ?" Duke called out. A flash of fire and smoke had blasted across the front cockpit window. The missile from Belikov's MiG shot overhead, missing by a scant thirty feet, then turned and headed for the ocean below.

Duke rocked the bomber. "Where *is* he?" he shouted to Koiser.

Koiser didn't answer, he was too busy searching the sky.

Duke then flipped the Nightstalker into a slicing dive and leveled at 300 feet above the ocean.

Belikov watched the missile just miss its target and crash into the water as the Americans banked away from him to the west, then back to the east. Well, the bomber would be no match when it came to the turning ability of his MiG . . .

He maneuvered his fighter back into position.

"This time there will be no mistake," he muttered, and lined up the MiG's HUD-mounted cannon-sight on the back of the enemy, which was 500 meters below him. He hit the cannon's trigger and held it down for a full second. As fifty 30-mm. cannon-rounds shot out the left side of his wing-root he followed the reddish orange tracers as they headed straight for the enemy bomber.

The first few rounds ripped past the B-2 by a few yards. But the next volley of heavy projectiles hit the right side of the stealth like thunder. A dozen cannon-rounds tore into the empty wing fuel-tank next to the engines, shattering the top of the wing. The bomber's wings shuddered badly under the force of the exploding rounds.

Just as Belikov readied another volley his helmet filled with a stronger, more defined high-pitched tone as his Aphids locked onto a new heat source. He checked the IR search-and-track scope. On top of the screen another target had appeared. This one's IR signal was strong and clear.

"An American interceptor," he said aloud.

He took a deep breath to steady himself and waited two seconds until the chirping tone was even. Then, without seeing what he was shooting at, he sent off two missiles and pulled his MiG up as the heat-seekers raced away. He watched their white trails of smoke until seconds later a bright flash told him they had found their mark.

* * *

"BREAK . . . *BREAK*," Cooper shouted as he watched two silvery smoke trails collide with his wingman's aircraft. His warning was too late. Both the MiG's missiles had found their mark, crippling the small fighter.

Cooper felt his heart move up into his throat. "EJECT, EJECT, *EJECT*," he called out. "This is Timber Wolf lead . . . I just lost my wingman."

The thought of his friend dying in a burning aircraft filled him with angry energy. His eyes went back to the smoke trails in the sky.

"I'm going to kill that son of a bitch!"

Then Cooper saw it. The thin gray profile of an odd-looking aircraft. And directly above it was a MiG-29.

Bowlings and Roundtree were fixed on the radarscope as the blip representing Timber Wolf two disappeared off the screen.

"My God. We just lost the number two Sixteen," Roundtree blurted out in disbelief. "General . . ."

"Damn it, I *heard*." Sweeny picked up the phone that gave him a direct line into Incirlik, Turkey. "They just shot down an F-16. I want S & R out there right now and get me two more Sixteens airborne. We'll vector them from here." He slammed down the phone. "How far out are they from the coast?"

"Nine miles and closing. They should be over it in about ninety seconds," Bowlings told him.

Belikov passed below and to the right of the fireball that had been an F-16 as it spun violently downward. Black smoke and flames spewed out of its tail and left-wing root. From the damage, one or two Aphids must have hit the same side of the aircraft, breaking it in half.

Belikov looked down at the bomber to be sure not to lose sight of it. White vapor trails streaked off its wingtips, now making it easy to spot against the silver-gray water. He glanced up in time to see the canopy of the fighter blow off and the pilot eject, watched long enough to see the American separate from his seat and become suspended by a multidomed parachute.

Belikov turned to check his six before he brought his attention back on the B-2. The fallen American's wingman would be close by, he realized as he rolled left into an inverted dive. The bomber was 800 meters below . . . and the Turkish coast was in sight.

He righted the MiG and looked behind him once again. Sure enough, he could make out a tiny gray spot circling in behind him. The other American fighter was coming around into firing position.

He only had a few seconds.

He centered the bomber on his HUD. Its wingtips touched each side of the plexiglass sight as it floated out in front of him. Skillfully he put the orange crisscross on the center of the B-2, and squeezed the trigger.

Duke heard the cannonfire hit the back of the aircraft with a deafening roar. The large-caliber bullets tore into the aft avionics-bay, turning it into a shower of sparks and ripping metal. Cannonrounds came right up the B-2's back into the empty weapons compartments. The exploding shells gashed holes in the top of the aircraft.

This time he was at least ready. He reversed throttles and pulled the stick back. The wounded Nightstalker responded. Relentlessly, as though it too had a mind of its own. Its nose started up, chugging, starting to stall. If Duke could force the B-2 up and then drop the nose to pick up airspeed, they could still break for the coast, he figured. Hoped.

As the front of the B-2 came up the cannonfire didn't stop. Flying shrapnel and smoke from a dozen projectiles cut into the bomber, filling the cockpit.

His vision suddenly was obstructed. He slammed the stick down and the throttles forward. Neither responded. The stick felt like dead weight and the throttles were loose and moved limply. Airspeed fell off. He pumped the stick down, and the B-2's nose slowly edged over and started to drop.

Duke cursed and tried to steady the B-2 as it came level and started to roll right.

Another round of bullets hit them, this time in the left wing next to the engines. The red fire-warning blinked on through the haze-filled cockpit.

"Fire," Koiser called out.

The center of the wing was spewing orange flames trailed by thick black smoke. Any moment it would spread to the wing-tank and explode. Duke hit the emergency engine shut-off and fire-suppression system, killing the engines.

Now the bomber was a giant glider.

The Turkish coast passed underneath them. The B-2 waffled into a shallow dive and rolled left.

Duke twisted in his seat and looked at Tucker slumped over in his ejection seat. Any second the B-2 could go up in flames and kill all of them. Even if he could bring the bomber in for a landing, chances were it would burn. Tucker for sure wouldn't be able to crawl to safety once they hit the ground. The only way Duke could hope to save Tuck was to get him out of the wounded plane. Fast.

He turned to Koiser—"Eject . . . *EJECT.*" He reached over and hit the ejection switch on the front instrument panel, and in a blast of fire and smoke Tucker shot out of the back of the cockpit.

"*Eject,*" he now said to Koiser. "Before she explodes . . ."

Koiser shook his head.

Cooper came out of a hard turn and leveled for an instant, then rolled forty-five-degrees so he could maintain eye-contact with the gray MiG and pointed the nose of his fighter straight up. At the same time he jammed the throttles forward, causing his GE F-100 engine to jump into afterburner. He felt his arms and head go heavy as the Gs built and his G-suit inflated, trying to compensate for the added pressure on his body. He knew if he was going to beat the MiG he would need an advantage—speed, then altitude.

*   *   *

Belikov waited until the last moment before peeling away from the bomber. There was no question in his mind that the American warplane was going down. But something inside of him wanted to *see* it crash and explode. On the other hand training and judgment told him to try to escape.

He turned left and advanced the throttles while turning his fighter away from the bomber, then with one thrust of his arm put his MiG into afterburner and accelerated into a vertical climb. Now his worry was the other American fighter. He turned his head until he caught sight of the F-16's glowing orange exhaust nozzle a few hundred meters above him . . .

Duke's arm ached as he fought to control the Nightstalker's glidepath. Airspeed was down to 280 knots and falling steadily.

The Turkish coast was a mile behind them. Koiser searched for a possible landing site—"*there . . .*" Koiser said, and pointed to a flattish stretch of ground between two small hills where they could at least try a gear-up landing.

Duke didn't argue. He pushed the stick right with all his strength. The B-2 shuddered and turned, its nose dropped a few degrees. He tried to swallow but his mouth was dry except for the blood bubbling from his left lung.

He struggled to level the Nightstalker and line it up with the center of the barren earth. With his left hand on the throttles he squeezed for air brakes to slow the bomber but they failed to open. He knew he was coming in too fast for a safe landing, and that there was nothing else he could do.

Koiser called off the altitude: "Fifteen meters . . . ten, a little right . . ." He kept his eyes straight ahead.

Duke tried to correct as Koiser requested, but the B-2's damaged flight controls wouldn't allow it.

"Five . . ." Koiser braced himself.

Duke eased the stick back. If he could bring the nose up enough it would slow the bomber . . .

The Nightstalker smashed the ground with a heavy thud. Duke's head snapped forward, breaking the front of the instrument panel. He instantly blacked out. Koiser put his head down a split-second before the window filled with brown dirt and dust as the bomber slid uncontrollably across the rocks and gravel. Its skin peeled away from its underside. Its left wingtip hit the ground first and ripped off next to the engine air-intake, causing the wing-root to explode.

Koiser felt the bomber spin around. He closed his eyes. A second later the bomber collided with the side of the nearest hill, crashed into a row of trees and bushes and splintered into pieces. The main part of the fuselage flipped over and rocked violently before coming to rest halfway up the hill.

Belikov hadn't thought it would be this easy. The American was still climbing above him only 500 meters away. The massive amount of heat being generated, while in afterburner, from the F-16's engine would make the American's IR signature easy to lock onto.

As he climbed through 3000 meters he slid in behind the F-16 and switched the armament-selection knob from his GSh-301 30-mm. cannon to AA-8 heat-seeking air-to-air missiles. His HUD told him he had only one left. Well, he decided, it was all he would need. He listened for the hum to change in his headset as the missile homed in on the heat.

Captain Cooper inched his stick back and leveled out upside down. He looked right and left until he caught sight of the MiG climbing directly at him, coming into position for a shot from below.

Belikov pressed the launch-button on his stick, sending the AA-8 infrared-guided missile after its target. His MiG shook slightly as the 121-pound heat-seeker left the rail launcher, automatically correcting its course as it sped away.

Cooper caught sight of a glimmer of light reflecting off the front control-fins of the AA-8 Aphid as it turned toward him.

He slashed his throttles, taking the F-16 out of afterburner and rolled upright, then snapped into a slicing right-hand turn as he hit the flare-dispenser button on the throttle. A trail of five white-hot flares tumbled from the underside of his fighter. He put the sun in the center of his HUD and flew right at it.

Over his right shoulder he saw the missile cut across the back of his fighter, and called on all his self-discipline to keep focused on the heat-seeker. If he could see it, he could outturn it.

Belikov watched as the AA-8 slashed through the first set of flares and exploded. He allowed his MiG to continue its climb as he came even with the F-16 at 4500 meters, then banked his MIG to the west and came in behind the American, leveling off.

I won't underestimate him again, he told himself.

He switched from the missiles to guns and adjusted his rate of fire from 500 to 1200 rounds per minute.

"*My* turn." Cooper was ready this time. He brought his fighter around into a tight 8-G turn, added power and watched his airspeed climb on the HUD. He was turning at 563 knots 13,900 feet above the filthy gray water of the Black Sea.

He held his breath and tightened every muscle in his legs and abdomen. He grunted, letting small amounts of air escape through his mouth as he tried to keep the blood from leaving his head and pooling in his lower body. His vision was narrowing as he caught sight of the red star on the portside tailfin of the MiG.

Almost there, Cooper thought. Just a few more seconds and I'll be in back of him . . .

Belikov was caught off guard. The turn-rate of the F-16 was apparently faster and tighter than he'd expected.

As he watched the gray-and-blue fighter turn into him, he realized that too soon the American would have the advantage.

He pulled the nose of his fighter straight up and went to full military power just short of afterburner. He hoped he could outclimb the American, do a quick barrel roll, force his nose down and bring his guns to bear.

Captain Cooper watched the MiG shoot up ahead of him as he came out of his turn and leveled his wings. He would only have the advantage for a moment before the MiG pushed over and headed back for the water to loop in behind him. His timing had to be just right.

He pushed the nose of his fighter up and slipped in behind the MiG. He could see its big dual tailfins and missiles hanging off its wings. The low-pitched tone in his headset signaled that neither one of his Sidewinders had locked up. Never mind. He had to try to force the Soviet into making a mistake.

He pushed the weapons-release button on the left side of his stick and sent one of his two remaining Sidewinders on its way. He added power and started to climb toward the MiG.

Belikov swung to the north and dropped the nose of his MiG, just enough dip in altitude to throw off the missile. He caught sight of the olive drab Sidewinder in his center rearview mirror as it streaked past his fighter fifty meters away and failed to explode.

He rolled over and dove straight down, watched his airspeed increase as he passed through 4000 meters at 700 knots, then pitched up the nose of his MiG by pulling back on the stick, completing a 9-G three-quarter loop.

The F-16 was above him only 1000 meters to the northwest.

He thrust his MiG into afterburner and closed the distance between himself and the American.

For a moment Cooper lost sight of the MiG. It had passed over him, dived and disappeared behind his right wing. By the time Cooper reacted he had misjudged the position of the Soviet. He was in trouble and he knew it.

* * *

At 500 meters below and to the south of the American, Belikov centered his gunsight. At 400 meters he began to put steady pressure on the trigger. Seconds later he saw the first tracer-rounds flash out of his wing root past the radome of his MiG, heading straight for the F-16.

The first rounds ripped into the engine compartment of the lightweight fighter, tearing into Cooper's turbofan. A second later compressor blades tore loose, slicing the Falcon's hydraulic lines.

The next set of cannon-rounds cut into the left wing and midsection of the fuselage behind the cockpit.

Cooper felt the stick freeze up just before he saw the fire-warning lights in his cockpit. He tried to force the nose of his fighter down but got no response. He watched his airspeed fall off, felt the aircraft shudder as he stalled and rolled to the right.

One more burst and the American would be dead. Belikov lined up the disabled F-16 in the center of his HUD as he opened his air brakes and cut his airspeed to under 300 knots. The American fighter was slowly falling, black smoke pouring out of large holes in the back of its fuselage.

Belikov's nose was still pointed up at a forty-five-degree angle as he climbed toward the American, then pulled the trigger and released a salvo of 30-mm. cannon fire.

The F-16 rocked back and forth as the armor-piercing projectiles slashed into its airframe . . . one pierced the cockpit, slicing into Cooper's left arm below the shoulder and severing his muscles. For a moment he blacked out from the shock of his arm being cut by the hot metal.

He felt his fighter roll over and head toward the water. He tried to clear his head . . .

*   *   *

Belikov unsnapped his oxygen mask and let it dangle from the hinge on his helmet, brushed sweat from his eyes and pushed the stick forward to level the MiG. The F-16 still above him was in a sluggish spin as it headed for the ocean below. He had won and not suffered a scratch.

Cooper drew in a long breath of oxygen. His cockpit was filling with smoke. He could smell the burning jet fuel. Energy was leaving his body. He tried to steady his fighter so he could eject without killing himself, moved the stick right to left and worked the rudder pedals.

Suddenly he spotted the MiG below him, crossing from the left. At first he didn't notice the tone in his helmet. The pain in his arm was so bad he could barely hold onto consciousness. Then he realized what the sound was. The high-pitched chirping in his headset was telling him his last Sidewinder had just locked up.

He pushed the weapons-release button on his stick, firing the missile, then pulled himself into a tight ball and yanked the ejection cord between his legs. In a shower of smoke and sparks, Captain Cooper left his aircraft.

It happened so fast Belikov did not see it coming. The Sidewinder hit the leading edge of his right wing, causing it to blow completely off and splitting his fighter in two. His MiG then went into a violent spin that pinned Belikov against the side of the cockpit. Metal pieces were then sucked up by the MiG's turbofans, shredding the engines and cutting the fuel lines.

As the MiG descended, its airspeed dropped, allowing fuel to mix with hydraulic fluid. The lethal mixture was then pumped into the engine compartment, where it exploded, tearing off the back-third of the aircraft.

Belikov reached for the ejection cord, too late. The secondary fueltank behind the cockpit caught fire and erupted into flames. The explosion's force split the cockpit into several pieces—instantly killing Colonel Belikov.

*   *   *

Captain Cooper looked up as he hung suspended from his parachute to see the MiG evaporate into a ball of yellow flames and smoke. As the airframe broke apart he looked for a chute—didn't see one.

In the distance he could hear the low rolling thunder of a helicopter drawing closer. It was a search-and-rescue team coming toward him. Cooper looked at the blood coming out of his left arm. Not good, but not fatal either. He'd survived, but he also felt restrained. The other guy had been a terrific opponent. It had been a hell of a fight.

24

ENDGAME

THE PENTAGON, NEXT DAY

Secretary of Defense John Turner wondered what if anything was left of the computer. From the size of the crater on top of the mountain ridge it was clear the entire complex had collapsed. The camouflage radar netting was gone and several Soviet military trucks were parked on the northern end. Obviously the PVO was assessing damage. The engineers at the DIA told him even if some of the computer's components could be salvaged, they would be too radioactive to use for many years, if ever.

He looked again at the last reconnaissance photo taken early in the morning, then put it back in the file. The Defense Secretary closed it slowly and set the folder on his desk, leaned back in his chair and glanced over at the captain's clock on the far wall—the present from his wife. It read 4:19 P.M.

DCI Tony Brady and Tom Staffer were sitting across the desk from him, having arrived minutes earlier from the CIA. They also looked tired, drained, yet all felt a certain exhilaration.

"This supercomputer-radar system of theirs could have thrown the whole balance of power their way," Brady was saying. "It would have been an *operational SDI. Our guys only just made it through . . . think of what the situation would have been if*

423

the whole system had been up and operating to the maximum . . .''

Staffer nodded. "And think how close we came to missing it."

John Turner, who had poured himself two fingers of bourbon, finished off the drink, stood up and said, "I say we call it a day, people. This is too much to sort out now, I'm just going to go home and enjoy it while I can. I suggest you guys do the same."

OAKTON, VIRGINIA

Mark Collins was sure he had turned his front porch light out when he had left his house three days earlier. It was still on. He slowly walked the fifty feet from the driveway, across the dry brown lawn to his doorstep, briefcase in hand. He fumbled for his keys a moment, turned the lock and went inside.

"Oh, God, you scared me," Christine said.

Collins smiled as he closed the door. "Christine . . . I didn't expect to see you here."

She held out the key in the palm of her hand. "Mr. CIA, you told me where this was . . . remember, the milk box? Besides, I've called your office about twenty times. I didn't believe the line Maddie was giving me about a trip to California. You would have told me." She moved up to him.

"Well, actually I was—"

She put her arms around his neck and her lips on his. "*Actually*, it doesn't matter. What counts is you're here and what comes next . . ."

THE PENTAGON

Jack Dawson had waited until the word came in that the C-137 had left Ramstein and was on its way to Turkey. He would feel better when the surviving crew members of the B-2 were back in the States. He was glad General Westcott had flown to Incirlik to take charge of the rest of the operation.

He slipped on his overcoat, wound his dark gray wool scarf around his neck, turned out the lights and closed the door. The halls in his wing were quiet and his footsteps echoed as he made his way to the nearest exit.

Dawson was no stranger to the emotional low he was feeling. He even had a name for it, postmission blues. Korea and Vietnam were the first places he had felt it. But this was different, it was a success . . . except for one dead Tucker Stevens, a badly wounded Duke James and a lovely aircraft called the Nightstalker that had died doing its job. Except . . .

He walked up to his waiting limousine and got in. The interior felt warm and comfortable. Unread copies of the Washington *Post* were on the sideseat. He motioned to the driver he was ready to leave, flipped the radio on and pushed the button to his favorite FM station as the driver put the car in gear and pulled away.

Sure, just another day at the office.

INCIRLIK AIR BASE, TURKEY

"Mrs. James, Mrs. James." The flight attendant touched her shoulder gently, and Katie James came out of her light sleep.

"I'm sorry to disturb you but we're almost there. The tower has cleared us for landing. We should be on the ground in five minutes."

"Thank you." Katie straightened up and brought the seat with her. She glanced out the window at the dark morning sky. The white lights of a small village slowly drifted below. There was still no hint of sunrise.

"Excuse me," she said.

"Yes?"

"What time is it?"

"Five fifteen A.M. local."

Katie looked back out the window. No wonder she couldn't sleep very well, it was only 7:15 P.M. in Rapid City.

Two seats back sat Charles Tyransky. He rested his head on a pillow between the seat and the window. He couldn't sleep either but not because of the time difference. It seemed the Air Force and CIA were up to their old games, nobody was telling him anything. Captain Koiser would need him and he was going to be on hand to help any way he could.

* * *

General Westcott watched the four-engine transport come to a stop a hundred feet from the main building. He waited for the pilot to reduce power and let the turbofans spool down before he exited the staff car he had been waiting in. He approached the plane as the ground crew wheeled the staired ramp into place below the front door, then hurried up the stairs into the jet.

"Katie . . ."

"General Westcott? I didn't expect to see you, is something wrong? Where is Duke?"

"He's okay, Katie, really."

"Oh, God, when I got your phone call—"

"I know." He put his arm around her. "Duke pulled through surgery without any problems. He said to tell you he missed the runway."

She had to smile as her eyes filled with tears.

"Come on." Westcott grabbed her coat and draped it over her shoulders. "I have a car waiting."

He turned to Tyransky. "Mr. Tyransky, it's good to see you again." He shook Tyransky's hand. "Please come with me, Captain Koiser has been asking to see you."

Ten minutes later they arrived at the base hospital.

"This way," Westcott said as he held the door open to the side entrance.

Tyransky followed a few feet behind Katie James as the three made their way down the white tiled hallway.

Westcott stopped halfway down the hall. "In here," he said.

As Katie moved toward Duke's bed a nurse whispered that he was still asleep. "Sit there," she said, and pointed to a chair next to the bed.

Katie took hold of Duke's hand as she looked at him. A pair of plastic tubes ran around his face and up each of his nostrils. The left side of his head was bandaged and she could see cuts on his neck and chin. An IV was connected to his left arm and both forearms were black and blue. His breathing was heavy and strained. She felt herself starting to cry and fought it.

The nurse touched her arm. "He's doing fine, the worst is over. The doctor will be with you in a minute."

Katie sat down, still holding Duke's hand. Westcott stood next to her.

"He's tough, Katie."

"I know. How is Tucker?"

Westcott knew it was no use stalling. "I'm sorry . . . he didn't make it. We found him a half mile from the crash site. The doctors are sure he was dead before he ever ejected."

"Dead? Oh God . . . how did he eject?"

"Duke ordered everyone out before the plane crashed. He went in with the plane."

"But where were they? What happened?"

"I wish I could tell you more, Katie, but I can't." He turned as the doctor came into the room.

"Does he know about Tucker?" she asked.

Westcott nodded.

"Mrs. James, I'm Dr. Caras," said the Air Force captain. "The colonel is going to be okay. We had to operate to repair some tissue in his left lung, but other than that it's some cuts and contusions. What he needs more than anything is rest. A lot of it."

Katie looked at her husband.

"He's pretty sedated right now, but you should be able to speak with him in an hour or so."

"Is it all right if I stay with him?"

"Sure, fine."

"I'll wait with you," Westcott said.

Koiser was wide awake when Tyransky entered his part of the room and smiled as his friend came around the corner.

"It is very damn good to see you, Grigory."

"It is good to see you, I did not expect you here—"

"How are you feeling?"

"I am fine, Charles. I got beat up some in the landing but that is all. I think the doctors are just watching me."

Tyransky sat down next to the bed. "I am amazed you are alive."

"Me too, Charles," Koiser said, and shook his head. "Duke James is an incredible pilot. We destroyed the computer, Charles . . ."

"Yes, I know. But there would have been no mission without you . . . Well, you can go home now."

Koiser caught the glimmer in his friend's eye. "Yes, home . . . America."

At first Duke didn't know who was holding his hand and calling his name. As he turned his head the image of his wife slowly came into focus.

"Katie . . ." His smile hurt his face.

"I heard you missed the runway."

"Yeah, you could say that." Duke could see Westcott in the background. "Hello, general. I heard we got it."

"You got that right. It's nothing more than a smoldering hole in the ground."

Duke nodded and looked to his wife. "Tuck bought it, Katie. I tried to—"

"I know you did all you could."

He tried to sit up and winced.

"Damn, I hurt like hell."

"Serves you right, taking off like that in the middle of the night." Katie lifted his hand and kissed it.

"Hey, I'm not that far gone," he said, pulling her to him and waving at Westcott to get out of his space.

EPILOGUE

They were sitting around the fireplace in their Georgetown, D.C., home, General Duke James, his wife Katie and his children Pamela and Matt. *General* James, he still had some trouble with that. He was no armchair type, and yet after the flight of the Nightstalker and knocking out the Soviet computer-radar complex, they insisted he was too valuable to reassign to line duty and had bumped him through the ranks to major general and put him on the staff of the National Security Council, grooming him, some said, for the top job of National Security Advisor.

Duke took plenty of ribbing about that, and he had plenty of reservations—he wasn't, he told himself and his wife more than once, another Colin Powell. He didn't take to the political bureaucracy and they weren't exactly enamored of him. But the President himself had told him they needed somebody like him, somebody who had been there in a way nobody else in the military had been. The irony was that after the remarkable flight of the Nightstalker neither side, not the U.S., not the then Soviet Union, ever announced what had happened. That was the deal. And it had worked out very well, indeed. In exchange for the U.S. not telling the world it had destroyed the Soviet's eyes and ears, its last and most formidable line of defense, the Soviets would not only sign a disarmament treaty far more Draconian in the reduction and destructions of its weapons than ever envisaged, but also would move to a policy of international cooperation, of openness—*glasnost*. The dissolution of the Soviet empire could not be far behind.

They could talk all they wanted about the bankruptcy of the communist system—and it was true, of course—but what pushed the General Secretary and his colleagues even in the military as much as any other factor was the destruction of the futuristic installation at Ramenskoye. Without that, the bear had his claws blunted for good. Peace and accommodation with the West were no longer a matter of choice. There was no other option.

Duke had heard all this from his superiors, and hesitated at first to think it could be so, wondering if they weren't giving his flight more credit than it deserved. But the more he thought about it, and saw the remarkable series of events and decisions out of the Soviet Union following the flight, the more he realized it must, in large part, at least, be so. More in his thoughts, though, was a man named Tucker Stevens, *and* an aircraft, the B-2 they called Nightstalker. Some said it wasn't worth the money. Tell it to the folks at Ramenskoye.

Don't talk about it, ever, he was ordered, not even to your wife. And he never had, although it hadn't been easy to resist her blandishments. But finally they both had better things to think about. Like another child, for example, which Katie was now carrying. It had been a long time coming, but as far as Duke James went, it was the definition of the real future for him, and beside its prospect, Ramenskoye's destruction, even the Nightstalker, could take a back seat.